"The year 2012 is synonymous with Doomsday, but what if the cause of the chaos to come was . . . Adolf Hitler? Read *SecondWorld*, a new treat from Jeremy Robinson."

—Steve Alten, *New York Times* bestselling author

"A harrowing, edge-of-your-seat thriller told by a master storyteller, Jeremy Robinson's *SecondWorld* is an amazing, globetrotting tale that will truly leave you breathless."

—Richard Doetsch, international bestselling author

"Robinson blends myth, science, and terminal velocity action like no one else."

—Scott Sigler, *New York Times* bestselling author

THRESHOLD

"One hell of a thriller, wildly imaginative and diabolical, which combines ancient legends and modern science into a nonstop action ride that will keep you turning the pages until the wee hours. Relentlessly gripping from start to finish, don't turn your back on this book!"   —Douglas Preston, *New York Times* bestselling author of *Impact* and *Blasphemy*

"Robinson's books have the necessary action and engaging characters to make the reader frantically turn the pages, but *Threshold* elevates Robinson to the highest tier of over-the-top action authors, like Matthew Reilly and James Rollins. Intense and personal, this book is a great launching point for new readers, and it delivers beyond the expectations even of his fans. The next Chess Team adventure cannot come fast enough."   —*Booklist*, starred review

"With *Threshold* Jeremy Robinson goes pedal to the metal into very dark territory. Fast-paced, action-packed, and wonderfully creepy! Highly recommended!"

—Jonathan Maberry, *New York Times* bestselling author of *The King of Plagues* and *Rot & Ruin*

"In Robinson's wildly inventive third Chess Team adventure, the U.S. president, Tom Duncan, joins the team in mortal combat against an unlikely but irresistible gang of enemies . . . Videogame on a page? Absolutely. Fast, furious, unabashed fun? You bet."
—*Publishers Weekly*

"*Threshold* is a blisteringly original tale that blends the thriller and horror genres in a smooth and satisfying hybrid mix. With his new entry in the Jack Sigler series, Jeremy Robinson plants his feet firmly on territory blazed by David Morrell and James Rollins. The perfect blend of mysticism and monsters, both human and otherwise, make *Threshold* as groundbreaking as it is riveting." —Jon Land, *New York Times* bestselling author of *Strong Enough to Die*

"Jeremy Robinson is the next James Rollins."
—Chris Kuzneski, *New York Times* bestselling author of *The Lost Throne* and *The Prophecy*

"Jeremy Robinson's *Threshold* sets a blistering pace from the very first page and never lets up. This globe-trotting thrill ride challenges its well-crafted heroes with ancient mysteries, fantastic creatures, and epic action sequences. For readers seeking a fun, rip-roaring adventure, look no further."
—Boyd Morrison, bestselling author of *The Ark*

"*Threshold* is my favorite Jack Sigler thriller so far . . . I hope one day to see the Chess Team materialize on the big screen. Robinson artfully weaves the modern-day military with ancient history like no one else has and I would love to see the adventures of the Chess team come alive in a movie."
—deadrobotssociety.com

"If you thought *Pulse* and *Instinct* were fun, just hold on tight, my fellow thriller lovers. Jeremy Robinson pulls out all the stops in *Threshold*, making this the most electrifying installment in the series so far. Robinson somehow takes the Tower of Babel, killer statues, giant lizards and insects, Stonehenge, and medieval lore and mixes it all together in this crazy, re-lentless story that is simply impossible to put down. . . . I have a blast every time I pick up a Jeremy Robinson novel and *Threshold* is no exception. I love authors who are dedicated to continually bringing fresh and original content to their fans, and Robinson continues to find ways to do this. If you are longing for a great thriller writer to follow and are tired of waiting a year or more between novels, then give Jeremy Robinson a chance. He's the perfect combination of quality and frequency in a market that is often lacking both."

—FictionAddict.com

INSTINCT

"*Pulse* was a videogame in print form, and [*Instinct*] is a tribute to James Cameron's film *Aliens*. Intense and full of riveting plot twists, it is Robinson's best book yet, and it should secure a place . . . on the A-list of thriller fans who like the over-the-top style of James Rollins and Matthew Reilly."

—*Booklist*

"If you like thrillers original, unpredictable, and chock-full of action, you are going to love Jeremy Robinson's Chess Team. *Instinct* riveted me to my chair."   —Stephen Coonts

"Jeremy Robinson is a fresh new face in adventure writing and will make a mark in suspense for years to come."

—David L. Golemon, *New York Times* bestselling author of *Ancients* and *Leviathan*

"*Instinct* is a jungle fever of raw adrenaline that goes straight for the jugular."—Thomas Greanias, *New York Times* bestselling author of *The Atlantis Revelation* and *The Promised War*

"Robinson's slam-bang second Chess Team thriller [is a] a wildly inventive yarn that reads as well on the page as it would play on a computer screen."   —*Publishers Weekly*

ALSO BY JEREMY ROBINSON

The Jack Sigler Thrillers

Pulse
Instinct
Threshold

The Chess Team Novellas

Callsign: Queen—Book 1
Callsign: Rook—Book 1
Callsign: Bishop—Book 1
Callsign: Knight—Book 1
Callsign: Deep Blue—Book 1
Callsign: King—Book 1
Callsign: King—Book 2—Underworld

The Antarktos Saga

The Last Hunter: Descent
The Last Hunter: Pursuit
The Last Hunter: Ascent

Stand-Alone Novels

Kronos
Antarktos Rising
Beneath
Raising the Past
The Didymus Contingency

SECONDWORLD

JEREMY ROBINSON

St. Martin's Paperbacks

This is a work of fiction. All of the characters, organizations, and events portrayed in this novel are either products of the author's imagination or are used fictitiously.

SECONDWORLD

Copyright © 2012 by Jeremy Robinson.
Excerpt from *Island 731* copyright © 2013 by Jeremy Robinson.

For information address St. Martin's Press, 175 Fifth Avenue, New York, NY 10010.

ISBN: 978-0-312-55245-9

Printed in the United States of America

St. Martin's Press hardcover edition / May 2012
St. Martin's Paperbacks edition / February 2013

St. Martin's Paperbacks are published by St. Martin's Press, 175 Fifth Avenue, New York, NY 10010.

10 9 8 7 6 5 4 3 2 1

For the real Roger Brodeur.
I apologize in advance.

ACKNOWLEDGMENTS

I've written acknowledgments so many times now, that I'm starting to run out of new ways to say thank you to the people who have helped, encouraged, and stood by me. So I've decided to write my acknowledgments in Klingon.

cha'DIch qo' 'oH naDev. 'uch lIj tlhuH!

Okay, that's probably a bad idea. I should probably just thank everyone.

First is my publishing team. Thanks to Scott Miller at Trident Media Group for being a supreme agent. At Thomas Dunne Books I have to thank my editor, Peter Wolverton, who has taught me so much about writing fast-paced thrillers, and Anne Bensson, who is always available to help me. I also have to thank Rafal Gibek and the production team, for copy-edits that make me look like a better writer than I am.

For help developing the crazy, but plausible, science at the core of the *SecondWorld* story, I must thank "Chemist-tree" from physicsforums.com, where I received ideas and advice from a number of scientists in a variety of fields.

For advance reading I have to thank Roger Brodeur, whose fate lies within these pages. I also have to thank Kane Gilmour, Stan Tremblay, Walter Elly, and Christopher Ouellette for listening to my crazy ideas and helping to make them crazier.

As always, I must thank the people who make all aspects of my life more fun, creative, and unpredictable, Norah, Solomon, and Aquila, my children. And thanks to my wife, whose unwavering belief that I could chase and catch my dreams allowed me to do so. Love you guys.

PROLOGUE

"I've never seen a person melt before," Dr. Kurt Debus said, twisting his skinny fingers together as though tying a knot.

"A *person*?" The deep voice oozed disdain.

Debus flinched in surprise and turned around. He had no idea how the two-hundred-pound four-star general and his polished boots, which normally announced his presence with the subtlety of a Clydesdale, had snuck up on him. He glanced at his counterpart, Dr. Walther Gerlach, and saw trepidation in his blue eyes. Fear threatened to crush Debus's heart, but he quickly regained control of his emotions and responded, "I was simply speaking in physiological terms, Obergruppenführer. They are only Jews, after all."

SS Obergruppenführer Emil Mazuw raised a skeptical eyebrow high on his broad, flat forehead. As one of the highest ranking and most honored officers in the SS, he commanded a level of fear and respect that only Himmler and Der Führer himself exceeded. And as the appointed head of the research project, he wielded that power without mercy. The FEP (*Forschungen, Entwicklungen, Patente,* translated Research, Development, and Patents) expected nothing less. Results were needed immediately if the tide of the war was to be reversed.

When discomfort crept back into Debus's expression, Mazuw grinned and placed a hand on the frail-looking scientist's shoulder. With a chuckle he said, "You have nothing to fear, Doctor. Had I thought you a sympathizer we wouldn't be talking, would we?"

Debus looked to the ground, unable to meet Mazuw's piercing eyes, which were surrounded by the scar-covered flesh of a man who didn't fear violence. "No, Obergruppenführer, we would not."

Mazuw turned toward Gerlach, who had made himself busy by straightening his bow tie. "Are we on schedule?"

Gerlach gave a nod as a stiff breeze snuck up behind him and tossed his white hair. He smoothed it quickly and said, "Yes, sir. We will begin in ten minutes." He glanced beyond Mazuw for a moment, distracted by the sight of so many people. Their entire science team was present—sixty-two men—which wasn't uncommon during tests, but the hundred Schutzstaffel soldiers behind them, armed with Sturmgewehr 44 assault rifles, unsettled him.

Mazuw noted Gerlach's distraction and looked over his shoulder. The line of soldiers straightened under his gaze.

"If you don't mind me asking," Gerlach said, but never had a chance to finish his sentence.

Mazuw anticipated the question and answered, "After today's successful test, the device will be dismantled and moved by Obergruppenführer Kammler."

"Moved?" Debus asked. "Where?"

Mazuw ignored him, turning back to Gerlach. "Ten minutes." He walked away, his feet clomping over the concrete ramp. The wind picked up again as he left, but the man's gray cap and stiff pressed officer's tunic seemed impervious to its effect.

Gerlach, however, was not. His body shook with a chill. He wrapped his arms around his chest. "I knew what you meant," he said to Debus. "About the persons."

"Will they really melt?" Debus asked. "Is such a thing possible?"

Gerlach ran a hand through his hair, which had begun falling out after being too close to the device during the first test. He had suffered no other ill effects, but the resulting widow's peak left him self-conscious. "I cannot explain it. It is better if you see it for yourself."

"You *can't* explain it?"

"I do not wish to." Gerlach let out a long, slow breath. "Come, they are almost ready." He walked to the side wall of the observation platform. They were a half mile away from the sight atop a two-hundred-foot hill that offered spectacular views of the test site and the large factory just beyond it. The factory produced bullets—or so the world thought. In truth, it served as laboratories and a fabrication area for the Third Reich's most classified project. The thick walls, coated with ceramic, provided protection from the effects of the project's outdoor tests, but because today's test would be at full power and involve a radical new phase against which ceramic could not shield, they had evacuated the faux factory.

Debus raised a pair of binoculars to his eyes, looking down at the test site. "They're nearly finished."

Gerlach's keen eyes didn't require the binoculars to make out what was happening. The last two of fifty Jews were being secured to a wooden post in the outer test circle. There were three concentric rings of posts. The first stood only fifteen feet from the test site's epicenter. The second was fifty feet away—the known limit of the powerful field that would be generated. The third ring stood one hundred feet away, well within the usual safety zone. But today's test, if all went well, would expand the lethality of the bell-shaped device Gerlach had dubbed the Beehive, a name that referred to the buzzing sound it made when activated.

The heavy clomping that marked the return of Mazuw tensed both men. Gerlach leaned in close to Debus. "That man will soon cause us both to lose our hair."

They shared a smile, which vanished when Mazuw spoke. "The bomber is en route. ETA three minutes. Are you ready?"

The question was asked in such a way that sounded more like "You better be ready." Gerlach looked through his binoculars, inspecting the site more closely. He could see the last of the support staff quickly vacating the area. No one liked being near the Beehive, especially when it was powered and ready to launch. He scanned over the rings of wooden posts. Each post held two Jews, strung up by their wrists. None of them struggled against their restraints. They'd long since become resigned to their fate, though Gerlach knew that fate would be far worse than any of them could imagine.

Still, he had no sympathy for them. Not only were they Jews, and thus subhuman, but he had also carried out similar experiments numerous times before. After the first successful test of the device, the one that had caused the recession of his hairline, he had vomited violently. He had never seen a man killed before, and he couldn't think of a worse way to die. In the past year, hundreds of men, women, and children had lost their lives in a similar fashion. The fifty down below meant little to a conscience that no longer existed.

"All is ready," Gerlach said. "You may proceed."

Gerlach typically started each test himself, but Mazuw wanted his full attention on today's events. He watched the general approach of the science team stationed at the portable control panel, which was really just a glorified on/off switch. The team responded to his commands, turning dials and watching gauges as power began to flow to the Hive. He glanced at Debus, who'd gone back to fidgeting his fingers. The man was clearly unnerved by what he was about to see. He'd been integral to this phase of the Hive's completion. While his official specialty was rocket science, and he'd made amazing contributions to the V2 rocket campaign, his true genius lay in the field of magnetic field separation. The resulting power supply made today's expanded test possible. With refinement, it might very well change the world.

But Debus had never witnessed the destructive power he'd helped create. And the impending test had him understandably nervous. Debus stroked the deep scar that ran from his cheek to just under his lower lip, possibly recalling the act of violence that had created it.

"You may close your eyes if you'd like," Gerlach said. While he had no sympathy for those about to lose their lives on the testing grounds, he felt protective of his team and colleagues. Debus was a good man. A good Nazi. But not everyone had the stomach for such things. "The general doesn't need to know."

Debus shook his head. "I helped create it. I must see."

A loud buzz rolled up the hill, cascading over the observation platform.

"It's beginning," Gerlach said.

Both men turned their attention to the bell-shaped Hive. Its brushed-metal surface reflected the sun's light and made it hard to look at directly. A concrete framework that looked like a modern Stonehenge surrounded the device and held four spools of metal cable, each attached to the base of the Hive.

The buzz grew louder and a flicker of blue light, brighter than the sun's reflection, pulsed across the Hive's exterior. Gerlach glanced at his watch. "Ten seconds."

Debus licked his lips.

And then it began.

Shrill cries of pain rose up from the valley below, so sharp that they cut straight through the droning buzz. Debus's hands shook as he witnessed the impossible. He focused on a single man, fighting the twisting knot in his gut.

The man's skin had been taut with hunger, muscles and bones clearly visible. All at once, the skin loosened and hung, as though his muscles had been liquefied. When dark red ooze began flowing from all of the man's orifices, Debus realized that was exactly what had happened. Different colors joined the mix, each substance of the man's internal organs flowing out as a distinct color, many of which he did not know existed within the human body. In ten seconds, the insides of his body had poured out of him, leaving a husk of skin hanging on bone. He thought that was the end, but then the skin began separating from itself, hanging in large sheets, dripping oily fluids before falling clean from the bones.

Debus bit his lip to hide its trembling, but couldn't stop a gasp of shock from escaping as the cartilage holding the man's bones together stretched out and then separated. The bones fell away, mixing with a puddle of what once was a man. The radius and ulna bones of the man's forearms hung from the rope bindings.

A second set of screams rose up from below.

"Has it reached the second ring already?" Debus asked, shifting his view.

"No," Gerlach replied. "They saw what happened to the others. It will reach them soon enough. But there are far more interesting sights at the moment." He took hold of Debus's binoculars and pulled them back toward the Hive.

Debus squinted at the bright blue light pulsing from the bell, but once his eyes adjusted he saw something amazing. The binoculars fell from his eyes. He looked up at his slightly taller counterpart. "It is flying?"

"Hovering. Thanks to your power supply."

A wide grin spread across Debus's face. A shift in the screaming below turned him back to the valley. He watched, without binoculars, as the invisible field emitted by the Hive reached the second ring. He could see the bodies shearing away from the posts. But movement took his eyes away from the silenced test subjects.

The Hive rose up into the air, slowly at first, and then rapidly. Fifty feet from the ground the metal cables snapped taut and the bell's ascent came to a sudden stop. It pulled against its restraints and for a moment Gerlach feared it might break free. But the cables held, and the now bright blue bell remained stationary.

"The bomber is inbound," Mazuw said. "Initiate stage two."

Gerlach didn't respond. He knew Mazuw wasn't addressing him and didn't want to miss what was about to happen. This was the second untested portion of this experiment, the first being flight. The second was something that if executed to its full potential . . . well, there was a reason this project alone had been deemed *Kriegsentscheidend*—decisive for the war.

"What's stage two?" Debus asked.

The buzz of the Hive was joined by the low rumble of plane engines. The roar of the plane grew louder, blotting out the sound of the bell completely as the large four-engine Fw 200 Condor passed just overhead. Papers and hats flew up and away in its wake. Gerlach held his wispy hair and silently cursed the plane. But he couldn't blame the pilots. He knew they had to skirt this hill, descending into the valley quickly so they could empty their payload into the energy field and pull up before careening into another hill. He gripped the handrail and leaned forward, eager to see if his theories would prove true.

The Condor's bomb bay doors opened. A massive gray cloud of fine particles poured out. The particles fell toward the bell slowly at first, held aloft by the valley's high winds. For a moment, Gerlach feared the wind would ruin the test, but then the cloud began to spin. A vortex formed at the middle, spinning faster. A bolt of lightning shot from the cloud, nearly striking the bomber as it banked out of the valley. A thunderous boom struck the observation platform.

With a flash of bright blue light, the storm of particles spun down into a small opening at the top of the bell.

What happened next left Gerlach, Debus, Mazuw, sixty-two scientists, and one hundred soldiers speechless. They gaped in silence as the phenomenon that followed descended on the valley. The screams of the remaining Jews in the outer circle became muddled by gagging. Then they too fell silent. A flock of birds sprang from the trees at the bottom of the hill. Thirty feet from the surface, their flight became erratic. As one, they fell back to the earth, dead.

Debus gripped Gerlach's coat sleeve.

"I know," Gerlach said. "It's amazing."

More birds rose from the trees, falling moments later.

"No, Walther. The birds."

Gerlach hadn't paid attention to the birds. He'd been too busy admiring his invention. But now that Debus had pointed them out, he saw what had the man concerned. He

felt a tickle on his head, and brushed his hair down. Then he
realized what was happening. The wind had turned in their
direction, and it was carrying the Hive's deadly product
toward them.

After spinning around so fast that he nearly fell over,
Gerlach shouted, "Shut it down!"

"What?" Mazuw asked. "Why?"

Gerlach stabbed a finger to the hill descending below
them. "The birds!"

Mazuw saw a fresh flock of birds take to the sky only to
drop dead seconds later. But these birds were only one
hundred feet away. Mazuw gave the command and the device was shut down. The buzzing slowed. They watched
through a red haze as the bell slowly descended toward the
launchpad.

Gerlach sighed with relief and followed it with a deep
breath. But the air in his lungs seemed inadequate. He took
a second breath and found no relief. His eyes widened as he
saw the others around him similarly affected. They had shut
down the bell, but not the wind. With the last of the air in his
lungs he shouted, "Down the hill! Run!"

One hundred sixty-five men abandoned the observation
platform, pounding down the hill away from the test site.
Men fell, cursed, and toppled over one another, but no one
slowed. Two hundred feet below the hill's crest, they stopped.
Gerlach gasped for air, terrified for several seconds until
the burning in his lungs began to ebb. The air was fresh and
full of earthy scents. Birds danced in the tree branches and a
few chipmunks stared at them. They were safe.

Mazuw stormed across the forest floor. His cap was missing. His uniform held sticks and patches of mud. And his
eyes burned with fury. "What happened?" he demanded
with a growl.

"The wind. It shifted the effects toward the platform."

"We were a half mile away," Debus noted.

Gerlach fought a widening smile, but could not contain it.

Mazuw took Gerlach by the coat, putting his bulldog face
within inches of the scientist's. "We were almost killed. *My*

men, who are the very best the SS have produced and represent the future of the Reich, were almost killed."

"I know."

"Then why are you smiling?"

"Because, Obergruppenführer, it worked. Beyond our greatest expectations. It worked."

Mazuw considered this for a moment before letting go of Gerlach's shirt. His expression became one of deep thought. "Well done," he said after nearly a minute. "You will speak of this to no one."

"But there is much to do if we are to use this against the Allies," Gerlach said.

"There is not enough time," Mazuw said. "The war is all but over."

"But—"

"Patience is as deadly a weapon as any, Gerlach. The device will be moved. Refined. And when the conditions are right . . ."

"Where are we going?"

"*They,*" he said, while motioning to his men, "are going with Kammler. To someplace you cannot follow. A man of your, and Debus's, renown will be sought after by the Allies when the war ends. Your disappearance would lead to questions. Do not fear, Doctor, we will be in touch."

"But . . . where will we go?" Debus asked.

"You will surrender, of course. Avoid the Russians. Find the Americans, if you can. Agree to aid them in any way, but *never* mention what you saw here today or any part of this project. We *will* rise from the ashes. Am I understood?"

Debus nodded, once again fidgeting with his fingers. "Yes, Obergruppenführer. I have but one more question."

Mazuw stared at him, waiting.

"What will happen to our team? Surely you can't—"

"Take aim!" Mazuw shouted. The forest filled with the sounds of weapons being readied and people shouting in fear. "Fire!"

SECONDWORLD
First Strike

1.

"Shit!"

The microwave door flew open and Rachel Carter reached her hand in.

The spoon, left in the bowl of oatmeal and heated along with the cardboard-flavored breakfast, had been shooting off blue sparks when she noticed it. Without thinking, she grabbed the spoon. A millisecond later, her mind registered the stupidity of her action, along with the searing heat. Her arm reacted quicker than her fingers, flailing backward. The spoon soared across the kitchen, weighted with expensive organic oats, and smacked against the stainless steel fridge, where both breakfast and spoon clung like Silly Putty.

Rachel turned on the tap and ran cold water over her pulsing index finger and thumb, her glare fixed on the spoon. It slid slowly toward the floor.

"You okay, Mom?" asked her ten-year-old daughter, Samantha.

"Fine."

Samantha walked past the fridge, paused, stepped back and looked at the spoon. She turned to her mother with an eyebrow raised. "Fine?"

Rachel forced a smile that communicated a single message: don't ask.

Samantha shrugged and pulled a chair up to the counter. She climbed onto the chair, then onto the counter.

"Get down from there!"

"I'm hungry."

"I made you oatmeal."

"You're gonna make me puke, too, if I have to eat that sludge."

With two granola bars in hand, she jumped down from the counter, swung the chair back to the table, and began unwrapping the first bar. Jake, the younger of the two siblings, strode into the kitchen, still in his footie pajamas, which he wore most days. "One of the advantages of being homeschooled," he was fond of saying. Samantha tossed him the second granola bar and they sat at the table, eating in silence.

Rachel sighed. She couldn't complain. At least they were eating granola bars and not fast-food egg and sausage sandwiches—which she suspected her husband, Walter, had been sneaking on his way to work. Again. She looked at the microwave clock.

8:30 A.M.

"Walter, you're going to be late!" she shouted after noticing the time. He worked for a big downtown marketing firm and had a major pitch to make that afternoon.

Walter slid into the kitchen, moving fast. He opened the cabinet, reached up, and took down the granola bar box. Empty. "Ouch. Epic fail." He looked at Rachel, who nodded toward the kids. Her grin said it all.

He took in their barely contained smiles. "Traitors!" He sighed. "I guess I'll just get something on the way."

"I'm sure you will," Rachel replied, drying off her still-stinging finger.

"What?"

Rachel stared intently at him, trying to convey her annoyance over his bad eating habits, without actually having to spell it out for him in front of the children.

Seeing her expression, Walter laughed. "I have no idea

what you're talking about! Now get out of my head, woman!"
He grabbed his bag and headed down the hallway for the
front door.

"Love you!" Rachel shouted as the door creaked open.

There was no reply.

No customary "Love you, too."

No closing door.

No starting car.

She was about to go check on him when Walter slowly
backed into the kitchen. He had his iPhone out and was
tapping the screen madly. This wasn't an uncommon activity, but the dire look on his face was far from normal. Rachel held her breath. The kids stopped giggling and watched
their father.

"What is it?" she asked. "Did the job fall through already?"

Walter shook his head and kept on tapping. Then he
stopped. "This is wrong."

"What?" she demanded, growing worried. "Is the phone
broken?"

He stared blankly down at the screen. "It's happening
everywhere—all over the world. Wait— Crap, I lost our
Wi-Fi connection."

"Walter . . ."

"The 3G network is down, too." He met his wife's eyes.
"It must be disrupting cell service."

She took his face in her hands, willing his stunned eyes
to meet hers. "Walter! What are you talking about? What is
happening?"

He glanced toward the still-open front door. She followed
his gaze and gasped.

The kids hopped out of their chairs to look.

"It's snowing!" Jake shouted, running for the door.

"No!" Walter jumped forward and snagged his son by the
sleeve. He looked at Rachel, his expression alarmed. "Close
any open windows. Tape the seams. Use the duct tape."

She nodded, feeling sick, and they both set off around the

house, closing doors and windows. Samantha and Jake went
into the living room, climbed onto the couch, and peered
curiously out the bay window.

"Why can't we go out?" Jake asked. "It *never* snows here.
I want to play in the snow!"

"Dad says it's not snow."

Jake looked grumpy. "Well, how does he know?"

"Because, silly, snow isn't red."

2.

Akiko Sato woke to a loud chime.

She reached for the alarm and hit the snooze button. The sound disappeared and she returned to sleep within seconds.

Moments later, the shrill electronic chime sounded again. Her mind, pulled from REM sleep by the first chime, finally registered the sound for what it was—her cell phone. She rolled over to look at the clock, but her tightly tucked-in sheets resisted her movement.

Had she missed her alarm? Was work calling to find out why she was late?

When she saw the time, she relaxed.

10:30 P.M.

She'd only been asleep for half an hour.

She brought the phone up to her eyes and squinted in the screen's bright blue glow as she read the caller ID. She groaned. *Tadao.* Her boyfriend. Soon to be ex-boyfriend. He was nice enough, but just too clingy for her. She hadn't called to say goodnight, and here he was, calling her instead. She popped open the phone and decided that she would break it off with the whipped pup of a man tomorrow. Tonight she had to sleep, and that meant saying goodnight now, or the phone would ring until morning.

"I was asleep, Tadao."

"Sorry, sorry. Right, it's late. But you have to see something."

Just say goodnight, hang up, and go to sleep, she willed herself. "I'm up at four thirty. You know that, don't you? I have to go."

"Wait! Just look out your window."

She glanced toward the drawn shades on the other end of her long, narrow bedroom. She lived on the thirtieth floor of a high-rise apartment building. The only thing to look at outside her window was other buildings. What could he want her to see?

A surge of nervous energy stirred in her belly. Normally reserved and always professional, Tadao sounded unusually lively. Like someone about to do something stupid. He was a system programmer, making it possible for hotels to control lighting and environmental systems from one location. He had, in fact, worked on several of the hotels within eyeshot of her building.

She had a feeling she knew where this phone call was leading.

"I'm going," she said as she yanked free of her sheets and stumbled over to the window. She hoped he wasn't going to take a picture of her in her nightgown, using some kind of long-range camera while she read, with a scowl on her face, his marriage proposal written out in lights on the side of a building.

She was positive that's what he had planned, because as reserved as Tadao was, that was exactly the stupid romantic kind of stunt he would pull.

She took hold of the curtain and held her breath. She'd never been one to climb slowly into a pool. She preferred to jump in. Let the shock hit her all at once and then fade all the more quickly. She counted to three, then jerked open the curtain, scouring the buildings for anything unusual.

Everything looked normal. Tokyo glowed brightly below her window. A thick haze filled the air, which was nothing new, though the color seemed more vibrant than usual. The streets were packed, which was typical.

Well, not quite typical, actually. Something was different. She pressed her nose lightly against the glass and looked down.

The streets were mobbed, but no one was moving one way or the other, simply standing frozen as they gazed upward in awe.

"Are you there? Do you see it?" Tadao asked. "Pretty amazing, right?"

She caught her breath. "I don't see anything."

"Step onto your balcony and look up."

Akiko did as she was told, more curious now than worried. She unlocked the slider, pulled it open, and stepped out into the cool night air. She breathed deep and sneezed immediately. The air was bad tonight.

But then she looked up and forgot all about the air.

The sky was ablaze with colors! Like a rainbow in motion, the atmosphere from horizon to horizon danced with vivid colors like the aurora borealis seen through a kaleidoscope. Hundreds, perhaps thousands, of bright streaks, like shooting stars zipping in and out of view, made the display even more spectacular.

She laughed.

"Beautiful, right?"

"Uh-huh."

"Like you," he said.

Akiko frowned, closed the phone, and tossed it back inside. It began ringing a moment later. She closed the door, blocking out the sound, and returned to watching the sky. Tadao could call all night if he wanted to. She doubted anyone in Tokyo would be sleeping tonight.

She turned toward the sky again as a collective "ahhh" rose up from the streets below. The shooting stars had picked up pace. They were everywhere. They were incredibly beautiful.

But somehow ominous.

She looked down at the people below again, all still looking up. Something major was happening. She followed their gaze and for the first time saw something in the night sky brighter than the neon city lights. The haze wasn't haze. It had a solid form to it.

Like snow.

Red snow.

She glanced down at the shoulder of her pale blue nightgown. What looked like ruddy dandruff, though some bits were more similar in size to a fifty-yen coin, covered the light fabric. Her entire nightgown was coated in it. Akiko gasped, breathing some of it in.

Tasting it.

She gagged and spit, trying to expunge the flavor from her mouth, but each breath only increased the potency.

The air tasted like blood.

3.

Fifty feet below the surface of the tropical ocean, Lincoln Miller cringed as his eyes locked onto the cracked portal window. A spiderweb of fissures spread out from the center, reaching for the edge like desperate fingers. He knew the glass would give way at any moment and ocean water would rocket into the research station, drowning whoever was inside.

Despite the dire circumstances, he had more urgent needs to attend to. He picked up the TV remote and paused the DVD before heading to the bathroom. The picture froze on the screen, stopping the first jet of CGI water as it rocketed through the portal.

As an NCIS (Naval Criminal Investigation Service) special agent currently tasked with investigating recently reported acts of ocean dumping over the coral reefs, Miller was technically hard at work. There were only three other people in the world who knew he wasn't—the director of the NCIS, the deputy director, and the executive assistant director for combating terrorism—his bosses. He had balked at the assignment when it landed on his desk. His skills were better suited to tracking down navy criminals on the lam or hunting seafaring terrorists. As a former Navy SEAL, now special agent, his skills seemed a gross overkill in the battle against glorified litterbugs. It wasn't until he arrived on-site that he realized the true nature of his assignment—a vacation.

He was scheduled to spend two weeks in Aquarius, an undersea research station run by NOAA (National Oceanic and Atmospheric Administration)—the world's *only* underwater research station. He was required to patrol the reefs surrounding the laboratory twice daily, searching for signs of recent polluting, and if possible, apprehend the culprits in the act. As a scuba enthusiast and lover of all things ocean, he looked forward to each and every "patrol."

Because Miller was an extreme workaholic, the NOAA assignment was the only way his superiors could get him to take his first real break in five years. It wasn't that Miller was performing poorly; quite the opposite. They simply believed that no engine could run forever without a respite. In truth, their actions were selfish. Were Miller to burn out, the loss would be significant to the organization. Not only was he a consummate investigator, but his time with the SEALs made him a man of action as well. The NCIS had plenty of both, but rarely in the same package.

With his first week of forced vacation over and his second week just beginning, he was feeling pretty good. The laboratory was cramped, but he had traveled by submarine several times as a SEAL and had no problems with claustrophobia. The lab was well stocked with every deep-sea movie and novel available. The lab's full refrigerator, air-conditioning, microwave, shower, and high-tech computer system, complete with video games, not to mention unlimited time to swim or even spearfish, made this place Miller's dream come true. Of course, he'd spent the last few days lazing about, watching movies, playing games, and reading books. He suspected the "ocean dumping" investigation was just a clever cover story for his vacation and had taken a break from his scheduled scuba patrols. There was plenty of time left to dive; he just needed some couch potato time first.

The facility was a forty-three-foot long, nine-foot in di-

ameter, eighty-ton cylindrical steel chamber separated into
two different compartments, each with its own air-pressure
system and life support. There were living quarters for sleeping and eating, and labs for work. At the far end, off the lab,
was a wet porch with an open moon pool for entering the
ocean. Miller had all of this to himself, plus—and this was
the best part—not a peep from the outside world for three
days.

It's not that he didn't like people. It's just that people
liked to talk, and after his first day aboard he had decided
the break would be good for him. Quiet was bliss. Years of
pent-up tension he hadn't realized he carried began to melt
away. So when the NOAA staff stopped checking in on
their laboratory, he didn't think twice about why. Instead, he
allowed himself to undergo an emotional readjustment. He
went over years of cases, of killers caught, of terrorists exposed, and the few who had slipped away. Then he moved
farther back, to the SEALs, and the event that had etched a
long scar into his leg and left a little girl dead. The tragedy
ended his career with the SEALs, but down here, fifty feet
beneath the surface of the ocean, he thought he might finally
make peace with his past.

After he finished the movie.

Finished relieving himself, Miller hustled back to his seat
without washing his hands. Why bother? Urine was sterile.
More important, no one was here to judge him. He'd let his
appearance slide over the past week, as well. His black hair
was uncombed, his face unshaven. Thanks to his half-
Jewish, half-Italian ancestry, Miller's week's worth of facial
hair was damn near a beard now.

The chair beneath him groaned as he leaned back and
propped his legs up on a work desk. With the remote back in
his hand, he waited, held his breath, and listened.

Silence.

Wonderful silence.

No worried NOAA voices. No traffic. No cell phone calls.
He thought about telling the director that the time off had
convinced him to retire. Sure, he was only thirty-nine, but

life without responsibility was fun. He held out the remote, positioned his thumb over the Play button, and—

Thunk!

The noise wasn't loud, but was so unexpected that Miller flinched, lost his balance, and toppled over. He struck his head hard on the metal floor.

"Son of a bitch!"

He lay there for a moment, wondering exactly how he'd ended up on the floor, and then felt the back of his head. One area, the size of an apple, was swollen, pulsing with pain, but there was no blood. He wouldn't need stitches, which was good because he couldn't get them here. In fact, if there was any kind of emergency, he was pretty much screwed. A nine-mile boat ride, and a fifty-foot dive, did not make for an easy 911 rescue.

He was on his own.

With a sigh, he rolled his head to the side and caught his reflection in the polished stainless steel base of a workbench. He grunted at the sight of himself. He flashed what he thought was a winning smile, sharpening the fine spread of crow's-feet around his blue eyes, but his current disheveled appearance hid his good looks. He hadn't seen himself look this bad since just after . . .

He pushed the images from his mind, still not fully prepared to deal with his past—not with a movie to finish, and a mysterious noise needing investigating.

He sat up. Pain surged through his head twice, following the rhythm of his heartbeat, and then faded away. When he stood, the pain rose up again, but only momentarily. Shuffling over to the fridge to grab an ice pack, he passed by the small bedroom containing six bunks, three on each side, with a large viewing portal between them. He stopped suddenly, his eyes focusing on the glass portal.

Something wasn't right.

It was a fish, not an uncommon sight, but something was odd about this one. Its movements were all wrong. He squeezed between the beds to get a better look.

Thunk!

The fish was back, this time smacking hard against the window.

Miller blinked a couple times. The fish, a black grouper, wasn't moving on its own. The ocean's currents were pushing it up against the hull.

Well, that's damn annoying.

He was about to head back to the fridge when something else flitted by the window. It looked like a large piece of fish food. This time, Miller focused on the water beyond the dead fish. There were other fish out there—scores of them—and they zipped through the water in a miniature feeding frenzy. The fish, normally concealed by the reef that Aquarius had been built to study, had come out of hiding, drawn by what looked like a Jolly Green Giant–sized handful of TetraMin. Most of the fish snatched up the flakes with gaping mouths, then spit the reddish stuff back out. If they were smart, anyway. Many fish, dumb enough to swallow the "fish food," floated belly-up. Poisoned.

Not seeing any large green legs in the vicinity, Miller searched his mind for answers and came up with only one— some jerks were *actually* dumping waste on top of the research station. Not only were they polluting and killing wildlife, they were also ruining his vacation. *Why couldn't you have waited just a few more days?* He was as pissed at these polluters as he was at the terrorists he helped track, and a piece of his mind was just the beginning of what he was going to give them.

Miller ran to the wet porch and hastily pulled on a full tank of air, dive fins, and a mask. In these tropical waters, he didn't need a wet suit, plus he was already dressed only in shorts—another perk of solitary living on board Aquarius.

He slid into the water and took in the scene around him. The flakes were falling everywhere. Fish, thousands of them, were either eating eagerly, twitching in violent death throes, or already dead. A few small white-tip sharks picked off the twitchers in the distance. The sharks didn't pose much of a threat, but he would have to watch out for tigers and bulls. All this action could draw their attention, which meant he could easily be mistaken for one of the twitchers—not that tiger sharks cared. He could be a car and they'd still take a bite.

He kicked out from under the Aquarius cylinder and looked up. What he saw made no sense.

The normally blue surface of the ocean . . .

. . . was red.

4.

Miller scanned the fuchsia waves above, looking for some sign of dumping—a thicker plume of material, for example, or better yet, a ship's hull. When he found what he was looking for, he intended to rise from the depths like the Kraken and bring a world of hurt to the people responsible. But he could see nothing to direct his anger toward, just an endless sea of red. Visibility had been cut in half, not just by the fog falling from above, but because much of the sun's light was being blocked by the maroon film covering the ocean's surface.

Miller looked down. The normally sandy brown seabed was coated in the ruddy ash; the coral reef had been buried. Dying fish thrashed about, sending plumes of the foreign substance upward like dust.

How had he missed this? It couldn't have just started. There was too much. He hadn't been outside Aquarius for days, but had he really not bothered to look out one of the portals?

A ladyfish struck his side, its silver body twitching as the last of its neurons fired. He took the fish by the tail and pulled it closer; its body went rigid, giving way to death. Pulling its mouth open, he peered inside. Red sludge lined the dark cave, thick as paint. He checked the gills and found the same phenomenon.

His eyes darted back to the snowy scene of death surrounding him. Some fish and the sharks in the distance had
taken to eating the recently dead instead of chasing after
the poisonous flakes. Perhaps they would survive? He hoped
so. A massive die-off in the Florida Keys would have a pro-
found effect on the surrounding ecosystems, not to mention
the many migratory species that passed through. A pod of
blue whales had recently been spotted heading north. The
red cloud, which looked like krill, would be absolutely irresistible to the one-hundred-foot giants.

A fluttering piece of red material, about the size of a corn
flake, caught his eye. He reached out and caught it in his
palm, then grasped it between two fingers. It was surprisingly firm. He squeezed and it broke apart. He rubbed his
fingers together, releasing a bloodlike cloud as the material
dissolved.

He took a deep breath from his regulator, tasting the
metallic-flavored air, and let it out slowly, releasing a cascade
of bubbles, which fled to the surface. His eyes followed
them. He knew the answer to this mystery lay up there. The
more he saw, however, the less he wanted to know what was
happening.

But he had no choice.

He kicked hard, pumping his muscles, an action that ate
up the air in his tank more quickly than would a leisurely
swim. He checked the pressure gauge—still plenty of air
remaining. This would most likely be a short dive, so he
could take the risk. Besides, the wet porch was only fifty
feet below and he could free dive that if he had to. Holding
your breath for long periods of time is a handy talent to have
as a SEAL, and one he had worked on over the years. The
skill had yet to save his life, but he had a feeling it would,
eventually.

As he neared the surface, the material grew dense, which
meant it was definitely coming from above and not being
pushed into the area by ocean currents. The material had to
be coming from a boat, or a plane, or . . . Well, he didn't

want to consider the last possibility, and wouldn't, until he confirmed it with his own eyes.

Through the haze he found the umbilical cord that connected Aquarius to its life support buoy, or LSB. The LSB supplied power and provided wireless communications and telemetry to the station and held air compressors, as well. It also made for a convenient viewing platform. While standing on top of the LSB, which was shaped like a super-sized yellow chess piece, Miller would be able to see from horizon to horizon. If someone was dumping this garbage, he'd spot them.

Approaching the buoy, Miller kicked harder, building speed so he could launch himself onto the platform. As he broke the surface, clumps of wet slime slid from his back and arms. A glob clung to his hair, but he paid it no attention. What he was seeing distracted him from doing anything else. He didn't stand, remove his goggles, or take out his regulator. He simply gaped.

The world was red. As far as he could see, a crust, like refrigerated pudding, coated the surface of the ocean. There wasn't a cloud to be seen, yet crimson flakes fell like snow from a sky that looked more purple than blue.

Heart beating hard, he stood up and looked in every direction. He spotted a sailboat off to the north, its sail limp as wilted lettuce, but nothing else caught his eye.

Miller tentatively held out a hand and caught another flake. Its surface felt rough and porous to his touch, like a petrified snowflake. Curious, he removed his regulator and placed the flake on his tongue. The flavor of blood struck him immediately. He gagged and spit several times, then took a deep, shaky breath. The air did no good. He felt winded, as though he'd just run a sprint.

He took another breath. His chest began to ache. He grew light-headed.

He took a third, deeper breath—

—and fell to his knees.

Was it poison? Could these flakes kill so quickly?

Spots danced in his vision as he realized the truth.

He was suffocating.

Drowning in the open air like a fish.

He shoved the regulator back into his mouth and breathed deeply, this time relishing the metallic-tasting air. He continued taking deep breaths until his head cleared and he felt relatively normal again. It wasn't until then that he let his mind fill in the blanks.

He couldn't breathe in the open air! What did it mean? What . . .

Oh shit! Miller thought. *I can't breathe because . . . there's no oxygen!*

5.

Miller shot up out of the water and into the wet porch, yanked out his regulator, and slipped out of his swim fins. During his frantic dive back to Aquarius he'd had time to run through some possibilities. This event could be local, regional, or—disastrously—global. All three scenarios were bad for him. With no oxygen in the air, rescue might be impossible.

If there was anyone left to rescue him.

He threw off his gear and raced to the computer terminal. He sat, still wet, in the computer chair, bouncing his legs while the system booted.

"C'mon, you son of a bitch. Start!" The computer's typical thirty-second boot time felt like an eternity. When the desktop appeared, he was forced to wait as programs opened in the background and the wireless searched for a signal.

"Connect . . . connect . . ."

A message appeared at the bottom right of the screen.

NO WIRELESS NETWORKS DETECTED

"Shit!"

He opened the network window and clicked Reconnect.

The same message came up. He had no Internet. No e-mail. No webcam.

But the life support buoy had a radio antenna. He rolled across the floor and wiped the bachelor detritus—wrappers, empty bottles, crumbs—from its surface, and switched the radio on. He quickly set the radio to broadcast on all frequencies and held down the Transmit button.

"This is Aquarius Research Station, nine miles south of Key Largo. Does anyone copy? Over."

He waited to a count of ten. "This is Aquarius Research Station, south of Key Largo. I seem to be experiencing some kind of atmospheric event. It's killing the fish. And . . . and the air. There's no oxygen in the air."

Oxygen.

His mind was trying to tell him something.

Air.

He let go of the Transmit button for a moment. Then his navy training kicked in and he pushed the button back down for a brief moment. "Over."

The microphone fell to the floor, dangling by its springy cord. He rolled back to the computer hoping he could still access the internal network. All of the station's systems could be checked and monitored from here—pressure, batteries, backup systems . . . and air. It was the last item on this list with which he was most concerned.

The digital gauges rose and fell as the system calibrated and then displayed the current levels. Miller leaned back in his chair, his jaw slack. The air gauge was near the bottom and blinking red, the universal signal for: You're screwed.

He punched up the maintenance schedule. The station was due for a recharge of air, pumped into the storage tanks from a ship that connected with the LSB. The refill had been scheduled for two days ago, but something had gone wrong. Miller was getting the awful feeling that a refill wasn't ever going to come.

According to the readouts, he had three more days of air left. The emergency reserve would give him another two after that. Plus, three high-pressure way stations sat approximately one thousand feet from Aquarius. They were originally meant to refuel the air tanks of divers on extended dives, but perhaps he could rig them so that they could supply Aquarius?

Which left him a definite five days to be rescued, maybe more with the air from the way stations.

And if he wasn't?

Then I'll die, he thought. *From a slow, painful asphyxiation.*

There had to be a solution. There had to be something he—

With the force of a train, something huge struck the side of Aquarius and tossed Miller into the air. His head struck the computer table as he fell, knocking him unconscious.

He woke a short time later to warm liquid oozing down the side of his face. He groaned at the pain in his head, and when he reached up to feel his skull for the second time in one day, he expected his hand to come away with a fresh coating of blood.

But there was no blood.

He leaped to his feet, realizing in an instant the awful truth. He fought to remain upright on a wet, steadily tilting floor. The Aquarius had sprung a leak and was leaning at a sickening angle. Miller turned toward the nearest portal. Something dark blocked his view. He hobbled to the bedroom viewport and found the same thing. Something massive had struck the research station and was now pinned up against it.

A pop followed by a metallic groan echoed through the cabin.

The weight of whatever was out there was tipping Aquarius over. If the station leaned too far, the ocean would pour in through the open wet porch. He could seal himself in the living quarters, but then what? Eventually, he would run out of air. And if Aquarius gave all at once, the wet porch might be slammed against the seafloor and he'd be trapped like a lobster in a cage.

He had to get out.

His thoughts raced. He needed to gather as many oxygen tanks as he could. Any supplies he could carry. And—

The lab tilted another ten degrees. He heard rushing water. He felt, more than saw, the lab continuing to roll. It was going to flip.

There was no time!

He ran for the wet porch, splashing through a foot of water. His foot caught on something sharp, sending a stab of pain through his leg. But he didn't slow down to check the damage. He could see water surging in through the open pool. And a shadow beyond it. He ignored the massive shape, thrust his hands into the water, and found his dive fins, mask, and air tank. He threw the tank onto his back and locked it in place. He took a small, portable pony bottle air tank and strapped it to his wrist.

He was reaching for a second pony bottle when a support beam gave way. Slowed by the tremendous amount of water pressing against the sides of the research station, the beam didn't buckle completely. It simply started to fall, then roll.

Realizing what had happened, Miller dove into the water and kicked hard without looking back. He was still holding the swim fins and the mask when he entered the water, but he knew how to streamline his body and swim efficiently with his finless feet. When a large pressure wave struck him from behind, he knew that Aquarius had hit the bottom. His home away from home was no more. He kicked until his lungs burned, then stopped, fumbled for his regulator, and thrust it in his mouth.

He put his mask on next, blowing out his nose to clear it. When his vision returned, he slipped on his swim fins and steeled himself for a shock. He turned toward Aquarius's position and saw the impossible. What had to be a hundred-foot blue whale was twisted about the station like a leech. The whale was dead. The ocean currents that passed by the station had carried the body, turning it into a deadly projectile.

Miller started kicking for the surface, but stopped short. Heading to the surface would do him no good.

There was no air up there. . . .

He took the air gauge in his hand and checked the pressure. Seeing how much time he had left, he felt tempted to remove the regulator from his mouth and let out a great, bubbly scream. He managed to stop himself just in time. He needed that air.

Then he remembered the way stations. Each was a thousand feet away. He could refill his tank at one of them, but how many times could he keep doing that? He shook his head in denial. The cold, hard facts didn't matter right now. He had no choice but to keep trying to survive. He kicked hard, heading north toward the way station.

And as he kicked, he prayed he could make the swim in twenty minutes.

Because that's all the air he had left in his primary tank.

6.

Each kick brought him closer to the way station. Each kick also used oxygen, of which he had precious little left. He checked the gauge. Four minutes.

Four minutes. For what? To live? To die trying?

He wondered for a moment if he should start contemplating the outcome of his eternal soul. If he didn't make it to the way station he would be dead in four minutes. Well, twenty minutes. The pony bottle would give him a little more time. But twenty minutes wasn't much time to figure out his fate.

He'd never been one to worry about religion, why start now? Without a priest, rabbi, or pastor around, how could he make up his mind anyway? Being totally uninformed, he would most likely choose the wrong religion and be doomed to Hell anyway. And he was pretty sure praying to a generic god wouldn't do him much good. All religions had their own steps to salvation you had to follow, or saints you had to pray to, or whatever else was being offered. He doubted simply shouting out to an "all of the above" god would seal the deal. So he ignored the question of how he was going to spend his eternity and focused on the here and now—finding the white, cylindrical way station.

He swam up and over the now ruddy reef, making sure to stay well above the ocean floor where the carpet of red flakes could be kicked up, further obscuring his flake-impeded view. It was like swimming through a snowstorm on acid. As he rose above the reef, he could see what looked like a large propane tank resting on the ocean floor.

The way station.

He glanced at his air-pressure gauge. Two minutes to spare.

His heart raced as he leveled out over the flat seabed, and then skipped a startled beat when a large object caught the corner of his eye. For a moment he wondered if he'd seen anything at all, then decided he had. The swirling plumes of flakes in the distance indicated something was out there. Something fast.

Miller kicked hard and performed the swimmer's version of a sprint. He went rigid, streamlining his body, pumped his legs, and dug through the water with cupped hands. As he closed to within thirty feet of the way station he relaxed. Whatever it was had either not seen him, or *had* seen him and not cared.

With one minute of air remaining, he slowed his approach, conserving the last few breaths in his tank before switching to the pony bottle while the large tank refilled. He'd never used the way station before, but could see the hookups clearly as he closed to within fifteen feet. It wouldn't take long to refill his tank, but—

Miller's entire body jerked violently, and then was yanked backward by his left foot. He spun about and the pressure on his foot dropped away. He was free, but ten feet farther from the way station. He glanced at his foot, which throbbed with pain. A quarter of the fin was missing, though his foot was still intact.

Or was it?

A brown cloud seeped out from inside the fin. Blood. He remembered cutting his foot as he was escaping the floundering Aquarius. He had left a trail of blood through shark-infested waters.

Idiot! Miller cursed himself, as he searched for the shark.

It circled, ten feet away.

A fourteen-foot tiger shark. It was second in size only to the great white, but its unpredictability and ferocity more than made up for the size difference. And right now it clearly had little interest in the tiny pink flakes or scores of small dying fish. It was interested in larger, still-living prey, most likely drawn by Miller's oozing blood and rapid heartbeat.

Staying alert, he moved carefully toward the way station while turning in time with the striped shark. He unstrapped the pony bottle and readied it for use. In about thirty seconds he was going to need it to breathe. He also planned to expel some of the air to scare the shark off. If the beast managed to get hold of him again, he could always use the bottle to pummel the shark's snout. Without help, without air, he wouldn't survive, anyway, but he'd rather not be eaten alive.

As the shark came between him and the way station, it twitched twice and then, with a snap of its tail, turned toward him. There was no time to blow the pony bottle. Miller reacted instinctively, kicking up and reaching out. His hands caught the shark's snout as it charged. He pushed up, moving his torso away from the open maw and squeezing the predator's sensitive, jelly-filled snout. The shark thrashed and slipped away from Miller's grip, but its large body smashed into him, spinning him around and knocking the pony bottle free. It sank to the seabed like a falling leaf. A puff of red debris exploded upward as the bottle landed.

He desperately wanted to swim down to that bottle, but his gut told him to watch out. He spun, looking for the shark, and found it bearing down on him from his left. With only a single breath remaining in the air tank, he removed the regulator from his mouth, held it out, and purged the tank. The shark veered off at the last moment, circling once again as it tried to figure out the best way to attack this defiant prey.

Miller let his last breath escape from his mouth and sank to the seafloor, never taking his eyes off the ocean's tiger. When he reached the bottom, he knelt by the pony bottle, picked it up, and put its regulator in his mouth.

He could breathe again.

He had fifteen minutes.

Staying close to the seafloor, Miller kicked toward the way station, hoping his proximity to the bottom and the large cloud of pink kicked up by his movements would confuse the predator. He reached the station, breathing heavily. He realized that if he kept sucking on the pony bottle like a hungry baby, it wasn't going to last nearly as long as it was supposed to. So he took one long, deep breath, and held it. After a count of three seconds, he slowly let out his pent-up breath, and, calmer now, set to work on refilling his air tank.

After removing his tank and detaching the regulator, he attached the tank to the way station valve, screwing the connector tight. The entire process took less than thirty seconds. He opened the way station valve and watched his pressure gauge.

It didn't move.

He closed and opened the valve again.

Nothing.

Panic set in and he began breathing heavily again. He'd done everything right. This was a basic setup! What could be—

Miller closed his eyes and shook his head.

The way station was empty.

But how?

As he searched his mind for answers, a looming shadow caught his eye. The shark still circled, but was now above him. As his eyes followed the shark around, his vision caught an aberration on the ocean surface. A long cigar shape.

A hull!

The sailboat he'd seen before.

Damn them! he thought. Whoever was on the sailboat had taken his air!

He pulled himself to the top of the way station. He was fifty feet down with a pony bottle and a fourteen-foot maneater. One fin was ruined and his foot was bleeding. He would never make it. With all the air in the world, he would never make it.

Then I'll make it with no air, he thought.

He removed the pony bottle from his mouth and looked at it. For all he knew, it contained all the breathable air left in the world. Maybe five minutes. But he could hold his breath for three. He took one last, long pull from the pony bottle, crouched, and as the shark circled closer, he banged the bottle's valve against the solid way station. A dull bong echoed through the water.

The shark jolted and turned toward him.

Miller struck with the bottle again.

The shark twitched its tail, moving in.

The third strike was followed by a loud hiss and a violent stream of bubbles. Miller twisted the bottle away from the boat's hull and let go. It took off like an injured fish. The shark snapped at the bottle as it surged past, then twisted around and gave chase.

Miller pushed off the way station and swam for the surface, holding on to that precious last breath of air.

Twenty feet from the surface, the urge to breathe welled up within him.

After another ten feet the desire became almost unbearable. The surface loomed and he kicked harder, adrenaline and fear for his life fueling his ascent.

With a quick glance back he saw the pony bottle resting on the ocean floor, still bubbling away its life-giving air. The shark had given up on the bottle and had returned its attention to Miller.

The predator rose from below, pumping its tail hard, gaining on its prey with the speed of a creature that moved much more efficiently through water than man did on land.

Miller knew that death would find him above the surface, just as surely as it raced to claim him from below, but he still did not want his last moment on earth to be one of violent gore. So he kicked hard and reached out as he approached the back of the hull. As his hands pierced the thick film coating the ocean's surface he stretched out and pushed down, hoping for a dive deck. He found one.

Using his momentum and several last frantic kicks, he flung himself from the water and onto the deck. A fin cut through the pink sludge inches from his leg, then slid beneath again, disappearing as though it had never been there.

Miller threw himself over the rail and onto the sailboat's aft deck. When he landed, he coughed out the air clutched within his lungs, and feeling safe for the briefest of moments, took a breath.

The painful sensation of drowning gripped his body like a python. His muscles tightened and he curled into a ball. Pain filled his body and clouded his mind. This was it. This was death. His vision grew blurry. His eyes darted frantically about as his body shut down. No one was aboard, he realized.

Not a soul.

He was alone, and his air—all of it—was gone.

7.

Nearly unconscious, Miller still wasn't quite ready to give up the fight. Eyes bulging, head pounding, he pushed himself to his feet. Staggering forward, he gripped the large polished wheel located at the back of the thirty-foot sloop, and it rolled under his weight, flinging him off. He hit the deck hard, landing in a thick pile of scratchy pink flakes. His fading vision darkened, but the white cabin door in front of him beckoned with hope. He reached for the small handle, yanked it, and forced his head up for a look.

His vision was nearly gone, but a familiar, bright yellow shape managed to make itself known. He dragged himself into the cabin, down the three stairs, and onto something soft. The air tank was sitting on the floor in front of him. He grabbed it and fumbled his hands all over the metal cylinder until he found the regulator hose. He yanked on it, but the hose resisted.

With the last of his strength—his vision dimmed to near nothing—he pulled again. The hose came free. Miller slid a trembling hand up the hose, found the regulator, and slammed it in his mouth. He breathed in.

After two deep breaths, he tasted the vomit. He wondered hazily if he had thrown up without knowing it, but decided he hadn't. The vomit belonged to whoever had used this regulator before him. A fierce wave of nausea swept through his body and he closed his eyes, forcing himself to fight it down. The taste in his mouth was horrible and sickening, but the life-giving air was delightful.

After waiting a full minute for his body and mind to return to normal, he opened his eyes. He found himself lying on his back staring at the ceiling. He could have sworn he had been lying on his stomach—most likely his oxygen-deprived senses were all twisted about.

He wasn't lying on the floor, he finally realized. He was lying on top of something.

He turned to the side.

Oh, God. Not *something*.

Someone.

He sat up fast and jumped to his feet. The regulator popped out of his mouth, weighed down by the heavy oxygen tank on the floor. Miller held his breath as he looked at the body.

It was a woman. Dressed in a yellow bikini with red polka dots. In life she would have been beautiful. Stunning. In death, surrounded by a pool of dried vomit, the graying corpse was hideous—the woman's mouth was frozen open in a gaping scream where the regulator had once been.

Miller knelt down next to her and picked up the oxygen tank. He placed the regulator in his mouth again, took one long drag, and removed it again. The sight of the dead woman combined with the flavor of vomit was more than he could handle at the moment. The door to the head lay open behind the body. He stepped over it, and in, yanking on the tap. The water flowed and he swiftly rinsed off the regulator, then popped it back in his mouth.

He held the tank by his side and stepped back into the hallway, eyes locked on the copious amount of vomit.

This woman didn't asphyxiate, he thought. *She still had plenty of air left in the tank. So what killed her?*

He decided it was a question better answered later, or not at all, and set about searching the rest of the sailboat. He moved quickly through the small hallway and opened the first cabin. A man lay splayed over the bed, tanned, muscular arms flung wide, like Jesus on the cross. His eyes stared at the ceiling and his mouth, wide open, was full of his own vomit. He'd drowned in it. The bedsheet, caked in the sour bile, stuck to the man's head.

Here too was an oxygen tank. Nearly full. Miller picked it up and headed for the second cabin. The wooden door opened smoothly and the afternoon light poured through the portal onto a stack of oxygen tanks. Six in all. Despite the gruesome surroundings, Miller smiled.

He quickly checked the tanks. All were full.

He shook his head. *Well, now I know who drained the way station.*

How many trips had they made back and forth? How long had they been here? And what had killed them?

Ignoring the questions that would normally have been important to him, he turned his attention back to the six tanks lying on the bed and the two in his hands.

Each tank held three thousand psi of air, which, at a sixty-foot depth, would last him about an hour. Here, in the open air, each tank would give him about two hours, maybe more if he could control his breathing. He had eight tanks.

Sixteen hours.

That was a great improvement from the sixteen seconds he had left to live upon boarding the vessel, but he was still nine miles from Key Largo. He couldn't waste any time.

He stepped into the hallway and over the woman, taking the stairs back out to the deck. He shuffled through six inches of the rose-colored flakes and sat at the helm. He looked over the controls. Everything was automated. He tried starting the boat. The engine wheezed and failed. He tried twice more without any luck. He couldn't get it to start. Then it hit him.

Oxygen.

Without oxygen there would be no combustion, which meant that any gas-fueled engines wouldn't work. Or generators, for that matter. He wouldn't even be able to start a damn campfire.

Miller glanced over at the furled sails. When he'd first seen the ship from the life support buoy he'd thought there was no wind to move the ship, but the sails had simply not been engaged.

He wiped dust away from the helm's console. The ship's batteries appeared to be working, which was one bright spot in an otherwise hellish day. The console buttons glowed dully in the afternoon sunlight. A button labeled ANCHOR was lit up. He pressed it and heard a winch start to run. The couple had dropped anchor right over the way station. The two sails were labeled as well: MAINSAIL and SPINNAKER. He hit both buttons.

Gears turned and winches spun. The sails unfurled and raised high on the mast. Before the sails had finished rising, the wind caught them with a *whump*. The boom swung around and snapped to a stop. The sloop lurched forward and accelerated.

Miller took the wheel and directed the ship toward the tiny sliver of land in the distance.

8.

The boat slid through the calm waters of Port Largo, a man-made river lined with docks and slips that gave the owners access to their waterfront homes. Several tributaries reached out from either side, extending the water's reach. It was like a street, really.

A dead street.

The only things moving were the palm leaves bending in the breeze and billowing clouds of red kicked up by the occasional gust of wind. The trees and large parts of several homes had been swept clean of the dust, which had gathered like snowdrifts against other homes.

Miller looked at the sky. The storm, if that's what it was, showed no signs of ending. Clouds of flakes fluttered down, spinning in the wind like great schools of fish.

Having made the nine-mile sail in just over an hour, he wasn't in a panicked rush, but with only fifteen hours of air remaining he needed to find more soon and then work out some kind of plan. Key Largo was a beginning, but he needed to reach a city—Miami for starters—where he hoped to find more air and survivors.

He remembered leaving from Port Largo only a week before. It had been a beautiful day. Dark cumulus clouds and high humidity foretold a coming thunderstorm. He'd flirted, for what felt like the first time in a long time, with the caretaker of Aquarius, a pretty blonde whose name he'd forgotten.

He pulled the sloop into the slip closest to the main street, Ocean Bay Drive. He tied the boat off and hopped onto the dock wearing an air tank on his back. He lugged along a second tank, just in case.

His first stop was the scuba shop. Dave's Scuba. He'd visited the seaside store briefly before heading out to Aquarius. Most of the tanks in the shop would likely be empty, but Dave also rented tanks to vacationers who wouldn't want to wait for one to be filled. Hopefully there would be some full ones left. Without breathable air in the atmosphere, the shop's compressor would do him little good.

He entered the store and found it free of the pink dust he'd shuffled through to get there. The place looked untouched, as though frozen in time. Wet suits hung on racks. Key Largo T-shirts dangled from the ceiling. Scuba tanks of all sizes lined the walls.

Then he saw a shoe.

He stepped around a rack of swim trunks and found a bare leg. The rest of the body was hidden behind the checkout counter. He peeked over the top. Despite the regulator covering the lower half of the man's face, Miller recognized him as the owner, Dave. His balding, slicked-back, long hair was hard to forget, or mistake.

The vomit surrounding his head was familiar. Dave, like the two people on the sloop, had not suffocated. They had plenty of breathable air when they died. Something else had killed them.

Miller glanced out the glass door. A sheet of red covered the parking lot. His eyes trailed down to his own body. He was covered in the stuff. Most of it was fine, powdery dust, but the occasional large flake clung to his shoulder and in his chest hair. Forgetting the air for a moment, Miller stepped over Dave and entered the small bathroom. There was a toilet, a sink, and a roll of paper towel hanging from the wall.

The cool water from the tap felt good as he toweled it

over his body. His red-hued skin soon returned to its formerly lightly tanned state. A pool of salmon-colored water surrounded his bare feet. He gingerly washed the sole of his wounded foot and checked the gash that had rung the tiger shark's dinner bell. It wasn't deep and had stopped bleeding, but it stung.

The still-running tap reminded Miller that he was desperately thirsty. He removed the regulator from his mouth, bent down to the tap, opened his mouth, and filled it with water. The taste hit him a moment before he swallowed. The water tasted metallic, almost like blood. He spit it into the sink, remembering the flavor of the first flake he'd placed on his tongue.

The water is contaminated with that crap, he realized.

He added water to the list of things he needed to find before leaving.

His stomach growled.

Food, too.

Miller headed back into the store and knelt by Dave's body. "Sorry, Dave," he said, his voice muffled by the regulator.

Despite some bloating, the boat shoes slipped off fairly easily, and fit well enough when he tried them on. He grabbed an I ♥ KEY LARGO T-shirt from a hanger. Holding his breath, he quickly pulled the shirt on and then restrapped the tank over his back. Dressed and feeling more human, Miller returned to the front desk. The tanks against the back walls would be the full ones. He checked them one by one, taking note of how much air was in them.

When he was done, he stepped back. Eighteen air tanks. *Eighteen.*

Thirty-six hours.

Combined with the air in the boat he could make it two days.

Feeling safe for the first time since he took that near-deadly breath of air at the life support buoy, Miller let his thoughts drift beyond his personal circumstances. He thought of his friends, the agents he worked with, and his former comrades in the SEALs. He had no idea if they were still alive. Hell, he might be the last person left alive on Earth. But he wouldn't give up fighting for his life. Wasn't in his nature.

He looked down at Dave, dead on the floor, and removed his regulator. "Thanks for the air, Dave."

As he turned away from the shop owner, a small blinking blue light caught his eye.

A laptop.

9.

The laptop sat on the floor, tipped on its side and opened partway. He could see the power cable plugged into the wall and a blue LAN cable that disappeared behind the shelf the machine had sat on before being knocked over. He slid on his belly toward the machine, righted it, and opened it up. He lay there on the floor, next to Dave's feet, like a child playing video games, and hit the Power button.

A Windows Vista logo flashed on the screen and Miller prayed the machine wouldn't be buggy. It started up quickly, though, and displayed a nice image of what Key Largo would have looked like a few days previous. A paradise.

But the image and all of Dave's files held no interest for Miller. Two icons flashing in the bottom right had captured his full attention. The first was a low-battery indicator. He had suspected there was no power, but the plugged-in laptop running off batteries confirmed it. The second icon revealed no network connectivity.

Hoping Dave didn't have his Internet history and cache cleared, Miller double-clicked the Firefox icon and a message appeared on the screen:

WOULD YOU LIKE TO RESTORE YOUR
PREVIOUS SESSION?

Miller clicked Yes and the Web browser opened. The cache did its job, filling in content that was no longer live, but still stored on the computer. Five separate tabs opened at the top of the browser. The first one was what he'd been hoping to see. A news station. He clicked on the tab and a video screen appeared. He tapped on the Play icon. The station's logo swirled dramatically onto the screen.

"Welcome to News Five at nine. I'm Rebecca Sanchez. We begin tonight's . . ."

The woman on-screen was a vision. Her voice comforted him as she welcomed viewers to the show. She was *alive*.

Was alive, Miller corrected himself. *Not anymore. Couldn't be.* The date on the newscast was two days ago.

He focused on her words instead, believing that this woman, like everyone else, was most likely dead.

"More disturbing news tonight, this time out of Washington. President Bensson has issued a state of emergency and imposed an eight P.M. curfew. He has asked that people in the affected areas remain calm, and in their homes. We here at News Five will stay at the station throughout the curfew and bring you updates as they come in."

She continued speaking for several minutes, repeating the same information in different ways, urging people to stay at home. Stay hydrated. Ration food. And watch the news. Then she switched gears.

"The rash of illnesses that swept across southern Florida and Tokyo, Japan, yesterday, in conjunction with the beginning of an atmospheric event that some are calling biblical, seems to have abated. Symptoms ranging from headaches to severe stomach pain afflicted most everyone in the region. It seems today that the worst is over as people, including myself, are finally feeling better."

The video ended.

Though he'd heard everything she said, only three small phrases really stayed with him: "affected areas," "swept across southern Florida," and, "afflicted most everyone in the region." He knew a lot of people had died. Key Largo was a city of red-coated corpses. But if this really was a regional event, maybe there was some hope after all?

Two small thumbnail images appeared on top, labeled *RELATED STORIES*. They were dated the day after the newscast. Unlike many of the blue text links on the page, these were highlighted in purple. Dave had watched them, too.

Miller clicked the first.

The news anchor appeared on-screen again, this time without the flashy graphic. The tired look in her eyes supported her claim that she and the crew had indeed spent the night at the station. She started right in on the story. No greeting. No hello. All business.

"We have just received word, and this has been confirmed by labs all over the world, that this is a natural event. A cosmic event."

She picked up a piece of paper.

"This statement comes from a NASA spokesman." She started reading it. "Last week, our solar system passed through a large cloud of naturally occurring iron particles. The massive iron cloud struck Earth's atmosphere at eight thirty, eastern standard time, on Wednesday morning."

The reporter inhaled deeply, and then did so again. She appeared overcome with emotion, and short of breath, but pulled herself together and continued.

"The reddish flakes falling from the sky are created when the iron particles strike our atmosphere and oxidize—"

"Rust!" Miller said with his teeth clenched around the regulator mouthpiece.

"—forming flakes of rust. There are two inherent dangers to watch out for during this phenomenon. The first, iron poisoning is . . ." The woman sniffled hard, let out a faint sob, then wiped her nose and continued. ". . . is caused by ingesting or breathing large amounts of iron. The symptoms of iron poisoning are . . ." She sighed. "Severe stomachache, nausea, and vomiting, followed by a day of apparent health as the iron penetrates deeper into the body and destroys internal organs, specifically the brain and liver, as metabolic acidosis sets in. Shock comes

next, severe vomiting, followed by death from liver failure."

She took another deep breath, put the paper down, and
continued.

"The second danger facing us is asphyxiation. That's like
drowning in the open air."

"Becky, you better read what they sent," came a whispered man's voice from off-camera.

"I've read it. They need to hear the truth, not a bunch of
technobabble!" Rebecca snapped. "When iron oxidizes, the
chemical change removes oxygen from the atmosphere. We
are being told that if this storm keeps up then it's possible
that the atmosphere will become . . ." Her lower lip trembled
and she looked close to breaking into tears. "Well, we won't
be able to breathe."

Her upper teeth clamped down on the quivering lip, and
after taking another deep breath, she began again. "The
president will be addressing the nation within the hour, but I
suggest you get in contact with your loved ones. Spend your
time with them, and if you believe in God, start praying. If
you're one of the millions who have suffered from the ail-
ments I listed off, don't bother trying to escape the area . . .
you're already dead."

An angry voice cut in, shouting, "Rebecca!"

The video stopped and once again showed two thumbnail
images. Most of what the woman said seemed accurate. The
effects of the storm had clearly been predicted correctly. It
had taken some time, but right now there was no air in the
atmosphere, though it seemed most everyone had died from
iron poisoning before the oxygen ran out. There was no escape, unless you happened to be in a sealed canister with its
own air supply.

Like he had been . . .

What didn't make sense was that an atmospheric event of
this magnitude could strike two highly populated areas on
different sides of the planet and leave the rest of the world
unscathed. Nature doesn't choose targets. People do. And

that chilled him more than the rest. To think that this might be a new weapon of mass destruction made his insides roil. The government had carefully worded their press release to avoid all-out chaos—which was almost certainly taking place anyway.

He turned his attention back to the computer screen. The battery indicator was flashing now. The screen showed two video thumbnails. The first video he'd watched and the second he hadn't. The thumbnail of the second video was dated the same as NASA's press release video, but the time was ten hours later. The still image looked poorly lit, and the reporter, Rebecca, looked like hell.

He clicked on the final video, wondering what Rebecca would have to say, knowing now that the end of the world was near.

She was in tears when the clip started. Her on-screen persona had completely vanished. She was now a terrified and angry woman, facing certain death. "You fuckers!"

Miller jerked back as though she had shouted at him.

"You won't get away with this! You can't!"

She wiped her nose, smearing her running mascara across her flushed cheek. The rage in her eyes faded as she addressed a different audience. "Anyone who is still alive . . . please listen to me. We just received an e-mail from a group claiming responsibility for everything. This didn't have to happen! If you survive, if you somehow make it through this, know that you are not alone. You are among enemies. And they're tagging the streets with their symbol."

She coughed violently, struggling for breath. She reached out her hand, snapping her fingers at someone. A piece of paper came into view and she took it. "This is their symbol. If you see it, either run the other way . . . or kill the bastards."

She held the image up to the screen, her hands shaking. It was eerily familiar, but he couldn't place it. And the longer he looked at it, the more his subconscious shouted, *danger!* As the screen went black and the laptop shut itself down, he closed his eyes and could still see the image clearly. He couldn't remember who it represented, but he recognized what it stood for.

Evil.

10.

Miller sat back from the laptop, stunned. Someone *had* caused the storm. Someone announcing their presence to the world through a symbol, someone who could kill millions without firing a weapon or even revealing themselves. What pissed him off was that the group responsible hadn't asked for or demanded anything in conjunction with the release of their symbol. In a firefight, when the enemy started by shooting two of your men, they had no intention of stopping to talk. More bullets would come until everyone was dead or you figured out a way to kill your enemy first. His instincts told him to get ready for a fight, but what could he do? He was alone in a dead zone of unknown size and had no way to get in touch with the outside world.

Or did he? He hadn't tried a landline yet.

Miller stood and searched the room. A phone hung on the wall above Dave's body. He picked it up and put it to his ear.

Nothing.

Anger got the best of him and he yanked the phone from the wall and flung it. Its old-fashioned bell rang out as the phone struck the front window and smashed it. The cacophony of breaking glass snapped Miller out of his anger as a cloud of red dust swirled into the shop.

Time to go, Miller thought. He needed to move—his life depended on mobility now—but he also needed supplies.

Over the next thirty minutes, Miller transported the air tanks from Dave's shop over to the sloop, which he now saw was named *Montrose.* After stepping over the woman's body three times he realized that his passengers had to go. He dragged the stiff bodies to the deck. At first he thought about burying them, but what was he going to do, bury every dead body he came across? It wasn't remotely feasible, and certainly not rational. Until he escaped this airless hell, his every action would be dictated by the need for survival. Burying two bodies would simply use up his limited resources. All he could do was apologize to the couple before rolling their bodies overboard.

With the air safely stowed in the *Montrose,* he turned his attention to the next problem—food and water. He could see a CVS pharmacy sign down the road, perhaps half a mile away. They should have what he needed.

He checked his air—forty-five minutes—then started to walk. Halfway there he found an abandoned bike. He hopped on and started pedaling. His speed doubled and his exertion lessened, which was good, but the street was littered with rust-covered bodies that he had to dodge. Staying upright became even trickier when the rust grew deeper. The tires slipped several times and he almost crashed twice. He hoped his tetanus shot was up-to-date. The vaccination was required by the NCIS so he thought he should be okay.

The CVS had been fairly well picked over, but people hadn't been thinking when they looted the store. Electronics were missing. Junk food and soda had been pillaged. But the good stuff, the food that would keep him alive, was still there. He took five boxes of energy bars, four large containers of chocolate protein drink, a bottle of vitamins, and two three-gallon containers of water. He double-bagged everything and hung the bags on the bike's handlebars, which made pedaling so unstable he had to climb off and walk the bike back.

Moving quickly, he returned to the store again, grabbing two more water containers and as many canned goods as he could hold. This trip went faster than the first and after returning everything to the sloop, Miller decided he had time for one last run.

As he moved through the aisles this third time around, he looked for anything he thought he might need. Batteries, flashlights, clothing, a raincoat, a knife set, and medical supplies. But one object that he required eluded him—a can opener. He hurried up and down the aisles three times, moving faster with each pass, until he saw a single can opener hanging above a display of nonstick pans on the endcap of the next aisle over. In his rush to reach the can opener, his clothing snagged on the corner of a sunglasses display. There was a hard tug from the display, but he yanked away, strode to the can opener, and picked it up.

He grinned at his success.

And then he *wheezed*.

He breathed again, but found no air.

He looked at the pressure gauge.

The air that was left was draining quickly.

He spit the regulator from his mouth and inspected the hose. Air hissed from a torn hole. And then, it stopped. The tank ran empty.

He hadn't snagged his clothing on the metal sunglasses display, he'd snagged the air hose. *Stupid!* Miller thought to himself.

There was a half mile between him and his air tanks. He cursed himself for not bringing a spare. His heart pounded with fear, realizing that death was two minutes away, three minutes at most. His last breath had not been deep and he already felt the need for another. Then he saw a sign on the back wall of the store.

PHARMACY.

He ran for it and jumped the counter. Pills littered the floor, where they had dissolved into sludge by some now-evaporated liquid. He had no interest in drugs or pills right now. Air was his drug of choice. Then he saw what he was looking for—an oxygen tank. Just one. The kind with which you see old folks shuffling around, or those attached to the electric go-carts of the morbidly obese. He picked up the white tank and set it on the counter. A plastic face mask in a sterile bag went next.

He ignored the reflection of his beet-red face in the reading glasses display on the other side of the counter and quickly attached the face mask. He loosened the valve. When the hiss of escaping oxygen hit his ears, he placed the mask against his mouth—and breathed.

After taking a few deep breaths, he realized that the air tasted different. Unlike the compressed air in the scuba tank, this was straight oxygen, meant to be breathed along with normal air, not in place of it. The tank would keep him alive, but it wouldn't be long before he started feeling loopy. He swiftly left the pharmacy, taking several pairs of sunglasses on the way, and transported his last shipment of goods to the *Montrose*. By the time he arrived and switched over to a new tank of air, he was feeling great. The weight of the air tank on his back felt heavy, but he was glad for it. The straight oxygen had worked wonders for his psyche, but too much would be deadly.

When the *Montrose* was loaded with enough food and water to last several weeks, and air to last for a little more than two days, Miller set sail for Miami.

11.

Only two hours of air remained when Miller caught his first glimpse of the Miami skyline. The doldrums had settled in over the ocean and left the *Montrose*'s sails limp. With no wind and no way to start the engines, the ship floated adrift for days in the now sludgy waters of the Bermuda Triangle. Surrounded by an otherworldly red ocean and pink sky, Miller had retreated to the cabin and tried not to think about his dwindling air supply. But that had been hard to do when eating meant holding your breath and sleep was interrupted every two hours by sudden asphyxiation.

When the winds returned, Miller had stumbled up on deck, unfurled the sails, and pointed the sloop west. With no idea how far out to sea he was, all he could do was pray for wind and stay the course. The wind blew gently—a breeze really—but it was enough to get him to Miami.

As the *Montrose* cut through the waters alongside Miami Beach's now pink shore—white sand mixed with red flakes—he kept a constant lookout for someplace that might have scuba gear. But all he could see were nightclubs and hotels. Having never been to Miami, he wasn't sure where to look. Rounding South Beach, he maneuvered the sloop into a channel. A buoyed sign read: MIAMI HARBOR—NO WAKE ZONE.

Miller looked at the harbor, dotted with large islands, and

the mainland beyond. Off the starboard bow he spotted a marina filled to capacity with massive white yachts. He spun the wheel, directing the *Montrose* through the maze of barriers that protected the marina from the open ocean.

With thirty minutes of air remaining, he didn't bother to find an actual slip. He simply pulled up alongside the end of a dock, hopped out, and tied the boat off. His footfalls on the dock echoed like gunshots in the still silence of the dead city. He could hear nothing else, save for the water lapping against the docks.

To his relief there was a sign at the end of the dock pointing toward Scuba Emporium. He followed it. One hundred feet later, he found a large shop, one of many, at the base of a sky-rise apartment building. The sign on the door read CLOSED.

He tried the door.

Locked.

Cupping his hands to the glass, he peered inside. The shop was expansive and well stocked—a scuba enthusiast's paradise.

Miller looked around for something heavy that could break the window. He found nothing in the immediate area, but as he was searching, he noticed something unusual. The walkway in front of the store was free of red dust. While much of the dust on the surrounding surfaces had been blown out to sea or piled high against buildings, a fine layer still coated almost everything—except for the space in front of the Scuba Emporium.

He kneeled down and looked at the walkway. Fine streaks of red stretched across the cement surface where a broom had passed over.

The rust had been *swept* away. With red flakes still falling from the sky, the sweeping must have been done recently.

Miller took a deep breath, removed the regulator from his mouth, and yelled, "Hello!"

His voice bounced off the city's buildings as though he'd just shouted into the Grand Canyon.

"Is there anyone here?"

No response. And his air was running low.

He took one more deep breath, removed the regulator again, and slipped out of the air tank. Holding it like a shot-put, he took two fast steps toward the glass door and let it fly. The glass exploded. Much of it fell straight down while the rest burst into the shop.

Miller entered slowly, aware of the glass shards poking out from the door's frame, and of the possibility of getting his head blown off by a justifiably paranoid survivor. The store, like the sidewalk in front of it, was immaculate—seemingly untouched and certainly not looted. He picked up his air tank, checked to make sure the regulator didn't have glass in it, and placed it back in his mouth.

Squeezing through several racks of wet suits, he cautiously worked his way to the back of the store, where he hoped he would find full air tanks ready for renting. He pushed the last of the wet suits aside, glad to be free of them. That is, until he saw the body that waited on the other side.

The man's death had been violent, and bloody, and the investigator in Miller wanted to look things over. The man had only recently died. But there was no time for that now. He needed air.

He tiptoed across the sticky swath of wet rug, stepped over the old man's body, and made for the back of the store. He quickly found a full air tank and switched it out. He took stock of the other tanks. Only ten.

Why so few for such a big shop? he wondered. *And with such wealthy patrons.*

Closed cabinets lined the back wall above the rack of scuba tanks. Miller smiled as he realized the answer to his question. *Because the people who shopped here could afford better.*

Miller flung open the cabinets. *Yes!* Inside were four black closed-circuit rebreather units, CCRs for short. A rebreather, as opposed to a standard scuba set, combines straight oxygen with exhaled air. The end result is smaller tanks, less weight to carry, and seventy-five percent more time per refill. Even better, he felt confident he could take any standard oxygen tank and adapt it for use with the rebreather. He would just need to make sure he had air or trimix on hand. Closed-circuit rebreathers required a diluting gas, in addition to oxygen, but the gas was recycled as he breathed and needed to be changed less frequently.

He knew it was odd to be smiling, but his life expectancy had just gone up. He also was no longer bound to staying on the ocean, or near the scuba shops that lined the shore.

He switched his air tank out for the rebreather, and was happily surprised to find a full-sized face mask. Not only could he breathe freely without a regulator in his mouth, he could also breathe through his nose.

Recharged by his small victory, Miller turned his attention back to the body he had stepped over. The one that hadn't asphyxiated. The one that didn't die in a pool of its own vomit, but in its own blood.

The man's body was round, perhaps from overeating, perhaps from gas built up inside. Miller wasn't sure which and didn't want to find out. He focused on the single wound—a gunshot to the man's head. The exit wound was a baseball-sized hole on the top of his skull. The gray eyes were wide and unblinking, looking up at the ceiling as though hoping for salvation. His mouth was frozen open, lips turned down in disgust at what he was about to do.

Miller reached out and touched the man's arm. The skin wasn't as warm as a living person's, but it lacked the lifeless chill of a long-dead cadaver. The man had killed himself within the last few hours.

The gun, a 9mm Parabellum, commonly recommended for home defense, lay on the floor five feet away from the body, beyond the pool of blood. A half-used air tank lay next to it.

He'd seen enough dead bodies over the past few days, and in his lifetime, that the old man's corpse didn't bother him, even though it was fresh. But it did seem a shame the man hadn't held on just a few hours longer. He could have escaped this mess with his life, as Miller intended to.

Miller stepped over the body and picked up the gun. He checked the clip, slapped it back in, chambered a round, and tucked it into his pocket. A city of dead people wouldn't be much of a threat, but the weapon made him feel more prepared to handle whatever lay ahead, whether it be a paranoid survivor, a stubborn lock, or someone sporting a circled lightning bolt insignia.

12.

After finding another bike and pilfering a map of Miami from the Scuba Emporium, Miller set off in search of the nearest hospital. According to the map, that was Mount Sinai Medical Center. If there were any survivors, he believed they would be there. Hospitals carried lots of oxygen, had backup power sources, and would be the natural place for other survivors to congregate. And if not, he had no doubt that there would be plenty of oxygen tanks that would work with his rebreather. He might find enough for months, though he hoped he wouldn't be breathing bottled air that long.

Wind had cleared away and piled up the rust against buildings and in alleys, making pedaling easier than it had been in Key Largo. The bodies remained a problem, though. In some places he had to get off the bike and carry it over what had once been a mob. The other new challenge was that the rebreather's mask had been made for underwater use and blocked his peripheral vision. He had to move his head fully from side to side to see what was around him and it made dodging the dead tricky business. He knew reducing the bodies' status to that of simple obstacles was a cold thing to do, but to give them any more attention would distract him from his own survival.

There was no way to know how far he might have to go to

escape the affected area, or if the attacks had already spread to the rest of the world.

He cut between neighborhoods composed mainly of tall, high-rent apartment buildings, some of which had caught fire. If not for the lack of oxygen in the atmosphere, those fires might still be burning.

Soon the right side of the road opened up into a massive parking lot. A line of palm trees swayed up ahead, and beyond them, something odd rose up from the ground, like a tree, but not.

Miller slowed as he approached the palm trees. The oddity appeared to be a statue of some kind. He pedaled harder and the rest of it came into view. It was a massive hand, its bottom seemingly torn apart. A red-tinged, lily-filled reflection pool surrounded the scene, and in the courtyard lay bodies; perhaps a hundred of them. Some were reaching up.

Alive!

Miller jumped off the bike and ran for the courtyard. "Hey!" he shouted. "Are you okay? I have air!"

His mask fogged over as he waded through the lily pond. Clouds of rust billowed around his feet. Reaching the other side, he removed the mask and looked at the people, wondering why they didn't respond. Then he realized the truth.

They weren't dead.

But they had never been alive.

Statues.

"Damn," he muttered before returning the mask to his face. As he turned, he noticed that the distortion from his curved mask, coupled with the statues' lifelike poses, created the illusion of life.

He spun around, taking in the scene. The bodies in the courtyard reached out for the giant hand. Intertwined bodies made up the base of the statue. The people looked tormented. Emaciated. Anguished.

Miller turned to the black wall of granite that encircled a portion of the round courtyard. The highly polished surface reflected the late-day sun struggling to shine through the haze of falling red flakes. He shaded his eyes to see the wall more clearly. "Son of a bitch," he said when his eyes focused.

There on the wall, spray painted in white, was the symbol from the news report—the lightning bolt encased by a crosslike circle. Beneath the symbol was a message, applied thick, with rivulets of white paint that had dripped down to the ground. It read:

Welcome to SecondWorld!

Miller realized that this wasn't just graffiti. A quick walk to the granite wall confirmed it. The first panel told a story dated 1933. What followed for two more panels was a complete history of what the Jewish people had endured during World War II.

This was a Holocaust memorial.

The target of this symbol and its message revealed a deep hatred, one straight out of history. His head snapped away from the wall as though struck. The symbol, in this context, became clear to him. The lightning bolt—no, the thunderbolt—was the Nazi symbol for the Schutzstaffel, Hitler's elite military unit known as the SS. They were the overseers of the Nazi death camps. The two S-shaped bolts, typically next to each other, had been combined.

Anger welled within Miller. He wasn't a believer in God,

but his great-grandfather had been, and he'd been killed by the SS in Auschwitz along with millions of other Jews across Europe. Thinking of Nazis, he recognized the rest of the symbol as a Celtic cross, which had been adopted by American white supremacist groups. The combination of the two symbols seemed to suggest that these were modern, American Schutzstaffel. The muscles on his back bunched with tension.

Whether they were still in the area, surviving from air tank to air tank like him, or holed up in a bunker, had yet to be seen, but they were prepared. And they had already named their post-genocidal world, SecondWorld.

This isn't over, Miller thought. *If they haven't attacked the rest of the world yet, they will soon.*

When he tore his eyes from the wall, he realized he'd been gripping the handgun in his pocket. A part of him hoped that whoever painted this symbol would show up. Give him an outlet for his anger. But nothing moved, other than the endless red flakes. Whoever painted this was long gone.

After returning to his bike, Miller cut through a large golf course free of bodies. Apparently, no one wanted to golf during the apocalypse. The open space increased his speed, but he felt exposed—watched. Leaving the golf course behind, he took to the sidewalks, preferring to stay in the buildings' shadows. He could be easily spotted in the stillness of the city, but he didn't like the idea of making himself an open target, just in case someone out there felt like taking a potshot.

He reached Mount Sinai Medical Center ten minutes later. The hospital was large and nicer than most he'd visited. In fact, with its light brown exterior and surrounding palm trees, the place looked more like a hotel than a hospital. As he approached the building, the doors to the emergency room slid silently open.

Emergency power must still be working, he thought, but forgot all about the door when he looked beyond it.

Miller jumped back. Bodies filled the emergency room—piles of them. Vomit covered several, as well as a dusting of rust. Strangely, almost all of the victims were covered in blood. Something awful—something terribly violent—had happened here. Did the people turn on one another, desperate enough for medical attention to kill off any competitors?

A little girl's face caught his eye. She was buried beneath three adults, her eyes closed. Peaceful. As though she had simply fallen asleep there. But Miller knew she hadn't. The death she had experienced would likely have been anything but peaceful.

Swallowing hard, he stepped back, out of the building.

The doors closed behind him.

He found the main entrance on the other side of the hospital and entered the lobby, steeling himself for a repeat of the emergency room scene. But there were only a few bodies here. He forced himself not to look as he moved past them, focusing instead on a wall-mounted map and directory off to his right. Reaching it, he ran his finger over each department as he read the list. He made a note of every place he thought might have oxygen tanks, then paused. His finger lay on the BURN WARD label. Fourth floor.

He knew that people with severe burns were sometimes put in oxygen tents. Could he spend the night in one? Breathing freely? He hadn't really slept since leaving Aquarius. As he assessed his need for sleep, he felt his legs grow shaky. His vision blurred. It was almost as though his body, knowing that sleep was near, began shutting down in preparation.

He knew he could sleep in the rebreather without issue. It was good for another twelve hours and he had two spare oxygen tanks strapped to his belt, not to mention a hospital filled with them. But to sleep freely, on a bed . . . well, that sounded like heaven. He headed for the elevators and pushed the button. The doors opened immediately.

Emergency power is definitely *still running.*

The elevator rose quickly. With a ding, the doors opened

to a stark white hallway. A dead nurse lay on the floor, crumpled up into the fetal position. He stepped out and the doors shut behind him. In the silence that followed, Miller thought he heard the wind. He held his breath and listened.

It wasn't the wind.

It was a child.

Weeping.

13.

Miller spun around, trying to discern the cry's source. He moved beyond the empty nurses' station, stopped, and listened again. The sound was faint, rising and falling in volume, but never loud. He moved down the hallway, passing open doors. Some rooms held corpses, some were empty, beds still made.

A shadow shifted in the room at the end of the hallway.

He ran toward it.

His chest pounding from excitement, he slowed as he approached the door, caught his breath, cleared his mind, and entered. The corner room had two walls of windows, one looking out to the north, up the coast, and the other back to downtown Miami, which was aglow with orange light from the setting sun.

An opaque sheet of plastic hung from the ceiling and descended over the room's bed like a tent.

A small body, obscured by the plastic sheet, lay on the bed. He couldn't be sure, but he thought the person was looking at him. The weeping stopped, followed by some sniffling.

"Are you here to rescue me?" a sweet voice asked. It was a child. A girl.

"Yeah," he said. "I am."

"You can come under. It's okay to breathe in here."

Miller looked beyond the tent. Next to the bed was an array of equipment including large tanks of oxygen and air. An oxygen tent. Was this girl . . . ?

He removed his mask so she wouldn't be afraid, knelt down, and lifted the plastic from the floor. He quickly pulled it over his head and let it fall again.

The girl, dressed in a hospital gown, smiled at him, but the smile only lasted a moment. Her lips were swollen and split in several spots. The skin on her left arm looked like it had melted. It was red, swollen, and in some places, cracked and oozing.

She noted his attention. "The bandages hurt when they dried out. I took them off." Her voice was weak. Frail. "There are other burns on my stomach and legs, all on the left side. Not as bad as my arm, though. The hospital gown hurts a little, but I didn't want to be naked. Just in case."

"In case of what?"

"In case you came."

"Me?"

"Or anyone else."

"Right."

"I'm thirsty."

He was sure she couldn't drink through those lips, though maybe a straw would work. "I'll be right back."

He slid out from under the sheet, donned his mask, and found her IV bag. Empty. She'd been dehydrating to death. Alone.

"I'm Lincoln Miller. You can call me Linc if you'd like. What's your name?" he asked.

"Arwen."

"Nice name."

"It's from Tolkien."

Tolkien? "How old are you?"

"Twelve."

"Listen, Arwen. I'm going to go get some supplies. Stuff to help you feel better. I'll be back in a minute."

"'Kay."

"Be right back," he repeated as he left the room. He

searched the hallways for a supply room, ignoring the bodies and his rising emotions. His focus was on Arwen now. He found a door with a brass label that read MEDICAL SUPPLIES. He tried the handle. Locked. After stepping back, he kicked the door three times, right below the knob. On the third kick, the door crashed open.

Cabinets and closets lined the walls of the room. Each was filled with impeccably organized and labeled medical supplies. He opened and closed five doors before finding a cabinet that held nearly twenty IV bags labeled *SALINE—0.9% SODIUM CHLORIDE SOLUTION.* He took five and left.

"I'm back," he said upon return to Arwen's room. He moved straight for her IV, checked the label to make sure he'd taken the right kind, and then switched them out. The liquid drip began immediately. Only then did he notice that Arwen had yet to respond to his entry.

Miller pulled up the plastic, climbed beneath, and found the girl lying still, her eyes closed. He pulled his mask from his face and knelt down next to her. He didn't dare check for a pulse for fear her red, swollen skin would crack open. Instead he held the back of his hand beneath her nose and watched her small chest.

He sighed as he felt air move across his hand and saw the subtle rise and fall each breath brought to her chest. She was still alive and she had moved over on the bed. Before, she'd been on her back at the center of the bed, now she lay on her unburned side at the edge.

She'd made room for him.

He shook his head, wondering who was taking care of whom. That small gesture of companionship, he realized, had rallied his fighting spirit. He slipped out of his gear, placing the rebreather, handgun, water bottle, and several protein bars on the floor next to the bed. The exhaustion, chased away by the adrenaline of finding Arwen, returned with a vengeance.

He climbed onto the other side of the bed, careful not to bump her little body with his. The bed was firm, but comfortable. The air smelled of burnt flesh and hair. He looked at the back of her head. Her blond hair had burned from the shoulders down, but the hair on top revealed the child she had once been.

He ran his fingers through her hair and wondered if she'd been in one of the apartment fires he'd seen on the way to the hospital. Or perhaps her burns had happened before the catastrophe hit. There was no way to know, not now, anyway.

As he stroked her hair he wondered what his life would have been like if he'd taken a different path. Could he settle down? Have kids? Could he put a little girl to sleep on a nightly basis? He wasn't sure and had no real frame of reference. Kids never really took to him. What he felt positive about was that he was damn glad to have found Arwen alive. On his own, he might get depressed, or distracted by the horrible setting. But with a child to protect, he'd be at the top of his game. He wouldn't let the kid die. Not this time.

He dreamed of the desert. Of *her*—nameless and beautiful— dark curly hair cut just below the ears to make her look like a boy. More memory than dream, the nightmare had plagued him for years. The girl was no more than ten years old. Her dark brown eyes tore into him across the distance and through the binoculars. He left the safety of his position and ran for the girl. She stood at the edge of the target zone—an Iraqi radar station—but without cover, she'd be cut down. Ten miles away, the BGM-109 Tomahawk missile called in by his team switched from a solid propellant to its low-heat turbofan engine, finalizing its descent. That's when she saw him coming . . . and ran the other way.

When he woke in the morning, he sat up straight, confused by the shield of white surrounding him. But then he remembered where he was and who he was with. He leaned over Arwen's little body and watched her chest. She was still breathing. It seemed, for the time being, that he had managed to save this child.

Stiff and sore, he climbed out of the bed. After donning his gear and switching out Arwen's IV bag he unwrapped a protein bar, lifted his mask, and took a bite. *Ugh,* he thought, looking at the label. Chocolate Cherry Nut. *Tastes like shit.*

Wandering over to the windows, he stared out at the world below. Orange light spilled over the city, reflecting off the high-rises and setting piles of red dust aglow. The sun rose over Miami, glinting off a distant billboard. The giant sign featured two sports cars, one red, the other silver. The logo read TESLA MOTORS.

Tesla Motors.

A grin formed on his face. He'd just discovered his first bit of good luck. Tesla cars ran completely on *electricity.* They didn't use combustion. They didn't require oxygen!

Miller squinted as he read the address given on the billboard. He quickly found it on his map, marked the location, and said, "Arwen." When the girl didn't respond, he repeated her name more loudly. She groaned as she awoke.

"You snore," she said.

Miller smiled. "Sorry, but listen—"

"I'm hungry. And thirsty. Weren't you supposed to get me something to drink?"

His smile broadened. He unwrapped a protein bar and slid it inside the oxygen tent. A bottle of water with a straw went next.

He watched the girl's silhouette move within the tent as she took a bite. "Gross," she said. "Tastes like shit."

Miller laughed loudly. "That's what I thought. But it'll keep you strong."

"Strong for what? I'm just lying here."

"Not for long," he said. "I found a way out."

14.

"I can't see anything under here," Arwen said from beneath the white tarp of her oxygen tent.

"You're not missing anything," Miller replied as he angled the modified gurney around the parched body of a woman facedown on the pavement. He'd rigged a white tent over the gurney and managed to attach two O_2 tanks and a saline drip. The end result was a crude but functional mobile oxygen tent.

He'd debated taking Arwen out at all, but when he'd mentioned the car dealership she refused to let him leave without her. Hearing the fear in her voice, he realized that leaving her behind would be cruel, even if there were people in the city gunning for survivors. If they killed him, maybe her blond hair and blue eyes would save her?

Not that it helped all the other white people living in South Florida.

The gurney bounced with a jolt that made Arwen groan in pain.

"Sorry," Miller said. He'd run over the dead woman's hand, which had apparently been separated from her body. *Must have been hit by a car,* he thought, and then lied, "Pothole."

"There aren't any potholes in Miami."

"There are now," he said in a tone that told her not to argue.

As he walked, Miller scanned for signs of life—both friendly and unfriendly. But with so many places to hide, and so many distractions for his eyes, he doubted he'd see anything. But the large red and white Tesla Motors sign was impossible to miss. He quickened his pace. They still needed to find a car and return to the scuba shop for his supplies before his air ran out—which would happen in just over an hour. Once all that was done, they could finally get the hell out of Dodge.

At least he hoped they could. Dodge could be the entire planet by now.

"Why are we going faster?" Arwen asked.

"Almost there."

"Go Percy. Go Percy! Go Percy, go, go!" she cheered.

Miller smiled. "Who's Percy?"

"It's from a cartoon of Cat in the Hat. Percy the Penguin races a seagull. I used to say it with my little brother, Sam, when we raced."

Miller sensed a dramatic shift in the girl's demeanor, which had remained stalwart and in good humor thus far. He slowed his charge toward the car dealership.

"He pronounced it 'Poucey.' " She sniffed back tears. "They're dead, right? My parents?"

Miller slowed almost to a stop. He wanted nothing more than to lift up the tarp and hug the girl. But the quickly-rigged tent would likely lose most of its air, she might see one of the many bodies around them, time was short, and even if he could get to her, he doubted he could hug her without causing extreme pain.

"I . . . I don't know."

He saw her lean up in bed.

"I could hear people dying. I saw the red snow. You don't need to lie to me."

Miller stopped moving and let out a deep breath that fogged the inside of his face mask. When it cleared, he said, "They probably didn't make it. So far it's just you and me."

"That's what I thought." She lay down again. "Let's go."

Without another word shared between the two, Miller pushed the gurney toward the dealership, happy to see the street ahead of them free of bodies. He stopped beneath the Tesla Motors sign five minutes later. Palm trees encircled the boxy gray building, which would have looked almost drab if you ignored the large glass windows revealing the rich, red interior. The red walls may have once invoked a feeling of power and superiority, but with most of the world presently coated in a red film, it just looked cliché.

If not for the sleek silver Model S electric car in the front window, he might not have given the building a second glance. But now he revered the sight like it was Jesus Christ himself returned to the Earth. The car represented salvation.

If he could get it started.

"We're there," he said, rolling the gurney to the front door. He tried it. "Damnit."

"Locked?"

"Yup." He pulled the gurney away from the door.

"What are you doing? One locked door and you're giving up? We're doomed."

Miller smiled, relieved to hear Arwen's spunk returning.

"Can you cover your ears?" he asked. "This is going to be loud."

Miller drew the 9mm and aimed it at the door. He was about to pull the trigger when he noticed that the showroom window was level with the sidewalk. Not sure if the garage doors could be opened without electricity, he turned the gun toward the window and fired.

"Too loud!" Arwen shouted.

But Miller barely heard her as he fired again. Cracks spidered across the window.

"Too loud!" she shouted again. "They're going to hear you!"

The third shot shattered the window and the glass fell away. It was only then that Arwen's last sentence sank in.

They're going to hear you. He ran back to her. *"Who* is going to hear me?"

"The bad men."

"What bad men?"

"From the hospital. I could hear them talking, even after everyone else died. Talked about killing people. Laughed a lot. Like the world ending was a party."

From the hospital? Miller's mind retraced their journey, searching for anything out of the ordinary. While *everything* was out of the ordinary, he hadn't seen or heard anything suspicious since they left the hospital. And the gunshots would echo off the city's empty buildings, disguising the direction of their source.

Then a chill ran up his spine. He'd been on the lookout for people all the way from the hospital, but hadn't once looked behind them. He slowly turned in the direction they'd come. What he saw quickened his breath and pulse.

"What is it?" Arwen asked in a whisper. "Is it them?"

"Yeah," he said, looking at a group of nearly fifty men, perhaps two football-field lengths away. They stood in the street, not moving under his gaze. They were dressed like casual Miami beachgoers—cargo shorts and tank tops in a variety of colors. But they all had shaved heads and every last one of them was white. Worse, they all wore identical black rebreathers, which implied preparation and foreknowledge about the impending attack.

Welcome to SecondWorld.

One of the men stepped forward and raised a hand in greeting. It was friendly enough, but when the group stepped toward him as one he felt like a wounded deer facing down a wolf pack. If they reached him, he was a dead man. And even if they spared Arwen, what kind of life would she live among men such as these?

Miller offered a wave back to keep the mob moving slowly. They'd probably been trained to not exert themselves and waste air. "Arwen, we need to move fast, okay?"

"It's going to hurt?"

"Probably for a few minutes, yeah."

"We in trouble?"

"Yup."

"'Kay."

Miller grabbed the gurney and slowly moved it toward the broken window. He kept an eye on the group of men as they watched him. The mutual suspicion quickly became apparent and more than the lead man could bear. He broke into a run and the rest followed.

Miller shoved the gurney inside the dealership, yanked open the rear door of the silver four-door sedan. He placed the unused oxygen tank on the backseat, twisted the valve open, and slammed the door shut. After opening the passenger's door, he scooped Arwen up, tent and all. She let out a cry, but held on tight. He placed her in the front seat and said, "Stay there, I need to find the keys."

He jumped over the vomit-covered body of a gray-haired man in a suit and made for the service desk. He hadn't yet reached it when he heard what sounded like an engine starting, but far more quiet. Remembering the car was electric, he spun around and saw the rear lights glowing red. The front window rolled down and Arwen shouted, "I had my foot on the brake, and pushed a button, and it started!"

The window rose again as Miller made for the car. He remembered seeing a car that could be started by a push button as long as the key—a small transmitter—was within a certain radius. He stopped at the dead body, patted him down, and found a small device bearing the Tesla logo. He snatched it up, afraid the car would stop if it got too far away, and dove for the driver's side door.

After throwing himself into the front seat and slamming the door, Miller threw the car into drive and said, "Hold on!"

The lead man of the mob reached the front of the store. He held a Heckler & Koch MP5 submachine gun, a compact, deadly weapon no civilian had any reason to own, and began raising it toward the car.

15.

The Model S had surprising kick. Glass flung from beneath its squealing tires, peppering the Tesla storefront. With the glass clear, the tires caught the slick linoleum floor and left twin streaks of black as the car rocketed out of the dealership and directly toward the man wielding a submachine gun.

As luck would have it, the gun-toting man had neither heard the nearly silent engine start nor recognized the Telsa brand. His eyes popped wide as Miller directed the silver missile toward him. The weapon lowered as he dove to the side.

Beyond the man, the mob, which was in no danger of being run over, began raising an assortment of weapons. Miller glanced ahead. The dealership sat across from a T intersection. If they could make it to the straightaway directly across from them, they might just make it. But the death squad to their left was about to open fire. And unfortunately, car doors are not as impenetrable as the movies portray. Most bullets, especially the high-caliber variety this bunch carried, could rip right through a car door. Though he was directly in their sights, Miller didn't duck or swerve. He simply pushed the Auto-down button on his window. While it lowered he took aim with his handgun and hoped the rest of the crew was as inexperienced and jumpy as their apparent leader. He squeezed off five rounds toward the group, not caring if he hit anyone or not. Miller watched as the group hit the pavement like his bullets had struck each and every one of them.

As Miller put the window up, the car tore across the intersection and shot down the side street, reaching sixty miles per hour in five point six seconds—the same amount of time it took the window to go back up. Miller glanced in the rearview and saw the mob rushing into the dealership. They'd have vehicles soon, too.

Miller turned left and pulled over. He turned to Arwen. "You okay?"

She looked small and frail in the seat. She had her seat belt on over the white tent tarp, which was wrapped around her like a blanket. When she gave him a small smile he realized she could breathe.

She noted his attention and said, "The air is okay. You opened the valve on the tank, remember?"

Miller removed his face mask, leaned forward, and shook out of his clunky rebreather apparatus, which had pitched him forward in the seat. He twisted the air supply valves to Off and put the whole thing in the back. The air inside the car smelled strange, but it was breathable. The car had become a mobile oxygen tent.

"We're going to have to do some more fast driving. Might get bumpy."

She grimaced.

Miller realized he should have taken some painkillers from the hospital. They'd probably been giving her morphine. He made a mental note to get something for the pain if they escaped the city in one piece.

Miller pulled away from the curb and wove his way through the city, avoiding bodies and the occasional abandoned vehicle as best he could. "We need to find the highway. Head north. Do you know your way around the city?"

She looked at him with squinty eyes. "You know I'm twelve, right? I usually read while my parents drive."

"Right. I think I need to—"

"What was that?" Arwen said, her voice tinged with fear.

Miller glanced at her as he rounded a body. She was looking beyond him, out the driver's side window. "What did you see?"

"Something red. Two intersections down. Thought it was moving."

Miller picked up speed, steering past obstacles like the street was a slalom course. He had no doubt that the red she'd seen was one of the two red Tesla Roadsters that had been on display at the dealership. They were two-seat sports cars and no doubt faster than his four-door sedan.

He turned right at the next intersection, hoping to put some distance between them and the red car. He glanced in the rearview after making the turn. The Roadster was cruising up behind them. One man drove, a second stood in the passenger's seat, weapon at the ready.

Miller pinned the gas pedal and shot forward. He did his best to avoid the bodies in the road, but knowing the bullets would hurt Arwen a lot more than bumps, he clipped a few arms and legs to maintain speed. He felt the tires spin whenever they hit a patch of rust flakes, like driving through sand, and adapted his driving to the conditions.

As they passed through the next intersection a streak of red to his left caught his attention. He turned to find the second Roadster aiming to T-bone them. He had no time to think about how insane the act was—the morons in the Roadster would almost certainly die. He acted on instinct, twisting the sedan toward the oncoming car and throwing on the parking brake. The Model S spun quickly through the red dust, kicking up a cloud. Miller saw the surprised look on the face of the Roadster's driver as the two cars came parallel to each other.

As the sedan's spin and forward momentum pulled it through the intersection, a loud metallic crunch filled the air as the pursuing Roadster T-boned the second. Miller saw both cars flipping through the street. A moment later, a body flew past, legs and arms sprawling out like a rag doll. He crashed to the street with a puff of pink dust. Miller twisted the wheel, straightening out the car, and zipped around the flung man's motionless body.

The encounter, while brief, had taxed Miller's body. He hadn't seen action like that since the SEALs. Adrenaline pounded his heart and made his hands shake. He gripped the steering wheel tight and slowed the car, catching his breath. Once he felt a measure of calm return, he looked to Arwen. She stared back at him with wide eyes. Her lips showed a slight grin. If not for the dry cracking on her lower lip it would have been a full-fledged smile.

"That was awesome," she whispered.

He smiled for her. "It was, wasn't it."

"Where'd you learn to drive like that?"

"Defensive driving course. Part of my job."

"That was *defensive*? What are you, in the army or something?"

"Or something— Whoa!" Miller hit the brakes.

Arwen became quickly frightful. "What is it?"

"Look," he said, pointing.

Arwen relaxed when she saw the Interstate 95 sign. "The highway!"

Miller checked the car's charge. It indicated they could travel an estimated two hundred miles before the car needed a recharge. He figured they had about five hours of oxygen left, too. And the rebreather tank if it came to that. He considered trying to find the scuba shop and all of his supplies, but a flash of blue passing through a faraway intersection in the rearview sent him toward the highway. Predators were still hunting in Miami.

They drove in silence until they reached the on-ramp for the highway. "We made it," Arwen said as they rode up the long, curving ramp.

When Miller saw that the double-yellow-lined road was almost completely free of cars and bodies, he powered up to eighty miles per hour and relaxed. The city of Miami, once full of life and never-ending parties, had been reduced to a red-hued ghost town hosting a gang of neo-Nazis somehow capable of reigning in their own SecondWorld. Leaving the city behind lifted a sinister weight from his shoulders.

As the buildings shrunk down to apartment buildings and then homes, Miller turned on the radio. He was greeted by static. He hit the Scan button and the numbers scrolled past until the cycle had completed and started over. Nothing but static. There were either no stations in range transmitting or something was blocking the signal.

Arwen leaned forward with a grunt and opened the glove box. It was empty except for one CD. "Score."

"I wasn't looking for music," he said. "I—" He saw the CD's label. *U2—War.* Score indeed. He took it from her and slid it into the CD player. Once "Sunday Bloody Sunday" started playing he knew the disc was kept in the car to show off its amazing eight-speaker sound system.

Miller and Arwen sat in silence as they cruised down the highway listening to an early Bono and The Edge pour their hearts into the music that made them famous. Red flakes danced on the breeze around them, flowing up and over the car.

Ten minutes into the CD, they passed an airplane that had crashed into the opposite side of the highway. It was big—a 747—and probably carried hundreds of people. Fire had consumed the middle of it, and Miller had to pull into the breakdown lane to skirt one of the destroyed wings.

"What happened?" Arwen asked.

"Engines can't run without oxygen," he said in a hushed voice. "They must have tried to land on the highway."

"Maybe the red stuff clogged it up?"

He nodded. "That, too."

Once past the plane, they fell silent again, neither wanting to talk about what they'd seen. After roughly twenty-seven minutes, nearly a minute into "Two Hearts Beat as One," Arwen turned down the music. "Enough old-people music."

"Old-people music? U2 is . . ." Miller paused. He was talking to a twelve-year-old. U2 *was* old-people music. "I thought you liked it."

"You thought wro— Ahh!"

A split second of confusion struck Miller as his ear picked up on Arwen's scream a fraction of a second before his mind registered what he'd seen—a bullet hole in the windshield. He yanked the wheel from side to side, hoping to throw off the sniper's aim. A second round tore through the windshield and blasted a hole out the back.

The third round found his left arm. Miller shouted in pain, twisting from the impact. He hammered the brakes as the car veered off the road toward a copse bordering an off-ramp.

16.

A wave of leafy bush branches covered the car as it sliced into the brush like a dull knife. Each shattered branch sent a jolt through the car, but ultimately helped avoid a bone-crushing stop against the guardrail, which was just a few feet beyond where the car came to rest. Once stopped, Miller took stock of the situation.

Arwen was still conscious, though dazed, and most likely in intense pain. He glanced at his shoulder, now covered in a maroon stain. A gash stretched across the side of his shoulder where the bullet had skimmed past. A little to the right and his arm would have been all but useless. He'd survived worse—much worse—and didn't give it a second thought. He couldn't see past the brush covering the car, but suspected the sniper had been on the overpass to which the off-ramp led. And since he couldn't see the overpass, the sniper couldn't see them, which meant he had a minute, maybe less, to figure out some kind of plan.

He ejected the clip from his handgun and checked the rounds. One in the clip. One in the chamber. Two shots. Against what? A lone gunman with a sniper rifle? Ten gunmen with automatic weapons? There was no way to be sure.

Arwen groaned. "What happened?"

Miller slid into the backseat and started putting on his

rebreather. There wasn't time to explain. "Stay in the car. No matter what you hear or see."

With the rebreather secured to his back, he slid the mask up over his head and secured it over his face. He adjusted the valves and took a breath. "Keep your head down. I'll be back soon."

"But—" Before Arwen could speak, Miller had slipped out the back door and closed it behind him.

Miller followed the rise of the off-ramp toward the overpass, staying well within the concealment of the tall bushes. The brush thinned out as several taller trees blocked out the sun. He paused at the edge of the brush, lowering himself down behind a leafy branch, and listened. His patience and instincts were rewarded thirty seconds later.

Fallen leaves and dry branches cracked beneath the careful approach of a lone figure. Miller watched him through the brush. He had the same look as the Miami gang—shaved head, blond hair, blue eyes, the military-grade rebreather—but a few details set him apart. He held the confident posture of a hunter. His black fatigues were similar to those worn by U.S. Special Ops on night missions. But his weapon stood out the most and made no sense. The Karabiner 98k was a five-shot bolt-action rifle sometimes fitted with an optical scope for sharpshooting. It was the standard infantry weapon of the Germans in World War II. But here it was, in the year 2012, held by the man who had just tried to kill him. In the open, with some space between them, the sniper had the advantage. Here in the brush, with twisting branches all around, the long rifle would be unwieldy. But if he reached the clearing . . .

Miller rose from his hiding spot and raised his weapon. The wound on his left shoulder pounded through him as he fired the first shot. The pain threw off his aim, and the bullet zinged past the sniper's head.

The man ducked and raised his rifle, but it snagged on a branch and his shot dug into the dirt at Miller's feet. As the man chambered a second round, Miller took careful aim. Before he could pull the trigger, he noticed the sniper was about to fire from the hip and ducked instinctively. Both shots went wild.

He had no idea how many shots the sniper had left in his five-shot magazine, but he knew how many he had left— none. He left the brush behind and charged through the sloped clearing. When the man charged as well, Miller knew they were both out of ammo. But the stranger still had the advantage. Not only was he not wounded, but the rifle had been fitted with a very sharp bayonet, which essentially turned it into a short spear.

The two met in the center of the clearing, both moving fast. The sniper thrust the bayonet toward Miller's chest. He spun like a football player, dodging the blade with his body, but felt a tug on something as he passed. He gave it no thought as he continued his spin and pistol-whipped the man in the back of the head.

The two men separated. As Miller watched the man stagger for a moment, he thought he'd gained the upper hand. But the man's smile, twisted by the thick plastic of his rebreather mask, revealed otherwise. Miller found out why a moment later.

He couldn't breathe.

The hose that supplied air from Miller's rebreather to his mask had been severed by the knife.

The ramifications of this struck both men at the same time. The sniper didn't need to fight. All he had to do was wait. Without air, Miller would soon drop dead without another blow landed.

The man turned to run, but stumbled, weakened by the hard blow to his head. Miller charged, his subconscious counting down the minutes his body could keep going without another breath, and then cutting that time in half because of the oxygen being eaten up by physical exertion.

Miller caught the man's shoulder and spun him around, but had to jump back as the bayonet swooshed past his stomach. The man's quick strike overextended his arms and Miller filled the gap, planting a punch into the man's stomach. The blow would have sent most men to the ground, gasping for air, but the sniper was a trained fighter. He flexed his stomach muscles and sucked in his gut, absorbing the blow's energy, and keeping his air—of which he had plenty—in his lungs.

In close, the sniper twisted the butt of his rifle up and caught Miller in the side of the head, sending him to the ground. Miller reached out as he fell and managed to pull the face mask from his attacker.

The effects of asphyxiation assaulted Miller. Dizziness and blurred vision blinded him to the man's approach. Then the man's weight was on his chest, forcing out what little air remained in his lungs. The sniper tore Miller's mask away.

The man grinned and spoke English with a heavy German accent. "It has been a long time since I took a life."

The man pressed his rifle's long barrel against Miller's throat and pushed, though it was really just a symbolic gesture since Miller couldn't breathe anyway.

Miller grasped the rifle and with the last of his strength, pushed back.

The German laughed. "Your struggle is admirable, but ultimately futi—"

Miller let go of the rifle and swung the bayonet, which he'd managed to unscrew with his fingers, into the German's side. But it didn't bite flesh. Instead, it stabbed through the man's rebreather and punctured something inside. As a loud hiss filled the air, the man turned toward the sound. Miller withdrew the bayonet and struck again, this time slamming the blade into the side of the German's head. The man slumped over without a sound.

Miller stood on shaky feet, his vision narrowing, his thoughts confused. He tried to reconnect his severed rebreather hose, but without tape to seal it back together, most of the air seeped away. All he could think about was the car and Arwen. He started back, stumbling through the brush, snapping branches and fighting to keep his eyes open. A glint of silver ahead shone like a beacon. He fell from the bushes, landing on the hood. Sliding along it, he found the door, opened it, and fell inside. With the door closed, he took several deep breaths.

Nothing. No improvement.

The car held no air, or at least not enough to help.

Arwen's silence confirmed it.

That's when he remembered the four golf ball–sized holes in the front and back windshields. He'd left Arwen behind, without air, to die on her own.

17.

Miller reached back and cranked the oxygen tank's valve all the way open. It hissed pure oxygen into the car. His head cleared and his vision returned. He checked Arwen and found a pulse. Unconscious, but alive. Next he removed his T-shirt and tore it into four pieces, balling them up and shoving them into the window's holes. They wouldn't stop all the air from escaping, but they were something.

Knowing the oxygen tank wouldn't last long, he pushed the car's starter button. When it clicked at him, he feared the car had been wrecked, but quickly realized the silent vehicle had never shut off. He threw the car into reverse and pulled back onto the highway.

Branches flew from the car and red dust billowed behind it as Miller hit the gas and pushed the vehicle to its top speed of 120 miles per hour. The highway passed in a blurry haze of red flakes.

Miller looked down at Arwen. She was tiny and frail and innocent. She didn't deserve to die like this. The millions of people lying dead in the city shrinking behind them didn't deserve to die like they did, either. He thought of the gang back in Miami. He saw the sick grin of the German sniper, leering down at him.

"Fuck you," Miller said to the red sky.

"Who are you talking to?" Arwen asked, her voice weak.

Miller breathed a sigh of relief. "The sky."

"What'd the sky do to make you so upset?"

Miller's tension bled away. "Aside from raining down oxygen-stealing red crap?"

Arwen glanced up. "Right. That." She wheezed. "Hard to breathe."

Miller motioned to the T-shirt-stuffed holes in the window. "We've got a leaky ship."

"We going to make it?"

There was no way to answer that question. Too many variables were still unknown. How far did they have to go? Had the rest of the world been attacked? How long would the oxygen tank last before it ran dry? The only real information he had was the battery charge. They had fifteen minutes left. Driving at full speed drained the battery fast. He'd been looking for signs of a drugstore or hospital close to the highway, but saw none. He'd considered slowing the pace, but if the air ran out before the battery, what was the point? Time was the enemy and speed was his only weapon.

Arwen coughed. "I'm sleepy."

"Try to stay awake."

The girl propped her eyes wide open, but the effort was short-lived. Her eyelids slid down to a tired squint.

Miller moved to touch her arm, but the sight of a body in the road snapped his hand back to the wheel as he yanked it to the left. The car jolted as they swerved one way, and then the other, nearly careening into the center guardrail.

"Sorry," Miller said, but was secretly glad to see the maneuver had woken the girl again.

"What's wrong with the sky?" she asked.

He looked up and saw an endless sea of red flakes. "What do you mean?"

"It's blue."

Miller looked again. Was Arwen hallucinating?

"Not up there." Arwen pointed straight out the windshield. "Out there."

Miller looked straight ahead. The change had been so subtle that he hadn't noticed the growing streak of blue at

the horizon. A blue sky lay ahead. And with it, the promise
of breathable air. If he could, Miller would have pushed the
accelerator farther down, but it was already pinned to the
floor.

"We're going to make it," he said, turning to Arwen, but
the girl had slumped to the side, her eyes closed.

He stared at her neck, looking for a pulse, and saw a
gentle twitch just beneath her skin. But it was faint.

With a suddenness that made his stomach churn, Miller
felt as though he'd just spun in circles. The world shifted
around him. He kept his arms rigid, maintaining a straight
trajectory. He took several deep breaths. His vision cleared
slightly, but he knew those three breaths had taken much of
what little oxygen was left in the vehicle—oxygen that Arwen needed as much as he did.

The blue sky grew larger before them, expanding fast as
they approached the border of the red storm.

As each breath became a wheeze, Miller knew the oxygen tank was empty. His vision became a blur, but he could
see the blue sky was nearly above them now. Another minute, maybe, and they'd be clear.

That's when the car's battery died. As the car slowed
from 120 miles per hour to zero, it carried them closer to the
blue sky, but stopped just short. While fighting the now-
familiar sensations of the onset of asphyxiation, Miller
stumbled out of the car and ran to the other side. He fumbled
with Arwen's seat belt, but got it free and scooped the still
form up.

He ran toward the blurry blue sky ahead of them. His
legs shook from the effort. Sweat poured down his shirtless
torso and red flakes clung to his skin. Through his waning
vision, Miller saw two things ahead of him.

The blue, blue sky.

And a wall, atop of which stood a line of armed men
wearing identical rebreathers.

"No," he whispered.

The men were moving now. Rushing toward him. Weapons raised.

"No," he whispered, and then fell to his knees. He placed Arwen down on the pavement and placed his body over hers.

"I'm sorry," he said with the last of his breath before falling to his side. Miller blinked at the red sky above and rolled his head northward. The blue sky was so close. Black military boots charged toward him. Loud voices shouted. His vision faded. The last thing he saw was the side of Arwen's neck. He fought against unconsciousness as he waited for the twitch of her pulse.

When none came, Miller closed his eyes and gave in to death.

18.

"Is he awake?"

"Not yet."

"Keep an eye on him."

Miller listened to the conversation with his eyes closed. He'd woken thirty seconds previous and attempted to determine his situation without opening his eyes. The sounds around him—feet walking in a hallway, the beep of a heart monitor, and a distant television—combined with the smell of antiseptic, told him he was in a hospital. Normally, this would be a good thing considering he was certain he'd died. But the line of men he saw before losing consciousness wore gear similar to that of the Miami gang and the highway sniper. He was alive, but was he also a captive?

When he heard the door close, he chanced a look. A lanky man stood at the door. His hair was blond and cropped close. Miller closed his eyes as the man turned toward him. He heard the man's footsteps round the bed and peeked again. The man's face was serious, his blue eyes intense. He wore a partially unbuttoned white shirt—sleeves rolled up. A 9mm Sig Sauer handgun hung on his hip. Miller sensed the man was dangerous, but he'd yet to see evidence that the man was his enemy.

Miller closed his eyes and pondered the notion for just a moment. That's when he realized the man wasn't wearing a rebreather. He breathed freely. And Miller wasn't wearing a mask either! He took a long slow breath, doing his damndest to not show a smile. The air was far from fresh, tinged with chemicals and detergents, but it smelled far better than his breath trapped within the confines of a plastic mask.

Feeling his strength return, Miller took stock of his body. A dull pain pulsed through most of his limbs, but felt sharp on his wounded shoulder. He could tell by the tightness of his skin that the gash had been stitched. A mild headache behind his eyes was bearable. Otherwise he just felt exhausted.

Through squinted eyes, Miller saw the blond man look out the window. He quickly searched the room. It was an average hospital room. Nothing special. The man's suit jacket hung from a chair. No balloons. No flowers. No get-well-soon card.

No Arwen.

A sense of urgency took hold. His muscles tensed. And without a second thought, he acted.

Miller sat up fast, happy to find himself not strapped down to the bed. He yanked the IV from his arm and jumped to his feet.

The man guarding him heard the movement and turned. For a moment he looked surprised to see Miller barreling toward him, but he quickly adopted a more menacing posture. For all the good it did him. The man reached out and started to say something, but Miller couldn't hear the words over the blood rushing past his ears. He took hold of the man's wrist, twisted it behind his back, and slammed him against the large window. The man's head struck the window with a loud bong. A moment later, Miller had the man's handgun pressed against the side of his head.

The man groaned, trying to turn in the direction of his twisted arm to reduce the pressure.

"Where's Arwen?" Miller said, his voice something like a lion's growl.

"Who?"

Miller tightened his grip. The man's voice had a slight

Southern twang. Combined with the blond crew cut and blue eyes, that was damn near strike three.

The man gritted his teeth.

"Arwen. Little blond girl."

"Covered in burns?"

"That's her."

"I'm not sure, she—"

Miller pushed the gun hard into the man's temple.

"I'm FBI!" the man shouted. "My badge is in my left pocket."

Miller considered this. Was it possible? Had they really escaped that pink hell?

"I'd have to let go of your arm to check the pocket," Miller said.

"You'd still have a gun to my head."

He had a point, and by now the man understood that if Miller wanted to kill him, he could. He released the man's arm and slowly reached into his pocket. A moment later he was looking at a photo ID badge that matched the man's face and read ROGER BRODEUR.

"This could be fake," Miller said, stepping back, but keeping the gun raised. "How do I know you're not one of them?"

"Have you looked out the window?" Brodeur said while rubbing his arm.

Miller turned his focus away from Brodeur and looked out the window. The first thing he saw was blue sky—an endless blue sky. He felt some of the tension in his chest fade. Then he saw the Capitol building far in the distance. "We're in D.C.?"

"George Washington University Hospital." Brodeur sat on the bed. "The National Guard picked you up at the redline—that's what they're calling the border outside of Miami. On account of the sky being red."

"I get it."

"How'd you survive?"

"Long story."

"S'pose it is."

"How many others survived?"

"The ones that thought to leave the affected area right away pulled through fine. Just over two hundred thousand people. The rest either never made it out or left after the iron had already poisoned their bodies. Nothing to be done at that point."

"How many?"

"You really should be resting."

"How many?"

"Two point two million dead. The affected area in the U.S. stretches from Miami to the Keys. Tokyo and Tel Aviv were hit too. We don't have the numbers, but the population of Tokyo alone is nearly thirteen million. If you apply the same survival ratio that we have in Miami . . ."

Miller shook his head. "Why?"

"No one knows."

Miller lowered the gun down and took a seat. He rubbed his forehead with his free hand. Two point two million people dead in southern Florida. It didn't seem possible. But he, perhaps more than anyone, knew it was true. He'd seen the bodies.

"Far as anyone can tell, you and the girl are the only survivors."

Miller shook his head. "No, we're not."

Brodeur's eyes went wide. "There are others? Where are they?"

"Right where I left them, would be my guess. Maybe forty in Miami. Another five in Hell." Miller stood. "Take me to Arwen."

"You're saying they're hostile?"

"I'll tell you everything I know just as soon as I confirm that the girl is safe."

Brodeur looked at the gun in Miller's hand. "Gonna shoot me if I don't?"

Miller turned the gun around and handed it back to Brodeur, who holstered it.

"You fight something fierce for an NCIS man."

With a grin, Miller said, "You know who I am?"

"Course," Brodeur said, motioning to a file folder sitting on top of the dresser. "Been here for ten minutes is all. Washington P.D. was guarding you until I got here."

"You're supposed to be my guard?"

Brodeur's face reddened. "Yeah, well, you kind of caught me with my pants down."

Miller looked down at his hospital gown. "Speaking of which, can I get some clothes?"

Ten minutes later, Miller was dressed in new jeans and a T-shirt. The hospital didn't have shoes, so he'd been given back the boat shoes he'd taken from Dave's Scuba back in Key Largo. He'd stared at the shoes for a moment.

"You okay?" Brodeur asked with a tone of genuine concern.

"They're not my shoes," Miller said.

"The nurse says you came in with them on."

"Took them from a dead man."

"Oh."

Miller stared at the shoes and then slowly slid them onto his feet. For a moment he felt the hot Miami pavement pounding beneath his feet as he pushed Arwen to the Tesla dealership, the tingle of his foot after he'd slammed the car's accelerator to the floor for an hour, and the slip of the dirt beneath his feet when he fought the sniper.

Brodeur's next words erased it all. "The girl—Arwen—she's in the burn ward."

Miller pushed past him, exited the room, and headed for the elevator. Brodeur did nothing to stop him. He knew better than to get in the way of a Navy SEAL, especially one tough enough to survive what Miller had.

With his finger hovering in front of the elevator button, Miller froze.

"Sure you don't want the doctors to check you out again, first?"

"Nothing's wrong with my body. I'm just not sure I can face her again."

Brodeur didn't ask, but the question hung in the air

regardless—why not? He looked at Brodeur. "If she's there. If she's real. Then it's all real."

"Then let me be the one to spoil things for you," Brodeur said. "It's all real."

Miller grinned. He was beginning to like Brodeur. The man didn't mince words. He pushed the Down button and said, "Well, then that sucks for you."

"Why's that?"

The doors opened and the pair stepped in.

"Because things are going to get worse."

The doors closed.

"A lot worse."

19.

Miller found Arwen in a hospital room very similar to the one in which he'd first discovered her. The only real difference was the number of windows and the view through them. The oxygen tent was clear plastic now, instead of opaque like the one she'd had in Miami, and he could see her lying there, looking toward the window. He imagined she felt skittish and afraid after everything they'd been through.

"How long does it take to get some pudding around here?" she said.

Or not.

"Sorry," Miller said. "I'm all out of pudding."

She turned toward him, smiling with her eyes, but not her hurt mouth. "Linc!"

"They didn't even offer me food," he said.

"You should have asked. Seriously. They'll get you anything you want."

Miller had no doubt she was right. They had survived the impossible, and she was a pretty girl with extensive injuries. If she asked for the moon it's likely someone would try to find a way to deliver it to her.

She lifted the tent up. "Better come in. They told me I needed to keep this down most of the time. Guess my skin didn't like all that time out in the open."

When Arwen scooted over, Miller noticed she wasn't wincing in pain. The burns still hurt, but the experiences of the last few days had toughened her. He could see it in her eyes. He climbed under the tent and lay next to her on the bed.

They stared at each other for a moment, for the first time without the fear of death between them. Arwen began to cry. "They asked about my family. Said I'd eventually have to go live with someone because they're all dead."

"No aunts or uncles?"

"They all lived around Miami."

Damn.

Miller searched his mind for something to say, but came up blank. He wasn't always great with emotions, and certainly not with expressing them—except maybe for anger. But then he understood what she was looking for. "I'm going to be here. I'll help figure things out, even if you have to come live with me."

She relaxed and laid her head on the pillow and wiped away her tears with her good arm. "Thanks."

"Okay," said a woman as she entered the room. "Pudding time." The nurse holding a pudding cup saw Miller and her face transformed from bubbly happy to righteous anger. "Hey, what the hell are you—"

Arwen leaned up. "It's okay. I want him here."

The nurse was confused by Arwen's defense of the strange man in her room. She was about to ask Miller to leave again when Arwen continued.

"Do you know who he is?" Arwen asked. "Don't you recognize him?"

The nurse looked from Arwen to Miller. Then her eyes went wide. "Oh . . . oh, I'm sorry."

Miller said nothing. He was too confused.

"No one offered him a pudding. Can he have one?"

"Uh, sure. What flavor?"

"Chocolate," Arwen said.

"Sure. I'll—I'll be right back." The nurse left.

"How'd you know I like chocolate?"

"Who doesn't like chocolate?"

Miller grinned.

Arwen frowned. "She didn't leave my pudding, did she?"

"Nope."

Arwen rolled her eyes, and said, "Some people, I swear."

Miller thought she must have been quoting one of her mother's catchphrases. All parents have them. The facial expressions and mannerisms were too adult. He knew he was right when fresh sadness crept into her eyes.

He distracted her with a question. "How did you know she would recognize me? Were you awake when they brought us in?"

"They had the TV on for me. Let me watch some cartoons. But the news came on after. Mostly it talked about Miami. And Tokyo. And a new attack in someplace called Tel Aviv. They said that people there knew what to do, though. Most of them got away." Arwen shifted, getting more comfortable. "Anyway, after that they talked about us. Said our names. Showed your picture a lot. Said what they knew about us, which was mostly about you. We're famous."

Miller wasn't sure how to reply. Arwen's face was a mix of emotions. She enjoyed the idea of being famous, but recognized that it was fame for all the wrong reasons.

Before he could speak, a quick knock on the door interrupted.

"Miller."

It was Brodeur.

"Can it wait?" Miller said.

"Wish it could."

Miller wanted to complain, but stowed it. They were on the same team and Brodeur was just doing his job.

Brodeur sensed his apprehension and added, "Someone's here to see you."

Miller raised an eyebrow. "Someone?"

"POTUS."

Miller's voice caught in his throat.

POTUS.

Arwen saw the change in Miller's body language. "Who's POTUS?"

"Someone you don't keep waiting," he said, sliding out from the tent.

"But *who's POTUS*?"

"Know what an acronym is?"

"I think so."

"Each letter of POTUS stands for a word."

"Like scuba? Self-contained underwater whatever."

"Exactly," he said as he closed the tent behind him. "You think on it. Tell me who it is when I get back."

"'Kay."

Miller stepped into the hallway, wondering why the president of the United States had come to see him at the hospital. Sure, he was one of two survivors to escape Miami, but Hell had come to Earth. If the president was here to pin a medal, or worse, use the meeting as a PR opportunity, then Miller would tell him to go fuck himself. He saw an army of Secret Service agents in the hallway ahead and made a mental note to use more polite terms when he told POTUS to go fuck himself.

When the waiting room door opened and Miller was ushered into the room, he saw the president's face and knew, without a doubt, that there would be no medals pinned, and no PR spun. The man looked like he'd gone a few rounds with the Grim Reaper, and the way he sat in the chair said that the next bell could ring at any second.

20.

Miller had never met President Arnold Bensson, but had seen the man on TV enough to recognize him as easily as family. He was a handsome African-American man with a manicured smile and casual and relaxed appearance. He spent a lot of time giving interviews to unusual media sources, including a lot of comedy shows. He couldn't play the sax like Clinton, but he knew how to work a crowd. But what Miller liked most about the president was that when it came down to the nitty-gritty business of armed combat and homeland defense, Bensson never backed down from the tough calls. And he'd made a few, even when they were unpopular.

Now, he looked defeated.

Or at least on the ropes.

"Mr. President," Miller said as he instinctively stiffened his posture.

Bensson stood and shook his hand. "You did good work out there, Miller."

Miller stopped pumping his hand. "Hope that's not what this is about."

A small grin appeared on Bensson's face. "I thought I'd like you." He returned to his maroon-cushioned chair and leaned his head against the wall.

Miller sat across from Bensson and saw him as just another man—tie loosened, shirt sleeves rolled up, looking desperate for a beer. "If you don't mind, sir, you pulled me away from a pudding date."

"She's a lucky girl."

"Hardly," Miller said, his voice taking on a hard edge. "Her parents, her brother, and every other member of her family are dead. She's been shot at, nearly asphyxiated on multiple occasions, and seen enough dead bodies to keep her in therapy for the rest of her life."

The president nodded. "Like I said. Lucky. It's a rare person that can face those kinds of odds and come out alive. You're that person. Without you, she'd—well, you know how things would have turned out."

"Please don't tell me you're here to pat me on the back."

"Not at all." Bensson leaned forward, elbows on knees. "I'm here because I trust you."

"Trust me? We've only just met."

Bensson nodded. "There are no microphones in this room. No cameras or recording devices. It's just us. Everything said will be between us. I had a ten-minute argument with the small army of Secret Service agents watching my back now. And they won't come in until we open the door."

That didn't sound very smart to Miller. "How do you know *I'm* not a threat?"

Bensson gave a sheepish grin. "If you wanted me to suffer, you'd let me live anyway. Death would be the easy way out of this mess."

"That still doesn't explain why you trust me. Or why you need someone you trust."

"I trust you because you survived."

"I got news for you. There are other survivors in Miami. And they're *far* from trustworthy."

With a slight nod, the president said, "We have satellite images of gangs roaming Miami. And we all saw the symbol on the news."

"They've been tagging it all around the city, too."

Bensson shook his head. "*Nazis*. It's just too much."

The president seemed to be fading into angry distraction.

Miller tried to pull him back to the conversation. "You were telling me why you trusted me."

Bensson looked up, his eyes focusing on Miller. "Mostly it's because of the girl." He took a photo out of his pocket and showed it to Miller. The image showed Miller on the ground. Arwen lay beneath him. This was the moment of their rescue. Of their near death. "You nearly died trying to save her. These SecondWorld bastards have so little regard for life that I can't see any one of them trying so desperately to save hers."

"That I'm an ex-SEAL and NCIS special agent has nothing to do with it?"

"Not in the slightest," the president said. "Ranks and titles no longer designate whether you're on the side of angels or demons. The line between friend and foe is smudged. That said, you being an ex-SEAL and NCIS agent are certainly helpful."

Something about Bensson's statement triggered Miller's subconscious. He'd said something without actually saying it. When it didn't come to him, he said, "Fine. But I'm still not clear on why you're here, talking to me."

"The nation is terrified. The economy is taking a dive. Things are falling apart fast and if we don't figure this thing out soon we're going to be looking at riots. Looting. Maybe worse. And everyone left in Washington is pointing fingers, but no one really knows who's to blame."

"What do you mean, 'everyone *left* in Washington'?" Miller asked.

The president frowned. "There are some people we have no doubt about."

Bensson's look of defeat returned. He rubbed his hands over his face and sighed. "About an hour before your return to the real world, the vice president's motorcade disappeared. We lost all contact. Secret Service followed the GPS tracking units in the vehicles. When they arrived, they found the VP missing and half of his guard dead."

"Half?"

"They'd been shot . . . by rounds issued to the Secret Service."

"Oh my God."

Tears formed in the president's eyes. "They were gunned down by men they'd served with for years."

Miller knew very little about the vice president, other than the fact that he was an older white man who seemed gentle and kind. But he'd clearly been living a double life.

"Twenty-five members of Congress have disappeared. Over one hundred thousand men and women in the armed forces have gone AWOL. In some parts of the South, entire towns have vanished."

"They're going to ground," Miller said. He was up and pacing now. "How's this possible?"

"There are a lot of religious groups and cults preparing for the end of the world. It's possible some of them have been fronts, allowing these neo-Nazis to prepare behind a veil of religious freedom. Hell, the Mormons have been building underground bunkers around the world for years. And either no one bothered to track their construction, or the information has been destroyed, because it's like they no longer exist. But we know they're there. Look, the point is, I'm not sure who I can trust anymore, but I *know* I can trust you. The reason for this conversation is twofold. The first is that I wanted to hear your story firsthand and unfiltered."

Miller gave a nod. Under the circumstances, his testimony would be unique and potentially beneficial to the ongoing investigation. If he had helpful information, it's likely the testimony could be altered before it reached those in power, or even altered by those in power. Miller empathized with the president's paranoia. Who could he trust? "That's why I was under guard," Miller realized and said aloud.

Bensson confirmed this with a nod.

"You know he looks very . . . German, right?"

"I didn't, but we can replace him if you'd like."

Miller smiled and shook his head. He couldn't decide whether the fact that the president took his joke seriously was funny or depressing. "He could have killed me if he wanted to."

"I doubt that very much," Bensson said. "I've seen your record."

"That was another life."

"We'll see."

Miller didn't like the sound of that, but before he could follow that line of thinking, Bensson looked at his watch and said, "I'm running out of time. Every move I make is being scrutinized. If I stay too long it might draw attention."

Miller caught the hint. Bensson wasn't worried about himself. He was the president of the United States during the worst act of genocide in the history of the world. Only the president's death could draw more attention to his office. Bensson was worried his presence would draw attention on *Miller.*

The story took ten minutes to relay. He told Bensson about the news report he'd seen, the spray-painted symbol, and his encounter with the well-equipped but poorly trained gang. The president didn't say a word until Miller relayed his encounter with the German sniper.

"You're sure he was German?"

"Even carried a Karabiner 98k with a mounted scope."

"What's a Karabiner?"

"Standard weapon for the Germans in the World War. But sharpshooters used it with a scope."

"World War Two?"

"Yes, sir. It's an obsolete weapon. But the way he handled it . . . he came damn near close to shooting me dead through a windshield while I had the needle pegged. That's a hard shot with modern sniper rifles, never mind an antique. For whatever reason, the Karabiner was his weapon of choice." Miller met the president's eyes. "You don't think the Germans are part of this?"

"God, I hope not." Bensson stared at the floor. "But it's safe to assume that our local neo-Nazis aren't operating alone."

"Well, that's pretty much the end of the story. You know

how it ended. It's not much, but I hope the Nazi angle gives
the agencies something new to go on. They can find his
body in the trees just after the off-ramp for exit fifty-seven.
Maybe he'll have some more intel."

"Good thinking," Bensson said.

Miller sensed the man had something more to say, but
felt uncomfortable saying it. "The agencies *are* on this,
right? CIA. FBI. Homeland."

"NCIS, too," the president confirmed. "But—"

Everything clicked into place as Miller's subconscious
finally found its voice. This meeting was never about getting
the story straight from the horse's mouth. It was about recruiting the horse. Miller stopped his pacing and turned toward Bensson. "But you don't trust them."

"Can't afford to."

"But—shit—you trust me."

"I do. You've seen combat. You're an excellent investigator. You're the one and only person alive who's drawn blood
on the other side of this thing."

"And you want me to what, chase down the bad guys?"

"I want you to try."

Miller began pacing again. "I wouldn't even know where
to begin."

"No one does."

"You do realize that I'm in pain from head to toe, that
I've got stitches in my arm."

"You've been through worse," the president said. "I would
give you the full support of my office. Money. Weapons.
Transport. Anything you need to get the job done. Unoffi-
cially. Off the record."

"In case I shoot the wrong person, you mean?"

The president ignored him. "I need a man I can trust."

Wounded soldiers in the field routinely requested to return to the front line. Sometimes out of loyalty to the men
they fought beside. Sometimes out of a sense of duty. And
sometimes because of baser desires, like vengeance. But the
SEALs were different. Wounded men were distracted,
slower, and more likely to make mistakes. Miller wanted to

help, but the discipline and self-regulation he learned in the SEALs told him to rest. There had to be someone else. "Sir, you *can* trust me. But I'm in no shape to—"

The president's eyes filled with a rage few ever saw in him. He stood face-to-face with Miller. "We might walk out of this room and find red flakes falling from the sky! Millions are dead! *Millions!*" Bensson reached into his pocket and withdrew a five-by-seven manila envelope. He handed it to Miller without opening it. He just sat back down and waited.

Miller opened the package and took out a stack of photos. The first was a satellite image. Green land and blue ocean could be seen at the fringe, but a big, dark red splotch filled the center of the image. Miller's back tensed. "What am I looking at?"

When the president didn't answer, he flipped to the next image. The red filled the photo. Barely discernable skyscrapers stabbed up through the pink. The next image was closer still, focused on an eight-block radius. He recognized a landmark that was taller than anything else around it. "Tokyo Tower." He looked at the president. "This is Tokyo."

"Next image," Bensson said.

Miller flipped to the next photo. Sun streaked down a long stretch of city street. It looked bumpy, but the long shadows weren't cast by poor paving. They were bodies. Millions of bodies. Miami had been a horrible sight, but he could navigate through the city. Tokyo was carpeted with dead. Miller sat down, speechless.

"These attacks were focused on the cities," Bensson said. "Of that, there is no doubt. But they affected the surrounding suburbs as well, which in Tokyo makes the death toll closer to twenty million. Frankly, we got lucky in Miami. It could have been New York or Los Angeles. We also got lucky that there was a southerly wind in Miami that day. Had it shifted north, up the coast, there would have been millions more dead."

"The wind?"

"We have no idea what kind of science is creating this effect, but once those red flakes appear in the lower atmosphere, they move with the wind, and a pocket of lethal air moves with them. On the northern edge of Miami, the wall of red flakes stayed consistent— on target—but to the south, it got dragged out to sea. That's how it reached you."

Miller stared at the photos in his hands. The bodies were so thick that they overlapped each other in red-dust-covered heaps.

"The clock is ticking," Bensson said, "and no one knows how much time is left. But we know the enemy is risking exposure by heading underground. Whatever else is coming, is coming soon."

He's right, Miller thought. But that didn't change the fact that he needed to rest, at least for the night. "I'll start tomorrow," Miller said.

Bensson took a deep breath and let it out slowly. He took an iPhone from his pocket and handed it to Miller. "That's a direct and secure line to me. I'm meeting with the remaining joint chiefs and a few generals I think I can trust. I want you there. Eight o'clock, sharp. I'll have a team look for that dead German overnight. With luck, we'll have a direction for you then. We'll have our best and brightest working every angle of this thing, but since I have no idea if they can be trusted, you're my point man on this."

"Copy that, sir. See you in the morning." Miller took the phone and pocketed it before heading for the door.

"Hey," Bensson said, stopping Miller at the door. He tossed a small pony bottle to him.

Miller caught it.

"Fifteen minutes of air," the president said.

Miller nodded his thanks and left. Fifteen minutes of air didn't sound like much to most people, but to Miller, fifteen extra minutes could change everything. It was a good gift. He just hoped he'd never have reason to use it.

21.

"Wow," Arwen said. "That's . . . a lot."

Miller leaned forward in his chair. "I know." After forcing Brodeur to wait outside Arwen's room, he'd taken a seat next to the oxygen tent and laid out everything Bensson had asked him to do. He probably should have checked in with Fred Murdock, the executive assistant director of the NCIS and the closest thing Miller had to a confidant, but he felt Arwen deserved to know everything—she'd earned it—and Murdock wasn't there. Hadn't called, either.

Her hand slid out from under the oxygen tent. She held an empty pudding cup. "All done."

He took the cup and placed it on the counter next to his, which he'd polished off in three big scoops.

"So what'd you say?"

"It's not something you say no to."

She was silent for a moment, and then asked, "You'll find me when you're done?"

The honest answer would have been, "If I'm still alive," but Miller said, "You'll still be here when I get back. Going to be in the hospital for a while."

"And if you *don't* come back?"

"That's not going to happen," he said. Miller felt guilty for saying it. She clearly knew the score, but he couldn't let her see his fear.

"You don't have to lie," she said. "It's okay to be afraid."

Son of a bitch. The kid can read my mind. "I'm *not* afraid," he insisted. It was a half-truth. Combat. Life-and-death situations. These things didn't frighten him. But he was afraid for Arwen. He felt guilty for leaving the kid. Had promised he wouldn't. If he didn't come back . . . Hell, if he didn't come back, it was likely she'd be dead along with the rest of the world.

"I didn't tell you how I got burned," she said.

"You don't need to." He didn't want her to relive that memory.

"I smelled the smoke. Did everything right. Stayed low. Checked the handles. Went to the sidewalk. This was before the red flakes, by the way. But the fire started in my brother's room. He couldn't get out."

Miller's hand rose to his mouth. "You went back in."

"He was my brother. I'd have done anything to save him. I don't remember the rest. My father pulled me out. The red snow started the next morning. I didn't see my parents after that."

"I'm sorry."

"The last thing my father said to me . . ." Arwen sniffed. Miller couldn't see her, but knew she was crying. "He said he was proud of me. And I know Sam is, too. Because I tried."

Miller rolled his neck and looked out the window. The sun hung low in the sky, casting a pink sunset that filled him with dread.

"You're like Frodo," she said, "You've been given a quest. To save us all. You need a fellowship, of course."

"What?"

"Never mind."

A silent beat passed between them.

"Before you go," she said, "take a shower. I can smell you even under here. The bad guys will smell you a mile away."

Miller smiled. "I don't live far from here. Going to take a shower, get some shut-eye, and then I'm off to the White House in the morning. And then . . . who knows."

"'Kay."

Miller stood and felt a wave of dizziness pass through him. He held on to the chair as his vision turned black for a moment. A single night's rest wasn't going to be enough. His body was still weak, and even a momentary blackout could mean the difference between life and death. *I'll rest on the move,* he told himself, stepping to the door.

"I *will* come back," he said from the door. The words were as much for him as for her.

"Linc," she said as his hand took hold of the doorknob. "Frodo was afraid, too. And he was a hobbit. Just a little guy. And he made it back."

"Copy that," he said, feeling stupid for using military lingo.

But when Arwen replied with a quick, "Over and out," he smiled. Had she been his child he'd see her as a chip off the old block. The kid had guts, nerves, and the spirit of a fighter. It kept her alive. Kept them both alive.

Miller opened the door and stepped into the hall, where he was greeted by the ever-vigilant Brodeur.

"I'm leaving," Miller said.

Brodeur frowned. "You said that like I'm not coming."

Miller set a quick pace toward the elevator despite the pain in his legs. "That's because you're not." To clear his head and rest, really rest, Miller needed to be alone. He had a lot to process and only one night to do it in.

"Going home, then?"

After stopping in front of the elevator doors, Miller hit the Down button and nodded. No sense in lying about where he was headed. "Cleaning up, getting some shut-eye, and meeting POTUS for a morning brunch."

"So that wasn't just a pat-on-the-back meeting?" Brodeur said.

"You sound surprised." The elevator failed to meet Miller's internal timetable. He found the door for the stairs and made for the stairwell. Brodeur shadowed him. Taking the stairs hurt far worse than walking, but Miller tried not to show it.

Brodeur noted Miller's slight limp. "You're not exactly battle ready."

"He was persuasive," Miller said.

"Dang, man," Brodeur said, his Southern twang coming through more clearly when unmasked by surprise. "What does he want you to do?"

Miller ignored the question, reached the ground floor, and exited the stairwell. He entered the lobby and headed for the reception desk. He tried to offer the portly man behind the counter a smile, but felt too uncomfortable to manage much more than an awkward grin that looked more like a grimace. "Can you call a cab for me?"

"Uh, sure," the man said, looking at him with wide eyes.

Miller realized the man recognized him. *Great,* he thought. He turned away from the desk and found Brodeur there, arms crossed, and a smile on his face.

"How are you going to pay for that?"

A quick pat of his pockets reminded him he didn't have a wallet. "Shit."

"Going to have to break into your apartment, too, unless you have a spare." When Miller said nothing, Brodeur flashed his ID and said, "I can make sure you don't get arrested for breaking and entering."

With a shake of his head, Miller turned to the man behind the desk. The man turned away quickly, looking at random papers on his desk in an attempt to hide his eavesdropping.

"Cancel the cab," Miller said.

The man's neck jiggled when he nodded. "Are you really him?"

Miller just turned away and headed for the door. Brodeur followed.

"I take that back about you being arrested," Brodeur said. "Everyone knows who you are, now. You're a celebrity."

Miller exited through the large glass doors at the front of the hospital. He stopped on the sidewalk as a breeze carried a waft of fresh air over his body. He breathed deep, intoxicated by the smell, by the feel of it in his lungs. He would never take it for granted again.

When Brodeur stopped next to him, Miller said, "A celebrity is someone people wish they were. No one wants to be me. Trust me. Where's your car?"

"No idea," Brodeur said. "I tend to misplace things."

Miller felt like slugging Brodeur, but held off when the man took out his keychain and pushed a button on a car alarm transmitter. A honk sounded in the distance. "That-away."

Brodeur led the way, honking the horn every ten seconds, honing in on the vehicle like a dolphin using echolocation. When they reached the car, Miller debated taking the keys from Brodeur and leaving him behind, but the man was just doing his job.

While Brodeur opened the driver's side door and climbed in, Miller looked back at the hospital. He found the fifth floor and followed the windows to the room he thought belonged to Arwen. It all seemed so normal. So simple. The hospital. The blue sky. It was hard to imagine that while part of the world had been transformed into hell, the rest was business as usual. He kept expecting red flakes to fall from the sky, or for the hospital to explode, or for a sniper bullet to find him.

When the doors unlocked, Miller jumped. *Relax,* he told himself. *Get a grip.*

After getting in the car and hitting the road, Miller discovered that his assessment of the world outside the Miami area was drastically incomplete. The world was anything but normal. In the fifteen minutes it took to get to his apartment they witnessed two stores being looted, several fights, and a standoff between a mob and D.C. police in riot gear.

When they turned onto Miller's street, he was glad to see it looked no different than the last time he'd seen it, nearly two weeks previous. Brownstone apartment buildings lined both sides of the street, most of which were concealed behind twin lines of maple trees heavy with green leaves.

"It's this one," Miller said, pointing to his building.

Brodeur pulled over.

"You don't have to stay," Miller said.

"You have your orders, I have mine," Brodeur said. "Won't be the first night I spent in a car."

"You're staying in the car?"

"Can't keep watch as well from the inside."

Miller knew he was right, but it still felt odd, having someone watch over *him*. He opened his door. "You sure?"

"Go," Brodeur said. "Sounds like you're going to need as much sleep as you can get."

"Thanks." Miller stepped out of the car and closed the door. He offered a nod and casual salute, and limped toward his front door. He strode up the granite stairs leading to the front entry of his building. He had planned to buzz a neighbor to let him in, but found the front door wedged open. The tenants sometimes did this if they were moving a mattress or TV, but no one was around. Assuming someone had just forgot, he kicked the rock away and let the door close behind him.

His pace quickened as he took the stairs toward his third-story apartment. It would feel good to just sit in his chair, which had conformed to the shape of his body. He took the last flight of stairs two at a time, working out his game plan: ibuprofen, shower, beer, chair, think, second beer, go to bed. As soon as he reached his door, the plan became moot. It would have to wait for another day.

The door was open.

Miller reached under his left arm, looking for a gun that wasn't there. *Shit,* he thought. He listened for several seconds, and after hearing nothing but the loud hum of his old refrigerator, slid into the apartment. Two steps into the apartment he saw that it had been tossed. The contents of every drawer and cabinet covered the floor. Paintings lay broken and torn. Cushions sat gutted.

At the center of it all, in the living room, stood a petite blond woman, gun in her hand and blood on her arm.

22.

Several options shot through Miller's mind. He could retreat and get Brodeur, who was armed. But that wasn't really his style. And the game could change by the time they got back. She might be watching the door, or have exited out the back. Leaving wasn't a viable choice. He had to take care of this here and now.

His way.

The woman held something in her free hand and was inspecting it closely. *No way she's a pro,* Miller thought. She'd left her back to the entrance and was totally ignorant of her surroundings. Still, she was holding a 9mm Glock and the blood on her arm suggested she knew how to use it.

Miller stepped quietly through the detritus littering the hardwood floors. With adrenaline fighting his fatigue, he managed to slide up behind the woman. Close up, he noticed a large purse at her feet.

Who brings a purse to toss an apartment?

Her clothes were all wrong, too. She wore tight-fitting jeans that showed off her short, but fit legs. Her red shoes looked like fashionable cross-trainers. And combined with her untucked white blouse and red, flowery purse, she looked like some kind of office employee on casual Friday.

Still, there was the gun.

A problem he would soon fix as he moved to within four feet of the woman. Close up, he could see that she was looking at the Purple Heart medal he'd been awarded for the greatest failing of his Navy SEAL career. He held his breath, pictured every move he'd make, and then acted. With one long step he closed the distance between them. He grasped the gun with his right hand and twisted, while with his left, he shoved her hard in the center of her back. The woman fell forward with a shout. The gun came free.

Miller turned the gun on the woman and took aim at her head.

She landed on the floor and spun around quickly. Her straight blond hair clung to her face, which looked wet. Through her hair, Miller saw her eyes, red-rimmed and wide. The woman was terrified. Not only was she not a pro, she wasn't even a killer.

"Who are you?" Miller lowered the gun a notch.

And then she spoke.

"Please, don't shoot me. I'm not your enemy." The request was simple enough, but every syllable she spoke held the unmistakable sharp sound of a German accent.

The gun came back up. "Bullshit."

"Please," the woman said, shrinking back.

"Who did you shoot?"

The woman looked confused. "No—no one."

Miller squinted at her. His logic said she was lying. After all, the last German he'd encountered had nearly killed him, and she had been standing in his ransacked apartment with a gun. But her eyes, blue and wet, looked honest. He quickly ejected the clip and looked at the bullets. Full. There wasn't even a round in the chamber. He slapped the clip back home and smelled the gun. If it had been fired recently and reloaded, it would still smell strongly of cordite.

He smelled nothing. Either the woman had reloaded and cleaned the gun, or she was telling the truth.

"Whose blood is that?" he asked, pointing to her arm.

She looked down at the blood, her eyes widening as though she'd seen it for the first time. With a shaky hand, she wiped at the dry blood, but it wasn't going to come off without soap and water.

Miller lowered the gun. Whoever this woman was, he could see she'd gone through hell.

"What's your name?"

When she kept wiping at the blood, Miller took her face in his hand and turned her toward him.

"What's your name?"

Her lips quivered for a moment, but after a deep breath, she found a measure of self-control and spoke. "Elizabeth Adler. I— I'm a German liaison for Interpol."

"Interpol?"

"I coordinate with the FBI and several European agencies on criminal activities that involve multiple countries."

"You're not a field agent?"

"Interpol has no field agents."

Miller's knowledge of Interpol came to him in a flash. The organization—despite what Hollywood and novelists would have the world believe—didn't hunt down criminals and solve cases. That's not to say they weren't important; coordinating police forces from multiple countries that might not always have the same agenda was no easy task. And thanks to their efforts, many international criminal organizations and terrorist plots had been uncovered. They were the good guys.

But, if President Bensson was right, even the good guys could be bad guys. Her being an Interpol liaison didn't necessarily make her trustworthy.

"Back to the blood," he said. "Whose is it?"

She glanced down at her blood-splattered arm, but didn't linger. She turned back to him and said, "My boss's."

"Is he dead?"

"I don't think so. I hit him with the gun."

"Why did you do that?"

"I have something important."

When Adler pronounced "something" as "somesing," Miller tensed. He wasn't sure if he could ever hear a German accent again without feeling threatened. Ignoring her accent as best he could, he listened to her story.

"Something about the iron."

"The attacks."

She nodded. "I took it to the local Interpol chief. After he saw it, he—" Her eyes shimmered with tears. "He tried to kill me."

She brushed her hair away from her face and neck. There was a cut just below the hairline on her forehead, but it was the ring of bruising around her neck that held his attention. Someone had damn near squeezed the life out of her.

"I got his gun. Hit him in the head. Here," she said, rubbing her temple.

"He fell on you?"

She pursed her lips. "I thought I would die beneath him."

"But you didn't. You got away. And . . . you came here."

With a sniff, she said, "Yes."

"Why?"

"The chief was on the phone when I entered his office, finishing a conversation and taking notes. Before he hung up, he said, 'I'll get word to the others. We'll find him and take care of the problem.'" Adler pulled herself up and sat on the edge of the cushionless couch. "After I knocked him out, I looked at the note." She reached into her pocket and took out a folded slip of paper. She handed it to him.

Miller opened the paper and saw just two handwritten words: *Lincoln Miller.*

"I had seen you on TV. After everything you'd been through, I knew they weren't looking for you to congratulate you. I wanted to find you first. The hospital said you'd left, so I came here. I thought I could trust you."

Miller shook his head. "You and everyone else."

"What?"

"Never mind. How did you find me?"

"I have contacts with the FBI and D.C. police. It wasn't hard."

"Okay. But what were you looking for? Why did you toss

my—" A warning Klaxon sounded loud in Miller's gut. He stood and raised his gun toward the empty apartment. "You didn't toss the apartment, did you?"

"No, why would—"

Miller held an open palm up. "Shh!"

Leading with the gun, Miller moved from the living room to the kitchen. The place wasn't big, but there were a few nooks and crannies that would make great hiding places, one of which contained some weapons he thought might come in handy.

"What are you doing?" Adler whispered. She was a few steps behind him, clutching her purse to her chest. "There's no one here. I checked."

"Whoever did this was searching for something. I—"

"What where they searching for?"

That was the million-dollar question. To his knowledge, Miller had nothing to hide, and certainly nothing to find. So if they weren't searching for something, what were they—

"Shit," Miller said, turning his attention to the open apartment door.

"What?"

"It's a distraction."

"For what?"

The answer came a moment later. Glass shattered in the living room. Miller spun, expecting to see someone swinging through the window. What he saw was much smaller, and much more deadly. The grenade bounced off the couch and rolled into the center of the living room. It wasn't a smoke or flashbang, either. This was the real deal—a frag grenade that would shred their bodies to pieces. Whoever had thrown it through the window had no intention of capturing them alive.

23.

Miller turned to Adler and was surprised to see her moving fast in his direction. Her open hands struck him hard in the chest and shoved him into the open bathroom. Miller saw where they were headed, spun around, and ran. He dove into the tub as Adler leapt atop him. The impact of striking the tub hurt like hell, but when the grenade exploded, they survived without injury.

Ignoring the loud ringing in his ears, Miller jumped up and pulled Adler to her feet. "Good reflexes for a liaison," he said.

She shrugged. "I played a lot of sports."

Good, he thought, *she's not falling apart.* Even soldiers sometimes check out when things start exploding. Adler was wide-eyed, but thinking clearly and still mobile. Knowing they most likely had just seconds, he yanked her out of the bathroom and into the hall. The living room lay in ruins. A three-foot-round hole had been blown through the floor into the apartment below.

Miller ran for the hole. There were two exits from his apartment—the main entrance and the fire escape. The metallic clang of footfalls on the fire escape were impossible to mistake. The shouts rising up the stairwell meant both exits were covered. That left them only one option.

"Into the hole," he said.

To his surprise and relief, Adler didn't question the order. She sat on the floor, dangled her legs into the hole, and scooted over the edge. He watched her land far more gracefully than he thought he would manage. When she stepped out of the way he noticed she was still holding on to her purse.

But there was no time to think about why the purse was so important. Red dots bounced on the hallway wall outside his apartment. The men coming up to greet him had weapons with laser sights. He took aim, waiting for the first man to show himself. Miller was outmanned and outgunned, but a single shot could stop an enemy cold. Precision often achieved the same level of shock and awe as brute strength.

When the first man's black-masked head rose into view, Miller squeezed off a single shot. The man toppled forward and dropped from view, leaving a splash of red on the opposite wall.

"Shit!" shouted a voice from the hallway. "Tango is down! Viper Two, Viper Two, target is alive and armed. Proceed with caution."

Miller's gut twisted. Everything about the attack screamed U.S. military.

"Copy that," came a voice from the back window of the kitchen.

As Miller spun toward the window and took aim, he heard the same voice shout, "Shit!" He squeezed off two more shots. He couldn't see who was outside the window, he just didn't want anyone to see his escape route. He knelt, fired another shot into the hallway, and then dropped through the floor.

Miller attempted to roll, but his body, already battered, resisted. With the wind knocked out of him, he fought to his feet.

"No one's here," Adler whispered, urging him on with her hands.

Something hard rattled across the floor of his apartment above them.

"Down!" Miller said, covering his ears as he curled into a ball.

The explosion was loud, but dulled by the floor above them. It was also far less violent than the first. A flashbang. But he knew what would come next. The assault team wouldn't take chances, and they had no reason to hold their fire.

"Ready to run?" he asked Adler.

She stabbed a finger to the second-floor apartment's exit. "Out there?"

"They think we're still on the third floor."

He sensed the argument would continue, but when the rapid-fire staccato of four assault rifles roared from above, she opened the door and dashed into the hallway. If they survived this, they would need to have a serious talk about tactics. He chased her out the door and was glad to see the stairwell leading up to his floor now empty. But that didn't mean they'd left the front door unguarded.

He managed to grab Adler's arm before she hit the last set of stairs and yanked her back. He held a finger to his lips. She instantly understood and moved so he could pass.

Leading with the Glock, he leapt into the stairwell and took aim at the man standing at the bottom of the stairs. But he held his fire.

Brodeur, gun in hand, saw him coming, and Miller's gun pointed at his face. "Miller, what in all hell happened?" He saw Adler. "Who's that?"

A red dot streaked across Miller's arm and danced on his chest. He saw it and dove to the side, shouting, "Look out!"

Brodeur dove to the side, but crossed through the line of fire when he did. The red dot appeared on his back. A moment later, two holes appeared. Brodeur hit the floor without a sound, his body motionless. Miller bounced back into the open doorway, aiming for where he'd seen the two muzzle flashes across the street. He fired twice and saw the man drop.

Echoing footsteps pounded down the steps above them.

The hit squad had either figured out the apartment was empty or heard the gunshots below. Either way, they were coming. The Glock 17 still held eleven rounds, but he had no idea how many men were coming down the stairs, how many were in the back, or if they'd lob another grenade. After quickly glancing at Brodeur and seeing two holes in the center of his back, Miller grabbed Adler and yanked her out of the apartment building.

"Where's your car?" Miller asked as they ran down the hard granite stairs.

"This way!" She ran down the street while pulling her keys from her pocket. She pointed the keys out in front of her. A honk came from one of the cars parallel parked on his side of the street.

"You drive," he shouted.

When Adler cut into the street in front of a tough-looking SUV, Miller felt a flash of hope. But she continued past it, opened the door to a pint-sized blue Mini Cooper, and threw her purse in the backseat.

"Europeans and your tiny cars," Miller grumbled before climbing into the passenger's seat. He didn't know exactly what kind of weapons the men carried, but there wasn't an assault rifle, or handgun for that matter, in the world that couldn't tear this car to bits.

The small engine purred instead of roared, but Adler worked the car like a pro, throwing it into gear and peeling out and around the SUV. She hammered the gas and tore down the street—straight back past his apartment building. A line of parked cars and the occasional maple tree would help shield them, but when five members of the assault team emerged, dressed in all black and carrying M4 carbine assault rifles, Miller knew they'd need a little more help. With the butt of the Glock, Miller smashed the passenger's window, took aim, and fired a volley of five rounds. The first struck a man's leg, toppling him down the stairs. The rest of the men dove for cover while the Cooper shot away.

Miller sat back in the seat and looked at Adler. She was focused on the road, emotions held at bay for the moment,

which was a gift not many people possessed. They'd both be
a mess when the adrenaline wore off, but the woman had a
dormant fighter at her core. "Turn right."

She did.

"Know how to get to the highway from here?" The question triggered Miller's memory. He'd asked Arwen the same
question back in Miami. This time he got a nod. Miller
watched Adler drive. She had the same blond hair, blue eyes,
and determination as Arwen, though her face was more an-
gular, more—

Adler noted his attention and glanced at him. "What?"

He cleared his throat and brushed the broken glass from
his leg. "How much cash do you have on you?"

The question caught her off guard for a moment. "Uh,
I— Nine hundred dollars."

She saw the look of surprise on Miller's face, and she
added, "I thought if people at Interpol were a part of the attacks, then maybe other agencies were, too, and I could be
tracked through my cards. I went to three ATMs."

A fighter and *smart,* Miller thought. "Good thinking.
When we reach Ninety-five, head north into Pennsylvania.
We'll get a room there."

Miller leaned back in the chair and closed his eyes.

"What are you doing?" Adler asked, sounding incredulous. "Taking a nap?"

"I'm thinking."

"About what?"

"About making a phone call." Miller opened his eyes and
removed the president's iPhone from his pocket. A single
number had been preprogrammed into the phone. He selected it and tapped the Call button.

SECONDWORLD
Return Fire

24.

The phone rang only once before Bensson answered. "You should be sleeping."

"No longer an option," Miller replied.

"What happened?" Bensson asked, getting straight to the point.

Miller gave him the short version of the story. "Special Ops squad took a shot at me. They missed."

"Are you okay?"

Miller thought about the question. He was far from okay. But his heart still pumped, which was more than could be said for Brodeur. "A little banged up, but they dropped Brodeur."

"Brodeur?"

"The FBI agent assigned to me."

"Do you want someone else?"

"I'm fine," Miller said. He'd trusted Brodeur, but didn't want to risk involving another stranger.

"Where are you?"

"Would prefer to keep that to myself."

"These phones can't be tapped."

As much as Miller trusted the president, he couldn't take the chance that the person who designed this phone wasn't a closet Nazi. There was no way to know, for sure, if their conversation was being listened to. He doubted it. But better safe than sorry. At least until he'd slept. "When I need you to know, you'll know."

Miller wasn't sure how Bensson would handle being denied by a subordinate, but the man remained composed.

"Fair enough," Bensson said.

"I might be a little late to that meeting," Miller said. "In fact, it might be better if we made it a conference call."

"You'd be safer here," Bensson said.

"Coming to you will put me back on the radar," Miller replied. "I'd rather be under it."

"Listen," Bensson said. "When you need something—anything—let me know and I'll make it happen. If they're already gunning for you, they know you're a threat." There was a pause before Bensson spoke again. "And I'm sorry about that. I can't help but think my visit in the hospital painted a target on your head."

Miller agreed, but didn't say so. The man didn't need more weight added to his already hefty burden. But he could help ease Miller's burden. "Actually, there is something you can do."

"Name it."

"Arwen."

"The girl from Miami."

"If they're gunning for me, they might try to use her."

"I'll assign a security detail to her."

"You'll assign more than a detail," Miller said. "The men who came for me were good, well armed, and weren't afraid to pull the trigger. If they come for her, the D.C. police and FBI won't be able to—"

"Secret Service," Bensson said. "She'll have the same level of protection as me."

Miller nodded and said, "That will work. Just make sure they look like Jay-Z's security."

After a chuckle, Bensson said, "Will do."

"I'm going to chase down a lead," Miller said. "I'll be in touch in the morning, but I'm hoping to—"

"A lead?"

Miller could hear the eagerness in the president's voice.

The FBI, CIA, and Homeland were most likely clueless, or being derailed from the inside. Bensson would be desperate for some nugget of good news. But he'd have to wait. Miller was in the habit of keeping his cards close during an investigation. It kept him from being distracted. Plus, he had no idea what Adler had in her bag or if it was worthwhile. "If it turns out to be big, you'll be the first to know."

"I knew you were the right man for the job," Bensson said.

"Thought I was the *only* man for the job," Miller said, half-smiling.

"You're both," the president said. "Godspeed, Miller."

"Thank you, Mr. President." Miller hung up, pocketed the phone, and stared out the tiny windshield of Adler's Mini Cooper. Night had fallen as they'd crossed into Pennsylvania. For a moment he just watched the reflective mile markers pass by, his anger slowly drifting away like steam.

He glanced over at Adler and found her wide eyes on him.

"That was the president?" she asked.

"The one and only," Miller said. "We go to the same church."

Her eyes widened a bit more, which seemed impossible.

The look of shock on Adler's face made her look like some kind of circus clown. Miller grinned, revealing the joke. His smile turned into a laugh, and Adler joined in. They laughed for nearly a minute, expunging the tension of nearly being killed. Miller watched her laugh. She was a stranger to him and nationality marked her as a potential enemy. But he felt glad to have her there.

Of course, that might change after he got a look at what was in her purse. Remembering the purse sapped the remaining humor from him and he turned back to the road. A Best Western sign appeared in the distance.

"Take the next exit," he said.

Adler's smile disappeared when she heard the serious tone in Miller's voice again. She put on the blinker and eased onto the off-ramp. Ten minutes later, they were checked into the Best Western, having paid in cash and used fake names.

The room was typical—two twin beds, a desk, two uncomfortable chairs, a large poster of a Western scene hung over each bed and screwed to the wall as though someone might actually steal them. The bathroom was small, but clean.

Adler opened the window.

"Better keep that closed."

"Smells in here."

She was right. The room reeked of cheap cleaning supplies. "You'll get used to it," he said as he stepped around her and closed the window.

"Why?"

"So we're not overheard."

A quick flash of fear appeared on Adler's face. She didn't know him any better than he did her. He realized this and said, "We need to talk."

Miller took a seat at the small round table and motioned to the other chair.

"About what?" Adler said, sitting down across from him.

Miller really wanted to take a shower. He'd never felt so dirty before and was sure the stench rising from his body would soon overpower the room's chemical odor. But the sooner he put his mind to work on what Adler was hiding, the better. "About what's in your purse and why your boss tried to kill you over it."

Adler sat still for a moment. Then her shoulders sagged. She lifted the large purse onto the table, opened it, and pulled out a small leather-bound book. "It's my grandmother's journal."

Miller fought against the sigh of frustration building in his chest. What could a grandmother's journal have to do with the attacks? And then she laid it out in the simplest terms possible.

"She was a mathematician and professor at the University of Königsberg. She was . . . brilliant." Her face churned with ancestral guilt. "They couldn't have done it without her."

25.

"Done *what* without her?" Miller asked.

Adler studied the table's drab mustard yellow surface for a moment. "The attacks. The timing. The ratios of iron to oxygen. Particle accelerations. All the calculations required to pull off the extinction of the human race. These things were not her ideas, but the math that made them possible was, is, hers."

"Your grandmother was a Nazi?"

"She was a German during the Third Reich. Many of the scientists that worked on projects for the Reich didn't agree with what they were doing. There was no choice."

"There's always a choice," Miller said.

"She would have been shot, and my mother with her."

"And yet here you are, risking your life to stop the same evil sixty-something years later. And if you die in the effort, your family's bloodline will end with you anyway. Sure, you might not have been born, and that's sad, but your grandmother handed over the keys to genocide to save her family? C'mon."

Adler's head bowed back toward the table. "You're right."

Miller took the book from Adler. The leather cover was worn and cracking. He opened it and found a name scrawled on the inside cover. "Elizabeth Adler. You were named for her?"

"I was her jewel, she said." Adler wiped a tear from her eye. "She was a good woman. A loving woman. She believed the SS men in charge of the project had died toward the end of the war. Some of the other scientists survived, but they became U.S. citizens."

Miller flipped through the diary. The first fifty pages were complex mathematical computations.

"She replicated the math from memory," Adler said. "And told my mother, and eventually me, that if red poison ever fell from the sky that we should get her diary to someone who could do something to stop it."

"And that someone was me."

"You weren't my first choice, remember?"

As she turned toward the window and looked at her reflection, he saw the bruising around her neck. He remembered.

"So this explains what, how it's done?"

Adler shook her head. "In theory, yes, but the equations are just part of the puzzle. There were others working on real-world applications. They never told her about the rest of the project, only what she needed to know to work out the math. But after calculating how much oxidized iron it would take to remove the oxygen from the lower atmosphere, she recognized the project's success could lead to a global mass extinction. She began duplicating her equations and keeping notes about everyone she knew to be involved and the small amount of information they revealed."

Miller flipped through the journal. The last one hundred pages were handwritten notes in German. "You've read this?"

"Several times."

"Other than the equations, is there anything that might help us?"

"Most of it is notes about her equations and what she believed the possible real-world applications of them could be, which may not be relevant because the world has already experienced the real-world applications. I'm not sure if the book will be of any use to anyone who can't understand the math."

"Which is both of us, I'm guessing?"

She nodded. "I took years of advanced math in the hopes that I could understand my grandmother's work. It's still like looking at hieroglyphics to me."

Miller flipped through the pages and stopped at a list of names beneath the word *Laternenträger*. "What's this?"

Adler leaned forward, looking at the open page. "*Laternenträger*. She called it Project Lantern Bearer, but that was just one of many names given to each individual aspect of the final project. The names are a list of everyone she believed was involved."

Miller read through the list of names.

— Admiral Rhein - Kriegsmarine
— SS Obergruppenführer Emil Mazuw
— Dr. Kurt Debus - Parameter und Messung, Hochspannungs-Stromversorgung, Mathematik
— Dr. Hans Coler - Physiker, Spezialisierung Strom und Magnetismus
— Professor Dr. Walther Gerlach - Spinpolarisation, Magnetismus Schwerkraft
— Dr. Hermann Oberth - Raumfahrt Theoretiker, Raketeningenieur
— Dr. Aldric Huber - Antrieb Spezialist und Assistent von Braun
— Dr. Wernher von Braun - Rakete Wissenschaftler, Ingenieur

"Wernher von Braun?" Miller said. The name sounded familiar.

"You know who he is?"

Miller looked at her. "Do you?"

"Only what it says there. That he was a rocket scientist and engineer."

Miller shook his head. "I guess that's why you're a liaison instead of an investigator?"

She bristled. "Hey, I didn't know if any of this was real

until a few days ago. I loved my grandmother, but she
wasn't lucid before she died. I wasn't— I wasn't sure it
was—"

"Don't worry about it." Miller had the phone out and
worked his fingers across the touch screen.

"You think this is worth taking to the president?" she
asked.

"Nope," he said, not looking up from the phone.

"Why not?"

"First, the math may reveal the scope and potential danger of the attacks, but like you said, we've already had a
taste of Grandma's secret recipe. Second, the president
won't understand a lick of this either and will have to turn it
over to NASA or DARPA. If he does that, there's a good
chance we'll tip off the bad guys and give them time to erase
the trail."

"What trail?"

Miller turned the iPhone around. A Web site was displayed showing a dapper-looking man in a gray suit leaning
on a desk in front of an American flag. Next to the photo
was the name: Dr. Wernher von Braun.

Adler took the phone and read through the text. Her expression became more shocked with each line. "Operation
Paperclip." Adler was familiar with the then-secret program
that brought the best and brightest Nazi scientists to the
United States and made them naturalized citizens. Many of
the great scientific achievements of modern America had
come from those German minds, including the atom bomb.
But she hadn't realized how much freedom those scientists
had been given. "*Mein Gott,* they made him director of the
Marshall Space Flight Center?"

"Wouldn't have made it to the moon without him. Says he
died in '75."

"Then what can we do?"

"Other than track down and interrogate his children?
Find out if Aldric Huber is still alive."

"Aldric Huber?"

Miller spun the journal around and pointed to the name

near the bottom of the list. "My German is rusty, but I'm pretty sure this says he was von Braun's assistant."

"*Ja.*"

Miller began dialing a number on the phone.

"Who are you calling?"

"Someone I trust."

After reaching the automated switchboard, Miller punched in the extension number. The line picked up a moment later. "You've reached the office of Executive Assistant Director Fred Murdock. Leave your name, number, and time and date of your call and I'll get back to you as soon as possible." The message beeped. "Fred, it's Lincoln. Sorry I haven't been in touch yet. But something fell in my lap and it can't be ignored. I need you to get me everything you can on a guy named Aldric Huber. Born in Germany. May be a naturalized U.S. citizen. If he's still alive he'd be old. Eighties. Maybe nineties. Keep it under the radar. Do the search yourself and delete it when you're done. Call me back at . . ." Miller quickly found the phone number under the Settings tab and read it into the phone.

When he hung up, Miller realized his instincts now controlled his actions. He was on the case. And that meant he'd follow this thing to the end, whatever that might be. Which meant he'd be breaking a promise.

He dialed 411 and got the name and number of the flower shop inside the George Washington University Hospital. After being connected he arranged to have a pack of chocolate puddings and a bouquet of flowers delivered to Arwen's room. When asked about the note for the flowers, he said, "Arwen, I'm taking the ring to Mount Doom. Love, Frodo."

The woman on the other end of the line got a laugh out of that, but Miller knew Arwen would understand the message. His quest had begun. He hung up the phone and turned to Adler, who waited with raised eyebrows.

"Now what?" she asked.

"Now," Miller said, "I'm taking a shower." He opened the Safari Web browser on the phone and handed it to her. "Find out what you can about the other names on the list. If anything stands out, make a note. After that, read and re-read your grandmother's journal. Flag anything that sounds like it doesn't involve Project Lantern Bearer. If Fred calls, come get me."

She looked surprised. "In the shower."

Miller gave a sarcastic nod. "That's where I'll be."

He stood and walked to the bathroom, wondering if it was even possible that a dead German scientist turned U.S. patriot and his assistant could help track down a modern Nazi cabal who'd shown they were fully capable of wiping out the human race. The truth was, he doubted it. He was grasping at straws. But the journal of a German mathematician had provided a few bread crumbs to follow.

Perhaps there would be a trail?

Of course, he didn't expect to find more bread crumbs. Blood seemed more likely.

26.

Miller left the bathroom thirty minutes later feeling clean for the first time in days. While he felt eager to hear back from Fred, he also felt thankful that he'd been given the time to just stand under the scalding water and decompress. The tension melted away from his back and the chaos in his mind eased.

When Adler looked up from her grandmother's diary, she noticed the difference immediately. "You look . . . better."

He sat down next to her. "I feel better." He tugged at his ill-fitting shirt. "Though we'll be picking up some clothes for me next time we get a chance. None of these are mine." He looked at the journal. "Find anything useful?"

"Obergruppenführer Emil Mazuw was general of the Waffen-SS—the Schutzstaffel, Hitler's elite—and one of eight Higher SS and police leaders. He was definitely involved in the development of secret weapons, but the Allies captured him at the end of the war. He served sixteen years for his part in the Holocaust, which included euthanizing Jews. After his release he got a job, lived off the radar, and died in 1987."

"Sixteen *years*?" Miller said, his jaw slack.

"*Ja*," she said. "They should have hung them all."

Miller smiled. Part of him expected Adler to be defensive, but her voice held as much venom as his.

"Dr. Kurt Debus. This may not be any help because he died in 1983, but he was also brought to the U.S. by Operation Paperclip and became the first director of NASA's Kennedy Space Center."

"Geez. Between him and von Braun, the U.S. space program was controlled by former Nazis." The ridiculousness of this made Miller wonder if Nazi sympathizers had infiltrated the U.S. system before the war had even begun.

"Dr. Hermann Oberth was actually von Braun's mentor and developed liquid-fueled rockets, including the V-2 rockets, for the Reich. He wasn't part of Operation Paperclip, but lived in the U.S. for a time before returning to Germany. He died in 1989. The last name on the list, Dr. Walther Gerlach, was interned by the British at the end of the war and some believe he helped develop their nuclear program. But he returned to Germany in 1946 and worked as a professor until he died in 1979. Another dead end."

"Literally," Miller said. "Anything on Huber?"

"Nothing. He's a ghost. If he exists, he avoided the history books."

Miller gave the journal a pat and said, "Not all of them." That's when he noticed a passage in the journal had been circled in fresh red ink. "Found something?" Even though he couldn't read it, Miller turned the journal around and looked at the text.

"I'm not sure. She mentions being asked to calculate the optimal temperatures for freezing and thawing bodies without damaging the cells. But she didn't believe a mathematical equation could help refine such a process without more data. She'd been disturbed when she was told that trials were being conducted and data would be delivered. But she never mentions it again."

"So she either didn't get the data, or just didn't bother to note it."

Adler didn't reply. Miller could see she was uncomfortable with the idea of her grandmother being involved with something as heinous as freezing and thawing living human beings. He knew that such experiments were conducted on the prisoners held in concentration camps, not to mention scores of other revolting experiments, but kept that to himself. He could see the weight of her grandmother's involvement tugging at Adler's shoulders. "You're right. Doesn't sound related." He passed the journal back to her. "But keep at it. You might find something."

The chime of the ringing phone made both of them jump. Miller accepted the call and placed the phone to his ear. "Miller."

"Damn, it's good to hear your voice, Linc," Fred Murdock said on the other end.

"Thanks for visiting me in the hospital," Miller teased.

"I didn't know you were there until you were gone," Murdock said. "Things are a little crazy right now."

"I'm sure."

"Where are you, anyway?"

"Better if you don't know."

"What, you think someone is going to torture me for the info?"

Murdock's tone turned grim when Miller didn't answer. "This is about that red shit, isn't it? Listen, if this Huber guy is a lead, I want in."

"That would be a bad idea, Fred."

"You're sure?"

"You've been out of the field for fifteen years and this isn't *Lethal Weapon*. You actually are too old for this shit. Just please, keep this quiet. If I need your help, I'll call. Until then, if even a mouse fart of this gets out, I'm going to feel some heat."

"I hear you, Linc. Loose lips sink ships. I know the drill."

"Thanks. What did you find on Huber?"

"Well . . ." Miller could hear papers rustling on the other end. "There wasn't much. The guy's led a quiet life. Came to the U.S. from Germany like you thought. Was only eighteen at the time, so he's eighty-five now. Lived in Huntsville, Alabama, for a long time."

"Huntsville? Isn't that where—"

"Home to the Marshall Space Flight Center, yup."

"Where is he now?" Miller asked, then snapped his fingers at Adler and pointed to a Best Western memo pad sitting on the room's dresser. She quickly snatched the pad and handed it to him. Using Adler's red pen, he wrote down the information as Murdock gave it to him.

"Last known place of residence is 23 Pinegrove Circle, Barrington, New Hampshire. I don't have a date of death on the guy, so he must still be there."

"Phone number?"

"None on record."

"Good enough," Miller said. "Thanks, Fred."

"If you need anything else—more intel, a wiretap, the cavalry—you let me know. Just stay alive, okay?"

"That's the plan."

Miller hung up the phone.

"So we're going to New Hampshire?" Adler asked as she read the memo pad.

Miller stood and picked up the car keys. "Yup."

"What, *now*?"

"It's at least an eight-hour drive. If we leave now we can be there in time to talk to Huber over donuts and coffee."

"You don't need to rest?"

Just hearing the question made Miller feel exhausted. He'd been pushing his body hard. But he'd been trained to deal with it. And if Adler wanted to be a part of this, she would have to do the same. "We'll drive in two four-hour shifts. I'll take the first."

With a tired sigh, Adler heaved herself out of the chair, put her scattered belongings back in her purse, and headed for the door with Miller. They were northbound on Route 95 five minutes later. Miller drove in silence as Adler slept. He felt the tug of sleep on his body, but his mind, firing on all cylinders, remained hypervigilant for danger. He half expected a bullet to zing through the window, or a storm of red flakes to descend. Danger felt inescapable—far worse than his combat experiences in the SEALs. Every enemy he'd fought in the military and every criminal he'd chased down for the NCIS had a face, a clear history, and a motive. But the enemy facing him now could be anywhere, anyone, and only God knew what they really wanted.

Would they make demands?

Would they instigate a third world war?

Or maybe just wait for the world to descend into anarchy?

They could deploy a weapon capable of killing millions. All from the shadows.

Doubt crept in when he thought about the immensity of what he was facing—he looked at Adler, sleeping in the passenger's seat—with a German Interpol liaison whose grandmother played a key role in the development of a doomsday weapon.

The odds were stacked severely against them, but the memory of how Arwen received her burns stuck with him. She had faced impossible odds when she raced into the fire to save her brother. She failed in the attempt, but she tried. She ignored the danger, plunged in, and fought the odds. Miller's odds of success seemed about as likely as Arwen's had been. Failure was likely. But he shared Arwen's spirit. He'd jump into the fire. Even if it killed him. As he turned away from Adler, he hoped she felt similarly. The fire was just getting started.

Four hours later, he pulled over at a twenty-four-hour rest area in Massachusetts. Adler woke up just as he finished fueling the car. She opened the door and got out. She stretched, yawned, took the keys from Miller's hand, and walked to the driver's side.

"Let's go," she said, climbing into the car and closing the door.

Miller grinned. He'd worried she might be a liability, but she was carrying her own weight, so far. After moving the Mini Cooper's seat all the way back and reclining it as far as it could go, Miller climbed in. "It's a straight shot up Route Ninety-five. Wake me up when we hit New Hampshire."

Adler gave a nod and hit the gas. Miller was asleep before they left the rest area's on-ramp.

He dreamed of a red sky and woke up to screaming.

27.

"Scheiße!"

The shouted word rocked Miller from a hard sleep. His eyes snapped open as he felt the car jerk hard to the left. He saw a flash of Adler's panic-stricken face. He drew the Glock, spun around, and searched for the vehicle that had tried to force them off the road.

There wasn't a car in sight.

Then he saw it. A massive bull moose stood in the middle of the road watching them drive away. The giant easily outweighed the tiny car and towered over it. If they'd collided, he had no doubt the moose would have walked away after turning the car and its passengers into a metal-and-flesh pancake.

"Sorry," Adler said. "Sorry."

Miller sat up, raised the reclined seatback, and closed his eyes. The close encounter had set his heart pounding and adrenaline surging.

"It stepped right out in front of me," Adler said, her voice full of apology.

Miller opened his eyes. "Haven't been to New Hampshire before, I take it?"

"No," Adler said. "Are moose common here?"

"They have bumper stickers that say, 'Brake for moose.'" He smiled. "I nearly shot the bastard."

"I don't think your nine-millimeter would have done much."

Miller looked at the gun. She was right. While it was great for putting deadly holes in a human body, the eight-foot-tall, fifteen-hundred-pound herbivore with a quarter-inch-thick hide would just be irritated by the small-caliber rounds.

"It's a good thing we're not going up against Nazi moose, then," Miller said. He took stock of their surroundings. They were on a small winding road that lacked signs or even a double yellow line. A forest of pine, white birch, and maples lined both sides of the road. The windows were open and the eighty-degree air smelled of earth and trees with a hint of something sweet. After breathing inside the rebreather for so long, the fragrant air felt like a dream to Miller. "Where are we?"

"You looked tired," she said. "I didn't want to wake you."

Miller rubbed his eyes. He probably could have slept for a few more hours, but felt a good deal better with the time he'd got. "Thanks."

"We're almost there. Maybe ten minutes out."

This came as a surprise to Miller. "How did you find the way?"

She pointed to the iPhone propped up on the front dash cup holder. A map displayed a moving car and a series of winding roads surrounded by a flat green landscape. "Phone has GPS. Two more left turns and we're there."

Miller picked up the phone and scanned ahead on the map. He followed the blue trail marking the roads they would take. A small bridge crossing the far side of a lake lay a mile ahead. A left turn after that would take them along the side of the lake and another left onto Huber's street, which looked like it crossed onto a small island. He zoomed in on the residence and found the house on the outer edge of the island, overlooking the lake.

Miller looked up and saw the bridge up ahead. It was big enough for just one car. A large lake emerged on the left of the bridge. A small pond lay to the right. Big houses with skylights, large decks, fire pits, and hammocks had been built along the shore. The water's edge was lined with docks holding Jet Skis, pontoon boats, and an assortment of smaller canoes and paddle boats. As they passed over the small bridge Miller looked out over the lake and saw a streak of white. A boat cut across the surface pulling a large inner tube to which a bikini-clad girl clung.

The peaceful surroundings and summertime scene gave Miller hope that things could return to normal. And maybe they could stay here in New Hampshire where there was no real target of significance to worry about. With the populations of most major U.S. cities dwarfing that of the entire state of New Hampshire, he doubted it was high on anyone's target list.

It was also the perfect place for an ex-Nazi to drop off the radar.

As they approached the left-hand turn just after the bridge, a large black SUV rounded a corner and headed casually toward them. Adler put on the blinker and waited for the beast on wheels to pass. Instead, it turned down the road before them.

"No one uses their turn signal anymore," Adler grumbled.

But Miller didn't hear her. He was focused on the SUV. Nothing about the vehicle stood out, really, but the men inside were a different story. He saw the driver through the front windshield as he steered the vehicle onto the street. He had a shaved head and pale skin. A man in the backseat was skinnier, but had the same close-cropped hair. Neither had the look of men about to hit the lake for a BBQ, fishing, or boating. Miller recognized the expression on their faces. He'd seen it on his fellow SEALs before every battle. They had the look of men about to spill blood. As they passed, he saw the silhouettes of two more men on the other side of the car. A hit squad if he ever saw one.

Miller tensed, hand on weapon, but the SUV kept on going, bouncing over a field of potholes before reaching the smooth pavement of the lake house association. *They're not here for us,* he thought. *They're here for Huber!*

"What's wrong?" Adler asked, looking down at the Glock clenched in Miller's hand.

"Get us up behind the SUV. But not too close."

"Why?"

Miller pointed toward the SUV. "There are at least four hit men on their way toward Huber and if we don't find a way to get there first, or stop them, we'll be interviewing a corpse."

The blood drained from Adler's face, but she nodded and steered onto the road. The SUV disappeared around a corner as the Mini Cooper struggled with the potholes. Free of the rough road, Adler punched the gas and shot forward. The road was still small, but the Cooper had plenty of room to maneuver and its low center of gravity made hugging turns a snap.

But they only made it around the first corner before everything fell apart. The SUV was parked on the side of the road. All four occupants were out, standing across the road, aiming an assortment of weapons straight at them.

"Steer left and get down!" Miller said, and jammed his foot on top of Adler's. The car shot forward as a barrage of gunfire peppered the front of the car. Glass flew. Adler screamed. A sound like giant popcorn kernels popping filled the car. The first impact to shake the car was accompanied by two shouts of pain. Their assailants' strategy had been sound, but they'd staged the ambush too close to the corner. There wasn't enough time for them to fire *and* get out of the way.

The second impact loosed a shriek of metal on metal. They'd struck the guardrail Miller had seen a split second before ducking. He sat up when the shriek stopped. They'd cleared the turn and had a stand of trees between them and the shooters.

"You hit?" he asked Adler as she sat up.

"I don't think so," she said, then looked out the windshield. "My car . . ."

The front hood had large dents on either side from where they'd struck the two men. The windshield had been shredded by rounds as the shooters had focused on hitting flesh first instead of stopping the car. But when white steam began billowing from the front of the car, Miller knew the engine had taken a few high-caliber hits.

Miller glanced at the iPhone map. They had half a mile to cover before the turn for Huber's street, and then a quarter mile to his house. "Gun it for as long as you can," Miller said.

Adler did an impressive job keeping the Cooper moving fast and on the street. But the increasing amount of steam and ruined windshield made it nearly impossible to see. Before Miller could tell Adler to pull over, the engine coughed and died. They rolled to a stop just thirty feet from the left turn onto Huber's road. The road dropped away on their left. The lake lapped against a rocky shore twenty feet down. To their right and directly ahead was nothing but forest.

"Get out!" Miller shouted as he snatched the iPhone, stuffed it in his pocket, and kicked open his door.

Outside the car, the roar of the approaching SUV echoed through the forest. Miller waved toward the road. "Run!"

Adler took off, running faster than Miller thought possible for a woman her size. Of course, when life hangs in the balance, most people can put a little extra pepper in their step. Miller, on the other hand, stood his ground and aimed back down the road. The SUV came thundering up over the rise and barreled toward him. A man leaned out of the passenger's window and opened fire with a submachine gun. Rounds sliced through the small car, but couldn't find Miller positioned behind the engine block and far-side tire.

As the shooter ducked away to reload, Miller took aim, held his breath, and squeezed off a series of rounds. The first four shots missed the target, shattering the headlight and pinging off the thick metal wheel well. But the fifth shot found nothing but tire. The effect was immediate and violent. The tire rapidly deflated under the SUV's immense weight. The rim bit into and shredded the rubber. The vehicle tilted toward the lake and the driver, fearing a twenty-foot drop, overcompensated. The SUV turned hard to the right, the tire tore away, and the rim dug into the pavement.

The giant SUV launched into the air, spinning like a flicked coin. The gunman was launched from the open window like a rag doll from a cannon. He flew three hundred feet, snapping dry branches from pine trees before having his head removed by a thick maple limb. Blood sprayed from his body as it spiraled toward the earth and landed with a thud in the forest's thick leaf litter.

The aerial arc of the SUV was much shorter, but no less dramatic as it flipped over the Mini Cooper. The roof of the SUV crushed the Cooper's as it rolled and nearly struck Miller, but its momentum carried it forward. The SUV bounced off the road behind Miller and spun into the open air above the lake. The vehicle fell, and with a loud *whoosh,* struck the lake's surface upside down. Water poured in through the open windows. Thirty seconds later, the SUV slid beneath the lapping waves.

Miller watched the SUV sink.

Adler ran up to him. "Holy shit!"

He just nodded and kept watching. After a minute, he felt satisfied that no one would be surfacing and checked the Glock's clip. One round left. He slapped the clip back in and started jogging toward Huber's road. "Let's go."

Adler followed, and had no trouble keeping pace. "You have nothing to say about what just happened?"

He looked at her. Her posture was perfect, her steps even. "You're a runner?"

"Yeah, but—"

"Endurance?"

"I've run a few marathons."

"Good," he said, before picking up his pace. She fell in line and became too winded to talk. There was no way to know if a second crew would be sent out, or if they were already on the way. And they still needed to find Huber, get him someplace safe, and hopefully get some answers to a growing list of questions.

They crossed a small stone bridge onto the island. The road became dirt and skirted the shoreline. They followed the road and soon came to the one and only house—Huber's.

The average-sized log home was in stellar condition and situated in the middle of a cleared section of land that ran down to the lake's edge. Miller saw an empty dock and feared Huber might actually be out on the lake, which would complicate things. Further out on the water he saw two men fishing from a canoe, but neither looked like an old man.

After slowing his pace and catching his breath, Miller entered the paved, and empty, driveway. A stainless steel carport stood to the side of the driveway, but there was no way to see inside without making noise. Weapon in hand, Miller took the three steps up onto the farmer's porch and silently stepped up to the red door. He gently took hold of the handle and turned. The door opened silently.

Adler stood next to him. "It's unlocked?" she whispered.

The same thing had concerned Miller, too, but then he once again remembered they were in the woods of New Hampshire. He suspected they'd find most doors unlocked, especially if the residents were home.

Miller and Adler crept into the house. It smelled of pine and woodsmoke and the temperature felt ten degrees cooler than outside. The front hall, which held a coatrack and welcome mat, opened into a dining area on the left and a small kitchen on the right. The table was thick and rough, sporting two long benches like a picnic table. The marble kitchen counters were spotless and reflected sunlight streaming in through the window over the sink. Directly ahead of them was a long living room that ran the length of the house. Mounted buck busts lined the outside wall above a line of windows that provided a stunning view of the lake. And it was that view that nearly cost Adler her life.

She stepped into the living room, eyes on the window.

Two metallic clicks pricked Miller's ears before he entered the room. "Elizabeth, freeze," he said.

"What? Why?"

The voice, that of an old man, came from the corner of the room, behind Adler. "Because, *fräulein,* I'm still deciding whether or not I should kill you."

28.

Miller hung back in the kitchen, out of view. Adler stood rigid in the middle of the living room, her back to the man that had just threatened her life.

"I've been expecting you for some days now," the man said.

"Expecting me?" Adler said.

"*Ja.* I knew you would come once I saw the shade effect over Miami. Though I must admit I am surprised you are a woman."

"Huber," Miller said.

"Don't do anything foolish," Huber warned.

Miller eased toward the living room. "I think you have us confused with someone else."

"You take me for a fool?"

"I'm going to walk in with my back to you." Miller eased into the living room. He held his gun out first and when he felt Huber could see it, he ejected the clip and dropped the weapon onto the floor. "I'm unarmed."

After three slow steps, Miller stopped next to Adler, his arms raised. Huber could kill them both with two quick pulls of the trigger, but Miller had to risk it.

"I heard gunshots from the road," Huber said. "Who did you kill?"

"Your neighbors are fine, if that's what you're worried about," Miller said.

"They have kids," Huber conceded.

"I can't say the same for the four men that were coming to kill you," Miller said.

"How do I know *you're* not here to kill me?"

Because you'd already be dead, Miller thought, but said, "If you'll let me turn around, I can show you."

"Slowly."

Miller turned around, keeping his hands high and his motions slow. As he turned, Miller looked at the line of mounted deer busts. If they were Huber's kills, the man knew how to shoot. Giving him a reason to pull the trigger would be a very bad idea.

Huber sat in shadow, but the double-barreled shotgun was easy enough to see. And while he couldn't clearly see Huber's face, Miller knew the old man had seen his. The shotgun lowered slightly as Huber leaned forward. He stood and walked into the light. His face was old and weathered, but his spectacled eyes burned with intensity. A full head of gray hair and a week's worth of stubble framed his confused expression. "Am I supposed to recognize you?"

"Most people seem to, these days," Miller said with a frown. If Huber didn't recognize him, his plan would go up in smoke. "My face has been on TV a lot lately."

"Do you see a TV?" Huber asked.

Shit. Miller didn't.

"Newspaper?" Miller asked.

Huber shook his head, no.

"How do you know what's happening in the world?" Adler asked.

"Radio," Huber said.

Miller realized he had just one hope. "Lincoln Miller, you know the name?"

Huber thought for just a moment. "The survivor from Miami, yes, but—"

"*I* am Lincoln Miller."

Huber looked at him like he'd just claimed to be Hitler himself.

"I'm going to reach into my pocket," Miller said. "For some ID."

"Slowly," Huber said, keeping his aim tight on Miller's chest.

Miller pulled out the iPhone and flicked it on.

"That's not a wallet," Huber noted.

"My wallet is under fifty feet of water off of Key Largo buried beneath a blue whale," Miller said as he opened the Web browser, opened a news network Web site, and watched the new headlines rotate. "Kind of hard to reach right now." When a photo of his face appeared in the rotation, he tapped the article to expand it and held it up for Huber to see.

Huber's face shifted through a variety of expressions. The article clearly showed Miller's face, name, and identified him as the man who'd survived the attack on Miami and saved a little girl, but didn't explain how Miller had gotten to New Hampshire, or why he stood in Huber's living room.

"I'm Special Agent Lincoln Miller with the NCIS."

Huber gave a small nod. "That's what it says under your photo, but—"

"I'm here at the behest of the president of the United States," Miller said.

That got Huber's attention. "Figured it out then, have you?" Huber motioned to Adler with the shotgun. "And you? *Sie sind Deutsche.*"

Adler turned around and eyed the shotgun pointed at her gut. "Elizabeth Adler. I'm a German liaison for Interpol."

Huber's eyes darted back and forth between the two of them, searching their faces for some sign of deception. Finding none, he lowered the shotgun.

Miller noticed the old man's free hand shaking. A trickle of sweat rolled down the man's face. Huber was terrified. "You have a beautiful home," Miller said, trying to put the man at ease. If he had a heart attack, he wouldn't be any use to anyone.

"It is my sanctuary," Huber said, returning to his seat.

A great stone fireplace stood to Miller's right, its chimney rising up through the center of the cabin. He stepped closer to the mantel lined with framed photos. Older pictures showed Huber with a woman, presumably his wife, and two young girls—daughters. Newer pictures showed an aged Huber with two older women—the daughters grown up—and a line of what had to be grandkids. "When did your wife pass?"

Huber sniffed. "Fifteen years ago. Cancer ate her alive."

"Sorry," Miller said.

Huber shrugged. "You're not here to talk about my family and I would prefer you had nothing to do with them. I am no longer burdened by the hatred of my youth. And up until this moment, I thought myself free of that past. But it seems history is repeating itself once again." He turned to Adler. "The evil born in our homeland has raised itself from the ashes once again."

"Millions are dead," Adler said.

"Sixty million lives were taken in the Second World War," Huber said. "What you have seen is just the beginning."

Miller stepped toward Huber. "The beginning?"

"Tests."

"For what?"

Huber leaned forward and pushed his fingers together. "Have you determined where the iron particles came from?"

Miller remembered the vague news report he'd seen in Miami. "I heard something about a cloud of iron that the solar system passed through."

Huber shook his head at the crude explanation. "The iron *is* extraterrestrial in origin—"

"Aliens?" Adler asked.

Huber laughed and waved a dismissive hand at her. "Nothing so foolish. There is a vast cloud of finely divided particles on the fringe of our solar system. It is typically held at bay in the heliopause by the sun's solar wind."

"Heliopause?" Miller asked.

"The heliopause is the region of space where the sun's ions meet the galaxy's. There are particles in this region of space, about one hundred and ten astronomical units from the sun—an astronomical unit is the distance between the Earth and the sun, nearly ninety-three million miles. During times of low sunspot activity, which occurs roughly every ten years, some of these particles slip through into the solar system. Many reach Earth and burn up harmlessly in the thermosphere. A period of extremely low sunspot activity occurred in 1933. Combined with an infrequent alignment of the planets, particularly the gas giants, a large cloud of iron particles entered the solar system and over the past seventy years has been journeying toward Earth."

"And it reached us a few days ago?" Adler asked.

"Oh, no," Huber said. "Those were small clouds that arrived in advance and allowed for the tests to be conducted."

"How do you know all this?" Miller asked.

"Because," Huber said, meeting Miller's skeptical gaze. "I was there when Wernher von Braun calculated its arrival." The old man craned his head toward Adler. "Of course, he wasn't absolutely sure until your grandmother confirmed the accuracy of his math."

29.

Adler's mouth hung open for a moment. "You knew my grandmother?"

"I met her twice," Huber said with a nod. "I was a youth at the time, working in von Braun's laboratory and living in his loft. She was a stunning woman. Taller, and fairer to look at than you, I'm afraid, but you share her eyes. She was instrumental in the completion of Lantern Bearer. Was she how you found me? Is she still alive?"

"She kept a journal," Miller said. "Your name was in it, among others."

Huber pinched his lips together, moving them side to side. "We always suspected her loyalties were not fully aligned with those of the Reich, but we never told the Obergruppenführer about our suspicions."

"Emil Mazuw?" Miller asked.

"The same. A ruthless man and stalwart believer in the superiority of the Aryan race. He would have had her shot."

"Why?" Adler asked. "Why didn't you turn her in?"

"Aside from the fact that her brilliance made our advances possible?" Huber settled back into his chair. "Tell me, what do you know of your grandfather?"

"My grandfather? My grandmother said he was kind and gentle."

"He was."

"And he died during the war. Allied bombs."

Huber shook his head. "I'm sorry to say, this is not true. Your grandfather died in 1979, just a few years after you were born, I suspect. He was ninety years old."

Adler sat down in the chair across from Huber, her hand to her mouth.

"He loved your grandmother very much and forbade the rest of us from turning her in. He was a dedicated Nazi, a valued colleague, and we trusted his judgment. And while your grandmother certainly helped with the success of several Nazi projects, many of them were born from the mind of your grandfather. In fact, without your family's involvement, the world wouldn't now be in danger."

To say that these revelations were stunning was an understatement. Adler had gone pale and had a lot to process. She felt guilty because of her grandmother's association with Project Lantern Bearer, but now her grandfather was involved as well, and on a much more grand scale. Her grandparents' hands were stained with the blood of millions. As horrifying as this was, Miller needed to keep the conversation on track. "What can you tell us about the project?"

Huber shrugged. "Everything I remember. But it won't help and I'm sure a lot has changed since we worked on the prototype."

"What do you mean, changed?"

"Debus, Gerlach, Oberth, and von Braun were all scientists of notoriety. The Allies were well aware of their keen minds and sought them out at the end of the war. If they'd been shot, or taken with the prototype—"

"Taken where?" Miller asked.

"We were never told." Huber cleared his throat and stood. He wandered to the fireplace and looked at the photos on the mantel. "Anything other than capture would have raised suspicions and begun a search. Turning themselves in kept attention away from the project long enough for it to disappear. It also served another purpose that allowed the project to continue into the present day."

"Which was?" Miller asked.

The old man rubbed a thumb over the photo of his grandkids—three smiling girls and two boys. "Recruitment."

The word twisted Miller's gut. Von Braun had been made the director of Marshall Space Flight Center and Debus the director of the Kennedy Space Center. They would have had access to the best and brightest U.S. scientists.

"I can see you understand the implications," Huber said, looking at Miller. "Our former affiliation with the Nazi regime was well known. We had no trouble finding like-minded scientists. In fifteen years, von Braun and I recruited more than thirty scientists from a variety of fields. Once initiated, they were picked up and we never saw them again."

Huber turned his attention back to the photos. "But we soon began having children, and grandchildren. And this was their home. Our families were American. And we came to love this country and its . . . diversity, as our own. We decided, as a group, to end the recruitment program. But it seemed our bold move was a hollow gesture. We were never contacted again."

"Why not?" Miller asked.

"Based on the events of the last few days, I'd guess it was because we sent them everyone they needed, and every time a recruit left, we ran the risk of exposing the program."

"So you just kept it all to yourselves?" Miller said. "Why didn't *you* expose the program?"

"Just because we weren't contacted doesn't mean we weren't being watched. We stayed silent for the same reason Walther Gerlach never visited his granddaughter." He looked at Adler when he said it. Gerlach was her grandfather. "A man will suffer a great deal of guilt to protect the ones he loves."

Miller got in front of Huber. "And now?"

Huber shook his head as a great sadness seeped into his expression. "Now, we're all going to die."

"When?" Miller asked. "How long do we have?"

Tears fell from Huber's eyes and landed on the photo of his grandchildren. "The second, more massive cloud of iron particulates will arrive in five days."

"And the targets?"

Huber's face screwed with confusion. "Targets?"

"What cities!" Miller said.

"There is only one target," Huber said.

One target? Miller thought. His mind ran through everything he knew. Millions were dead. Three major cities had
been struck, but how could just one more achieve anything?
Washington, D.C., would kill a lot, but the government
would be evacuated as the first red flake fell from the sky. In
fact, most cities were already preparing large-scale evacuation plans and casualties would be minimized. Hitting a city
like Jerusalem might set off a regional war, but after the attack on Tel Aviv, not even the Arab world was blaming Israel.
The weapon's initial success came mostly from its effects not
being known. But now, unless you were trapped with no way
out, escape should be possible.

But there is always someplace to go, Miller thought, *unless . . .*

Oh no . . .

"The planet? They're going to wipe out every living thing
on the planet?"

"No . . . ," Adler said.

Huber confirmed it with a low nod.

"But won't they be killing themselves?"

"They will survive underground. In bunkers stocked with
enough raw material, seeds, and animals to begin again."

"How will they begin again without any oxygen?" Miller
asked.

"Only the lowest levels of troposphere are affected. The
oxygen above that layer will remain, as will the oxygen trapped
in the water and the Earth's crust, of which forty-six percent
by weight is composed of oxygen. It will not take long to re-
plenish the troposphere and make the Earth habitable again.
They've been working this out for seventy years. I assure you,
every detail has been well planned." He looked at Miller. "Except for you, of course. The survivor. I don't know how you
escaped Miami, but it is nothing short of a miracle that you
walked out of that red hell so long after it descended."

"You believe in miracles?" Miller asked.

"I believe in the ingenuity of man," Huber said as he walked to the window and looked out at the lake. Miller stood behind him and a little to the side. "Perhaps you can find a way to stop them. To save my family."

As Huber turned toward him, Miller caught sight of the canoe out on the lake. One of the men was missing and the second held what looked to be a short fishing pole. Miller realized what it was a moment too late. "Get do—"

Two shots rang out.

Glass shattered.

Blood sprayed from Huber's chest as his body arched in pain. He hit the floor hard, facedown. Two holes had been punched in his back.

Miller dove down to the old man and turned him over. Blood oozed from his mouth, but a glint of life still remained. Huber took Miller's arm and pulled him close. He shook, gasped, and then whispered, "The bell tolls."

Huber's arm fell to the side and the muscles in his face relaxed. The man, and his secrets, were gone. But that was just the beginning of their problems. There were two killers lurking outside. Miller had no idea where the second man had gone, but the sniper in the canoe had put two rounds in Huber from one hundred yards away while sitting in a wobbly boat. He had no doubt that if they tried to run, bullets would find their backs. Problems like this were best tackled head-on.

Miller crawled to his Glock and slammed the clip back home. There was only one round left, but it was better than nothing. "Stay here," he said to Adler, and then pointed at the shotgun. "Use that if you have to. Just check your target first. Make sure it's not me you're shooting at."

Miller crawled to the back door on the opposite side of the living room.

"Where are you going?" Adler hissed.

"For a swim," he said, then cranked the door handle, gave it a shove, and ran toward the lake.

30.

The man in the canoe took aim as Miller burst from the cabin's back door. He fired a moment later.

And missed.

Anticipating the shot, Miller dove right, rolled to his feet, and continued his charge toward the lake. Two tall pine trees stood between the cabin and the lake and Miller put the first tree between him and the canoe. Behind the tree, there was no fear of being shot, but he'd eventually have to leave its protection to cover the distance to the dock.

When he reached the first tree, he stood sideways against it to make sure his body didn't show, and began stripping. He kicked off his shoes, peeled off his T-shirt, and slid out of his pants. Anyone watching would think he was just an eager skinny-dipper. To live through the next portion of his journey, his timing would have to be perfect and he couldn't allow anything to slow him down, not even his clothes.

After hearing the shooter's weapon three times he felt fairly certain he knew the make and model. He'd seen and heard one just like it just a few days previous—a Karabiner 98k. If he was right, the man in the canoe had two shots left in the clip. If Miller could get him to waste those two it would be a race between Miller's legs and the shooter's re-load speed.

After three quick breaths Miller peeked out from behind

the right side of the tree, made a note of the man's position, and ducked back just as the man fired. Sharp bits of pine bark stung Miller's face and the sound of breaking glass filled the air as the deflected bullet shot through one of the cabin's windows. Miller rolled out from the other side of the tree, took aim, and fired.

The round sailed over grass, then beach sand, and finally water before it struck the canoe just inches from the shooter's leg. The proximity of the shot made the man flinch. The canoe rocked and the man had to brace himself to keep from tipping.

In that moment of lost balance, Miller made a dash for the dock. He ignored the second pine tree and continued forward. The downward slope of the yard allowed him to pick up speed quickly, but the grass ended at a four-foot drop-off to the beach, from which the floating dock extended out over the water.

The shooter found his balance just as Miller reached the wall and jumped. The shot passed just beneath Miller's airborne body and pinged off the rock wall that rose from the beach to the yard.

Five shots, Miller thought just before he landed, rolled back to his feet, and began his sprint across the ten-foot beach and twenty-foot dock. He could cover the distance in two seconds, which he knew would be about the same amount of time a skilled shooter would need to reload.

His footfalls thudded loudly across the dock, scattering the fish hiding beneath it. As he reached the end of the dock, Miller saw the shooter raise his rifle. But there was no place to hide, so Miller did the only thing he could—he dove. And as he sailed through the air, he saw the man look down his sight, tracking Miller's arc through the air. Miller raised the empty Glock at the man, and for just a moment the man flinched. When the assassin pulled the trigger, Miller's body was already disappearing beneath the water.

The cold embrace of the lake water reinvigorated Miller. As a Navy SEAL, the water was his element. No matter how cold, violent, dark, or murky, Miller could not be topped in the water. *Except by a tiger shark,* Miller reminded himself. He pumped toward the canoe, angling himself deeper. He had no fear of being shot while under the water—most rounds would mushroom and break apart just feet from the surface—but he wanted his arrival to be a surprise.

After nearly a minute of swimming without a fresh breath, Miller saw the canoe's hull outlined by the blue sky above. The man's shimmering form could be seen, too. He stood in the boat, scanning the water with his rifle, no doubt hoping the afternoon sun would reveal Miller's approach. Not only was Miller thirty feet down, skimming the bottom of the lake, but he was already behind the canoe.

With the burn in his chest just beginning, Miller planted his feet on the lake's bottom, bent down, and pushed off hard. He shot toward the surface, kicking with his feet. Unhindered by wet clothing, he rose quickly and shot out of the water like a breaching whale.

Before the shooter could react, Miller reached around the man, took hold of the rifle on both sides, and held on as gravity pulled him back to the water. The man shouted something unintelligible, though it sounded German to Miller, and fell back into the water.

Miller held on tight, pinning the rifle against the man's chest. Treading water with the man firmly in his grasp, he shouted, "Who are you?"

The man said nothing. Instead he roared and leaned forward; for a moment, his voice bubbled as his head entered the lake. Then he flung himself back. Miller tried to duck to the side, but his proximity to the man made dodging the blow impossible. The back of the man's skull connected hard with Miller's forehead.

The two men fell away from each other, both dazed by the impact.

He's lucky he didn't knock us both unconscious, Miller thought as he fought to regain his senses and find his target. When he found the man, Miller had only a moment to open his mouth and suck in a lungful of air. Then the man, who was much larger than Miller thought, reached his arms around Miller and squeezed him in a bear hug.

With his arms pinned to his sides, Miller couldn't fight back, and as they slid beneath the water even a head butt would do little good as his movements would be slowed and the force dulled. When fighting underwater, brains always won over brute force. Of course, without a body to control, all the brains in the world wouldn't be much help.

They sank quickly, weighed down by the man's clothing and belt, which held pouches of spare clips, a handgun, and a sheathed knife. With his hands free, Miller could have used the man's weapons against him, but now he could do nothing but push against the man's muscular arms in a fight to keep the air in his lungs.

The man snarled at Miller with gritted teeth. His brown hair was cut short; his hazel eyes burned with hatred.

Miller stopped fighting and just returned the man's stare.

I've got you now, asshole, Miller thought when the man grinned. Miller let his body go limp, feigning death.

The man's grip loosened.

Miller blinked, erasing the man's smile.

The shooter made a halfhearted attempt to crush Miller again, but all he managed to do was further deplete his own oxygen supply.

Miller smiled at the man.

In the fading light, Miller saw the man's face go red with the realization that Miller had been drowning *him*.

The crushing force on Miller's body fell away a moment later. The man kicked frantically for the surface, fighting against the weight that had pulled them both down, using up even more oxygen.

Miller casually reached up and held the man by the ankle. The man kicked violently.

The kicking became shaking.

And then he was dead.

With his lungs craving air, Miller swam up to the man and quickly checked his pockets. Finding nothing, he removed the man's handgun—a semiautomatic 9mm Walther P38—once again a standard weapon for Germans in World War II. Miller then took the man's knife and swam for the surface.

He drew in a loud, deep breath when the midday sun struck him. He leaned back, breathing hard, and thanked God there were no red flakes falling from the sky.

Yet, he thought, and climbed into the canoe.

Inside the canoe he found two fishing poles, neither of which held lures, two paddles, and a small notebook.

He flipped through the notebook. Sketches of Nazi symbols covered the pages, no doubt scrawled while waiting for his targets. He paused on a page that held a full-page sketch of the thunderbolt inside a Celtic cross that symbolized the joining of American neo-Nazism and Heinrich Himmler's World War Two elite Schutzstaffel. The man had written *ZweiteWelt* beneath the drawing.

SecondWorld, Miller thought with a shake of his head. Outside of an all-powerful God, the idea of wiping the world clean of all life seemed impossible. Hell, the idea of a global flood supposedly caused by God had always struck him as crazy. But here he was, facing global genocide that would be caused by mankind. Of course, when the storm of oxidized iron receded and the air became breathable again, the world wouldn't be repopulated by a handful of God's chosen, it would be dominated by a worldwide Aryan race that defined "pure" in an entirely different way than the God of the Old Testament.

Miller turned the page and found a list of ten names. The first three had been crossed out and he didn't recognize them. The fourth name was Huber's. Miller mentally crossed him out and read the next three names, which had also been crossed out. Three names remained at the bottom, all written in a different color ink, mostly likely added recently.

The first name was his.

The second, Adler's.

And the third belonged to a man named Milos "Wayne"

Vesely. Except for the "Wayne," which appeared to be a nickname, the name sounded European. It was the only other name not yet crossed off. And, hopefully, that meant he was still alive.

A shotgun blast rolled over the lake.

Adler!

Miller placed the notebook, handgun, and knife by his feet, picked up the paddle, and stabbed it into the water. He paddled hard for shore, hoping that Adler's first shot had found its target.

A moment later, he knew it hadn't.

The shotgun's second blast echoed across the far shore. New Hampshire was known for its hunters, but the sheer volume of gunfire coming from the area over the past few minutes had no doubt garnered a few 911 calls. While he'd normally welcome police backup, Miller had no way of knowing just who would be responding to the call. Even the police would be suspect, and he fully intended to be gone by the time they arrived.

Hopefully with Adler alive.

The canoe slid up onto the sand. Miller snatched the notebook, knife, and handgun and jumped onto the beach.

That's when Adler screamed and Miller knew he might not be quick enough to save her, just like he'd been too slow to save the brown-eyed girl in Iraq.

The gunshot that followed confirmed it.

31.

Miller's heart hammered painfully in his chest. Not from exertion, but from the fear that Adler had been shot. He had only just met her, but the bond forged by combat—like with soldiers in the trenches—was strong. He'd lost men before, and it rattled the soul every time. But something about the idea of losing Adler seemed worse. Perhaps because she wasn't a soldier. She worked for Interpol, but spent most of her time behind a desk and on the phone. A bullet had no right to take her life.

Ten feet from the door, Miller checked the Walther P38 and flicked off the safety. The door hung at an odd angle and a jagged chunk of its side had been blasted away, like a giant had taken a bite out of it.

One of Adler's shots, Miller realized. Seeing no blood splatter, he knew the shot had missed.

He entered the living room like a missile, but found no target. Huber's body lay on the braided rug, which had absorbed much of the dead man's blood. Adler lay just beyond him. When she lifted her head, he felt relieved, but the feeling vanished when her eyes went wide and she shouted, "Behind you!"

The impact came before she finished shouting her warning. Miller sprawled forward and landed on his back. Through fading vision he saw a tall, lanky man with a crooked smile.

He wore beige Dickies pants and a plaid shirt that made him look like a local. His hair was slicked to the side in a style that looked straight from the 1940s.

Miller blinked, trying to find his bearings. He no longer felt the weight of the gun in his hand. But even if he had it, he doubted he could hit the man. The room spun around him, so much so that he barely registered the tall man who leaned down, raised his weapon, and slammed it into his forehead.

Miller woke to an argument. The voices—one female, one male—sounded furious. But he couldn't make out a word of it. He remembered being struck and wondered if the blow had injured his ears, or rattled him so thoroughly that he couldn't make sense of the words being spoken.

Miller forced his eyes open when he realized the verbal combatants spoke German.

Adler, he thought, and opened his eyes.

The room swirled above him and sparks of lights, like fairies, danced in his vision. A swirl of nausea twisted in his gut. The copperlike smell of blood reached his nose. Blood. His, Huber's, or Adler's, he wasn't sure.

Miller closed his eyes, turned his head toward the side, and opened his eyes again. The spinning worsened. He closed his eyes to keep his stomach under control. In that brief, turbulent look, he saw Adler on the floor, propped up on her hands. The tall man stood above her. He held a World War II–era Sturmgewehr 44 assault rifle—the first of its kind— but didn't have it aimed directly at her.

"Begleiten Sie mich. Ende dieser Dummheit," the man said. *"Eine schöne, reine deutsche Frau wie Sie wäre eine gute Ehefrau in den kommenden ZweitenWeltkrieg zu machen."*

Miller opened his eyes. The spinning seemed less violent, and he saw Adler looking up at the man, her expression torn between fear and deep thought. While the man's focus remained on Adler, Miller slowly slid a hand beneath his side. He could feel the cold knife against his back. He'd been holding it in one hand when he'd been struck and had fallen on top of it. He slowly wrapped his fingers around the handle.

The man reached a hand out to Adler. *"Kommen Sie."*

Was he inviting her to join him? Miller wondered as he slowly slid the knife out from under himself.

When Adler reached her hand up to the man and said, *"Ja.* Okay," Miller's suspicions were confirmed in the worst way possible. The man offered her an invitation and she accepted.

How could she? Miller thought. He tightened his grip on the knife. Despite her poor choice, he couldn't let the man take her.

He took aim.

The room still spun.

Shit, he thought. The odds of the knife striking flesh were good, but with Adler and the man so close, he couldn't be sure which one of them he'd hit.

Adler linked hands with the man. He pulled her up, but her motion didn't stop. She pulled down on the man's hand, pulling him forward slightly. Before he could react, she brought her other hand up and around and smashed the butt of the shotgun into his forehead.

The strike wasn't hard enough to incapacitate the big German, but he let go of Adler's hand and stumbled back. The man quickly realized he'd been duped and brought his weapon to bear. But Adler was one step ahead of him. Holding the shotgun like a baseball bat, she swung out.

The blow fell just short of the man's head, but connected solidly with the side of his nose. Cartilage tore, bone cracked, and blood sprayed. The man shouted in pain, and fired off a slew of German curses. But he didn't lose his composure, or his aim. Instead, he lost his life.

When Adler struck the man, he stumbled back, and stopped just a few feet away from Miller. With a quick jerk, Miller sat up, raised his arm, and plunged the knife into the man's back. With the assault rifle pointed at Adler, he needed the wound to be an instant kill. Anything else would give the man time to pull the trigger and then turn the weapon on Miller. So when he struck, Miller aimed for the man's spine.

The jarring blow and instantaneous collapse of his target confirmed his accuracy. He should have felt relieved—that the attacker was dead, that Adler hadn't actually betrayed him—but all he felt was dizzy. Miller leaned over and held his head.

Adler crouched beside him and placed a hand on his back. "Are you okay?"

Miller opened his eyes. The room spun a little less. "You had me fooled."

"What?"

"I thought you were going with him."

"I wanted to be an actress when I was in college," she confessed.

"Could have made a fortune," Miller said with a grunt. "Actually, you could have been the first woman in the major leagues with that swing."

"I was terrified."

Miller pushed himself to his knees. He kept his eyes closed to minimize the nausea. But he could do nothing about the throbbing pain emanating from his head and rolling down his body in sickening waves. Adler held on to his arm and helped him stand.

He opened his eyes and looked at Adler. "You did good."

She looked back at the two dead bodies. "Doesn't feel that way."

Miller knew what she meant. He'd met many soldiers who felt guilty about what they did. Even if they saved lives, they likely took a few in the process. Adler fought to save the world, but had aided in the taking of a life.

Another life.

They'd left a trail of death in their wake.

And for someone new to the business of war, adjusting to carnage took time. Unfortunately for Adler, time was short and adjustment a luxury. Sirens rang out in the distance, growing louder by the moment.

"We need to go," Miller said. Moving as fast as he could without falling over, he snatched up the small notebook and pistol taken from the man in the canoe. He handed the pistol to Adler, who took it without comment, and turned his attention to the fresh corpse.

"Did he say anything useful?" Miller asked as he searched the body.

"After I missed my first two shots, he taunted me," she said. "Forced me to scream and then fired a shot."

Miller shook his head. He'd been lured into a trap and if the man had shot him instead of knocking him unconscious, the trap would have worked. "Why didn't he kill me?" he wondered.

"I think he wanted to question you," she said. "He knew our names."

"We're on the list," he said.

"List?"

"I found a hit list on the other shooter. Our names were recent additions."

The sirens grew louder still and Miller guessed they'd reached Huber's road. They had maybe two minutes before the place swarmed with police who might or might not be friendly. He took the assault rifle and a second Walther P38 from the dead assassin. "What is it with these guys and old weapons?"

Miller stood and stumbled to the back door.

"What do you mean?" Adler asked as she helped him walk. "Where are we going?"

"To the canoe," Miller said, and they started across the grass. Miller pointed to his clothes. "Grab my clothes. The phone is in my pocket."

Adler let go of Miller's arm and retrieved the clothes. He stumbled, but remained upright and mobile. "All of their weapons are World War Two relics, like they want to be authentic SS soldiers."

"Strange," Adler said as she jumped from the grass to the beach and helped Miller down. "I noticed something, too."

"What?"

"The way he spoke—" she said, then paused to think. "It sounded, I don't know. Language changes over time. Certain inflections and words are more common during different time periods. They can define the way a generation speaks."

Miller knew what she meant. He imagined that he could peg the time period of any movie from the past seventy years just by listening to the dialogue.

He reached the canoe and pushed it into the water. They put the weapons and his clothes in the canoe. Standing in waist-deep water, Miller held the boat steady as Adler stepped in and sat down. After she was in, he flung himself over the side and landed on the bottom of the canoe, too exhausted and dizzy to move. The bobbing of the boat didn't help any, and he fought to stay lucid. "You paddle," he said. "Take us along the shore. Get behind the trees."

Adler picked up the paddle and got them moving. She struggled at first, but quickly found her rhythm, stroking twice on one side and then twice on the other.

Once they were behind the tree line, Adler stopped paddling and looked at Miller. "He sounded old."

"How old?" he asked. The man in the boat looked to be in his midtwenties. The man now dead in Huber's living room couldn't have been much over thirty, right around the same age as Adler. His speech pattern shouldn't have been all that different from hers. But something about it had rattled her.

She looked up at the sky, paddled twice more, and stopped again. The words were hard to say, but she forced them out. She motioned to the collection of World War II weapons on the floor of the boat next to Miller's feet. "As old as those weapons."

32.

After taking the canoe a mile along the shore without seeing any sign of police or men with World War II weapons, Miller sat up. The dizziness and nausea had faded, but his head pulsed with pain.

"Got any painkillers on you?"

Adler pulled the paddle out of the water. "I think so." She rummaged through her purse while the canoe drifted forward, past a string of tall pines lining the shore.

"Found something."

Miller noted how the "someing" sound of her voice no longer grated on him. In fact, after everything he'd been through over the past days, her voice, like Arwen's, kept him thinking straight.

"It's ibuprofen," she said. "You want two?"

"Make it four."

She tsked and said, "You're going to melt your liver."

"Odds are I'll be shot first so it won't matter much, will it?" Miller took the pills and popped them into his mouth. Unlike the macho men in movies who could not only swallow pills dry, but roughly chew them first, Miller couldn't take pills without a drink. He dipped his hands into the lake and drank. The water was gritty but felt cool and refreshing. When he leaned back up, Adler was staring at him, a look of disgust frozen on her face. "Once again, I'm more likely to get shot before I die from dysentery. This isn't Oregon Trail."

"Oregon Trail?"

"A video game. Forget it." Miller turned toward the shore. The trees suddenly gave way to a long public beach. The beach wasn't crowded, but there were more than a few people sitting on the sand and enjoying the water. Good for them, Miller thought. While much of the nation had taken to looting or holing up in their homes, these folks had continued on with their lives, refusing to live in fear. He wondered if they would do the same if they were in the city instead of New Hampshire, or if they knew the world had only five days left.

For a brief moment, Miller realized he was still dressed in just his boxers. But then they passed by an overweight shirtless man standing waist deep in the water. The man held a beer in a bright orange cozy and had enough hair on his body to be mistaken for a yeti. Miller glanced at the other beachgoers and saw more skin than clothes. No one would notice his lack of clothing.

The fat man raised his beer at them as they glided past him. He gave a nod and said, "Live free or die."

Miller grinned and gave the man a casual salute. He liked New Hampshire. He looked back at Adler. "Take us to the far end of the beach. We need to find a new car."

Adler took up the paddle again. "Thank God. My arms are killing me." Sweat dripped down her forehead and she'd undone the top few buttons of her blouse so that a hint of cleavage showed.

Feeling self-conscious again, Miller gathered up his clothes.

Adler noticed his haste. "Don't worry. You're not that bad on the eyes."

Miller smiled as he slid slowly into his pants, trying not to tip them in the process. "Thank you for choosing the Love Boat," he said as he picked up his shoes. "We hope you enjoy your—"

Adler stopped laughing when Miller's grin disappeared.

He stared at the boat shoes in his hands. At some point they'd stopped being Scuba Dave's shoes and become his. But there was blood on them now and he remembered, in fresh detail, where they came from. He pursed his lips and sighed.

"What is it?"

The boat slid onto the sandy beach and they were embraced by the cool shade of the nearby trees. "Back when I was sixteen, I somehow managed to get a girlfriend, and one day after school we found ourselves alone at my house. I don't think I've felt so nervous and excited since that day. It took us thirty minutes to work up the guts, but then we were on the bed. Half naked. I'm rounding the plates like a son of a bitch." He looked up at Adler. She stared at him with a single raised eyebrow and an unsure smile, no doubt wondering how hard he'd been hit. He continued, "I stand, drop my pants, and then, *wham!* The front door closes and my mom announces that she's home." He held the shoes up. "These shoes are like my mother."

"Your mother?"

"A wet blanket."

"A wet blanket?"

"You know. Like when— Forget it. We need to go."

"I think I understand," she said, and took the shoes from him. She gave them a once-over, shrugged, and then tossed them over her shoulder. They hit the water with a splash and floated away.

"What?" she said when Miller just stared at her.

He pointed to the woods. "I don't know how far we have to walk, do you?"

She shrugged. "You're tough."

Miller smiled. He wouldn't admit it, but being free of those shoes was a relief. At first he thought they were a good reminder of what the enemy intended to do to the world. But their repeated attempts to kill him kept their lethality on the forefront of his mind. He said a silent thanks to Dave, wrapped the guns in his shirt, and headed for the woods.

The half-mile walk over a pine-needle-covered path

actually felt good on his bare feet. The dirt parking lot filled with jagged rocks, not so much. But he quickly found a vehicle that would suit their needs.

The black pickup truck had a sticker of Calvin—from the *Calvin and Hobbes* comic strip—peeing, a set of rubber "truck nuts" hanging from the rear hitch, and a bumper sticker that said YANKEES SUCK. While none of these things made the truck desirable, they did ease Miller's conscience about stealing it. And the toolbox in the bed made it possible.

"Hop in," Miller said. He opened the driver's side and placed the shirt-wrapped weapons on the seat. Then he headed for the back and opened the toolbox.

Adler looked around nervously like a true first-time thief. "What if someone shows up?"

"I'm a Navy SEAL, remember? And we have guns." He paused. "Of course, if skinhead Nazis show up, be sure to let me know." A moment later he found what he needed and joined Adler in the truck's cab.

He placed a flathead screwdriver in the ignition and held it tight. "Give me a little room," he said, raising a hammer. Adler leaned back and Miller gave the screwdriver two hard whacks. He gave the screwdriver a twist and the truck roared to life.

He hopped out of the truck and patted the driver's seat. "Slide over. You're driving."

She complied, but asked, "What are you doing?"

"Research," he said. "But first I need to castrate this truck." Walking around the back, Miller kicked the oversized rubber testicles from the back of the truck and then got into the passenger's seat. He closed the door. "Let's go."

"Where are we going?"

"I'll let you know when I figure that out. For now, let's just get out of here before Bubba comes back."

The truck rumbled out of the dirt parking lot and onto a narrow paved road. Miller took out the iPhone and flicked it on, but before he could get it to work, Adler hit the brakes.

"Shit," she said.

Miller looked up and saw two police cars ahead. "Don't slow down!"

Adler flinched. "You don't want me to ram them?"

"No. Just don't act nervous."

"But they're looking for *us*."

"We don't know that."

When they were twenty feet from the squad cars, an officer stepped forward and raised his hand, motioning for them to slow down. The officer, who couldn't be over twenty-five, approached the passenger's side. Miller relaxed when he saw the officer's dark black hair and Hispanic facial features. Racial profiling probably wasn't the best idea—people could be bought—but he doubted there was a good reason for a small-town Hispanic police officer to be on the take. He rolled down the window and leaned out casually. "Something going on?"

"There was a shooting across the lake," the officer said. "You folks didn't see anything . . . weird? Or hear anything?"

"Heard the gunshots, I think," Miller said. "Thought they were fireworks at the time."

The officer gave a slight nod, and then leaned down. "How 'bout you, miss?"

"No. Nothing."

Miller heard the same thing the officer did. "Nothsing." Adler tried to mask her German accent, but failed miserably. At first, Miller wondered why she bothered, but when the officer stiffened and stepped back, he understood. Being white and German in a country on high alert for Nazis made Adler a potential enemy. Everyone was profiling.

"Could you step out of the car," the officer said, hand moving to his hip.

"Don't do that," Miller said. "Please."

Keeping his hand on his sidearm, the officer reached his free hand up to the radio strapped to his chest. Before he could speak, Miller pulled a Walther P38 out from under his shirt and pointed it at the officer, just feet from his face. The man froze.

"Toss the gun," Miller said. "Now."

The man slowly drew his weapon and tossed it into the woods behind him.

"What's your name?" Miller asked.

"Miguel Lewis."

"Officer Lewis," Miller said. "Look—"

Before Miller could speak again, a loud voice shouted, "Everything okay, Lewis, or do you need a real cop to come do your job?"

A large white man leaned out of the second squad car. Jowls hung from his portly face. The officer took off his cap and stepped out of the car. Miller doubted the man could run fifty feet, and the walk to the truck winded him.

Miller pulled his hand with the gun back in the car, and gave Lewis a look that said, "Not a peep." Lewis gave a nervous nod.

The heavyset officer bumbled up to the driver's window. "Now what the hell is taking so long?" He stopped to look Adler over and grinned. Then he looked up and saw Miller's face. The smile fell away and was replaced by recognition. And not the happy kind.

Miller couldn't see the man's hands, but he could tell he was fumbling for his gun. "Don't," Miller said.

"Barnes, don't," Lewis said. "He's—"

Barnes was a surprisingly fast draw once he found his gun. He whipped it up and squeezed off a round. Miller was a little faster, firing three rounds in the same time, and much more accurately—two to the chest, one to the head. Barnes fell away, dead.

Miller spun, expecting to find Lewis taking action, but the man was nowhere in sight. A cough drew Miller's attention down. Lewis lay on the ground, a wound in his chest. Miller flung open the door and knelt by the fallen man, lifting his head. He inspected the wound. There was nothing to do for the man. He was already dying.

Lewis tried to speak, but only managed a gurgle before he died.

Miller laid Lewis down and shook his head. *How many*

of these assholes are there? he thought. Without another word, he stood, got back in the truck, and closed the door.

Adler rubbed her ears, which rang from the gunshots, and looked at the body of the fat, dead cop. "Should we take their guns?"

Miller rolled his head toward her and held up the German pistol. "This seems to work fine."

"But—"

"Just drive," Miller said. "Please."

Adler steered the truck onto the intersecting street and drove away from the two fresh bodies.

As the woodsy air erased the smell of cordite from the truck's cab, Miller leaned his head back. There was a lot to figure out, but they had a new problem to take care of first. His face was becoming a liability. And to a certain extent, Adler's was, too. With every sleeper Nazi in the country taking potshots they might never make it out of New Hampshire, never mind find Milos "Wayne" Vesely, the mysterious last name on the hit list. "Stop at the first drugstore or grocery store you see," he said. "It's time to say good-bye to your pretty blond hair."

33.

Miller sat in the cab of the truck, elbow propped in the open window. He'd just eaten a cheeseburger and was waiting for Adler to complete her makeover in the fast-food restaurant's bathroom. They had found a pharmacy in town where they bought supplies and changes of clothes. Now dressed in cargo shorts, a T-shirt, and a pair of cheap sandals, he looked like any other summertime local. He'd also shaved his facial hair into a goatee, trimmed his hair to a quarter inch, and donned a green John Deere cap. He completed the disguise with a pair of NASCAR sunglasses. Not even his mother would recognize him.

With his stomach full and the pain in his head dulled by drugs, Miller switched on the iPhone and connected to the Internet via Wendy's free wireless connection. He opened Safari and then did a Google search for "Milos Vesely."

The first return was a Wikipedia page about a Czech bobsledder. He opened it, scanned the contents, saw nothing of interest, and decided he'd found the wrong man. Heading back to Google, he scrolled through the rest of the top results. There were a slew of Facebook pages and message board entries, but still nothing that would make any of them a person of interest to Nazi assassins. Nothing he could see, anyway.

He went back and searched again, this time for "Milos 'Wayne' Vesely." The first hit—a book—caught his attention.

"*Nazi Wunderwaffe and Secret Societies*," Miller read. "By Wayne Vesely."

This is more like it.

He clicked the link and was surprised when the complete text of the book opened in Google Books. The black cover held a hand-drawn sketch of a bell surrounded by what looked like electricity, or fire. The poor skill of the artist combined with low resolution made it hard to tell. He jumped to the end of the book and found an About the Author section. A black-and-white photo of Vesely showed him wearing a cowboy hat, aviator sunglasses, and a cocky grin. A paragraph of text below the image read:

> *Wayne Vesely is the author of three previous books,* The Nazi UFO Connection, The Zero-Point Reich, *and* The United States of the Fourth Reich. *When not preparing for what he calls the Fourth Dawn—also the title of his next book—Vesely can be found lecturing throughout Europe. When not traveling, Vesley resides in Český Krumlov, the Czech Republic.*

The guy's a conspiracy theory nutjob, Miller thought. *But if they're after him, he must have got something right.* And that meant he might have answers.

It took Miller just one minute to access the white pages for the Czech Republic, type in "Milos Vesely," enter "Český Krumlov," and get the man's phone number. Being so easy to find, Miller thought for sure the man would be dead already, but when he dialed the number, a man answered on the second ring. *"Ahoj?"*

"Ahh, hello," Miller said. "Is this Milos Vesely?"

There was a silence on the other end for a moment, followed by a tentative, "You are American?"

Miller noticed that the man's accent sounded like Chekov from *Star Trek* and said, "Yes." For a moment he considered posing as a publisher interested in his books, but there wasn't time to play games. Vesely might have answers and his life was certainly in danger. "Am I speaking to Wayne?"

The tone of the man's voice changed again, this time to a hush. "How do you know that name?"

"It's on your books."

"But *Milos* is not."

Miller looked at the book. He was right. The hit list revealed his full name.

"Listen closely, you now have thirty seconds to explain who you are and how you obtained my name," Vesely said. "I'm counting."

It took Miller ten of those seconds to decide on the one and only explanation he felt wouldn't result in the man hanging up. "I found your name on a hit list I took off the body of a Nazi assassin."

Miller waited for some kind of explosive reaction, but heard only silence. Then breathing. Vesely hadn't hung up.

"And who, my American friend, are you?"

"Lincoln Miller. My name is two spots above yours on the list."

"Miller? The Survivor?"

"Why is everyone calling me that?" Miller asked.

"It is the news," Vesely said. "They have deemed you The Survivor. Capital T, capital S. It is a good code name, no? *Survivor.* You may call me *Cowboy* if you like."

"Listen, Milos—"

"Cowboy."

Miller sighed. "These guys are going to come for you."

"I am ready for them."

"Ready for them?"

"I am Cowboy. Gunslinger."

The nickname "Wayne" suddenly made sense. The man fancied himself an honest-to-goodness cowboy. A UFO-hunting, conspiracy-junky cowboy. *Great,* Miller thought, wondering how difficult it would be to separate fact from fiction. Then he wondered aloud, "How did you know they're after you?"

A red Mustang pulled up next to the truck. Its loud engine and pounding bass made Vesely's next words hard to hear.

"I knew when I saw the red sky," Vesely said. "I predicted it."

"Bullshit," Miller said. If someone like Vesely knew about the attack, someone in power would have figured it out, too. The Mustang's engine cut off. The music fell silent. The driver got out of his car and said something, but Miller wasn't paying attention.

"And yet you say they are 'after' me. *Probudit se*. Let me ask *you* a question. Why should I bother speaking to you? Hmm? I have been publishing everything I have uncovered about the Nazi secret programs for years. The Wunderwaffe. The Bell. The experiments. I have written letters. No one listens."

"Hey! Who are you?" an angry voice interrupted. Miller glanced up and saw a burly man with a long beard approaching.

"Why should I believe you will be any different, Survivor?" Vesely asked.

"I know you stole Steve's truck," the bearded man said as he stopped just shy of the driver's side door. His clenched fists and body language said he was ready for a fight. "Heard you even left the nuts behind. Now get the fuck out before I knock—"

Miller's already worn patience snapped. He pulled the door handle and kicked the door open as hard as he could. The hard metal doorframe connected a solid blow with the man's forehead. He sprawled back, rolling over the hood of his Mustang, and collapsed onto the parking lot.

Miller didn't give the man another second of his time and seethed his anger into the phone. "You will listen to me because I just came from the home of Aldric Huber, who helped recruit the science team behind these attacks. Because I've killed more than fifteen of these Nazi assholes already. Because I have a direct line to the president of the United States. And because I'm the goddamn fucking Survivor."

A moment of silence. "You met Huber?"

"Yes."

"And he was forthcoming?"

"Until a sniper put two bullets in him."

"*Hovno.* What did you learn?"

"That United States scientific superiority has Nazis to thank."

Vesely responded with a sniff of a laugh that said, "Duh," and followed it with, "Anything else?"

"Just your name from the sniper's dead body."

"Huber could have told you everything. . . ."

Miller would have strangled the man had he been present. "I *know*."

"But," Vesely said, "now you have the Cowboy."

Miller heard three dull thuds in the background. "What was that?"

"Hold on," Vesely said.

The banging came again. Miller recognized the sound as someone pounding on a door. "Vesely! Damnit!" With no reply, all he could do was listen.

He could hear the tinny voice of the drive-through attendant, the squeaky brakes of a car stopping at the road, and the sound of a baby crying from one of the other parked cars, but not a sound through the phone. A stream of curses ran through Miller's mind. If they lost Vesely, he and Adler would just be two names on a hit list who posed no threat. Five days later, they'd be corpses along with most of the Earth's oxygen-dependant life.

Miller pressed the phone hard against his ear when he heard footsteps and heavy breathing.

"Survivor," Vesely said. "Are you there?"

"I'm here, Cowboy."

"They are here."

"Can you get out?"

"I am gunslinger."

Miller appreciated the man's confidence, but didn't share it. The men he'd faced were well-trained professionals. The only reason he'd survived was because he was better. "We need to meet."

"Agreed. One hour at—"

"I'm in the United States."

"Can you get here?"

Miller considered this and said, "Yes. I can be there tomorrow." The president could make it happen.

The banging on the door grew loud. They were kicking their way in.

"Wunderwaffe," Vesely said quickly. "Page one forty-two!"

The door shattered.

Miller heard shouting.

Gunshots.

Then a dial tone.

Miller stared at the phone. Had Vesley been killed? He hated being one step behind, especially when every step forward resulted in someone dying.

The passenger's door opened and a woman with short black hair and large sunglasses got in. Miller nearly pulled a pistol on the woman, but then she spoke.

"How do I look?" Adler said. "A good disguise?"

Miller took a deep breath and leaned his head back. "I damn near shot you."

Adler looked at the phone in his hand. "Who were you speaking to?"

"I found Vesely. We're going to meet him."

"But that's great," she said. "Why do you look so upset?"

Miller handed the phone to Adler and started the engine. "Because he might be dead when we get there."

34.

"Four hours," Miller said before hanging up the phone with President Bensson. Normally, he'd consider arranging a covert international flight in just four hours good time, but under the circumstances it felt like an eternity. Of course, with commercial flights grounded and the military full of homegrown Nazi spies, there were very few options on the table. The president's solution would be hard to miss, but would nicely conceal the true purpose of the flight—to deliver him to a secret rendezvous with a Czech conspiracy theorist who might have information that could save the world.

Miller leaned back in his green metal chair. He looked at the clear blue sky and saw no hint of red. He allowed a slight grin to form on his face. In addition to providing a flight, Bensson had delivered some good news. Brodeur survived, thanks to a bulletproof vest Miller didn't know the man was wearing. The impacts had knocked him unconscious and bruised his ribs, but he had suffered no serious injuries. That didn't mean he'd be happy about being back on duty. Brodeur was one of the few men Miller currently trusted, and he'd requested that the FBI agent be on the flight when it arrived at the nearby Portsmouth International Airport at Pease—formerly known as the Pease Air Force Base until 1991 when the Strategic Air Command closed up shop. The base was still home to the Air National Guard and a variety of specialized military refueling aircraft, but the majority of the two-hundred-acre base had been converted for civilian use.

"One cheeseburger with Swiss, mushrooms, Thousand Island, and enough calories to kill you before the Nazis get a chance," Adler said as she walked out of the seaside grill carrying two red baskets filled with sandwiches and fries. She put Miller's burger down on the table and joined him. The restaurant stood on the bank of the Piscataqua River in Portsmouth, just ten minutes from Pease. "You realize you had a burger a half hour ago, yes?"

"Who knows when our next meal will come," Miller said. "Calories equal energy."

Adler smiled. "Like a seal storing blubber for the winter?"

"Actually," Miller said, took a bite, and offered a food-muffled, "exactly."

The pair dug into their food and ate quickly. When their sandwiches were gone and they turned to the fries, Adler restarted the conversation.

"Any luck with the president?"

Miller ate a French fry and nodded. "We'll be airborne in four hours."

Adler froze with a fry halfway to her mouth. "What? How?"

"You'll find out when we get there." Before Adler could object, Miller added, "Brodeur, the FBI agent from my apartment. He's alive. He'll be joining us."

She placed the fry down and rested her head in her hands, as though she'd found out she hadn't been convicted of a crime. "Thank God."

Her reaction surprised Miller at first, but then he understood. "You've been blaming yourself for what happened?"

"If I hadn't been there, things would have turned out differently."

"Actually, you're right," he said.

She looked up at him.

"If you hadn't been there, I would have been in the shower when they stormed the apartment. I would be dead."

Adler sat back. "But Brodeur nearly died."

"It's likely he would have been shot either way."

"But—"

Miller grew serious. He leaned forward, elbows on the red-painted picnic table. "Elizabeth. We are at war. We are outgunned, outnumbered, and have zero intel on the enemy. It is very likely more people are going to die. Including me. Including you. You need to be prepared for that. We are the last-ditch effort to stop this thing. If I die, you and Brodeur will take it to the end, even if it kills you both. If you die, I won't stop to mourn your death until these people are stopped or I'm dead, too."

Adler pushed her remaining food away and leaned back. She crossed her arms. "That's cold."

"Going to be a hell of a lot colder when six billion people are asphyxiating in five days." He pushed her food back to her. "Finish it. Might be your last real meal."

"Because I might be dead, you mean?"

Miller gave a nod. "And because as soon as we take off, we're not going to stop moving until this thing is run down."

He gave that a second to sink in. She sat forward and continued eating, although each bite was now forced. But the reality check would help keep her alive.

Miller turned his attention back to the iPhone. It was time to find out what was on page 142. He'd called the president first because he needed to set things in motion. But the pilots wouldn't know where they were flying until Miller told them. And Miller wouldn't know where that was until he reopened the digital copy of *Nazi Wunderwaffe and Secret Societies*.

The opened the e-book and scrolled through pages. As he neared page 142 a chapter heading caught his attention. "The Bell."

"What?" Adler asked.

"The Bell. It's the title of the chapter Vesely sent us to."

"Is it a church bell?"

Miller ignored her. Something about the words sounded familiar. Then he remembered. "This is it!"

"You found something?"

"The Bell. Before Huber died, he said, 'The bell tolls.' I thought he was talking about his death, but he could have been referring to this."

Adler slid her chair around the table and they read it together.

The Bell was one of many code names for a secret project that the Nazis began in 1944. The sole goal of this *Wunderwaffe,* or "wonder weapon," was mass destruction on a grand scale. The program grew in tandem to the nuclear arms development in Germany, but was considered a higher priority. While weapons like atom bombs, fuel air bombs, guided missiles, stealth planes, sound cannons, and a variety of other exotic weapons were classified as *Kriegswichtig,* or "important for the war," the Bell had been deemed *Kriegsentscheidend,* which translates to "decisive for the war."

The project was seen as a game changer. Something so important that only those integral to the project's success were allowed to live to the war's end. The pages mentioned several names Miller now recognized and explained the parts they played in the weapon's development. Debus, Huber, Oberth, Gerlach—they were all there, including—

"Oh my God. My grandmother."

Dr. Elizabeth Adler. University of Königsberg. Mathematician, unknown specialty.

Miller turned the page. Seeing her grandmother's name listed among those Vesely had determined to be working on a project that might now be threatening all of humanity clearly weighed heavily on her, but easing her conscience could wait. He was more interested in what the Bell supposedly did and where they would be meeting Vesely.

An image on the next page showed a drawing of a bell-shaped object that was clearly not a bell, primarily because the bottom was not open. A block of text described the interior of the bell as two metallic cylinders that rotated in opposite directions. The cylinders were covered with mercury and attached to a hollowed-out core that held a purple liquid theorized to be composed of a thorium-beryllium-mercury compound designated Xerum-525.

Miller shook his head. It sounded like the same conspiracy theory bullshit that surrounded almost everything the military developed. He reminded himself that Vesely's name sat just beneath his own on the hit list for a reason, and jumped back into the text.

Liquid nitrogen cooled the interior of the device, which stood at nine feet tall, five feet wide at its middle, and eight feet wide at its base. Vesely theorized that something called zero point energy, developed by Dr. Kurt Debus, provided over one million volts of current and powered the device. A quick peek ahead confirmed that an entire chapter had been dedicated to the subject. But Miller didn't really care how the device was powered. He skimmed ahead until he came to a section that revealed the device's effect on the human body.

He didn't like what he read.

Just looking at the Bell from a distance required wearing special red goggles. A little closer and you'd enter the outer rim of some kind of energy field produced by the powered device. Just a few seconds of exposure would leave subjects with red, irritated skin resembling a sunburn. Closer still, the test subjects died due to radiation exposure. They died slowly and in agony. But the fates of those closest to the Bell seemed cruelest of all. The test subjects' bodies turned to jelly from the inside out. The elements composing muscle, fat, blood, and other tissues separated. Bodies slid apart, as though melted.

The image reminded him of Indiana Jones, tied to a stake, at the end of *Raiders of the Lost Ark,* while the Germans around him melted away. Perhaps Spielberg had heard of the Bell and used the scene as a kind of catharsis.

"That is sick," Adler said.

"Yeah, but it's not very helpful," Miller replied. "There's nothing here about red flakes or iron clouds in space. It's just as outlandish. It doesn't match up with what Huber told us."

"Turn the page," she said. "One forty-two is next."

A black-and-white photo of a concrete structure resembling Stonehenge sat at the top of page 142. Beneath it was a drawing of the same henge, that diagrammed a concrete basin, tunnels for cabling, electrical ports, and several metal rings where chains may have once been attached.

"That's where they tested it?"

"Looks that way," Miller said. "But I don't see a location."

"There it is," she said, pointing to the next page. "Ludwigsdorf, Germany."

Miller studied the images, hoping to glean more information from them. The information in this book, if accurate, was interesting to say the least. But it didn't reveal anything that might help them track down modern-day Nazis. Miller was convinced that Vesely had yet to publish the information that posed a threat to their enemies. If he had, they would have no reason to kill him. But he'd been attacked and that meant he knew something important; something worth traveling halfway around the world to discover. Miller looked at Adler, whose brows were furrowed. "What is it?"

"There is no Ludwigsdorf in Germany," she said. "Not anymore. After World War Two, the village was given to Poland. I think it's named Ludwikowice Kłodzkie now. I've driven through a few times. A beautiful place."

Miller closed the book. "Looks like we're going to Poland."

35.

"*Scheiße,* that is Air Force One," Adler said when she saw the large blue and white Boeing VC-25, which was a highly modified 747, taxi toward them. It turned parallel to them and stopped, revealing the big UNITED STATES OF AMERICA painted on the side.

Miller stood next to her on the tarmac, a grin on his face. The president had come through nicely. "Actually, it's technically *not* Air Force One right now because the president isn't on board. 'Air Force One' is the designation given to *any* military airplane carrying the president, whether it's this giant or the Red Baron's biwing. If he's on a civilian plane, it's 'Executive One.' "

"If the president's not on board then what—"

A strange-looking truck with a staircase on top of it pulled up to the plane. The "air-stair" vehicle stopped and raised its staircase up to the door, which opened a moment later. A tall, blond-haired man wearing a suit coat that screamed "FBI" gave a wave in their direction. Miller waved back.

Adler craned her head toward him. "*This* is our ride?"

"Yes, ma'am." Miller headed for the stairs. It felt strange, boarding a plane without a carry-on, never mind without the weapons he had gathered. He felt naked out on the tarmac. But better gear and weapons were waiting for him on board.

"It works out well, actually. When I told Bensson about the five-day deadline he realized it was time to get out of Dodge and find an underground shelter. But he also knew the enemy might be gunning for him. So they deployed all of the presidential aircraft and ground vehicles, hoping to confuse anyone that might want him dead."

"So should we just paint a big target on the side?"

Miller laughed and motioned to the plane. "These are the safest aircraft in the world. We'll be perfectly safe." Twin rumbles announced the presence of their guards. He pointed at the two F-22 Raptor fighter jets circling the airfield. "And we have two of the deadliest watchdogs in the world escorting us across the Atlantic. There is no faster or safer way to get us to Poland in under twenty-four hours. I promise."

"I can't believe you left me, you son of a bitch!" Brodeur said when he reached the bottom of the air-stairs. He sounded serious, but wore a smile on his face and extended his hand. "I ought to kill you where you stand."

Miller shook his hand. "Quit whining. You're fine." He slapped Brodeur's shoulder and laughed when the man cringed.

"By the way, thanks for getting me back on duty," Brodeur quipped. "I hate resting after being shot. *Twice*."

"You see?" Miller said to Adler. "This is why I joined the NCIS instead of the FBI. They're all a bunch of pussies."

"Ugh," Adler said, then pushed past the pair and started up the stairs. "Please tell me I do not have to sit with you two."

"Other than the two pilots, we have the whole bird to ourselves," Brodeur said. "You can sleep in the president's bed if you fancy."

Miller hopped onto the steps with a chuckle. "C'mon, Fancy Nancy. Let's get a move on."

Five hours later, the 747 cruised over the North Sea, just east of England, at thirty thousand feet. At seven hundred miles per hour, it was one of the fastest passenger jets in the world. They had completed the majority of the nearly four-thousand-mile flight in just five hours—one to go. They would soon land at the Strachowice Airport in Poland and

take a car to Ludwikowice Kłodzkie, where they would
have to track down the strange concrete henge. Total time
since hanging up the phone with Vesely—twelve to fourteen
hours, maybe a little longer if the henge's location wasn't
well known by locals. Not bad for a last-minute, round-the-
world meeting. But Vesely had not given a time. They might
miss the man, or end up waiting ten hours for him, especially if he was on the run. Of course, the wait would be
much longer if he'd been killed.

Miller sat in a brown leather executive chair at the head
of a long oak conference table. He'd changed into a dark
gray T-shirt and black cargo pants that could hold a good
number of supplies and concealed weapons. He would have
preferred a jacket, too, to hide more weapons, but it was
summer and a jacket would make him stand out and sweat
like a bastard. With his shaved head and dark garb he would
look "military" but hoped the bright green John Deere cap
would offset the look.

Brodeur sat kitty-corner to Miller, still dressed in his black
suit and red tie. An array of weapons rested on the table.
Miller looked the weapons over with satisfaction.

Two MP5 submachine guns and six spare clips.

Three Sig Sauer P226 handguns. Two spare clips for each.

A single SEAL team knife, delivered at Miller's request,
rounded out the armament. The SEAL knife underwent the
most rigorous evaluation program for a blade in military
history and beat out even the fabled KA-BAR blade favored
by certain Delta operators he knew. Its seven-inch blade
could chop, slice, penetrate, and saw almost anything it encountered.

Miller would have preferred a couple of M4s added to the
mix, but they'd be impossible to conceal. And since there
were only three of them, there were plenty of weapons to go
around. He took the two MP5s and slid them to Brodeur.
"Keep them under your jacket."

Brodeur grinned. "Yehaw."

"I'll keep two of the Sigs for myself," Miller said, pulling
the weapons and four clips.

Brodeur motioned to the open double doors with his head. "Can she handle the third?"

"Yes," Adler said, appearing in the doorway. "*She* can." She took the gun, two clips, and sat down across from Brodeur. She wore black pants and a dark short-sleeve blouse that matched her now-black hair and made her blue eyes stand out like LED beacons. But for all the color in her eyes, they looked heavy.

"Couldn't sleep?" Miller asked.

"You could?"

Miller had slept for four solid hours, but didn't bother mentioning it.

"There's some instant coffee in the kitchen," Brodeur said.

"That would be great," Adler said. "Thank you."

Brodeur sat in the chair for a moment while Adler stared at him. "You want me to make it?"

"Sounded like you were offering," she said without a hint of humor.

Brodeur pushed up from the chair. "Fine. Fine. But be warned, I make my Joe with some kick."

"Make it two," Miller said as Brodeur left.

They sat in silence as Brodeur's footsteps faded.

"How did you do it?" Adler asked.

"Do what?"

"Survive."

Miller frowned. The topic of his survival grated on him, but he knew the question would be asked from now until the day he died. Even after they wrote books, and made movies, people would still want to hear the story from his lips. The air. How it tasted. The whale. The shark. The bodies. The close calls and the battles with Nazis. He'd prefer to forget it all.

But then Adler clarified the question. "I don't mean physically. Breathing and all that. Most people would have given up. I have no idea what you saw. I don't really want to know. The little I do know is enough to convince me I wouldn't have pushed on. I wouldn't have survived."

"You're here, aren't you?" he said. "You're a survivor, too."

"Not without you." She placed her hand on his forearm.

"I need to know. In case it happens again. In case I need to survive."

He looked at the table, reliving the emotions of survival. "At first, my reactions were guided by instincts and training. SEALs are conditioned to survive the harshest conditions on Earth. It's what we do. I saw a news report saved on Scuba Dave's laptop—"

"Scuba Dave?"

"The guy I took the shoes from. I saw a report about a group claiming responsibility for the attack. I guess revenge became my motivation. I wanted to survive long enough to take a shot at whoever was responsible. Had I met the SecondWorld assholes before Arwen I might have stayed in Miami until each and every one of them lay dead."

"But you met Arwen first."

He nodded. "She probably saved my life, too, though. As much as I'd like to think I'm invincible, it's likely I would have been killed in Miami. Lack of air or neo-Nazis; one of them would have done me in eventually. Saving her became my motivation."

"And it still is, isn't it?"

"Yeah, Oprah, it is. Her and everyone else. But vengeance is still a close second."

They smiled together, but Miller's smile disappeared a moment later. He cocked his head to the side, listening.

Brodeur returned with a tray holding three steaming coffee cups and a box of biscotti. "Java is serv—"

Miller shot an open palm in Brodeur's direction and shushed him loudly.

The room fell silent.

The noise that had been at the edge of his hearing grew louder—the rumble of a second, very large, plane.

"What the hell is that?" Brodeur asked.

Miller jumped from his seat and headed for the cockpit. Adler and Brodeur followed.

As he pounded toward the cockpit, Miller glanced out the hallway windows. The deep blue sky of a new day greeted him. The sun was rising. Four days left. He quickened his pace and after reaching the cockpit door, gave it a firm knock. "It's Miller."

The cockpit door opened a moment later. Colonel Keith Wallman, who they'd met upon boarding, smiled at them. He had a friendly manner and a kind smile.

"I hear a second aircraft," Miller said.

"What?" Wallman replied. "Oh! That's the KC-10."

The McDonnell Douglas KC-10 Extender was an air-to-air refueling plane that serviced all branches of the U.S. Air Force. It explained the noise, but not why it was here. "We're on a 747," Miller said. "We could probably make the round-trip from New Hampshire to Poland without refueling."

Wallman offered a nod. "And then some. This is the president's plane, after all. The KC isn't here for us." He stepped to the side, revealing the rest of the expansive cockpit, which held more gauges, buttons, and lights than seemed reasonable.

The copilot, Lieutenant Colonel Matherson, gave a wave and turned back to his job.

"Take a peek," Wallman said.

Miller stepped forward and looked out the cockpit window. The ass end of the massive KC-10 hovered above and to the right of them. One of the two F-22 Raptors was attached to the long boom that sent fuel from the larger plane to the fighter jet. It made sense now. The Raptor's range was far shorter than the 747's.

A moment later, the Raptor disengaged from the KC-10 and fell back. A second Raptor skillfully dropped into view and approached the boom. The boom found its target and linked the two planes in midflight.

That's when the Raptor exploded and all hell broke loose.

The last thing Miller heard before being flung to the floor was Matherson's voice shouting, "Missile lock! Missile lock! Missile lock!"

36.

"Deploying chaff!" Wallman shouted as he lunged into his chair and toggled a switch. A distant *choom, choom, choom* sounded out from behind the plane.

Miller gripped the cockpit door and hoisted himself to his feet. Matherson had banked hard as soon as the missile-lock warning sounded. The sudden movement had thrown him to the floor, but he was uninjured.

For now.

He glanced back at Brodeur and Adler. "Get to a chair and strap in! Now!" He thought for a moment that both of them would object. But they turned and ran for the chairs lining the hallway just beyond the cockpit doors. Miller sat in the cockpit's third chair, just behind the copilot.

Choom, choom, choom.

More chaff.

Chaff was a missile countermeasure that confused missile radar systems by dispersing a cloud of aluminium, plastic, or metallized glass. The sudden appearance of a secondary target, sometimes several, can wreak havoc with the guidance systems of radar-guided missiles. But the system was far from perfect. Modern missiles were often smart enough to stay on target.

The radio came alive with shouted reports from the KC-

10. "Eagle One! Eagle One! Be advised, attacker is Eagle Three! Repeat, attacker is Eagle Three!"

A momentary silence filled the cockpit.

Eagle Three was the second F-22 Raptor that had been escorting them across the Atlantic. Its pilot had waited for Eagle Two to connect to the fuel boom, effectively making the plane defenseless, and then destroyed it. Now it had turned its deadly sights on the 747.

Miller did a quick calculation in his head. Time to live—five minutes. Tops. Make your peace with God and kiss your ass good-bye. The F-22 Raptor was a stealth fighter jet, which meant they had no way to track it. It could fly circles around them at Mach 1.82 (1,674 miles per hour) and while the 747 could fly far higher, the six AIM-120 AMRAAM missiles it carried weren't called "beyond visual range" missiles for no reason. The fire-and-forget, active-guidance missiles could track them down at any altitude.

The only positive of the situation was that they were aboard the world's toughest and most heavily defended aircraft. Of course, the escort comprised a large part of that defensive capability, but if any aircraft stood a chance against the Raptor, the president's transport was it.

The last hope they had was that the mayday Wallman called out while Matherson communicated with the KC-10 would be responded to quickly. There were air bases all over Europe and he had no doubt that jets could reach them in minutes. But minutes was all they had.

The silence in the cockpit ended with Matherson stating, "Missile lock, off."

The chaff had done its job for the moment.

"Hawk Ten, Hawk Ten," Wallman said into the radio transmitter, speaking to the KC-10 refueling plane. "Can you confirm hostile as Eagle Three? Are you sure?"

"Hell yes!" the man on the other end shouted. "The boom operator saw it with his own eyes."

"Eagle Three," Wallman said into the transmitter. "Stand down!"

No reply.

"Listen, you son of a bitch," Wallman said, seething with anger. "If you—"

And shrill alarm sounded.

"Missile lock!" Matherson shouted.

Wallman toggled the chaff switch again. "Deploying chaff."

Choom, choom, choom.

"Missile away!"

An explosion shook the plane from behind, but the plane was intact.

"Doesn't this thing have any offensive weapons?"

Wallman shook his head. "Even if it did, the Raptor's invisible."

Miller hated being helpless. He wanted to fight. To shoot back. But there was nothing he could do but watch, and hang on tight.

Matherson banked hard to the right. The plane rumbled. A warning blared along with a flashing light.

"An engine is on fire!" Adler shouted from the hallway.

"Shutting down engine four," Wallman said. The alarm fell silent.

Choom, choom, choom.

The sky behind them filled with chaff.

An alarm blared.

Before Matherson could shout out a warning, a second explosion shook the plane.

And still, they flew.

Three missiles left, Miller thought. *Just three more.*

"Take us up," Wallman said. He sounded calm now. In control.

The three remaining engines whined as the plane angled up and gained altitude. But Miller knew that all the altitude in the world couldn't save them from the AMRAAM missiles. "Why up?"

"Because when—if we fall, we'll have more time to jump."

"Jump?"

"Parachutes, but odds are we won't need them." Wallman looked back at Miller. "We're either flying away from this or going up in a big ball of flame. If one of those missiles connects with a fuel tank there won't be much of a plane left to jump from."

Choom, choom, choom.

The plane continued to climb. Miller watched as the altimeter reached thirty-five thousand feet, which was the Raptor's ceiling.

"What the hell is he waiting for?" Miller asked.

Choom, choom—

"That," Wallman said. "We're out of chaff."

Miller's respect for Wallman grew as the man reacted to the development as though they'd just flown through turbulence. He realized the pilot had another trick up his sleeve just before he spoke.

"Deploying ALE-50."

Muffled clucks rang out. The ALE-50 countermeasure was a towed metal decoy that provided a large radar cross section and lured missiles toward it. The plane shook as the cables connecting the 747 to the ALE-50 snapped taut. The jolt felt stronger than Miller expected. "How many of them did you deploy?"

"Four."

Four countermeasures against three missiles. Could be worse.

"Missile lo— Incoming!" Matherson shouted. "Two from behind."

Was the enemy pilot hoping to sneak one of the two missiles past the countermeasure, or was he hoping the shock wave from the dual explosions would shake them apart? Miller didn't think the latter was possible. The 747 was armored like a flying Abrams tank. It could take a beating. Of course, the engines were another matter. They were vulnerable to shrapnel. Hell, a gaggle of geese in the wrong place might be enough to foul the engines.

Twin explosions rocked the plane from behind. They pitched forward.

"Engine two is hit," Matherson said as he shut the engine down. "Losing speed. Altitude."

"Hold us," Wallman said.

Matherson fought to retain their altitude.

Wallman scanned a line of warning lights. "We lost three of four ALEs."

"Shit," Matherson whispered.

"Just keep us steady," Wallman said. "Wait for it."

Miller realized that this was a pivotal moment in the battle. The Raptor held just one more missile. If it could be avoided without losing another engine, they might limp their way all the way to Warsaw. If not . . .

"Missile launch!"

"Take us down!" Wallman shouted. "Go, go, go!"

The plane's nose dipped toward the earth as Matherson pushed the control column forward. The whiny pitch of the engines increased as, thanks to gravity, they gained speed. Behind them, the ALE-50 followed the plane's arc, descending behind and above the plane.

A jolt shook the plane as the last of the six missiles struck the countermeasure. But there was no secondary impact. The missile had been traveling horizontally, and most of the shrapnel continued harmlessly in that direction.

Miller felt a rush of relief. "Now I know why you guys fly for the pres—"

A roar filled the cabin as the F-22 rocketed past beneath them.

Matherson leveled out the 747 at thirty thousand feet. They watched in silence as the fighter jet became a speck in the distance.

"Eagle One. Eagle One," said the KC-10 pilot. "You guys okay?"

Miller looked out the window and saw the big KC-10 about a half mile ahead and just above them.

"We're down two engines," Wallman replied. "But we're still— Holy shit!" He grabbed the controls and rolled the plane to the right.

Miller saw a flash of tracer fire zing past, followed by the roaring Raptor. The thing still had a M61A2 Vulcan 20mm rotary cannon hidden within its stealth body. The cannon was drastically harder to aim than a guided missile, but the 747 was a big target, and they couldn't afford to lose another engine.

"I'm starting to think a missile or two might not be a bad idea," Wallman said, his lips twisted in a deep frown.

The 747 couldn't be maneuvered like a fighter jet. Avoiding a constant stream of fire from the Raptor would be impossible. Miller pictured the jet looping around for another run, this time from behind. Unseen. They didn't stand a chance.

Or did they?

Miller unbuckled and stood between the two pilots, gripping their headrests to stay balanced. "Keep us steady," he said.

Matherson started to protest, but Miller spoke over him. "Is there a way to contact the KC-10 without the Raptor hearing us?"

"KC-10," Wallman said. "Initiate communication protocol Whisper Seven." He changed the channel and waited. "It's a predetermined emergency channel for all aircraft that come in contact with Air Force One. He'll have to look up the right frequency."

"Won't the Raptor know it, too?"

"Escorts have a separate emergency channel," Wallman said. "And it's a single-pilot plane. He wouldn't be able to look it up even if he had the option."

The radio crackled. "We're here," the KC-10 pilot said.

Miller took the transmitter and spoke to the pilot of the KC-10. "KC-10, are you able to purge the fuel you're carrying?"

"Yeah, but—"

"Position yourself just in front of and below us. When I tell you to, purge *all* the fuel."

"What!" The KC-10 pilot sounded like he'd just been told he had a second head growing out of his ass. "Who is this?"

"Just do it! We don't have much time."

Miller could see Wallman nodding slightly as he understood the plan. The man lifted the protective plastic cover from a button labeled FLARES.

Wallman took the transmitter. "This is Colonel Keith Wallman. Do what he said."

The KC-10 dropped down and flew in front of them for a moment. The 747 shook in the wake of the giant fuel plane. Then the KC-10 was below them.

"Get us closer," Miller said.

Matherson throttled forward until they were just fifty feet back from and above the other plane. If they flew through a batch of rough turbulence, which could drop a plane one hundred feet in just seconds, a collision might be hard to avoid.

Miller's gut told him the Raptor would be behind them now. Approaching fast. "Keep us steady . . . steady . . ." He took the transmitter. "Start dumping the fuel."

A billowing cloud of fuel shot from the back of the KC-10. Thousands of gallons of highly combustible fuel.

A loud metallic ticking came from the back of the 747. They were taking fire.

The Raptor was right behind them.

"Now!" Miller shouted at Wallman, and then in the transmitter, "Stop the purge!"

Wallman pressed the flare button, unleashing twin cascades of super-hot flares designed to defend against heat-seeking missiles. Instead, they became a fuse.

The air behind the two planes exploded like napalm, enveloping the F-22 and its pilot.

Matherson veered the 747 away from the KC-10 as the shock wave hit both planes and shook them violently. A second explosion marked the destruction of the Raptor.

The 747 leveled out. The KC-10 flew ahead and to the right. Both planes had survived the explosion. All three men relaxed. Miller gave both pilots pats on their shoulders. "How's that for a countermeasure?"

"We'll call it the BAE," Matherson said. Sweat covered his forehead, but he was all smiles.

Miller figured out the acronym—big ass explosion—and laughed. "Good flying, gentlemen," he said before leaving the cockpit to check on Adler and Brodeur. He felt the same elation as the two pilots—they'd survived an impossible situation—but he doubted the two men would be smiling if they knew he was the one and only countermeasure standing in the way of the Fourth Reich.

His smile faded as soon as he left the cockpit.

37.

The ground crew at Strachowice Airport had been nervous about receiving Air Force One. The small regional airport featured just one terminal and had little in terms of security. They were ill-prepared to handle the sudden arrival of the U.S. president, and voiced their concerns several times over the radio when Wallman requested permission to land. When he explained that they'd been attacked and had two engines out, leaving out the fact that the president wasn't actually on board, permission came quickly. The runway was short for a 747, but Wallman and Matherson handled it with ease. Even with two engines out, they managed to land the plane more smoothly than the three passengers had experienced on a plane.

The forty-minute drive from the airport to Ludwikowice Kłodzkie felt like a roller-coaster ride in comparison. Miller, Brodeur, and Adler had squeezed into a small red Opel Corsa—a two-door hatchback with a whopping ninety horses under the hood. But the small size was only half the problem. Adler, feeling at home on the curvy European country roads, pushed the vehicle to ninety miles per hour every chance she got.

"Just happy to be alive," she said.

"Well, let's try to stay alive for a bit longer," Miller replied, but she had got them to the small village quickly. The

terra-cotta-colored roofs and stark white walls of Ludwikowice Kłodzkie's homes and buildings, glowing in the late-
morning sun, came into view after only thirty-five minutes.

Adler slowed as they entered the town on Route 381. The
majority of the village was situated around the road, which
cut through the center of a valley. Green slopes and patches
of forest completed the image of a picturesque European
village that most would see as a perfect getaway, but Miller
knew it hid dark secrets of the not-too-distant past. Still, the
cool breeze and pleasing scent of fresh-cut hay did a lot to
ease his nerves.

They pulled into a small roadside shop. Adler put the car
in park, took a deep breath, and let it out with a smile. "I
love this area," she said.

Miller and Brodeur looked far less thrilled.

"Just get me out of this rodeo car and let me stretch,"
Brodeur said.

Miller opened his door and tilted the front seat forward
so Brodeur could get out.

Adler rounded the car and headed for the shop. "I'll see if
I can get directions to the henge."

Brodeur climbed out of the car, removed his suit jacket,
and stretched with a grunt, first touching his toes and then
leaning side to side. An old woman with wrinkled jowls and
cold blue eyes rode past on a bicycle. A basket on the front
held several jars of pickles. Brodeur gave a wave and said,
"Howdy," but the woman just kept on riding.

"Well, she's a grumpy old gal," Brodeur said.

"You look like a Mormon warming up for a round of
door-to-door evangelizing," Miller said. "She was probably
worried about you taking her bike."

Before Brodeur could come up with a comeback, Adler
exited the shop. "We just missed it."

Miller stood by the tilted seat and swept his hands toward
the backseat, motioning for Brodeur to enter. "Your chariot
awaits."

"I'm starting to hate you," Brodeur said, but quickly entered.

Adler spun the tires as she turned the car around and went back the way they came. After just three hundred feet, she made a hard left turn and sped up a small, roughly paved road. The street, lined with a mix of oak and pine trees, reminded Miller of their brief visit to the New Hampshire lake house. His discussion with Huber already felt like a lifetime ago.

They passed beneath a tall railroad bridge and watched as another mile of unremarkable terrain went by, along with a few nondescript but large buildings. Then, the road on the right cleared and the ruins of a massive building came into view. The building was long and tall, and clearly not that old, but looked as worn as the Roman Colosseum. The only sign of recent use was phallic graffiti covering several of the walls. The images were impossible to miss, but no one remarked on them. They were close and eager to find the henge, and hopefully Milos Vesely along with it.

Miller racked the slide of each handgun, chambering rounds in both. Adler holstered hers at the hip. Brodeur threw his jacket on, despite the heat, to hide the two MP5s strapped beneath his arms.

Gravel crunched beneath Miller's feet as he exited the car. The air here felt warmer, and smelled of dust.

"Around the back," Adler said.

The threesome walked slowly and quietly around the building. Bees buzzed in the overgrowth rising up through the cracks of what was once a large area of concrete. When they reached the back of the building and saw more of the same, Miller said, "This doesn't look anything like the picture in the book."

"Through the trees," Adler said, pointing to a stand of leafy trees that swayed in the breeze. The swishing leaves transported Miller back to Key Largo again, where the dry palms scratched against each other. He looked up at the sky, confirmed it was still blue, and struck out for the trees.

The temperature dropped in the shadow of the woods, and Miller drew his weapon.

"Hear something?" Brodeur asked, his hand inside his jacket, ready to draw an MP5.

Miller shook his head. "Just tired of being caught with my pants down."

Brodeur pulled out one of the MP5s and gave a nod.

The trees began to thin and Miller saw the unnatural straight lines of human construction in a clearing ahead. He motioned for Adler and Brodeur to wait and moved ahead alone.

The concrete henge stood half in the forest and half in the clearing. Trees had grown up around it in the past years and a few small saplings rose from its center. Eleven interconnected concrete columns formed the modern monolith. Within the ring, the ground dipped down, revealing where a basin had once been before the forest reclaimed the site. The place felt otherworldly, as though torn from the pages of a fantasy novel. Miller entered the clearing of tall grass, scanning back and forth, looking over his gunsight. Other than the henge, he saw nothing important.

No hostiles.

No Vesely.

"Survivor?"

The voice startled him and spun him around. It sounded like Vesely, but he wouldn't let his guard down until he erased all doubt. He saw no one and realized that he must have walked right past Vesely. *Where the hell is he?*

"Is that you, Survivor?"

The repeated use of Vesely's code name for Miller made him realize it was an identity test. Only he and Vesely knew of the names the man had given them both. "It's me, Cowboy," he said, and lowered his weapon.

The ground in front of him came to life. Leaf litter fell away from the lanky man's body. He wore blue jeans, a plaid flannel shirt with rolled-up sleeves, a pair of leather boots, and a cowboy hat. Vesely slapped the dirt and leaves off of his hat and placed it back on his head. He flashed Miller a smile, strode right up to him, and shook his hand.

"I am happy to see you," Vesely said.

"I'm happy you're alive," Miller replied. "Things didn't sound too good before we were disconnected."

"Meh," Vesely said, giving a dismissive wave. "They sent only two men." He looked down at his belt where two .38 Supers were strapped to his hips. The .38 Super held six rounds, each easily powerful enough to make a one-shot kill, even if the head or chest weren't struck—people missing limbs tended to bleed out fairly fast. "I had enough for twelve."

Miller smiled. The man's thick accent, eccentric dress, and cocky attitude amused him. But he knew Vesely had been attacked, and had somehow survived, so despite his comical appearance, he might actually know how to use the handguns.

"Just so you know, I'm not here alone," Miller warned.

"This is good. A battle of this size should not be fought by just two men. How many do you have?"

Miller called out, "Come on out," into the woods. He knew Vesely would be disappointed when he saw the army of two come out of the woods, but hey, now there were four of them. Arwen would be proud. His very own fellowship. Now they just needed a few elves and hobbits and they'd be all set.

Adler came out of the woods first, putting her handgun away.

"Gut, Sie kennenzulernen," she said. *Good to meet you.*

Vesely's head cocked to the side. "You are German?"

"Ja. I'm an Interpol liaison to the U.S."

He squinted at her. "Have we met?"

Adler fought a smile. "I think I would remember if we had."

"It's your eyes," Vesely said, then shrugged. "I must be mistaken. What is your name?"

Adler held out her hand. "Elizabeth Adler, nice to finally meet—"

Faster than Miller had ever seen, Vesely drew his .38 and leveled it at Adler's forehead. Not only did the man know how to use his weapons, Miller had no doubt his quick draw could match Billy the Kid.

"You colored your hair," Vesely said, "but you cannot hide your grandmother's eyes."

38.

"Do you know who this woman is?" Vesely said to Miller, his voice filled with suspicion.

"Her grandmother worked for the Nazis, yes," Miller said, and then pointed to the .38. "Mind putting that down?"

Vesely kept the gun raised. "They couldn't have done it without her. She brought the red sky on all of us."

"I am not my grandmother," Adler said, her hands raised.

"And we wouldn't be here without her," Miller said. "She kept a journal detailing her calculations and everyone involved. It's how we found Huber."

Vesely looked Miller in the eyes. "You have this journal?"

"It is in the car," Adler said, thankful that she'd managed to hang on to her bag through all of their journeys and chases.

"You trust her?" he asked Miller.

"With my life."

Before Vesely could lower his weapon, a gun pressed between his shoulder blades. "Put it down, cowboy."

The Southern drawl of Brodeur's voice put a smile on Vesely's face. "You are from Texas, no?"

"You got it."

"Where in Texas?"

"Amarillo," Brodeur said. "Born and raised in the panhandle."

"Then you are for-real cowboy?" Vesely asked, excitement creeping into his voice.

"I'm for-real FBI, and if you don't lower your weapon, I'm going to put a for-real hole in your for-real back. You following me?"

Vesely holstered the weapon and turned around to look at Brodeur. He looked him up and down, scrunching his face like he'd just smelled something foul. "FBI, yes. Cowboy, no. From Texas and not even boots." He shook his head.

"I drive a car, too," Brodeur said. "Hard to catch bad guys on horseback these days."

Vesely let out a hearty laugh and all four relaxed. "I will call you Tex." He looked at Adler, suspicion creeping back into his eyes. "And you . . . you will be Chameleon because I suspect you have yet to reveal your true colors."

Adler shook her head with a roll of her eyes. "*Genug!* We just flew halfway around the world to meet with you."

"Of course," Vesely said. "What would you like to know first?"

"We know what was in your book," Miller said.

"You have my book?" Vesely looked pleased.

"It's on Google."

After muttering a string of Czech curses, Vesely said, "Then you know its general construction, who was involved—" He gave Adler a sideways glance. "—and the effects it had on anyone unfortunate enough to stand too close to it." He looked at the concrete henge. "Were we standing this close during a test, we would be dead in seconds, the fluids and materials that make up our bodies separated. Is like melting."

Miller remembered the description from Vesely's book. "The problem is, people aren't being melted. They're being suffocated in the open air. So far, nothing we know about the Bell explains how iron clouds from the solar system's heliopause are being oxidized in our atmosphere."

Vesely's eyes widened. "Heliopause? What is this you speak of?"

"Huber told us about it," Adler said. "It's a place beyond our solar system. Something about the solar wind, and the galaxy's ions. It's where a vast cloud of refined iron particles was trapped until low sunspot activity and a specific alignment of the planets allowed the particles to enter the solar system."

"Ahh," Vesely said. "That is where the iron is coming from. I wondered how they could reproduce the tests done here on such a grand scale."

"Miami, Tokyo, and Tel Aviv were tests," Miller said. "The grand finale involves the whole planet."

Vesely nodded and wandered away. He bent down, plucked a long, dry strand of grass, and put it in his mouth. "I should have known."

"How could you?" Brodeur asked.

"Is my job to know. Or at least to surmise. But I did not think even they would commit global genocide. The first targets made sense. Miami is major U.S. city known for its . . . alternative lifestyles and has large Cuban population. Tokyo was targeted, I suspect, because the Nazis held a grudge against the Japanese. Had they not attacked Pearl Harbor, the Americans might not have entered the war and things would have most likely ended very differently. And Tel Aviv, well, that's obvious. I thought more attacks would come. That they would follow pattern. Domination, not eradication." Vesely removed the grass from his mouth. "But if they are dependent on the solar system to deliver iron particles, perhaps we can predict when they will strike next?"

"Huber already did," Miller said. "We have four days."

The news seemed to weaken Vesely. First he lowered his head, then knelt down on one knee. "We must move quickly," he said. "There is much distance to cover. But first I must show you."

Vesely tore away clumps of the tall grass, revealing a

patch of topsoil. "The connection between the Bell and the attacks is here, in the earth." He dug into the dirt, scooping out handfuls of dark brown soil. After digging down eight inches, he sat back and let them see his handiwork.

Miller noticed the oddity first. The top layer of soil was dark, composed of fresh decomposition. Beneath that was a band of drier, lighter brown soil, and beneath that a sandy layer full of small stones and chips of concrete. But it was the thin layer separating the soil from the sand that captured his full attention. He immediately recognized the horrible red hue. "Rust," he said.

"For nearly half mile in every direction, radiating out from this site. I discovered it years ago, but never knew what it meant until I saw the pictures of Miami on TV. Red rust falling from the sky. It has only happened one other time that I know of, here at the henge—the test site of the Bell."

"Son of a bitch," Brodeur said, running a hand through his hair. "But how can something created during World War Two be doing this now?"

Vesely looked up from where he squatted next to the hole. "Because they have been working on it, perfecting it, for seventy years."

"We would know about it," Brodeur said.

"There are strong ties to Nazi Germany in all areas of United States government. Operation Paperclip infused thousands—*thousands*—of Nazi scientists into system. Financial sector was controlled by families who had supported the Nazis—the Harrimans, Rockefellers, and the Bushes—all of them financed Nazi war machine. The Bush family remained on the corporate boards of many Nazi front companies even after they were exposed. When war ended, America reached out over the game board like greedy child and pulled as many pieces into itself as possible. The result was Nazi infection that festered in the political, military, and social aspects of your country. If they wanted to stay hidden, they could."

"He's right," Miller said. "We've been attacked by our own people several times. Even the president doesn't know who to trust. The entire system is corrupt. Hell, the vice president is in on it."

"*What!*" Brodeur said. He looked like he'd been slapped in the face. "You left out that detail." He rubbed his head. "*Man alive.*"

"So how does the Bell work?" Adler asked.

"Surely you know. You have seen calculations, no?"

"That doesn't mean I understand them," Adler said, her voice full of vitriol. "I only know what little Huber told us, and what my grandmother's notes explained, and she said nothing about how a device strapped to a concrete henge could pull iron out of space, oxidize it, and destroy the world's oxygen."

Vesely twisted the grass between his lips and leaned against one of the concrete columns. "When Miami is explored again, we will not find Bells attached to sites such as this."

"Then where are they?" Miller asked. "We need to find them. Destroy them."

"They are out of reach," Vesely said. He motioned to the ring of columns. "Tell me, what do you think this construction is for?"

Brodeur ventured a guess. "It held the Bell above the ground."

Vesely took off his cowboy hat and looked at the structure. "Close. Device was tethered, but not to hold it aloft. It was to keep it from *leaving* the ground. To keep it from going—" Vesely pointed to the blue sky. "—up there."

"They can fly?" Adler asked.

Vesely nodded. "I suspect there are hundreds of them in Earth's orbit by now. Perhaps thousands."

Miller wasn't buying it. "We would have seen them."

"Even if those in charge of the observation centers that had capability to locate and track secret satellites were *not* part of the plot, it is well documented that Nazis spent significant resources developing stealth technology. Where do you think Americans got it from? Hiding a satellite from radar and the naked eye would be a simple thing."

"But we would see them being launched into space," Adler said.

"Once again, I must remind you of the scope of what we face. The roots of many American corporations can be traced back to Nazi Germany. Siemens, Bayer, Volkswagen, IBM, Ford, GM—never mind families of super-rich I mentioned earlier. If they wanted satellite in orbit, it could be done without raising eyebrows. But, when satellite is capable of flight on its own, and cannot be seen, one does not need rocket to get it in Earth's orbit. Once there I suspect magnetism attracts the iron to the devices. The Bell produced powerful fields and may be used to shelter the particles as they are forced into upper layers of our atmosphere at superhigh speeds. It's when they strike lower troposphere that the fast-moving particles are exposed to friction, rapidly heat, and oxidize."

"This is hogwash," Brodeur said with a shake of his head. He looked at Miller. "Flying bells? The thing doesn't have wings, never mind an engine."

"Antigravity," Vesely said.

"Antigravity. That's great," Brodeur said. "Next thing, Engineer Chekov here is going to tell us they have bilithium crystals."

"Scotty was the engineer of the *Enterprise*," Vesely said with a grin. "But I can see how my accent has you confused. And for record it is dilithium or trilithium crystals. There is no such thing as bilithium crystals."

Brodeur looked like a sarcastic mime when he thrust both hands toward Vesely in a motion that said, *see!*

Vesely got a crafty look in his eyes, the kind a man gets when he's about to win a game of chess. "Tell me, Tex, what do you know about Roswell?"

39.

"Roswell?" Brodeur said with a scoffing laugh. "Lots of people dressed up like freaks selling alien cookies, hats, T-shirts, and thongs that say 'I got probed at Roswell.' Hell, you'd fit right in."

Vesely shrugged and raised his eyebrows as though to say, "This is true," and said, "Actually, forget Roswell."

Brodeur threw his hands up in the air and walked a few feet away. "Now he's backpedaling. I'm going to wait in the car. Come get me when we need to figure out our next move."

"Roger," Adler said, then looked at Miller. "You are just going to let him go?"

"I'm going to follow him in a minute, if Cowboy doesn't start talking some sense."

Vesely held up his hands. "Okay, okay." He took the strand of grass from his mouth and twisted it between his fingers. "Foo fighters. You have heard of them, yes?"

"Yes," Miller said. "World War Two pilots reported a lot of flying lights."

"And you take this subject seriously. The witnesses are credible?"

Miller nodded. If just one pilot made a report, he might dismiss it, as would have the military. But the sheer number of reports by Allied pilots meant that there really had been something unexplainable in the skies over Germany.

"Okay. These objects, these lights, they weren't seen until near end of war. Some say that they were angels come to witness war's end. Some say they were, and are, aliens come to observe mankind from another planet. These lights could move horizontally and vertically far faster than any plane. They could not be engaged, or captured. Superior to Allied planes in every way. And they began appearing shortly after successful antigravity tests, including the Bell. Declassified British and American documents reveal this to be true."

"But they never attacked," Miller said.

"That we know of," Vesely corrected. "Had any pilots been attacked by such craft I do not think they would have lived to tell the tale. That being true, I believe that foo fighters were simply extended tests of mobility, stealth, speed, and maneuverability when facing enemy aircraft. Shortly before war ended, foo fighters disappeared."

Vesely looked Miller and Adler in the eyes for a moment, then continued. "Until 1947."

"Roswell," Miller said. He'd seen enough cheesy late-night specials to know the date.

"Follow me, I want to show you something." He led them into the woods toward the abandoned factory and continued speaking. "I'm sure you know story. A strange flying object crashed at a ranch in Roswell and was recovered by air force. A press release was issued saying that they'd recovered a flying disk." He held a tree branch aside for Miller and Adler and then continued with his story and walk. "A day later, same air force people said the flying disk was actually a weather balloon."

Vesely paused and looked at Miller. "Do you think you could confuse a weather balloon for a flying disk?"

Miller grinned. "Probably not."

"You see? And you are navy." Vesely led them out of the woods and approached an open hole in the brick back wall of the factory. "Before air force collected the object, several people saw it, and some describe strange-looking text, almost like hieroglyphs, etched into the metal. Remember that for later. No one saw object before it crashed so is hard to say if it was truly disk shaped, balloon shaped . . . or bell."

They entered the large open factory floor. The place smelled of dust, mold, and animal piss. The building had been gutted for the most part. No furniture remained. No assembly lines. Just a lot of graffiti, broken glass, and beer cans.

Vesely walked to a partially torn-down interior wall and leaned against it. Miller could see that the wall had once been part of an enclosed space, but two of the interior walls had been torn down and removed.

"December ninth, 1965. Kecksburg, Pennsylvania. Many people saw and reported UFO crash in the woods, just outside town. Several witnesses went in search of the object. They described what they found as acorn shaped. Some said it was shaped like bell. The dimensions were similar to those of the Bell tested here and some people described hieroglyphic-like text surrounding the outer rim of the device."

"Are there any photos?" Adler asked.

"There was no time for photo-taking," Vesely said. "The military arrived quickly, led by two men in trench coats who announced the area was under quarantine. But the strange text is important. It links this craft to the one found at Roswell, and both craft to Bell."

"How so?" Miller asked.

"Hitler dabbled —'dabbled' is too weak a word—Hitler pursued the occult. He sent teams around the world in search of arcane and supernatural powers, of mystical artifacts, like the Spear of Destiny, the supposed spear used to pierce Jesus's side on cross. And we sometimes find strange, possibly occult languages etched into many of the more fantastic Nazi experiments."

"Are you saying the Bell is supernatural?" Miller asked, a hint of skepticism returning.

"No, no. Not at all. As Tex would have learned if he had remained with us, I believe people often use the supernatural, and now aliens, to explain things they do not understand. Even the Nazis. They made leaps in science, but didn't fully understand what they had done, so they deemed it supernatural. The occult. When the outside world sees that same science—UFOs—we say it is work of extraterrestrials. But it is far more likely that neither is true. That the foo fighters and the various UFO crashes around world are of terrestrial origin."

"But—" Adler started.

"Wait, wait, wait. Back to Pennsylvania. Object is quarantined. Military controls the area. But several locals see large, bell-shaped object obscured by a large tarp taken away by military truck. Two days later, Wright-Patterson Air Force base, only two hundred fifty miles away, orders sixty-five hundred double-glazed ceramic bricks. Delivery truck driver later reported that he saw large bell-shaped object in the hangar where he dropped off the bricks. He said they wanted to enclose the object. Entomb it."

"Holy shit," Miller said.

"What?" Adler asked.

"I wondered how long it would take you to see it, Survivor," Vesely said with a lopsided grin.

"See *what*?" Adler said.

Vesely knocked on the wall behind him. "Double-glazed ceramic brick, perfect for insulating electricity and heat, but is also resistant to radiation, and I suspect also contains the fields produced by Bell."

"The field that melts people," Miller said.

"The same," Vesely said. "I believe UFO crashes in New Mexico and Pennsylvania, and a few others around the world, were test flights of the objects now threatening the human race."

"But if the military recovered them—" Adler stopped when both Miller and Vesely gave her dubious looks. "Right. They had Nazis in the military and science communities. Maybe that's why they got there so fast?"

"To Pennsylvania," Vesely agreed. "They reached Roswell a day too late."

"All right," Miller said. "Let's assume you're right. That the Nazis achieved antigravity. That UFO sightings and crashes starting at the end of World War Two are actually the Bell—"

"Bells," Vesley corrected. "There would be thousands of them by now."

Miller continued. "So there are thousands of Bells— killer stealth antigravity satellites—orbiting the Earth waiting for a massive cloud of refined iron to reach the planet, at which point they will pull the iron in, speed it up, and launch it at high speed into the lower atmosphere— protecting the iron from friction by whatever body-melting field it produces—and when the iron hits the lower atmosphere it superheats, oxidizes, and kills everyone on the planet."

While Miller took a deep breath, Vesely clapped his hands. "Yes, yes! You have it exactly."

"Don't tell me they did all that on U.S. soil," Miller said. "I don't care how many Nazis are embedded in the military, they'd need a full-scale base and lots of space to fabricate thousands of these Bells. It would be impossible to hide."

"You're right," Vesely said. "Americans filtered money, personnel, and resources, but the technology was developed somewhere else."

"And you know where that is?" Adler asked.

"I do," Vesely said, "but . . ."

"But what?" Adler said.

Miller knew exactly what the man wanted. He had spent his whole life researching this subject; in essence, preparing for this fight. "He wants to come with us."

"I don't think—"

Miller cut Adler off. "Done."

"Yes!" Vesely said, thrusting a victorious fist in the air.

Adler looked incredulous.

"We don't have time to beat the information out of him," Miller explained. "And I've seen the way he handles a gun. Might come in handy." He turned to Vesely. "So, where are we going? I suspect it will be far from the eyes of civilization."

"Correct again, Survivor. We're going to Antarctica."

Neither Adler nor Miller spoke. It was too crazy. Too far. How could they get there?

Vesely spoke, his voice serious. "I can see you need to be convinced. Let's start before war. In 1938, Germany launched expedition to Antarctica under supervision of Reichsmarschall Hermann Göring, who would later become Oberbefehlshaber or Supreme Commander of the Luft-waffe, Germany's air force, and after war was tried and convicted of war crimes and crimes against humanity. He committed suicide before being hanged. I say this because Göring's promotion may be result of his success in the Antarctic. They took a seaplane carrier, the *Schwabenland,* to Queen Maud Land, a region of Antarctica claimed by Denmark. They flew over area, dropping clouds of tiny, spiked flags bearing swastika, and renamed region Neuschwabenland. They also took thousands of photos of coast, mountain ranges, and ice sheets. A large team of scientists including biologists, geologists, and climatologists scoured the land and claimed to have found geothermal hot springs—free of ice and home to algae. They spoke of deep, heated caverns, noted food sources such as penguins, walruses, and whales, and without saying so directly, made a convincing argument that this area, with its harsh terrain, freezing temperatures, and geographic isolation, would make perfect place for a secret base.

"Göring returned to Germany five months later, made his report, handed out medals, and never, not once, spoke of mission again. Flash forward to end of the war. The Allies are advancing on all fronts. The war is essentially over. Obergruppenführer Hans Kammler not only oversaw con-struction of the concentration camp system, extermination camps, and all cremation facilities used on prisoners, but also ran a think tank that developed secret weapons projects including the Messerschmitt ME 262 fighter jet, V-2 rock-ets, and the Bell alongside Obergruppenführer Emil Ma-zuw. More than that, he also oversaw relocation of the Reich's R and D facilities to underground locations, some-

thing he apparently had previous experience with before
war. He was also in charge of a special evacuation plan developed by Martin Bormann, personal secretary to the Führer. The plan detailed how Hitler, key scientists—ones that
would not be missed—personnel, supplies, and projects like
the Bell, would board several Junkers 390 transport planes
just miles from our current location, at the very same place
Kammler was last seen alive. There are several contradic-
tory reports of his death, but many believe he simply vanished. The plan had the Junkers fly to the coast of Norway
where all materials and personnel would be transported to a
fleet of waiting U-boats, several of which were advanced
XXI variety—wire-guided torpedoes, magnetic proximity
fuses—advanced for the time.

"Three days after Hitler supposedly killed himself—"

"What do you mean, *supposedly*?" Adler asked.

Vesely shook his head. "You are German. You should
know this."

Adler crossed her arms. "Some Germans don't like talking about Hitler. I'm not as fascinated by the man as you
apparently are."

"Fascination is the wrong word," Vesely said. "Prepared."

"Know your enemy," Miller chimed in. "Finish your
story. Please."

Vesely looked at the factory ceiling, recalling where he'd
stopped talking, and said, "The Russians told the world that
Hitler committed suicide, along with his wife, Eva Braun,
by shooting himself. They claimed his body had then been
covered in gasoline and set on fire. They recovered two
charred bodies and a skull fragment. There was never a positive ID made from body. No DNA tests. And the Russians
cremated the remains a second time, in 1970, and scattered
the ashes. Many believe the Russian claims were simply propaganda that U.S. and England went along with because they
did not want the world to know that Hitler still lived, and
they could not find him."

"A World War Two Bin Laden situation," Miller said.

"Exactly. That one man cannot be found by world's superpower would have been as embarrassing then as it is now." Vesely stretched and continued. "Three days after his supposed death, Kammler's disappearance, and the mass killing of sixty-two scientists that worked on the Bell, a flotilla of U-boats left coast of Norway and headed for Iceland."

"This is part of the plan?" Adler asked.

"No," Vesely said. "This is history. The submarine fleet made run south between Iceland and Greenland, where they encountered an Allied battle group. The result was an epic battle, perhaps the last of the war, that left only one Allied survivor, the commander of a destroyer, who told of an overwhelming naval force of advanced submarines that, after wiping out the Allied fleet, powered south and were never seen again."

Vesely held his hands out to his impatient-looking audience. "I am almost finished. In 1946, U.S. Admiral Byrd led fleet of seaplane carriers, destroyers, fueling ships, and submarines to Neuschwabenland, the region claimed by Germany before war. The expedition was prepared for eight-month stay. Forty-eight hours after reaching Neuschwabenland, they were ordered back to the States. No official reason was ever given for mission's cancelation, but I suspect Nazi influence in upper echelons of American power was already at work."

"That's all very interesting history," Miller said. "And I admit that I'm intrigued, but how can you be sure that after seventy years, the Nazis—including Hitler and Kammler—are still hiding out in Neuschwabenland?"

"Because," Vesley said, "a U.S. aircraft carrier group has been stationed there for the past five months."

"How can you know that?" Adler asked.

"Aircraft carrier groups are hard to hide," Vesely said. "Even in Antarctica. Several whaling, fishing, and scientific expeditions have come across the fleet, and I make it habit to keep track of such things."

Miller took out his phone and prepared to call the president. If Vesely was right and there was an aircraft carrier group at the German-claimed territory, he required no more convincing. In part, the presence of an aircraft carrier was good news because they would have a place to land and a jumping-off point to Antarctica. The bad news was, a portion of the crew, and most certainly the officers, were part of the Fourth Reich. A warm welcome might include surface-to-air missiles.

But if that's where the enemy hid themselves, that's where he would go. Miller's thumb hovered over the Send button, but a loud booming voice stopped him from placing the call.

"To jest policja. Wyjdźcie z podniesionymi rękami!"

Miller, Adler, and Vesely all snapped toward the sound of the amplified voice, just outside the factory.

"It's police," Vesely said, "They want us to come out."

40.

"They sound angry," Adler said as the officer repeated his command.

"If they found Brodeur and his two MP5s they're probably pissed," Miller said.

"Backup is probably en route," Adler said.

Miller clenched his fists. "We don't have time for this."

Vesely whipped off his belt and holsters, tucked the two .38s into his pants behind his back, and headed for a hole in the front wall. "Watch my back, Survivor?"

Miller wanted to object, but Vesely stepped into the sunlight before he could say anything. The police started shouting a moment later. Miller peeked through a hole in the wall and saw Brodeur lying against the hood of one of two police cars, hands cuffed behind his back. Two officers stood beside him, weapons drawn and pointed at Vesely, who strode confidently toward the men.

That's when Miller noticed the weapons the officers carried were Micro-Uzis, which from a distance looked like standard handguns, but could actually fire 1,200 rounds per minute. Two things quickly occurred to him. First, these weren't police. Second, they were about to tear Vesely apart. But it was too late to warn the man without revealing himself as well.

Vesely approached the officers calmly, open passport clutched in one of his raised hands. His body language was relaxed and the faux police approached him less aggressively than Miller expected. That was, until they got a look at the name on his passport.

Both officers took a reflexive step backward, Miller assumed because they didn't want to get splattered with Vesely's blood. The step only took a second, but it was longer than Vesely needed. The man's hands came down and behind his back in a blur. He drew both .38s, leveled them at both men's chests, and pulled the triggers. Twin explosions of blood and gore burst from the two men's backs as the high-caliber rounds tore through them.

Miller charged out of the factory as two more officers appeared behind the cars, which left only their heads for targets. Miller fired twice and one of the officers' heads snapped back. He dropped down behind the car. The second officer opened fire, causing Miller to dive for cover. But the man only got off three shots before Vesely turned one of his hand cannons on the man and fired a single round. Unlike the man Miller had shot, this man's head burst like a melon.

"Good God, man," Brodeur said from the hood of the car, where he still lay, cuffed. "You could have shot me!"

"I do not miss," Vesely said.

"Right, you're a cowb—"

A single shot rang out. Vesely spun, but not in reflex. He'd been struck in the shoulder.

Miller turned toward the sound of the shot and saw another officer standing at the corner of the factory. The man's Micro-Uzi was already leveled at Miller, who knew he wasn't nearly as fast a draw as Vesely.

Fortunately, he didn't need to be.

Three shots fired.

The first two struck the officer's chest, twitching his body with each impact. The third shot punched a hole in the man's nose. The round, slowed by bone and brain, didn't exit the skull, but the effect on his body was no less dramatic. He fell in a heap.

Miller turned and found Adler by the ruined factory wall, gun still raised in a solid shooter's stance. "Thanks."

She kept her weapon raised and stayed silent. Together, she and Miller scanned the area for more hostiles and peeked around the factory corner. All seemed quiet. When they turned back to the cars, they found Vesely holding a hand over his shoulder, which was wet with blood. Brodeur was still cuffed, but stood on his feet. His cheek was swollen.

"What happened?" Miller asked Brodeur.

"I was in the car. Didn't hear them coming." He pointed to his injured cheek. "Sucker punched me through the open window, dragged me out, cuffed me, and threw me on the hood."

"Why did they not shoot you?" Vesely asked.

"How the hell should I know?" Brodeur said, his typical good nature fading fast. He locked his eyes on Vesely. "Maybe because my name's not on the list. It was *your* name they reacted to." He shook the cuffs at Miller. "Can you please get these off of me?"

Miller searched a body and found the cuff keys. He freed Brodeur and turned to Vesely. "How's the shoulder?"

"Is nothing. The man's aim was horrible."

Adler lifted Vesely's hand away, found the hole the bullet had torn in his shirt, and ripped it open. She inspected the wound. "Looks like it could use a few stitches."

Vesely waved her off. "Let it heal. Will leave scar. Women will like it."

Adler smiled and tore the sleeve the rest of the way off, ignoring Vesely's protests. She tied the sleeve around his shoulder. "Keep it there until the bleeding stops. Then you can look tough *and* not bleed to death."

Vesely chuckled, but then grew serious. "Survivor, before I risk my life for this cause, I would like to know how they found us."

"Maybe a local called it in to the police?" Adler asked.

"Police in Poland do not carry Uzi," Vesely said, picking up one of the weapons and showing it to her. "They came for me." He nodded to Adler and then to Miller. "They came for both of you." He turned to Brodeur. "But not for him."

"If you're implying that—"

"I imply nothing," Vesely said. "He was not on the list, yes?"

"No, just the three of us," Miller confirmed.

"Then perhaps this is why you were not shot. Or perhaps they simply did not want to reveal their presence. I cannot say. What I can say is that they knew we were here."

"Maybe they followed you?" Brodeur said.

"Is not likely," Vesely said. "I was very careful. But is possible. If they are embedded in the U.S. military as deep as we suspect then perhaps they are watching us even now."

All four turned their faces to the sky, as though they could see the satellite watching them. Vesely lifted his fist and extended his middle finger.

"What are you doing?" Adler asked.

"I am sending message," Vesely said. "I say, fuck you."

"Great," Brodeur said. "Can we leave before a drone shows up and blows us to kingdom come?"

After squeezing into the small rental car, they left the five officers—if they were indeed officers—dead where they lay.

"Where to?" Adler asked as she sat at the steering wheel.

"Back to the airport," Miller said. "I have some flights to arrange."

He took the iPhone out of his pocket.

"Do not use that!" Vesely shouted. "Don't you know it can be tracked?"

Miller shared Vesely's paranoia about the phone, but it was a necessary risk, so he decided to put the Cowboy's mind at ease. "Not this phone," Miller said. He dialed, glanced back at Vesely, and said, "Mr. President, it's Miller."

Vesely's eyes opened wide as he realized to whom Miller spoke. But then he turned to Adler and whispered, "Perhaps it is the president who betrayed us?"

Adler turned back to Vesely and whispered, "I don't think the *black* president of the United States is a Nazi."

Miller ignored the conversation happening around him and focused on the president. The man sounded stressed, but still in control. Still fighting.

Miller quickly relayed everything that had happened

and explained that the military should be trying to find and destroy stealth satellites in Earth's orbit. He then relayed a list of required equipment, where he needed to go, how he needed to get there, and his suspicions about the aircraft carrier group stationed off the Antarctic coast.

"Shit," Bensson said. "We've had reports of friendly fire from most of the deployed armed forces, but it's hard to believe an entire battle group could be compromised. Though, at this point, anything is possible. I have a growing list of generals and admirals I believe to be trustworthy. They are in the process of reestablishing a chain of command while doing what they can to root out this cancer infecting our country. I'll do my best to make sure your pilots, and escorts, don't try to kill you."

"Appreciate that," Miller said.

"I'll call with details as soon as I have them."

"One more thing, Mr. President," Miller said.

"What is it?"

"Can you track this phone?"

"If I needed to, I could; even if you're out of cell range, I could trace the GPS. But no one else can track it if that's what you're—"

"Not at all," Miller said. "If you haven't heard from me, and red flakes start falling from the sky, track my phone's location and drop a nuke on it."

"Are you serious?"

"If you don't hear from me, it means I'm dead and you are out of options."

"Okay . . . okay, I'll see to it."

Miller hung up a moment later and turned to find three sets of wide eyes on him.

"Let me get this straight," Brodeur said. "We're going to Antarctica because of intel you got from *him*—" He motioned to Vesely. "—and you've just turned your cell phone into a targeting device for a nuclear missile."

Miller glanced back. "That a problem?"

"Course not," Brodeur said. "Be a helluva way to die."

41.

"I've got fifteen men in the brig. The world is on the brink of war. And you want to use four F/A-18 Hornets and their pilots as glorified taxis!" Commander Aaron Brown had his arms crossed over his khaki shirt and wore a deep scowl on his face that, for the most part, hid beneath a prodigious gray mustache. He hadn't liked receiving the orders to send four jets to Antarctica, but he absolutely loathed the idea when he got a look at whom his precious jets would be ferrying to the underbelly of the world.

After flying from Poland to France, Miller, Adler, Vesely, and Brodeur had boarded a Blackhawk helicopter and flown out over the Mediterranean where they rendezvoused with the USS *George H.W. Bush*, a massive Nimitz-class aircraft carrier. When the chopper had landed and Vesely got out, clutching his cowboy hat to his head, Brown's face had turned two shades redder.

Brodeur had followed wearing a bloodstained white shirt—the red tie long since removed. Adler went next, clutching her purse containing her grandmother's journal. Miller brought up the rear, and since he was the only one of the bunch who looked like he had any business in a war, Brown directed his comments and anger toward him.

"They told me you were Navy SEALs!" Brown shouted. "There's no way I'm giving you four of my birds."

"I *am* a SEAL," Miller said, trying to keep his cool. He'd been attacked enough by the enemy. He had little patience left, even for a navy commander. "And we need those planes. Now."

The commander gave Miller a once-over. He shook his head in disgust. "Bullshit." He turned away. "I'll be damned before letting a couple clowns take my—"

Miller caught the commander's arm and spun him around. It was a move he would never have considered while enlisted, but he was a civilian now, and had the backing of the U.S. president.

The two men accompanying the commander tensed and moved their hands to their sidearms. Vesely, who had kept his .38s tucked into his pants, once again proved he was the fastest draw in town. He leveled the weapons at the two sailors and shook his head.

"What the hell is this?" Brown asked.

Miller took out his phone, initiated a video call, and waited for the other end to pick up. "I told you he would need convincing," he said when the call was answered. "Here he is." He handed the phone to Brown.

The man's beet-red face went white when he saw the president's face staring back at him. His scowl flattened out. His deeply furrowed eyebrows rose. He turned away and walked a few steps so the group couldn't hear what Bensson was saying, but they could hear Brown's quick replies. "Yes, sir. I understand. But— Yes, sir. I will. I will." The call was ended from the other end. He turned to face Miller again and handed the phone back.

"Stand down," Brown said to the sailors, whose hands were still perched over their weapons. They complied and Vesely did as well. "Take off the hat and glasses," Brown said to Miller.

He did.

"Why are *you* here?" Brown asked.

"Long story," Miller said. "If we both live past the next few days, I'd love to tell you all about it, but right now, I need four planes."

The commander nodded and sent the two sailors away with a "Do it." Then he turned back to Miller. "You'll need to rendezvous with refueling planes three times, and that's already been arranged. The flight will take roughly six hours at top speed."

Miller could hear the "but" coming, and added, "*But . . .*"

"But we haven't been able to reach the USS *George Washington.* She's been stationed there, running cold-weather drills, for some time. But she's not replying to us, or anyone else. We know she's still there. You can't hide a ship like that short of sinking it, but either no one is home, or they've got a mutiny on their hands. I caught thirty-two traitors trying to sabotage my ship. It's possible the ship is no longer under U.S. control."

"Guess we'll find out in six hours," Miller said.

"If they don't welcome you with open arms, you'll be too low on gas to make it back, and there are no other places to land."

"We will eject over target area," Vesely said.

Miller couldn't help but smile. He appreciated the man's spirit, and he'd just taken the words out of his mouth.

"You do know it's winter in Antarctica? It's going to be below freezing, windy as hell, and dark for most hours of the day. The odds are against you surviving."

"Thanks for the pep talk," Brodeur said.

"The odds against *you* surviving are one hundred percent if we don't go," Miller said. "That's not a threat. It's a guarantee. The entire world is going to look like Miami in three days."

"Then why aren't we flying a battalion down there?" Brown asked.

"I'd rather fight with three people I trust," Miller said, motioning to the others, "than an army that's already tried to stab me in the back on more than one occasion."

Brown stared at him for a moment, and then nodded. "Good luck, then."

They were in the air twenty minutes later, speeding around the globe at Mach 1.8. The four F/A-18 Hornets flew high and fast, and carried no ordnance, to stretch fuel as far as possible. Each fighter jet carried one passenger and one pilot, and after Miller requested his unlikely band of heroes use the flight to catch up on some sleep, conversation between the planes had stopped. They all knew the next few steps in the master plan were up in the air. And speculating on what they might find in Antarctica, or worrying about the welcome they might receive on the *George Washington,* served no worthy purpose. So he'd ordered them to sleep.

He quickly fell into a deep REM sleep, and dreamed of Miami.

Pink corpses littered the streets.

Rainbow swirls of dust fell from the sky and clung to the buildings, like children's glitter.

He could hear engines roaring in the distance, mixed with racial slurs.

Dread consumed him.

He ran, pursued by something unseen.

Pink sludge clung to his legs, slowing his flight.

"Lincoln," a voice said.

He turned toward it. A short figure stood in front of him, covered in pink. Blood oozed from its chest in the shape of a swastika.

He looked for a weapon and snapped the antenna off of a car that looked just like the station wagon his parents had when he was a kid. He held the antenna like a sword and stabbed the figure twice.

The pink melted away. For a moment, he saw Arwen's face beneath the pink, but then she melted, too, saying, "Can you hear me?"

"No!" he screamed, reaching for her. The girl's hand turned to scalding hot liquid in his hand. He lurched back, tripped, and fell—

Miller gasped as he awoke with a spasm. He'd fallen. He swore he'd fallen. It felt so real. But he was still in the F/A-18, strapped in and immobilized, miles above the Earth.

"You okay?" the pilot asked, clearly concerned that his passenger might be mentally unstable or having some kind of seizure.

"Bad dream," Miller replied. "I'm fine." But he didn't

feel fine. His subconscious was clearly worried about Arwen, and that was bad enough, but there were a billion innocent kids just like her.

Flashes of the dream repeated as exhaustion moved through his body like a force. The dream, and the emotions it triggered, began to fade. His internal clock told him he'd slept for just ten minutes, and as he closed his eyes again, he said, "Wake me when we're within radio range."

He felt his consciousness fading quickly, but the pilot's reply slapped him awake. "We're there now, sir."

The fog of sleep rolled away from Miller as a tornado of questions flooded his mind. "Have you tried reaching them?"

"Twice. No response."

"ETA?"

"Twelve minutes, but I don't think they're hostile, sir."

"Why?" Miller asked.

"Because we're in missile range and they're not—"

A loud beeping filled the cabin.

"Shit," the pilot said. "Scratch that. They're locked."

"Can we make it to land?" Miller asked.

"They're between us and the land," the pilot said.

Then a voice came over the radio. "To, uh, the four incoming craft. Please state your reason for being here, or we will fire."

Not only did the speaker lack confidence, but he also had very little experience when it came to bluffing. Miller had that in spades. He picked up the transmitter, depressed the Speak button, and said, "USS *George Washington,* this is Lieutenant Lincoln Miller, stand down now or we will attack."

Silence.

Miller filled his voice with fire and brimstone and said, "We are here under order of the president of the United States of America. Stand down now, or we will launch a tactical nuclear strike on your position in three . . ."

It was a ridiculous bluff, but the voice on the other end sounded like it belonged to a kid.

"Two . . . one . . ."

42.

"Okay, okay!" the voice shouted over the radio. "What do you want?"

"First, I'd like to know who I'm speaking to."

"Uh, CS James Hammaker, sir."

CS? Miller had to think for a moment to recall the rank. Culinary services! "You're a chef!"

"I'm rated E2, so I mostly wash dishes, sir."

"What are you, twenty?"

"Eighteen."

Miller could see the pilot in the front seat shaking his head. He couldn't believe what he was hearing either. "Hammaker, why am I speaking to you?"

"Um, I think it would be better if you spoke to Ensign Partin in person, sir. He's on the flight deck now."

"Why *Ensign* Partin?" Miller asked, suspecting the answer, but hoping it wasn't true.

"Because, he's the highest-ranking officer left alive. Sir."

Miller felt the angle of the F/A-18 change and knew they were already on approach. They'd be standing on the gigantic aircraft carrier deck in just a few minutes, so he decided not to press the kid. There was only one explanation for the comm being operated by a CS and an ensign being in charge of a skyscraper-sized war machine.

Mutiny.

* * *

The landing was textbook smooth. The deck crews operated expertly, guiding each fighter jet down, and taxiing them out of the way so the subsequent jet could land. Miller stepped onto the deck before the last of the four planes taxied into position. The flight suit he wore did little to stop the arctic cold. He took a breath through his nose and felt the sting of freezing flesh. He wrapped his arms around his chest and looked for the welcoming committee.

Three men approached him, one dressed in purple, one in red, and one in white. They all wore protective headgear, wind visors, and bright-colored vests that identified their deck crew job. This would be a very different greeting than he'd received on the *George H.W. Bush,* mainly because as a lieutenant, a rank he received shortly before retiring from the navy, he was the highest-ranking officer on the ship.

The three men gave casual salutes as they neared. Miller noticed all three were armed with sidearms—certainly not standard issue for deck crews. The man in the middle, dressed in white, had dried blood on the front of his shirt.

"That your blood?" Miller asked.

The man looked down. "No, sir. I'm not sure whose it is." He lifted his wind visor, revealing dark brown eyes. "I've killed a lot of men."

Miller looked over the deck. A rainbow of men and women stood motionless, watching the conversation play out. "Which one of you is Ensign Partin?"

The man with blood on his white vest gave a nod. "I am. This is my ship now."

Miller felt a challenge in the man's words. "I outrank you, Ensign. While I'm on this ship, I'm the commanding officer." Miller had no scruples about leaving out the fact that he was actually Lieutenant Lincoln Miller, Retired. He was here under presidential orders and had already bossed around a commander.

"You'll find your rank doesn't hold much weight around here right now," the man said.

Miller eyed the deck crew again. All of them were armed.

Some with handguns, others with assault rifles. "We're on the same side, Ensign."

"You sure about that?"

Miller nodded to the man in purple, who was black. "Well, since he's still breathing, yeah, I think it's safe to say that you're not Nazis. And if we were the bad guys, why would we land on a ship full of the enemy. We're not here for you, Ensign, we're here to find, and kill, *them*."

The three men relaxed a little.

"Care to tell me what happened here?" Miller asked.

"Mind if we go inside?" Partin asked, rubbing his arms.

Miller would have preferred rapid answers to his questions, but the look in Partin's eyes said he'd seen and done things that would mark him for life. He nodded and waved for Adler, Vesely, Brodeur, and the four pilots, who had been unloading gear, to follow them inside. On the way to the bridge stairs Miller saw more than one dark red stain and the occasional bullet casing. By the time they reached the warmth of the bridge he'd counted twenty-two spots where he believed someone had lost their life.

A war had been fought on this ship.

Goose bumps covered Miller's body as he stepped out of the cold and onto the bridge of the USS *George Washington*. He saw a young man sitting at the comm station looking nervous and insecure. "Hammaker?" he asked.

"Yes, sir," the man said, standing to attention.

"For future reference," Miller said, "F/A-18s don't carry tactical nukes."

Hammaker looked to the glossy blue linoleum floor. "Yes, sir."

Miller gave the kid a pat on the shoulder. He suspected Hammaker had been through a lot. "It was a nice try, though."

The kid smiled and sat back down.

Miller turned when he heard the bridge door close behind him. Adler, Vesely, and Brodeur stood just inside the door. Ensign Partin gazed out of the long strip of windows lining the front of the high-tech bridge. His helmet had been removed, revealing a gleaming white bald head. The pilots and the two other deck crew members hadn't joined them.

"Did the president really send you?" Partin asked.

"Yes, you can confirm it by—"

"We have no long-range communications," Partin said. "Something is blocking satellite communications, from the carrier, the planes, everything. All we have is local radio."

"Some kind of jammer?" Vesely said.

"Or they just turned the satellites away," Miller said, then looked at Partin. "You'll just have to take my word on it. Can you tell me what happened here?"

Partin took a deep breath and let it out with a hiss. "We've been here for I don't know how long—"

"Months," Hammaker added.

"Months." Partin turned away from the window and looked at Miller. "Cold-weather training exercises. We put birds in the air every day. Several times a day. And caught them when they came home. It's what we do on deck. The conditions are beyond miserable here, but harsh-weather exercises test the deck crews as much as the pilots and planes. We did our jobs. No questions asked. A few weeks in, we started sending teams over to the continent. Might have been SEALs. Maybe Rangers. We didn't ask even though we knew sending troops to mainland Antarctica is against international law. But we're damn good at our jobs. *Damn* good. Maybe better than they thought."

Partin chewed his lower lip for a moment. "They started coming home with more men than they left with. At first it was subtle. One here. Two there. But occasionally there would be ten extra soldiers. Grim-faced sons a bitches, too."

"They ate like robots," Hammaker said. "We've got some good chow pounders here, but these guys didn't miss a beat." He motioned with an imaginary spoon, acting out two scoops per second. "And they did it in unison."

"In unison?" Adler asked.

"Like when the North Korean Army marches," Hammaker said. "One, two, three. Scoop, scoop, scoop."

Partin stared at Adler. "Where are you from?"

Miller quickly understood Partin's suspicion of Adler's accent. He stepped forward. "Sorry I haven't introduced my team yet. This is Elizabeth Adler, she's a German Interpol liaison." He motioned to Brodeur. "This is Special Agent Roger Brodeur with the FBI. The man in the cowboy hat is Milo Vesely, a special consultant from the Czech Republic. I can vouch for every one of them and expect them to be treated with the same respect given me. Back to the visiting soldiers."

Though he was clearly still uncomfortable with Adler's accent, Partin continued. "They kept to themselves and never spoke to us, which was fine because they scared the shit out of the crew. Then, one day, they were gone. I supervise most flights on and off this ship and I didn't see them leave. A few days later, the helicopter crews started bringing in big wooden crates, then long metal containers. They stacked them up on the deck like wc were a cargo ship."

"What was in them?" Vesely asked. "Were there any insignias on the wood?"

"I didn't see any," Partin said. "But then they started transferring the crates to the support vessels."

Several ships typically supported an aircraft carrier. Two sub destroyers, two guided-missile cruisers, two antiaircraft warships, a submarine, and two fuel ships. Now that Partin had brought it up, Miller couldn't remember seeing any support ships surrounding the carrier. "Where are the support ships now?"

Partin shrugged. "One morning, I came on duty and they were gone, along with each and every crate. Crew members who asked questions were thrown in the brig. A group of us started looking for answers. We discovered they were going to the United States, but not what they were taking or their final destination. That's when we found out about Miami."

The man leaned forward, clutching a radar console. "I had cousins there." He looked up. "Did anyone make it out?"

Miller met the man's eyes. They'd heard about the attack, but not its outcome. "Not many. Millions died."

"It happened in Tokyo, too," Adler said.

"And Tel Aviv," Vesely added.

With a shake of his head, Partin pulled himself out of his despair. "We knew the truth when we heard men cheering. Most of the officers. The commander. Pilots. MPs. Thank God most of the Special Ops guys left with support ships or what followed would have turned out differently. We spread the word and staged a coup that night." He rubbed a hand over his bald head. "The fighting lasted three days. We lost communications almost immediately and they disabled the screws. We were dead in the water and cut off from the world. Four thousand two hundred men and women served aboard this ship when we left port. I suspect at least two hundred had already left with the support ships, more if you count the newcomers, and we outnumbered them, two to one, but most of us were support crew—flight deck, engineers—" He motioned to Hammaker. "Cooks. We fought guns with knives, with hands, with anything we could find. When their ammunition ran low, we took the ship. There are nine hundred crew members alive. Some are on the fence. We put their numbers close to seven hundred, leaving us with twenty-four hundred dead. We're still collecting bodies from the lower decks."

Miller felt sick. War was one thing. The battlefield made sense. The men around you were brothers. You bled for each other. But what happened on this ship was an affront to everything he believed about the U.S. military. He pushed aside his rising anger and asked, "Do you have prisoners?"

"In hindsight, prisoners would have been a smart idea," Partin said. "But we—we were afraid. We killed the bastards and threw them overboard. Our dead are in the hangar, covered with sheets, but the smell is getting bad and we'll need to give them sea burials soon." Partin looked up as he remembered something. "We checked the commander's quarters. Found lots of Nazi and white supremacist paraphernalia. Same with the senior officers. Small flags. Old uniforms. Guns. I don't know if they had it all along, or if it came from the mainland, but it helped with the guilt." He looked at Miller. "Nazis. Can you believe it?"

"You have no idea," Miller said. He stood in front of Partin. "Listen, Ensign, what you did here; you can't be thanked enough. If I get my way, each and every member of this crew will get the Medal of Honor. But this thing isn't over. The world is still in danger."

Partin listened intently, his eyes locked on Miller's.

"Can you take us to the mainland? I need to see what's there."

"I've got plenty of helicopters," Partin said. "But no pilots. They're all gone, or dead."

"I took lessons," Vesely said.

"How many?" Miller asked.

"Two. But only piloted once. No takeoff. No landing."

Miller silently cursed, then saw a hand rise in his periphery. He looked over and saw Hammaker, hand raised. He stood, looking unsure of himself, and said, "I can fly."

"No way are we letting the kid fly us to Antarctica," Brodeur said.

"My father is a helicopter pilot for Fox News in Chicago. He taught me how to fly. I have a commercial license."

"Why are you a cook?" Brodeur asked.

Hammaker shrugged. "Never told the recruiter. Joined to pay for school and didn't want to risk getting shot down. Figured the galley of an aircraft carrier was a safe place to be. Didn't turn out that way, though."

"Well, it's about to get worse," Miller said. "You're hired." He turned to Brodeur. "He's all we've got. Unless you know how to fly a helicopter."

He didn't.

"How long will it take to prep a chopper?" Miller asked Partin.

"I can have you in the air in ten minutes."

"Do it."

Partin left. Hammaker followed him.

"Suit up," Miller said to Adler, Vesely, and Brodeur.

Adler opened the duffel bags containing white snow gear and an assortment of weapons they'd commandeered from the USS *George H.W. Bush*. The four of them stripped down and donned their winter gear, perhaps the first people in the history of the modern navy to change clothes on the bridge of an aircraft carrier.

Vesely grinned as he pulled up his white thermal pants. "We are like the Allies," he said. "People from around the world, joining forces. The new Allies. No?"

Miller shook his head with a grin, which felt completely inappropriate, considering what they were up against and what had happened on this ship. But the man was right. They were a ragtag group of allies going up against a technologically advanced Nazi force with the world hanging in the balance. The difference was, there were only four of them—five if you included the kid—and he had no doubt this flight would take them into the heart of the enemy's preparations.

He could be dead within the hour.

He looked at his watch, still set for eastern time.

The whole world could be dead in sixty.

43.

"You all right?" Miller said into his headset microphone. He sat in the helicopter's copilot seat, across from Hammaker. The large CH-53 Sea Stallion transport helicopter had lurched hard to the left as they descended over mainland Antarctica.

Hammaker gave his nose a twitch, like it itched, but refused to take his hands off the controls. "Sorry about that. Felt like we flew into a wall of wind."

"Katabatic winds," Vesely said from his seat in the back of the helicopter. "Cold air from the mountains is denser and pulled toward the coast by gravity."

The chopper could hold up to twenty soldiers and equipment. Right now the only passengers it held were Vesely, Adler, and Brodeur. Ensign Partin had offered more men, but Miller still had trust issues. Though the men and women of the *George Washington* were true patriots, there was no way to know if any of the enemy still lurked among them. And seeing as how most of them were deck crew, engineers, galley staff, and cleaning crews, they'd be more likely to shoot each other than the enemy. They might be good with kitchen knives and broom handles, but Miller's four-person team now carried MP4 assault rifles, 9mm sidearms, and had enough ammunition to stage a mutiny of their own.

"Whatever it is," Hammaker said, "I've got it under control."

Miller noticed that Hammaker's lack of confidence had disappeared when he sat down behind the helicopter's controls. The kid's claim to be a helicopter pilot proved true. While the cockpit contained a lot of buttons, switches, and gauges he didn't recognize because they had to do with weapons and defensive systems, the flight controls for most helicopters were universal.

The GPS coordinates recovered from the previous flights made by the mysterious missing aircraft carrier crews had been punched into the helicopter's GPS system, which had a larger-than-average display screen. The target area showed as a green pushpin. The red blinking circle representing the helicopter was almost on top of it.

Miller leaned forward, but couldn't see much over the nose of the helicopter. "Take us around," he said to Hammaker while twisting his finger around in the air.

The kid gave a nod and banked the helicopter, taking them in a clockwise circle that gave Miller a clear view of the land below. He felt thankful he'd thought to wear anti-glare sunglasses, because all he could see was white snow blazingly bright. Of course, the bright white snow would soon fade to pitch darkness. Night would arrive soon and last well into the following day. If they didn't locate Vesely's Nazi hideaway quickly it might be eighteen hours before they got another chance.

"Can you take us lower?" Miller asked.

Hammaker replied by dropping the helicopter down to just one hundred feet above the surface.

Miller saw what he was looking for right away—a square of white that didn't shine as brightly. The white-painted landing pad would be impossible to see by satellite. He pointed to it. "There. Take us down."

Hammaker saw the landing pad and gave a nod. The Sea Stallion swung around, leveled out, and dropped down onto the landing pad. A tornado of snow churned by the rotor whipped around the helicopter.

"Good job, kid," Miller said. "Keep her warmed up and ready to go."

"I'm not coming with you?" Hammaker said, clearly not pleased about being alone.

"If we need to make a quick exit, I want you ready." Miller handed Hammaker a 9mm Glock. "If you see anyone that is not one of us, shoot them. No questions asked."

"Yes, sir."

Miller climbed into the back of the helicopter, joining Vesely, Adler, and Brodeur, who were dressed in white from head to toe and held their MP5s at the ready.

"What is plan, Survivor?" Vesely asked.

"I'm going to take a look," Miller replied.

Adler put her hand on Miller's arm. "Not by yourself."

"If there are snipers, I don't want all of us exposed," Miller said. "And we still don't know where we're going." Before Adler could object, Miller slid open the side door, jumped out into the bitter cold—made worse by the rotor-fueled wind—and closed the door behind him. Now on the ground, he could see a one-foot-tall rim of snow that had been cleared from the landing pad. With his assault rifle up, he scanned the area, searching for targets, and clues. Thankfully, he found the latter and not the former.

A portion of the snowy rim looked trampled. He headed for it and found a trail of footprints that led to a white metal hatch large enough to drive a truck through, had it been on a wall instead of in the ground. He waved to the chopper. Vesely, Brodeur, and Adler quickly joined him.

"We'll never get that open," Brodeur said when he saw the hatch. "There has to be another way in."

"Always so negative," Vesely said, inspecting the hatch.

"You see an alternative?" Brodeur asked.

"Other than knocking," Adler added.

Vesely and Miller scoured the hatch, checking every crack, rivet, and indentation.

"Here," Miller said. He'd found a circular recess with a bar across it, perfectly sized for a human hand. He tried turning it, but it wouldn't budge.

Vesely dashed to the far side of the large hatch. "There

is another here." He knelt by it and gripped the bar. "Perhaps if we turn at the same time?"

"On three," Miller said. "Counterclockwise."

"Lefty-loosy, as you Americans say," Vesely replied with a nod.

"One, two, three."

Both men twisted.

The bars rotated ninety degrees and sank in an inch. But nothing else happened.

"Twist again," Vesely said. "One, two, three."

The bars rotated another ninety degrees. This time a dull clunk sounded from beneath the door. Then it shook.

"Get off!" Miller said, diving away from the hatch, which had already begun rising. Four massive hydraulic posts pushed the door skyward. It stopped twenty feet from the surface, leaving a square hole in the ice large enough to drive a tractor trailer through. Miller stood and approached the hole. A ramp descended into the ice, and then stone, where it merged with what could only be described as a road—a paved road, under the Antarctic ice.

"Watch our backs," Miller said to Brodeur, then headed down the road. Twenty feet from the surface he found a large metal switch he suspected would open and close the hatch, but let it be. He wanted the hatch open for the same reason he left Hammaker behind with the helicopter.

The tunnel, which had been cut through solid stone, made a sharp right turn one hundred feet down. Miller slid his head around the corner, ready for a fight, but instead found something amazing.

The road continued down in a series of switchbacks, but it was no longer encased in stone. The road led down the side of a massive gorge, perhaps five hundred feet deep and half as wide. Huge steel beams cut across the top of the gorge, supporting a wire mesh. Ice and snow, which glowed white from the lingering sun, covered the mesh, making the gorge impossible to see from above.

As Miller stepped out of the tunnel and into the gorge,

the temperature shift struck him. His thermal winter gear, rated for negative fifteen degrees, suddenly stifled him. He peeled off his white mask, which no longer provided camouflage, and took a breath. The air was humid and smelled of wet earth, and . . . flowers? The roar of flowing water reached his ears as he crept toward the edge of the road and looked down.

"My God," he said. The giant crevice stretched for half a mile in either direction. Far to the right, a waterfall emptied, perhaps carrying fresh glacial meltwater. The waterfall ended in a large pool that became a fast-moving river. The water cut through the center of the valley, billows of steam rising from its surface. And lining the shores—*son of a bitch*— were leafy green plants. Patches of mushrooms grew near the walls. Green algae coated most stones, and the gorge walls fifteen feet up. The gorge was like a tropical oasis, except instead of being in the desert, it was beneath Antarctica.

"Wow," Adler said as she slid up next to Miller.

Vesely crouched at the edge of the road, balancing on his hands. He pulled his mask off and revealed a huge grin. "The Antarctica Shangri-La. Is real."

Brodeur said nothing. He removed his mask and looked out at the valley. "I think we should move."

Miller stepped back from the edge, realizing that the beauty of the place had distracted him and endangered them all. "Lose the suits."

The four shed their white outer gear, revealing the black BDUs beneath. Feeling less conspicuous and much cooler, Miller led the team down the switchback road. He hugged the walls all the way down, looking for trouble, but only seeing paradise. He stopped at the bottom. A bridge led across the steaming water, which he could now see bubbled with heat.

Vesely stopped next to him and pointed to the water. "Geothermal vents. Whole river is heated."

"That's great," Miller answered, "but I'm more interested in what's on the other side of the river." A massive door, like an oversized bank vault, had been built into the wall of the gorge—locked tight.

A modern-looking keypad was attached at the side of the vault door. There was no way to figure out the combination, so Miller dug into his supply belt and took out some small bricks of C4. The vault door looked tough, but he wasn't going to blow the door. He was going to blow the stone around it.

While Miller assembled the charges, Brodeur walked up to the keypad.

"You're not going to get it open," Vesely said. "Not without code."

Brodeur ignored him and kept fiddling. No one bothered watching as Miller handed each of them an armed explosive charge to hold while he rigged more.

A sharp beep spun them around toward Brodeur.

The vault door slid open silently. Brodeur stepped aside, revealing the now pried-open keypad. "Standard code lock. FBI trains on them. Piece of cake."

"I'm impressed," Vesely said. "FBI is more competent than I believed."

"Glad you approve," Brodeur said sarcastically.

Miller quickly switched off the detonators and plucked them from the C4. With everything back in his supply belt, he crossed the bridge and stood in the open door. A tunnel, lit by hanging bulbs, led deep into the stone, no end in sight. No guards, either.

Miller led the team in, feeling like he'd entered the throat of a giant who might swallow him whole. But he had no choice. Answers waited in the darkness.

Though he suspected more than answers lurked beyond, Miller began to jog. Then ran. He reached the end of the tunnel a minute later and stopped. He heard the footfalls of his team approaching from behind, but when he looked at the open space around him a bomb could have detonated and he wouldn't have heard it.

44.

A cavern bigger than Miller thought possible opened up before him. Hanging stalactites meant the cavern was at least partly natural. But the walls and floor had been smoothed. And a grid of metal poles held a maze of beams from which hung an endless sea of grated lamps.

While much of the floor was smooth matte stone, shiny walkways had been buffed into the floor. The path Miller now stood on ran toward the center of the space where it split and wrapped around an octagonal control center lined with modern computers. Miller noticed that while the lights were on, there wasn't a soul in sight. He headed for the command center.

"I think we're alone," Miller said to the others, keeping his voice quiet. "But stay ready for anyth—"

A distant high-pitched whir filled the air. It reminded Miller of the remote-controlled car he had as a kid. So he wasn't surprised when the small, modern-looking vehicle rolled into view. To Miller it looked like a land mine on wheels, but sleek and modern.

The device spun around, stopping when a small red LED light faced their direction. Miller got the distinct feeling that the device was looking at them.

"Looks like Roomba," Vesely said.

And he was right. The device did resemble the robotic

maid, but Miller didn't think it was left behind to keep
the floor looking good, clean as it may be. He tensed when
the device approached. When it closed to within twenty-five
feet, Miller raised his weapon.

Brodeur shoved the weapon down. "Might be explosive!"
Miller held his fire. Brodeur was right.

Miller scanned the area. One hundred feet to the left of
the walkway was what looked like an empty hangar bay.
Large metal frames, now empty, lined the walls. An assembly line, like that of a car factory, complete with robotic
arms, stretched down the center of the hangar. This massive
fabrication plant had been operating for seventy years, em-
ploying scientists recruited from America, financed by
American dollars, and hidden by American politicians and
military personnel.

Miller turned to the right and found a tall, metal, capsule-
shaped object. Its smooth surface appeared to be copper, or
lead, and had a sheen like brushed metal. A vertical seam,
framed by strips of silver, ran around the outer edge, disappearing around the top and bottom. Its metal base was bolted
to the floor. Next to it stood another. And another. There
might be a hundred of the things. The rows of metal cylinders looked like giant capacitors arranged on a circuit board.

Miller was about to order the group into the maze of cylinders when the red light atop the Roomba-thing began
blinking. *Not good.* The round device was composed of two
sections. Wheels could be seen at the fringe of the outer
ring, so Miller assumed it also held the engine and whatever
else it needed to function. But the disk at the center could be
anything. When it began to spin, Miller assumed the worst.
"Get down!"

Miller, Vesely, and Adler dropped to the floor. Brodeur
dove toward the cylinders, which he was closest to.

The spinning disk sprang into the air. There was a sound
like a thousand puffs of air, which was immediately followed by the ticking of metal balls bouncing off the wall
and rolling over the floor. Somewhere in the chaos, Brodeur
shouted in pain. The center disk fell to the floor next to

Miller, spinning like a flicked coin. He slapped his hand down on it, silencing the thing.

Free of its payload, the rover just sat in place, its red light now extinguished.

"Is modern Bouncing Betty," Vesely said, standing up.

Miller picked up one of the marble-sized metal balls. They were everywhere. Vesely was right. The Bouncing Betty, formally known as an S-mine, was used extensively by the German army in World War II. When triggered, the spring-loaded mine would bounce two feet into the air and explode, sending a ring of metal balls and shrapnel flying into anyone standing nearby. Unlike conventional mines, enemies didn't need to be close by to be injured, and those close, well, some men were cut in half. This device was more sophisticated. It fired its payload of metal balls as the disk launched into the air. The attack was silent compared to the explosive force of the other mine. And as demonstrated, this device didn't have to wait around to be triggered, it could seek its enemies out.

The question nagging Miller was whether or not this was some kind of automated defense, or was it sent?

Movement in the field of metal cylinders reminded him that he'd heard Brodeur shout. Had the man still been standing? Why didn't he duck with the rest of them? "Brodeur, you hit?"

A blur of motion, black like Brodeur's clothing, caught Miller's eye. But Brodeur wasn't responding. Why would he be running, but not talking? Was there another mobile Bouncing Betty?

The black blur passed through another opening as it closed the distance.

Then it was followed by a second.

Acting on instinct, Miller drew his knife and whipped it toward where he expected the first man to appear.

Adler began to protest. "Miller, wh—"

Thuck. The blade buried in the chest of a tall man whose face and head were covered by some kind of solid mask that reminded Miller of a luchador wrestler, but the eye slots were covered by some kind of tinted glass. The man also wore body armor, but like all bulletproof vests, which stop the blunt impact of bullets, it proved ineffective against the slicing power of a sharp blade. As he spilled to the floor, he pulled the trigger of his Sturmgewehr 44 assault rifle. The cacophony of rounds, fired into the stone wall, acted as a kind of catalyst. At least ten men, most dressed in white lab coats, shouted and charged through the maze of cylinders. The second man dressed in black saw his partner drop and ducked back in time to avoid being shot by one of Vesely's high-caliber pistol rounds. The shot, however, ricocheted off of two cylinders and struck one of the white-clad men in the chest. He fell to the floor, gasping for air. The man next to him shouted in fright.

They're not soldiers, Miller thought. The two dressed in black were killers, no doubt. But the rest were science personnel, or maintenance. A few carried handguns, but most held whatever tool had been in their hands when they became aware of the team's presence —a wrench, a screwdriver; one man even carried a ceramic mug. Vesely and Adler could handle them. But the soldier, Miller knew from experience, needed his personal touch. He'd been lucky with the first, who probably assumed they had been injured by the Betty. But the second, with time to regroup, could be dangerous.

"Take care of them!" he shouted to Vesely, pointing at the approaching group of workers.

Vesely drew his second pistol. Between the two, he'd have eleven shots. Miller knew he'd need just nine to finish the job, but when Adler took up her solid shooter's stance next to the cowboy, Miller didn't think the man would even need both guns.

Miller ran right, sprinting through a row of cylinders. He quickly lost sight of the mob, but knew their fate when he heard the occasional boom of Vesely's handguns, each, without doubt, a well-placed kill shot. The single cannonlike rounds from Vesely were complemented by the less loud triple shots that Miller recognized as Adler. Two to the chest, one to the head. With very few shots fired in return, and lots of screams off to his left, Miller knew the pair had the situation under control.

Miller, on the other hand, did not. An arm stretched out in front of him and caught Miller across the chest. Miller fell backward, but his forward momentum turned the fall into a slide. As he slipped across the polished floor, he leaned back with his MP5. Aiming upside down while sliding would have been a challenge, so he just pulled the trigger and let loose a barrage that sent his attacker diving for cover before he could get off a shot.

Miller got to his feet and dove behind the nearest cylinder. As he rolled to his feet, he ejected the MP5's magazine and slapped in a new one. The staccato roar of his enemy's rifle, accompanied by the ping of bullets on metal, echoed through the chamber.

Miller leaned out and fired a volley, then ducked as his adversary took a turn. They could go at this all day, or until one of them ran out of ammunition, Miller realized. *Lucky I came prepared*. While the other man finished his volley, Miller pulled the pin on a flashbang grenade and tossed it toward the man's position. While the weapon wouldn't kill the man, it would effectively render him blind and deaf, and confused as hell.

Miller closed his eyes and covered his ears. The explosion wouldn't be close enough to render him helpless, but it would still hurt like hell. When it came, the *boom* hurt his ears, but it wasn't enough to slow him down. Miller whirled around the cylinder. He planned to come around behind the man and finish him off without a fight. But as he rounded the cylinder behind which the man hid, he realized his plan had a fatal flaw.

The man's strange mask. The tinted lenses protected him from the flash. And the rest clearly protected him from the noise. Miller would have a ringing in his ears for the next week and this man was no worse for the wear. The man saw Miller coming and spun his weapon toward him.

Miller knew the bullets wouldn't pierce the man's armor, but he unloaded anyway as he continued his charge. The kinetic force of each round was diffused by the thick armor, but a series of high-speed projectiles in a row at close quarters was enough to send the man reeling. As he spilled back, the man pulled the trigger, firing the full contents of his clip toward Miller.

But Miller wasn't there.

When the man caught his balance again, and began to reload, Miller jumped out from behind the man and leapt onto his back. He got his arm up under the man's mask and squeezed. The man's armor could deflect bullets and his mask could ward off the effects of a flashbang grenade, but the man still needed to breathe. The man slammed Miller against one of the cylinders and nearly shook him off, but when the man tried again, he missed. The pair fell back onto the floor. With his leverage gone, the man was defenseless. He died thirty seconds later.

Miller shoved the man off of him and stood, listening. The gunshots had stopped, but he could hear Adler shouting. He couldn't make out what she was saying, but he didn't need to. He bolted toward the voice, weaving in and out through the endless rows and columns of the strange devices.

When Miller reached the end, he found Vesely aiming a gun at a white-clad man standing at a mobile computer console. It wasn't plugged into anything, so he assumed its power source was inside the big black plastic case beneath the computer. And if it was connected to a network, it was wireless. The man's finger hovered over the Enter key of a computer keyboard. Adler stepped closer to the man, hands raised. "Don't do it," she said.

Miller didn't know what "it" was, but doubted the man was about to send out a blog entry. Though it could be a communication. Or something worse. Miller gave the slightest of nods to Vesely, who pulled the trigger. But the man must have seen the gesture, because a microsecond before his brains exited the back of his skull, he pushed the button.

In the silence that followed the cacophonous gunshot, Miller heard the rev of a tiny engine. The man had triggered another of the killer Roombas. But then the engine sounded different. Louder. When the small robotic Bouncing Betty rounded the corner from the far end of the cylinder field, Miller knew why.

The man hadn't activated one Betty.

He'd activated hundreds.

45.

The robotic army's whirring engines grew louder as they closed the distance. Miller rushed to the computer. The screen was covered with text, flashing and moving as the system worked. The text scrolled faster than he could read. He moved the mouse, but nothing happened. Whatever kind of operating system this was, it made little sense to him.

Adler sidled up next to him. "It's Linux based," she said. She typed in a command faster than Vesely could quick draw, but nothing happened. She tried several different keystroke combinations and nothing happened. "The program is locked," she said.

"Please hurry, or start running," Vesely said. "Roomba army approaches."

Miller glanced up and saw an endless sea of red LED lights. They were going to have to run in a second, but he doubted they could hide for long. And lying down probably wouldn't work. One of the Bettys would eventually fire at an angle, assuming that's how they all functioned. Some might just be bombs.

Adler pointed back toward the entrance. "Cowboy, run that way."

"Happily," Vesely said, and then ran toward the exit.

A burst of text flowed onto the screen in response to Vesely's movements.

"There!" Adler said. "The robots' movements are being controlled, or at least coordinated by the system. There must be sensors throughout this whole place. Maybe cameras. Motion sensors. But they are being controlled by the network. If the computers go down—"

Miller took aim at the computer.

"No!" Adler shouted. "The entire networked system. Shooting one computer will not stop it."

"Then what will!"

"Fork bomb," Adler said.

Miller had no idea what a fork bomb was, but said, "Do it!"

He watched as Adler struck three keys and opened a new window. It was a basic text system, like old DOS. She quickly typed in a seemingly random grouping of symbols.

$:(){ :

"A fork bomb is a bash function," Adler said. "It is called recursively and runs in the background. Once it is started, it cannot be stopped. It opens itself again and again. It starts slow, but each function continues to operate. It is exponential so once it begins, it can happen quickly depending on the power of the networked computers."

She finished the sequence—

$:(){ :|:& };:

—and hit Enter. "There!"

A single robot Betty rolled around the console. Too late! As the disk at the center of the mobile mine spun up, Miller tackled Adler to the ground. As they fell he realized he would be on top of Adler and quite possibly in the thing's kill zone, even if it didn't tilt.

They hit the floor together, each letting out an "oof!" But the puff of air and clack of metal balls never sounded. The disk hit the floor next to Miller, but this time it didn't spin. It fell flat to the floor, heavy with unfired rounds. Miller leapt up, afraid the thing might fire in his face. He pulled Adler up, too, and then turned to face the rest of the robotic horde. Not a single red light glowed. He looked at the computer screen. Black and dead.

Adler had done it. Before he could thank her, Vesely shouted, "Safe to come out now?"

"*Ja*," Adler said.

Vesely slid into view from behind one of the cylinders. He looked down and then stopped. He crouched, scrunched his nose, and then said, "Survivor. Come see this."

"What is it?" Adler asked.

"Come and see!" Vesely said. "Is labeled with man's name. Rolf Bergmann."

Miller stood next to Vesely and looked at the name etched into the base of the strange device. Several gauges and valves lined the base next to the name. Three metal tubes on the far side exited the base and stretched out toward an identical device.

Miller guessed there were at least one hundred of the things. But what really bothered him was that beyond cylinders left behind were several hundred more empty bases. Had they never been filled or were these things part of what had been transported out?

He couldn't imagine what they were, but they looked like futuristic giant-sized vertical coffins. He knocked his fist against it twice. It rang hollow.

"Here," Vesely said. "Is handle." He took hold of a handle on the side and pulled. It stuck for a moment, held closed by a small amount of suction, and then opened. Cool air seeped out, steaming as it rolled around them. The inside of the device was cushioned with red rubber. Several tubes dangled from the side. But it was otherwise empty.

The shape of the cushioning—perfectly fitted for a six-foot-tall man—held Miller's interest. "I think these held people," he said.

"Cryogenics," Vesely said.

"That's not possible," Adler said. She moved a hand to play with her hair, but her blond locks had been cut. She squeezed a fist instead.

Vesely turned to Adler. "The Nazis did many experiments on humans. Jews and Russians at Auschwitz were

stripped naked. Placed in freezing water with temperature
probe in rectum. Is documented. Test subjects were kept in
water until death, or near death. Then, they would attempt to
resuscitate the victims. Heat lamps. Internal irrigation—
scalding water in throat, stomach, and intestines. And bath
in near boiling water. To my knowledge, all victims died.
But it seems process was perfected."

"*Mein Gott,*" Adler said. She walked along the line of
cryogenic tombs, reading the names to herself. "There are
so many. But where are the others?"

"That's what we need to find out," Miller said. He turned
toward the command center and saw Brodeur sitting at a
computer, its screen glowing brightly. He'd apparently recovered from the attack, booted the system back up, and got
back on task. His fingers clacked over the keyboard.

"Where were you?" Miller asked.

Brodeur glanced up for just a moment and gave an awkward smile. "Got lost. By the time I came back the army of
killer gizmos was on the loose. When they shut down, I got
to work."

Miller headed toward him. "Why did you scream?"

Brodeur's smile turned sheepish. "I tripped."

Before Miller could tease the man, Brodeur finished his
flurry of keystrokes. "To quote *Spaceballs,* I ain't found shit.
Can't make heads nor tails of this operating system, never
mind that everything is in German."

Miller looked at the screen. Like the mobile computer,
Miller couldn't make sense of what he was seeing either. It
looked something closer to the Windows operating system,
but the learning curve would be steep with everything written in German. But Adler seemed to know her way around a
computer.

Vesely entered the command area and whistled. They
were surrounded by computers, servers, and bundles of cables
that descended from the grid of metal beams above them. As
his eyes followed the cables up, Vesely went white and fell
back. He landed in one of the floor-bolted swiveling chairs
and would have spilled out if Miller hadn't caught him.

"You okay, Cowboy?" Miller asked.

"No. I am not." Vesely looked beyond Miller's face, toward the ceiling. "Am terrified."

Miller looked up and saw what had Vesely so frightened. The Bell.

It hung from the stone ceiling, fifty feet above their heads.

"Is that what I think it is?" Miller asked.

"I do not think it is prototype, but it resembles Bell, yes. I do not think this is meant for flight, though."

"Why?"

Vesely looked at Miller like he was crazy. "Because is mounted to ceiling."

Adler joined them, looking up, looking nearly as pale as Vesely. Then she saw the computer screen. "Have you found anything?"

"Everything is in German," Brodeur said.

"Let me," Adler said, motioning Brodeur out of the seat. She looked the screen over for a moment and said, "Linux, same as the other. Should not have any trouble accessing anything that is not encrypted." She looked back at Brodeur. "You are lucky starting the system did not restart the robots."

"Actually, I think it did," Miller said, pointing out the red lights gleaming like a horde of angry, midget Cyclopes. "It just didn't restart the last command."

"Well, good. Knock yourself out," Brodeur said. "I'm going to do some recon and make sure there aren't any stragglers."

"Cowboy," Miller said. "Go with him."

Vesely didn't look happy about the order. Neither did Brodeur. The two men had rubbed each other the wrong way from the beginning. But he didn't like the idea of any of them being alone. After the two men left, Miller watched over Adler's shoulder as she worked her way through the system.

A series of folder icons appeared on the screen. She translated them. "Assembly. Stasis. Facilities. Schedule."

"Facilities," Miller said.

Adler opened the folder. The first name on the alphabetical list was "Auschwitz."

The number of sites was mind-blowing. Adler opened one at random and found several more subfolders, everything from schematics to construction reports to photos. They scanned it all, quickly realizing they were looking at the plans for an underground bunker and the evidence that it had been completed.

"Go back to the list," Miller said. If these bunkers had been built to survive the coming storm, and he believed they were, then one of them might hold the key to stopping it. He scanned the list.

Several names sounded familiar. Some sounded foreign. One of the names had caught his attention. "Dulce."

"Have you been there?" Adler asked.

"It's a base so secret it's kind of a modern myth. I served with a guy who claimed he served at Dulce. Said they had—shit—he said they had UFOs. Was real proud of it. Come to think of it, he was a racist prick, too. It's our best bet so far."

"What about Area Fifty-one? Aren't they supposed to have UFOs?"

"They've got stealth bombers, which will probably turn out to be Nazi technology, but I don't see Groom Lake on the list."

"I think I can print this if you want."

"Don't need to." He reached into his pocket and took out a thumb drive he'd requested along with the rest of the equipment. Nothing worked better for high-speed, mobile data transfers. "Thought it might come in handy. But don't just copy the Dulce folder. Copy it all."

He handed it to her and she plugged the small device in the computer's front side USB port. She went back to the display of the four folders, selected them all, and started the transfer. Ten gigabytes of information in ten minutes. Not bad. If they found nothing else, Miller would take the information back to the *George Washington* and have a team of people sift through it. He suspected Dulce was important and didn't want to stay in the Nazi stronghold any longer than he had to.

"You think that's what we came for?" she asked.

"We'll find out when we—" A horrible thought occurred to him. "Can you open the personnel file while that's transferring?"

She did. Three new folders appeared.

Current.

Deceased.

Stasis.

Miller's stomach churned. "Open the stasis folder."

Adler's shoulders shrunk in. She'd figured out what had him concerned. "You don't really think?"

"Just open it."

Inside the folder was a single file. She opened it.

A long list of names, in no discernible order, opened on the left side of the screen. As she scrolled through the names using the arrow keys, a photo and profile for each person opened on the right side of the screen. Images and text flashed past.

"Stop!" Miller said. He moved her hand away from the keyboard and hit the Up key three times. A face he'd hoped to never see again appeared on the screen. *It's true,* he thought. *Vesely is right.*

He scanned the man's profile. Ulbrecht Busch. Born in 1921. Member of the Schutzstaffel—Germany's elite SS. He served in World War II under a man named—

"Mazuw," Adler said. She'd seen the name, too.

Miller nodded, "I'm willing to bet most of the men in this database served under him, perhaps were handpicked by him."

"You recognized him?"

"I killed him," Miller said. "In Miami."

He scrolled through the names again. Images of grim men flashed on the screen, but his eyes were on the names. The first name he recognized sent a chill through his body.

Hans Kammler—the man who'd overseen the building of extermination camps and many of the Reich's more exotic weapons, including the Bell.

A second name caught his attention as it quickly scrolled past and made his knees nearly give out.

Before he could think about the discovery's ramifications or point it out to Adler, she said, "Stop!" and brushed his hand away. "The names on the left, highlighted in red. I think they're the men who have been revived already."

Miller scanned the list, looking for the name. It was colored mustard yellow.

That was good.

Above it, near the top of the screen, Kammler's name appeared in red.

Not so good.

Toward the end of the list, most of the names were in red. "Look," she said. "Rolf Bergmann."

The name from the cryogenic chamber. It seemed Adler's assumption was correct. She scanned through the red names slowly. A face appeared that they both recognized.

"The asshole from Huber's," Miller said. "Who wanted to marry you."

Not wanting to look at his face any longer, Adler tapped the Down arrow and immediately felt far more violated by what she saw than when the large Nazi manhandled her at Huber's cabin.

Miller let out a drawn-out, whispered "Fuuuck."

While he and Adler once again both recognized the face, the name—Lance Eichmann—didn't make sense. They knew him by a different name.

"I don't look bad for ninety years old," Brodeur said from behind them. The Southern accent was gone, replaced by a thick German zing. He punctuated the statement by chambering the first round of his assault rifle. The message was clear: if they moved, they were dead.

Miller turned around slowly, fire burning him from the inside out.

Roger Brodeur was Lance Eichmann.

A Nazi.

46.

"You didn't bypass the outer door," Miller said. "You knew the code."

Brodeur grinned and shrugged. "I may have exaggerated my skills."

Miller fought back visions of tearing Brodeur's head from his body. Losing his cool now would be a mistake and would likely result in him and Adler lying in a pool of their own blood. Of course, that seemed the most likely scenario, anyway, but no need to rush things. He really only had one hope left. The Cowboy. "Where is Vesely? Did you kill him?"

"The clown is alive. Wandering the hallways in search of little green men. Bringing him was a mistake, Miller. The man's not a soldier. Doesn't follow orders. Of course, if he'd listened to you and followed me, he would be dead. Darwin was wrong, sometimes the stupidest of us survives." Brodeur grinned like a demon. "Though not for much longer."

"Is that what you're doing now?" Miller asked. "Following orders?"

"Right now, I'm improvising." Brodeur adjusted his aim from Miller to Adler and then back to Miller. "I was tasked with following you and reporting everything you discovered."

"To monitor what the president knew," Miller guessed.

He nodded. "I've become quite good at intelligence gathering."

"How is this possible?" Adler asked. "You're an FBI agent."

Miller realized Adler could easily put the pieces together herself. She was stalling for time as the data transfer progress bar scrolled across the bottom of the computer screen behind them. But then what? Did she think he had a plan? Because aside from being Superman or the Flash, there was no way he could cover the distance between himself and Brodeur without being cut down.

"I was brought back in 2000. My first year included painful physical therapy. But I regained my former strength, and then surpassed it. For a year I studied modern American culture—learning about all of the silly ways you waste your lives. I perfected my Southern accent and then, in the wake of nine-eleven, when the military and law enforcement agencies began recruiting for the War on Terror, I was inserted into the United States with a complete history—passport, driver's license, medical history, diplomas, everything I needed to join the FBI. I have enjoyed rapid promotion since." He smiled. "I will be an Obergruppenführer in the SecondWorld."

"But you almost died," Adler said. "Several times."

"A cause not worth dying for is a cause not worth following," Brodeur said. "While I am thankful I will survive to witness the new world's arrival, I would have gladly given my life, along with yours, to stop your progress."

"Why not kill us yourself?" Miller asked.

"I considered it," Brodeur replied. "On many occasions. But I could not risk exposing myself, and my superiors, if you survived the attempt. Better to die with you."

Miller could feel the muscles of his back knotting. He understood how the president must have felt when he learned about the vice president's involvement. "My apartment. Huber's lake house. The attack on Air Force One. The police in Poland. Those were all you?"

"I cannot take credit for the lake house, but the rest . . ."

The man just couldn't keep himself from grinning. He took a small phone from his pocket. "You have your phone. I have mine."

All of this was disturbing news, but a realization began forming in Miller's mind. "Huber was already on the hit list?" Miller asked.

"He was."

"But you wouldn't send six men to kill an old man. The Germans. The men like you—"

Brodeur's smile faded slightly. He gripped the MP5 tighter. "Were friends of mine."

"They were there for Huber. But the other four. They were there for us."

Brodeur said nothing, waiting for Miller to figure it out.

"And you didn't know where we were."

"Not at all," Brodeur confirmed.

"No . . ." Miller's thoughts came clear. "Fred Murdock." His friend. His boss. Who he'd worked with and fought alongside for years.

Brodeur laughed. "He detests you. Has spoken of you on several occasions. The half-Jew mongrel. Firewood for the oven."

Miller took half a step forward wondering how many rounds he could take and still break Brodeur's neck. Adler's hand on his wrist stopped him from moving.

"You shame Germany," Adler said, her voice seething spite.

Brodeur's eyes zeroed in on Adler's hand gripping Miller's. His nose twitched with disgust. "It is not *I* who have betrayed his heritage. Yours surrounds you even now. All of this was made possible by your grandparents. How proud they would have been to see this. How pleased they would be to know you lived to see SecondWorld."

"I would rather die here," Adler said.

"I'm afraid I cannot allow that. You will be coming with me."

What is it with these guys and Adler? Miller wondered. But quickly realized the truth. The Nazis were all about

purity—good breeding. Genetics. Adler's grandparents
were Elizabeth Adler and Walther Gerlach. Genius-level genetics. And given Adler's pure white skin and bright blue
eyes it seemed clear that her mother's last name wasn't
Hernandez. She was a prize to these men in a world where
many once "pure" bloodlines had been mixed as skin tone
became less of a problem and more of an attraction. And
he knew from his time with the NCIS that the majority of
white supremacists in the United States were undereduc-
cated, and mostly men. The willing and available women in
SecondWorld might not meet the stringent standards of the
thawed-out Nazis, but Adler . . . she was—Miller looked at
her—stunning, intelligent, and pure-blood German. A wife
like that didn't have to be willing.

Miller pulled Adler behind him. It was a useless gesture.
Brodeur could shoot him where he stood. But if he was
about to die, and she could make it out alive, then there was
still hope—as long as she thought to take the thumb drive
from the computer while Brodeur couldn't see her.

"Please," Brodeur said, looking at Miller. "Stand to the
side. You don't want her harmed as much as I."

The man was right. Miller steeled himself for pain and
death and—

"Hey, Survivor!" Vesely's voice was distant, and excited.
He had no idea what was happening in the control center,
and the surrounding equipment would keep him from seeing
Brodeur's MP5 leveled at Miller's chest. But his appearance
unnerved Brodeur and kept him from pulling the trigger. At
least for the moment.

"I found a UFO, Survivor. You need to see for yourself!"

Miller looked over his shoulder. Vesely stood one hundred feet away between two of the cryogenic chambers. If
Brodeur took a shot and missed, Vesely would have plenty
of cover and an MP5 to defend himself with, not to mention
the two .38 Supers still strapped to his hips. Brodeur had
seen the man's speed and aim. His first shot had to be a kill.

"Tell him to come closer," Brodeur said.

"I can't hear you, Cowboy," Miller said. "Come closer."

"Have you found something interesting?" Vesely asked, stepping toward them.

"Come take a gander for yourself," Brodeur said, his German accent replaced by the Texas drawl.

"A gander," Vesely repeated with a smile as he walked toward them. "This Texas accent never gets old. Like old Westerns, you know, Survivor?"

Was Vesely trying to tell him something?

"No offense, Survivor, but I think sometimes you would be better off if you were more like John Wayne."

He was definitely trying to tell him something. John Wayne. How could being more like John Wayne help him? The man played gunslingers, but was actually a slow draw. What else was there? The only other thing he knew about Wayne was that the doors on his movie sets were made in miniature to make him look bigger. *Because he was short!*

Miller ducked.

Brodeur adjusted his aim toward Vesely.

Three shots rang out.

A shout of pain followed.

Miller recognized the voice as his own.

47.

Lancing pain came next.

Miller recognized the burn in his left arm. Brodeur had pulled the trigger a moment before clearing Miller's body. Two shots left the barrel of the assault rifle. The first struck Miller. The second headed toward Vesely.

But the third round Miller heard fired still echoed in the massive chamber. Cowboy's .38 Super. He had gotten off a shot.

Miller rolled over and pushed himself up. He saw his MP5 lying a few feet away and reached for it.

"Don't move!" Brodeur shouted.

Miller stopped mid-reach and looked up.

Brodeur stood near the exit of the octagonal control center. He held Adler by the hair and had his assault rifle pressed against her back. With most of his body concealed behind Adler, not even Vesely could get a clean shot.

"If you come after me, I'll kill her," Brodeur said.

Miller wasn't sure exactly how valuable Adler was to him, but didn't want to put it to the test. He could do nothing but let her go. He stood and saw Vesely, unharmed and .38 raised toward Brodeur.

"I can hit him," Vesely said quietly.

"Hold your fire," Miller commanded.

"But—"

"Cowboy. Do *not* take the shot."

His eyes were locked on Adler's. He saw sadness for a moment, but it was replaced quickly by determination. She opened her hand and let the flash drive slide out. She struggled for a moment, concealing the noise the small device made when it hit the floor.

Then he watched them go. But not toward the exit. Brodeur dragged her in the direction Vesely had come from.

"He's taking her to the flying craft," Vesely said. "To the UFO."

Miller stood still, waiting for Brodeur to lose sight of him before picking up the flash drive. If the man suspected Adler's defiance he might kill her out of spite. Adler remained silent, keeping her eyes locked on Miller until she was dragged around a corner.

Miller dove to the floor and scooped up the flash drive.

When he stood back up, pain radiated from his arm and through his body. A droning buzz filled his ears. He thought for a moment that he might pass out, but the pain became manageable. The buzzing, however, grew louder.

He ignored it and headed after Brodeur.

"Survivor!" Vesely called.

Miller ignored him.

Vesely took Miller's arm—his injured left arm—and turned him around. Miller shouted in pain and yanked away. "I'm not letting him leave with her."

"You must," Vesely said, his eyes pinched with fear.

The well-trained soldier in Miller knew he was right. They had the flash drive. The answers to questions that might save the world were literally in the palm of his hand. But another part of him, the same part that charged into a missile strike to save a girl he did not know, the same part of him that dragged a little girl out of Miami, couldn't stand for it. "I can't."

This time when he pulled away, Vesely gripped his wound, sapping his strength, and pulled him back. Before

Miller could protest, Vesely shouted, "There is no time! Listen!"

As soon as Vesely's words sank in, Miller heard the buzzing again. "It sounds like a beehive."

"The Beehive! It was code name for Bell!" Vesely pointed up. A dull white glow pulsed at the base of the bell device attached to the ceiling. "The Bell sounded like angry bees when it was powered up! When it was charging field. Field that *melted* people!"

Miller's mind focused upon hearing the word "melted." He dashed to the computer and hit the three keys Adler had used to open the text window. It popped open just like before. He began typing the fork bomb code, but the loud buzzing sound distracted him. He couldn't remember the order of the symbols. He gave up and shouted, "Let's get the hell out of here!"

They left the control center and ran for the exit. They'd only gone a few steps when the buzzing suddenly intensified. A wave of nausea sent both men to the floor, but it passed quickly.

"The cryogenic chambers!" Vesely shouted. "They *must* be shielded from the Bell's effects."

They ran to the cryogenic chambers and yanked two of them open. Miller felt sure he was looking at the plush red interior of what would be his coffin, but then his skin began to burn and he didn't hesitate. He climbed into the cryogenic chamber, pressed himself into the man-shaped indentation. He reached out, took the door, and pulled it shut with a clang.

Darkness consumed him.

The buzzing disappeared.

He took a deep breath.

Relaxed.

And then screamed in agony.

A wave of energy passed through him.

It felt like his body was being torn apart.

He saw stars.

Tasted blood.

And then, nothing.

* * *

Hell feels cold.

It was Miller's first thought upon waking.

The last thing he remembered was Adler being taken away. And then what? Something had happened. Something bad.

He remembered . . . heat. And feeling sick. And buzzing.

Like bees.

Like a beehive.

The Bell.

His memory returned painfully. Adler was gone and he was stuck inside the Nazi base, trapped in a cryogenic tube.

But he hadn't melted.

And while that was the world's shittiest "bright side" ever, he *was* still alive.

He could move, though his muscles ached and his injured arm throbbed. He'd probably lost a good amount of blood already, which didn't help his spinning head. He couldn't hear the buzzing sound, but he remembered not being able to hear it after closing the hatch.

The only way to find out if he'd be melted upon opening the door was to open the door. He had no idea how long he'd been unconscious. Could have been thirty seconds. Could have been ten minutes.

Or longer.

The cold struck him again. He shivered.

That's when he remembered that he was in a functional cryogenic chamber.

Miller felt stiff as he reached out and pushed on the door. The metal stung his flesh. He pushed harder, waiting for the suction to give way. But the door held strong.

It can only be opened from the outside, he realized.

When Miller was ten, he was short and scrawny. While visiting his Italian cousins one Sunday, after they'd been to Mass and were feeling fully absolved of their sins, the two older boys took him into the garage. They'd found a row of lockers at the dump and brought it home. The lockers held bats, balls, hockey sticks, and, later that day, Miller. They locked him in and left him there, kicking and screaming, for thirty minutes. Ten years later Miller could look at the cousins and send them running, but that memory always stuck with him. It replayed in his mind now as he kicked and punched at the door.

"Hey!" Miller shouted, his voice echoing loud and close. "Vesely!"

He shouted until his voice grew hoarse.

He stopped pounding when his knuckles bled.

But he kept kicking. Hoping that Vesely would somehow get free.

Miller realized there might be a handle on the inside. He searched for it with his hands, but found nothing, and couldn't bend over to check below his waist.

He shouted in frustration and kicked the door again.

The door burst open.

Miller fell forward.

And was caught.

"Sir!" Hammaker shouted. "I have you."

Hammaker laid Miller on the hard stone floor. "Sir, what hap—"

"Vesely," Miller said through chattering teeth.

"Vesely did this?"

"N-no." Miller pointed to the cryogenic chamber Vesely had hidden in. "In-in there. Vesely."

Hammaker understood. He jumped up and yanked open the door. Vesely fell out, eyes closed. But was he unconscious, or dead? The kid laid him down next to Miller and checked for a pulse.

"He's alive," Hammaker said. "But his pulse is weak. We need to warm him up. Warm both of you up."

"The river," Miller said. "Take him-m to the-the river."

Hammaker nodded, shoved his hands under Vesely's arms, and lifted him up. "I'll come back for you."

As the kid dragged Vesely toward the large exit, Miller noticed he could barely see them. *It's dark,* he realized. The lights were all out. He could only see because Hammaker had left a large blue glow stick on the floor next to him. He looked back up at the kid and saw that he had a small flash-light clutched between his teeth.

Though his body revolted, Miller forced himself up. Holding on to the cryogenic chamber, Miller lifted the glow stick and looked at the control center. In the faint blue glow he could see that every portion of the control center that had been made of plastic had melted. A surge of panic gripped him. He dug into his pocket, found the small device, and pulled it out.

The flash drive appeared fine. But while Miller hadn't been melted, some of the Bell's effects had pierced the cryogenic chamber. There was no way to know if the data recovered from the computers remained intact.

Nausea slammed Miller as a violent shudder shook his body. Darkness loomed again.

"Sir!" Hammaker said as he approached. He took Miller's arm and threw it over his back. "Put your weight on me."

Miller held the flash drive up. He would have preferred to keep it, but knew it probably wouldn't survive a dip in the river. "Everything depends on this. Keep it safe."

Hammaker took the flash drive. "Yes, sir."

As darkness reduced his vision to pinpoints, Miller asked, "How long?"

"What?"

"How long have we—"

The kid understood and said, "I waited five hours, sir. Spent another hour looking for you."

Six hours.

Brodeur could be halfway around the world with Adler by now if he really did have access to a modern-day foo fighter. Miller was about to ask the kid to make sure he woke him up soon. The world didn't have time for him to be unconscious. But the darkness claimed him before he could open his mouth.

He woke just minutes later, screaming, as searing heat consumed his body.

48.

Miller thrashed as liquid fire enveloped him. The burn stung his skin like a thousand bees. His heart raced. Stabbing pains pierced his limbs. He fought to free himself, but a tight pressure on his shoulders held him down—*someone held him down*. He reached up to grab his attacker, but found his arms too weak.

"Stop fighting!" a voice said close to his ear. "The water only feels like it's burning because you're so cold."

The voice sounded familiar.

His vision cleared and he saw water. It bubbled from below.

Boiling!

He fought again, but this time the voice shouted at him. "Stop moving, sir! You need to warm up!"

Sir.

The word identified the voice.

Hammaker.

The kid.

Miller trusted the kid. Remembered being taken out of the cryogenic chamber. Dragged down the hallway, to the— Miller looked at the water. He sat in the river heated by geothermal vents.

As he relaxed and Hammaker loosened his grip, the burn

began to fade. The water still stung for sure. It *was* hot. But
he'd been in hotter Jacuzzis. He leaned his head back on
the soft, moss-covered shoreline and looked at Hammaker's
upside-down worried face. He was cast in blue, lit by the
glow stick. Night had fallen. "Where's Vesely?"

Hammaker tilted his head to the right. Miller followed
the motion, his head spinning as he moved, and found
Vesely lying in the water next to him, unconscious and un-
moving.

"He didn't wake up when you put him in?" Miller asked.

"Moaned," Hammaker replied. "But nothing since.
Think he'll be okay?"

"He's tough," Miller said. "Hey, kid—"

Hammaker looked him in the eyes.

"Nice work."

The kid smiled.

"Can't believe they made you a cook."

"Thank you, sir."

A strange euphoric feeling came over Miller as the heat
worked its way into his body, melting the tension away.
"You can stop calling me sir. I'm Survivor." He looked at
Vesely. "He's Cowboy. And now you're The Kid. I think
Cowboy will like it."

"The kid?"

"Capital T, capital K. And we'll write it with two Ds so it
looks cool."

Hammaker grinned, but his eyebrows still bent up in the
middle. "You need to rest."

"Uh-uh," Miller said, and tried to push himself up. "We
need to leave. Adler. She—"

Hammaker pushed Miller back down. "Your lips are still
blue. You need to get warm. Besides, it's nighttime and a
storm blew in. I'm a good pilot, but I can't fly in that."

Miller felt too tired to be angry. He blinked, but had to
force his eyes back open. "There isn't time. The red sky
is . . . We only have two days left. Just two—"

Miller's vision blurred as sleep claimed him once more.

* * *

He woke to the sound of voices.

The river still flowed around him like a wet electric blanket. His head rested on a mossy cushion. The scent of plants and something—coffee?

The smell of fresh brew sat him up.

"Survivor!" Vesely's voice was loud and cheerful. "You have cheated death once again."

Miller rolled over and pulled himself from the water. On shore, bathed in blue light, he found his clothes were missing. *Naked on Antarctica and not cold,* he thought, before wondering what happened to his clothes. Before he could ask, he saw a small fire burning next to the gorge wall. His clothes dangled from the rocks, drying.

Vesely, who was also naked, waved to him from his seat on the gorge floor. Hammaker sat next to him. Both were lit by a large rectangular light that blurred Miller's vision. He squinted, rubbed his eyes, and then saw the light for what it was—a laptop.

Hammaker noted Miller's attention. "I went back up to the helicopter after Vesely woke up. Got supplies and the laptop. The flash drive works fine."

"And it is treasure trove of information," Vesely added. "Come! See!"

The flash drive! Miller quickly joined them by the laptop, his nudity forgotten. He felt a chill for a moment as the water evaporated from his body, but the air at the bottom of the gorge felt tropical. His muscles ached as he sat down, but the pain was bearable. The throbbing in his arm was another matter. He grunted as he put weight on it. The wound had been bandaged.

"It's a clean shot through the side," Hammaker said.

"You dressed it?" Miller asked.

"After I sewed it," Vesely said. "I'm afraid your scar will be as ugly as mine." He patted his injured shoulder, which also had a new dressing.

Miller flexed his hand. The pain was immediate, but wouldn't incapacitate him. He knew morphine would help, but didn't want to dull his senses or reaction time. He'd need both in the coming days.

Days.

"How long was I out?"

"Four hours," Vesely replied. "I've been awake for an hour."

"He nearly killed me when he woke up," Hammaker said.

Vesely shrugged. "I was confused. Last I remember I am being frozen. I wake up in hot water."

Miller looked at the computer screen and saw a mass of open files. "What have you found?"

"A lot," Hammaker said. "And honestly, a few days ago I wouldn't have believed any of it. There are records going back to World War One. Science staff. Military. Engineers. Support staff."

"Not to mention traitors, spies, moles, and saboteurs," Vesely added.

Miller knew that it wouldn't be hard to weed out the majority of turncoats based on who had gone AWOL shortly after the attacks on Miami and Tokyo, but hard proof was always a good thing to have. And there were obviously a good number of traitors still embedded in the actively deployed military. They would need to be exposed and dealt with as well. But not right now.

Vesely read his mind. "But that's not important right now. I think I figured out where they went."

Miller remembered. "Dulce."

"How did you know!" Vesely said, his thunder stolen.

"I'm an investigator," Miller said. "I investigated. Before Brodeur tried to kill us."

"Have you been there?" Vesely asked.

Miller shook his head. "I've only heard of it once."

"Is in New Mexico. Little is known about base, and government denies it exists. In 1997, Dulce Papers were released. There was video. And photos. And supposed quotes from guards about internal layout and alien breeding chambers. Tall tubes. Metal. One guard spoke of pale, skinny being removed and placed in tube of hot wat—"

Vesely and Miller looked at each other and then to the river of hot water.

"He saw a cryogenically frozen Nazi," Miller said. "Being thawed."

The revelation further solidified Miller's opinion that Dulce was the place to go.

"Dulce is underground base. Some say tunnels from base stretch far away. Some say across continent. But most believe a tunnel—a high-speed rail—goes to Los Alamos."

"The laboratory?" Hammaker asked.

Vesely nodded. "If they can become directors of NASA, why not national laboratory? If Kammler wanted a modern think tank there is no better place to start."

Miller stood, walked to his clothes, and picked up his underwear. Warm and dry. He slipped them on. "So what's our move? Infiltrate Los Alamos and search for the rail? Or go straight to Dulce and kick in the front door?"

Hammaker raised his hand. "Do I get a say, since I got a code name?"

"He gave you a code name?" Vesely said.

"The Kidd," Hammaker said. "Two Ds."

"Like Billy the Kid," Vesely said. "I like."

"I knew you would," Miller said, and turned to Hammaker. "What are you thinking?"

"Kick in the front door," The Kidd said. "Kill every Nazi son of a bitch you find."

Miller grinned as he pulled his black pants up and cinched the belt tight. "That's exactly what I was thinking." He put his shirt on next. "But the only way that's going to happen is if we leave. Now."

Vesely stood and began dressing.

"That's not possible." Hammaker looked from Vesely to Miller. "There's hundred-mile-per-hour gusts up there. Blinding snow. Twenty feet visibility if we're lucky. And it's night. Going to be for like eight more hours."

"We don't have eight hours," Miller said. "We've been here too long already."

"But—"

"Kidd, impossible sums up my entire week. I survived Miami, two hit squads, a rogue F-22, a traitor, *and* I was almost melted alive. There is no way I'm going to let a little wind and snow stop me now. I know you weren't looking to take risks when you enlisted, but you did enlist, you're here, and if you want to keep that code name, you better grow a set of balls right this second and say you're going to fly us out of here."

Hammaker looked on the verge of panic, but dug down deep, set his serious eyes on Miller's, and said, "On one condition."

"What?"

"I want in," he said. "On all of it. Dulce. Los Alamos. Whatever. I want in."

Miller nodded, slung his MP5 over his shoulder, and took the flash drive out of the laptop. "You got it."

Ten minutes later, after leaving the gorge and entering the below-freezing Antarctic storm, both men reconsidered the wisdom of their decisions. But there was no turning back. The white flakes that shot through the nighttime air and stung the skin like angry wasps were nothing compared to the red flakes that would soon envelop the planet.

49.

The big helicopter lurched to the right just ten feet above the Antarctic landing pad. Miller couldn't see the ground—the nighttime sky and blanket of snow blinded him—but his stomach and the helicopter's altitude indicator twisted in tandem. If they rolled much further, the rotor blades might strike the ice and their flight would be one of the shortest in the history of avionics.

Several warning indicators flashed. Alarms sounded. Miller wanted to slap the helicopter. Tell it to stop screaming like a little girl. But all he could do was hang on and trust The Kidd.

Hammaker fought the storm for control of the aircraft. While they were still far from vertical, the altimeter showed them rising slowly. At an angle.

Miller searched his memory. What had the surroundings looked like? They were surrounded by flat ice, but there had been mountains inland, to the east. He found the compass. They were facing north, but moving west.

As they continued to rise, the helicopter's roll leveled out. Hammaker turned to Miller. "Sorry about that. Wind was intense."

"That Katabatics," Vesely said from the back. "Luckily they flow out to sea, which is where we want to go."

"We'll make it to sea," Hammaker said. "But landing

on the *George Washington* in this mess is going to be a trick."

The chopper shuddered and dropped fifty feet.

"Storm is reminding us who is in control," Vesely said.

A gust struck the chopper's side, rolling them to the left. Miller sensed that if he could see, he'd be looking down at the ground through his window. The helicopter was close to tipping.

Either God heard someone's quickly-said prayer or Hammaker was the best damn closet-pilot in the navy, because the helicopter righted and all three men sighed with relief.

Miller looked at the GPS screen. They were headed in the general direction of the *George Washington,* but couldn't see beyond the helicopter's nose. He picked up the radio transmitter.

"*George Washington, George Washington,* this is Lieutenant Lincoln Miller. Do you read? Over."

There was a moment of silence and Miller opened his mouth to repeat his message, but then heard, "Miller, this is the *George Washington,* Ensign Partin speaking, reading you five by five. Are you all safe? Over."

"That remains to be seen," Miller said. "We are en route, over."

"Did you say you were on your way here?" For a moment, Miller waited for the man to say over, but the surprise in his voice marked a shift in the conversation from trained radio operators to normal conversation.

"We're a mile out and closing on your position," Miller said. "But we can't see anything. Do me a favor and light that boat up like it's the Fourth of July. Over."

Miller expected a statement of shock or outrage, but all Partin said was, "Copy that. Consider it done. Out."

For a moment he thought the change in the man's demeanor was strange, but then he remembered that the ship was missing the majority of its crew, and Partin might actually have to run around switching on the lights himself.

Two nerve-wracking minutes passed as the helicopter

pitched, rolled, and shook. Had the helicopter been a news chopper and not an aerial tank designed to handle extreme weather and machine-gun fire, they would have crashed long ago. That wasn't to diminish The Kidd's piloting abilities. He was better than he claimed. But the chopper was a beast.

"There she is!" Hammaker shouted.

Time seemed to pass more quickly as they closed the distance to the ship, but as soon as they descended over the *George Washington*'s deck, a new level of hell gripped the helicopter. The lower they flew, the stronger the wind became. The Katabatics rolled down Antarctica and spilled out over the ocean. That was normally bad enough, but the storm added power to the wind and turned the normally unidirectional force into an omnidirectional maelstrom. Giant waves, fifty to seventy-five feet tall, hammered the aircraft carrier. The massive vessel surged up and down, its decks repeatedly drenched with freezing seawater.

They could see the lights blazing on the deck, rising and falling with the waves, but there were no colorfully clad crew on deck to guide them down. No one was that stupid. They were on their own.

The helicopter spun as Hammaker guided it down. Sweat dripped down his forehead. "C'mon," he said to the helicopter. "C'mon!"

A gust of wind sent them flying to the side.

Miller saw the control tower come into view as they flew toward it, seconds away from becoming a bloody, oily smear on the metal wall. Then they tilted away. After leveling out again, Miller could see the deck just ten feet below.

"Almost there!" he shouted.

Then the deck fell away.

"Why are you pulling up?" he asked Hammaker.

"Not me," Hammaker said. "The ship's in a wave valley. I'm still descending."

Miller saw the deck lights rising to meet them.

Fast.

"Pull up!" Miller shouted, but he was too late. The giant deck of the aircraft carrier slammed into the bottom of the helicopter. Its legs folded and its belly struck hard.

The impact hammered the three men inside. Miller felt his head spin.

"You okay, Survivor?" Vesely shouted from the back.

He shook his head, shouted, "Yeah," and looked over at Hammaker. The Kidd was unconscious.

A blast of ocean foam struck the helicopter's windshield. When it cleared, Miller saw the *George Washington*'s deck. It was slick with snow, ice, and ocean water. The ocean lay beyond the deck, lit by the ship's array of exterior lights. And it was getting closer.

No, Miller thought. *We're getting closer!*

The aircraft carrier had entered another giant wave valley and pitched forward, its slippery deck acting like a slide—straight into the water.

Miller shouted as the ocean reached up to swallow them. "Oh shi—"

An impact shook the helicopter.

Water surged over them.

Miller's thoughts flashed back to his Navy SEAL training. Thirty months of the worst the military could legally put a man through. The infamous "Hell Week" alone included sitting in freezing water, endless running, miles of swimming, and pushed the human body to ten times the amount of exertion of which the average person was capable. He could overcome almost anything. A dip in the Antarctic Ocean on its own could kill a man   any man—in two minutes. But being sandwiched between giant waves and an aircraft carrier would mean a much quicker death. Granted, being crushed by the hull of an aircraft carrier would be a merciful ending as compared to freezing in the water, but Miller didn't like either option.

When the water fell away, Miller saw the ocean recede. The *George Washington* rose above the waves. The helicopter sat ten feet from the edge of the deck. Then fifteen. Then twenty. They were sliding back as the ship rose up the next wave.

Miller knew the ship would pitch forward again after cresting the wave and had no doubt the ocean would swallow the chopper whole when it did.

"Get ready to jump!" Miller shouted to Vesely.

The man already had the laptop, secured in its case, in one hand, and his other on the door handle. *He would have made a good SEAL,* Miller thought, and then turned his attention to Hammaker's unconscious form. The SEALs had a long tradition of teamwork. It was essential to everything they did. And as a result, they had never—not once—left a man behind, dead or alive. Miller wasn't about to let Hammaker be the first.

As the metal underbelly of the helicopter struck a clear portion of the deck, it screeched and came to a stop.

Miller heard the back door slide open. A burst of cold air filled the cabin with a violent swirl of snow. He leaned over to Hammaker and fought to unbuckle him. His sore arm and the weather slowed him. As the ship, and helicopter, pitched forward once again, Miller heard Vesely shouting his name like a distant foghorn. But he wouldn't leave Hammaker. He couldn't.

Then he remembered Adler. Captured.

And the rest of the world. Red flakes would soon fall from the sky and kill every last non-Nazi on the planet.

For a moment, he considered leaving Hammaker, measuring one life against billions. But then he thought of Arwen. She wouldn't leave the man. She'd die trying to save his life.

He pushed Hammaker forward, thrust his arms under the man's shoulders, and dragged him into the passenger's seat. The pain in his left arm was excruciating, but focused him on the task.

The helicopter skidded over the ice again, headed for the ocean.

Miller twisted the door handle, pushed hard with his

legs, and emerged from the door like a penguin leaping from the water.

He hit the deck hard. Hammaker landed on top of him, knocking out the little air left in Miller's lungs.

The helicopter, riding on a bed of smooth metal, slipped past them.

There was a crash.

The sting of freezing water covered Miller's body.

He heard shouting voices, but couldn't make out the words.

All of his effort went into one thing—holding on to Hammaker.

Even if it meant they would die together.

50.

Miller was back in the cryogenic chamber. Cold stabbed his body with icy talons, piercing his muscles and scraping his bones.

But his arms locked around Hammaker's body and never let go. Not when frigid salt water filled his mouth. Not when the stitches in his arm popped like over-tight guitar strings. Not even when he felt himself lifted up and dragged away.

When his senses returned he found himself on a stretcher covered in heated blankets, being carried through the delightfully warm hallways of the *George Washington*. He recovered from the cold more quickly than when he was in the actual cryogenic chamber, and realized that the burn of recovery lacked the intensity of his time in the heated river.

Exposure must not have been that long, he thought.

He looked for Vesely, somehow knowing the man would never leave his side. He found him following the pair of medics carrying the stretcher. "How long were we out there?"

The man smiled wide. "I told them you would not stay unconscious long."

The man carrying the stretcher confirmed it with a grin and a nod. "He did."

"More than once," said the other man.

They turned the corner and Vesely said, "You were hit by two waves. Nearly swept you off deck."

"Was it you?" Miller asked. "Did you pull us off the deck?"

"No," Vesely said. "Was them." He motioned to the men carrying the stretcher. Miller looked at them. Their faces were red from exposure to the elements.

"Thank you," he said to them.

"Just doing our jobs," said the man in the back.

Miller had never felt more proud of his navy service. Never mind the fact that a portion of the armed services had been infiltrated by the enemy, those that were true Americans never ceased to make him proud.

Like Hammaker.

Miller opened his mouth to ask about the man, when Vesely said, "Kidd is unconscious, but alive. Hit his head hard, they think. Getting X-rays. Will live, but will not be coming with us."

Probably for the better, Miller thought. The Kidd was brave as hell, a good pilot, and had earned his Vesely-style code name. But his inexperience in a down-and-dirty, no-holds-barred firefight could be a liability. It was always harder to kill people when you were worried about someone else's well-being. Vesely had no formal training— that Miller knew of—but had proven himself more than once.

"Did he just say 'coming with us'?" asked one of the men carrying the stretcher.

"He did," Miller said, sitting up. His head ached, as did most of his body, but he pushed through it. The motion caused the two men carrying the stretcher to stop. Miller spun his legs around and got to his feet. Veseley helped keep him up, but he stood on his own after a moment. He turned to the first man. "Find someone who will patch me up fast. Meet me on the bridge. Go."

The man nodded quickly, impressed and intimidated by Miller's show of strength, and then hurried off. Miller turned to the second man.

"How long is this storm supposed to last?"

The man nodded. "Four hours, tops."

"Any F-22s on board?" Miller asked.

"Yes, sir," the man replied. "Four of them."

"Find Ensign Partin. Tell him I need two F-22 Raptors and two F/A-18s fueled and ready to leave the second this storm lets up."

The man nodded and left.

Miller looked back to Vesely. "Go find our pilots. Bring them to me."

"Is fun to see you in action, Survivor," Vesely said with a grin, and then went in search of the pilots. Satisfied that the three men would follow his orders, Miller headed for the bridge, and when he got there, he cranked up the heat.

The storm let up three hours later, just as the black sky turned a dark hue of purple. The sun would rise slowly, peek over the horizon for a few hours, and then begin its slow descent. But Miller planned to be in an entirely different hemisphere by the time that happened.

His wounds had been expertly attended to. His body temperature had been brought back up. He'd received two IV fluid bags and a bag of blood to replace the amount he'd lost—it wasn't a dangerous amount thanks to Vesely's stitching, but his body would tire more quickly if it was fighting to restore his blood supply while he was in the field. The stitches were tight and dressed properly. He'd been given some heavy-hitting antibiotics to fight off any potential infections and took eight hundred milligrams of ibuprofen along with six hundred milligrams of acetaminophen for the pain. His stomach would be spared discomfort because he'd eaten a lot of food with the drugs, but his liver would be working overtime. He had the same dosage in his pocket and would take the drugs again before landing. But even with the high double dose, the pain would merely be dulled, and only for a few hours. After that, pain would consume his body.

After learning what Miller was up against, the medic had

given him a small vacuum-sealed preloaded syringe of morphine. "It might make you a little loopy," she'd said, "but it will keep you in the fight if the pain gets too bad."

To stay awake he'd been given a pack of caffeine gum, which the medic wouldn't normally recommend, given his condition, but knew he'd be going back into the fight with or without it, and she'd managed to talk him out of the strong caffeine pills. He'd burned through half of the gum already and cut himself off when the storm began slowing. He didn't want to be fidgety while sitting in the backseat of an F/A-18. He could chew the rest when they got nearer to their destination—which had been the subject of debate for the past hour.

Miller wanted to kick in the front door, guns blazing. But Vesely had put the kibosh on that idea. Dulce was an underground base, mostly likely designed to survive a nuclear assault. A direct hit might do them in, but short of that, the base could very well be locked up tight—at the ground level, which was little more than a group of faux buildings anyway.

Vesely believed Los Alamos and its fabled underground high-speed rail to be the best entry route. With both facilities likely under the enemy's control, he thought the rail would be up and running. They would go in quietly. Covert. No guns blazing. No doors kicked in. No trail of dead neo-Nazis. The plan did little to sate Miller's anger at being duped by Brodeur, the kidnapping of Adler, and the murders of millions of people. But he ultimately agreed.

Miller went over the plan in his head one more time while the F/A-18's canopy closed over him and the pilot. There was a lot of guesswork involved, despite the intel they'd gathered at the Antarctic base, but it was the best they could do. And since the skeleton crew of the *George Washington* had not yet discovered how their long-range communications were being jammed, they were on their own. An ex-Navy SEAL. A Czech conspiracy theorist/wanna-be cowboy. Two F/A-18s. Two F-22s. And four pilots. They were all that stood in the way of the rise of the Fourth Reich.

"Hey, Cowboy," Miller said into his headset. They'd be using code names from here on out. Vesely named the pilots White Horse, Red Horse, Black Horse, and Pale Horse after the Four Horsemen of the Apocalypse. The Pale Horse brought Death, and he sent his victims to Hades. Miller understood the analogy and appreciated it because the Pale Horse was his pilot, and it carried him. He was Death and had every intention of sending the men he killed to Hell.

"I'm here, Survivor," Vesely said. He was in another F/A-18 waiting for Miller's to take off.

"Just wanted to say I appreciate everything you've done," Miller said. "Thought I should say it now in case one or both of us die."

He heard Vesely laugh for a moment. "Two things, Survivor. One, you need to work on motivational speeches. Watch locker room speech from *Any Given Sunday.* Will help. Two, you are *Death* now. Riding on Pale Horse. Leave emotions on boat. It does not matter if I die. Only thing that matters is that our enemies die. That we stop the red sky. 'When Lamb opened fourth seal, I heard voice of fourth living creature say, "Come!" I looked, and there before me was pale horse! Its rider was named Death, and Hades was following close behind him. They were given power over fourth of earth to kill by sword, famine, and plague, and by wild beasts of the earth.' *We* are wild beasts, Survivor. We are sword. Plague. Is time to slay our enemies."

Miller grinned, gave his pilot's helmet a tap, and said, "You heard the man, Pale Horse; is time to go."

Engines roared. Adrenaline pumped into Miller's body as the F/A-18 rocketed across the *George Washington*'s deck. G-forces pinned him to his seat as they tilted up toward the now blue sky and accelerated toward Mach 1.8. He heard Vesely cheer as his F/A-18 followed close behind. A moment later, the two F-22s followed.

The Four Horsemen of the Apocalypse were airborne.

SECONDWORLD
War

51.

Despite the distance from the *George Washington* to United States airspace over southern Texas being a 6,600-mile, five-and-a-half-hour flight, there was no time to rest. While Miller and Vesely discussed various aspects of their not-so-perfect plan, the pilots arranged for refueling flights en route. Miller kept expecting to be attacked as they reached out to every air base on the way, but they were left alone. Perhaps they flew unhindered because two F/A-18 Hornets and two F-22 Raptors would be a losing fight for anyone not flying similar aircraft, but Miller didn't think so. With Huber's five-day time limit just twenty-four hours away, the remaining Nazi elements embedded in the military would be seeking shelter.

They passed over Texas in what felt like just minutes, the whole state sliding beneath them as a beige blur. Three hundred miles from their target, the two F/A-18 Hornets reduced speed and dropped down to one hundred feet, hugging the ground. While it would be hard to escape any radar systems protecting Los Alamos forever, they could get lost in the ground clutter—buildings, trees, hills, and mountains—for as long as possible. The two F-22s, with their transponders switched off, were invisible to detection and remained at a higher altitude.

As Pale Horse guided the jet across the terrain, Miller

took the second megadose of ibuprofen and acetaminophen. His immobilized body had grown stiff, and would
ache like a bastard when he started moving again. Even more
when the fighting started. He followed the pain relievers
with six sticks of caffeine gum. The stimulant would wake
him up, but also rush the pain medication into his system. It
was far from a perfect solution—like duct tape on a submarine leak—but if it kept him going for the next few hours, it
might be enough.

"Pale Horse, this is Red Horse. Over."

"I read you, Red Horse. Over."

"Are you guys seeing this?"

Miller heard a tinge of nervousness in the man's voice.
Red Horse, whose real name Miller never learned, struck
him as the strong, silent type. Followed orders. Flew with
precision. And was absolutely deadly behind the controls of
the world's most sophisticated fighter jet.

So what's making him afraid? Miller wondered.

Tick.

The sound was barely audible.

But it repeated.

Tick.

Tick, tick, tick.

Miller looked out the window. The ground flew past in a
blur of desert sand, trees, cacti, and boulders. They followed
the twists and turns of a dry riverbed, allowing them to
travel well under the radar. Everything was a blur, though.

Tick, tick, tick.

He looked up, wondering if he might see the F-22s, but
saw nothing.

Or did he?

As his eyes adjusted to the distance, his view of the deep
blue—almost purple—New Mexico sky appeared hazy.

Static-filled.

"Survivor," came Vesely's voice. "I think Huber's predic-
tion was off by a day."

Tcktcktcktcktck.

Miller gaped in silence as his mind struggled to comprehend the unthinkable. The sky was filled with red flakes. Oxidized iron. The process of purging oxygen from the Earth's lower atmosphere had begun. Their twenty-four-hour window had just been reduced to hours. It would take time for all of the oxygen to be used up, though many people would be poisoned beyond recovery long before that. If they didn't find a way to stop the cosmic attack in the next few hours, it would already be too late.

The red flakes triggered several memories for Miller. Surfacing at the Aquarius life support buoy and taking his first breath of blood-flavored, oxygenless air. The tiger shark. The pink-covered streets of Key Largo. Miami. Arwen. The gang. It all felt like a lifetime ago. So much had happened in the past few days.

Another memory came back, slapping him out of his reverie. He'd told the president, "If you haven't heard from me, and red flakes start falling from the sky, track my phone's location and drop a nuke on it." That time had come.

Hopefully the president would realize that his current Mach 1 speed meant he was still fighting and would delay a strike for as long as possible, but he couldn't bank on it. He'd tried calling the president several times already, but never found a signal. He wasn't sure he'd find one in the middle of New Mexico, either, but had to try.

"Any cities ahead?" Miller asked Pale Horse.

"Passing by Santa Fe in a few minutes. We'll reach the LZ ten minutes after that."

"Are you there, Survivor?" Vesely asked.

Miller held the phone up, watching for a bar to appear. "Going to make a phone call. See if we can avoid being nuked for a few more hours."

"Is good idea," Vesely said.

A bar appeared. Then two. Then three. Miller knew they would leave the cell tower's range just as quick as they'd entered it. He hit the Call button, heard just a single ring, and then—*shit*—voicemail.

Are you serious? Miller thought, but then realized the president was most likely already underground.

Beep.

"Bensson, it's Miller. If you get this, hold off on that nuke for as long as you can. In case I don't make it there, the target is Dulce Base in New Mexico. That's the stronghold. That's where I'm headed. If you can, get a message to Arwen for me. Tell her—"

Beep, beep, beep.

Signal lost.

Miller was about to let loose with a string of curses, but Red Horse interrupted.

"We have incoming. Six bandits—F-16 Falcons. Closing fast from the north. ETA five minutes."

Five minutes. They would be intercepted before reaching Los Alamos. If they could survive the next ten, the plan might still work, but being shot down over the New Mexico desert would put a rather large wrinkle in things.

"Can we outrun them?" Miller asked.

"F-16 is light and fast. Our top speed is Mach one point eight. Falcon is Mach two."

"Do we have any advantage?" Miller asked.

"Just one," Pale Horse replied. "Better pilots."

"Don't forget us," said Black Horse, the second F-22 Raptor pilot.

"Yeah, yeah," Pale Horse said. "White Horse, stay on my six. Let's cut the grass and hit the gas."

"Copy that," White Horse said.

The ease with which the four pilots coordinated made Miller relax. They had the element of surprise with two F-22s, and their goal was only seven minutes out now. All they had to do was make it there. What happened to the planes after that didn't matter.

Miller felt the anti-G suit he wore expand on his body as the jet rocketed toward a violent encounter. Bladders within the suit expanded as the G-forces increased, keeping his blood from rushing away from his brain. Without it, he and the pilot would have fallen unconscious.

They were so close to the ground now that Miller felt sure they'd be leaving trails of kicked-up dust behind them.

"I have visual," Black Horse said. "Coming your way. Over."

"They're not locking missiles?" Miller said.

"They'll swing around behind us for a better lock. Head on, this close to the ground, it's nearly impossible to get a— Holy shit!"

Miller's world spun upside down and righted itself so quickly he wasn't sure what had happened, but he'd swallowed his gum. He had a brief memory of seeing another plane, headed in the opposite direction, but nothing more.

"Sons a bitches tried to ram us!" Pale Horse said. "White Horse, you still with us? Over."

"On your six," White Horse said. "Black Horse, would you mind showing these kamikaze assholes how to fight? Over."

"Shit!" It was Red Horse. "Bogey on our six! Black Horse is down! Black Horse is down! Missile lock! Deploying countermeasures!"

Static.

"How did they take down an F-22?" Miller asked, fighting his rising fears.

"Snuck up behind him."

"What can sneak up on an F-22?"

"Another F-22."

"White Horse, this is Pale Horse. Open it up. Let's give 'em a run for their money."

"Copy that," White Horse said.

Miller's anti-G suit grew tighter as Pale Horse pushed the F/A-18 to its top speed, just fifty feet from the ground.

"We'll be there in four minutes," Pale Horse said to Miller. "Be ready."

A loud beeping filled the cabin.

"Missile lock," Pale Horse said. "Here we go."

Miller was expecting a rapid turn or ascent, but when Pale Horse pointed the plane down, just fifty feet from the ground, Miller knew he had half a second before being pancaked on the New Mexico desert.

52.

A valley opened up in front of the Hornet and swallowed it whole. Stone walls flashed past on either side. Pale Horse guided the plane through the wide twists and turns at ridiculous speeds.

An explosion from behind shook the plane.

Vesely.

"You still with us, Cowboy?" Miller said.

Vesely's reply was shouted, but not with fear, with excitement. "Is like *Star Wars* Death Star trench run!"

"The explosion was one of the bandits," White Horse said, his voice cool and collected. "Clipped the top of the valley trying to follow us in."

A sharp turn squeezed Miller's body as the anti-G-suit bladders expanded. He looked to the left and saw the valley floor not far below. The plane righted and Miller's head spun. Anti-G suit or not, this flight was taking a toll on his body. The military's ground forces, including the SEALs, tended to give pilots a hard time. Had all sorts of unsavory names for them. The impression was that they flew above all the action, all the danger, but Miller realized that wasn't necessarily true. This was intense on the body and mind in a way he hadn't experienced before.

An explosion rocked the valley wall ahead of them. Boulders and debris shot out.

The anti-G suit nearly crushed him this time as Pale Horse hit the brakes. White Horse pulled up and roared over them, spinning as he cleared the falling debris. The maneuver was an act of aerial acrobatics that looked well rehearsed, but Miller knew had more to do with training. Pale Horse pulled up over the debris, and then punched forward again, closing the distance between the two planes.

With White Horse in the lead, Miller could see just how close they were coming to the valley walls. As a child, Miller often closed his eyes at scary movies and a part of him wanted to do that now. But if he were going to die, it would be with his eyes open.

He looked to the side and saw the top of the valley wall. "We're going up?"

"Valley ends up ahead," Pale Horse said. "We're going to be exposed for about thirty seconds before entering the next valley that will take us to the DZ."

The DZ was the drop zone, and "drop" was a nice word for what they were going to attempt.

As soon as they left the valley behind, warning lights flashed and alarms blared.

"Missile lock," Pale Horse said. "Hold on to you   "

The alarms went silent.

"I got your backs, boys!" Red Horse shouted. "Just needed to swat a fly first."

"Glad to hear it," White Horse said from the lead plane.

"You still have four bandits on your six. Over."

"Keep them occupied for another minute," Pale Horse said. "Then bug out. Over."

"What?" Miller said.

"We can use them," Pale Horse said.

"Copy that," Red Horse said. "But if it's okay with you, I'm just going to hang back until you're on the ground and then shoot the shit out of them. Over."

"Sounds like a plan."

Miller saw White Horse dive into the ground and disappear from sight, so he was prepared for the motion, but the feeling of falling fast still unnerved him. He'd flown a lot.

Jumped out of planes. Off of buildings. Never mind experiencing aerial combat onboard Air Force One, but after this dogfight, he was going to swear off fighter jets.

They entered the valley moving slower than the last. With Red Horse making the bandits' life a misery of missile locks, they had less to worry about. That is, if you didn't count the narrow valley walls squeezing them on either side. Happily, this valley was nearly a straight shot toward the DZ.

"Thirty seconds," Pale Horse said.

Miller tensed. He knew what was coming. And he knew it would hurt.

A bridge appeared in the distance. He recognized the shape. Los Alamos National Laboratory lay on the left side of the gorge. The rest of the city to the right. The only way in was to cross what had been dubbed the Omega Bridge— a 106-foot tall, 422-foot long steel arch bridge that connected one side of Los Alamos Valley to the other.

The valley widened, exposing them to attack.

"Red Horse, let them off the leash," Pale Horse said. "Over."

"Copy that," Red Horse replied. "Good luck and happy hunting. Out."

Alarms sounded a moment later.

"Lock," Pale Horse said.

The bridge loomed ahead. It was empty.

"Missiles away."

Missiles. Plural. The enemy was unloading.

Warning beeps sounded. *Beep, beep, beep.*

"Here we go," Pale Horse said.

White Horse passed under the Omega Bridge a split second before Pale Horse followed.

Beepbeepbeepbeep.

Both planes pulled up.

Spun sideways.

And exploded.

Miller felt the heat of the explosion, but it lasted only a fraction of a second. He felt a pressure beyond anything he had experienced while flying in the plane. The anti-G suit tried to compensate, but Miller's vision began to fade. A split second before the missiles had struck the jets, Miller, Vesely, White Horse, and Pale Horse ejected. The rocket-propelled ejection seats launched from the cockpits like missiles, carrying them two hundred feet in the blink of an eye.

The twin explosions of the Hornets, along with several missiles striking and decimating the Omega Bridge, hid their escape from the bandits, which rocketed past a moment later.

The ejection seat jolted Miller hard as the parachute deployed. His vision returned in full a moment later. He saw the ground approaching fast. They'd ejected at an angle that launched the seats up and out of the valley. When the chutes deployed, they were only three hundred feet above the ground. Miller braced himself, but the impact didn't play out exactly how he expected. He slowed suddenly, and then swung in an arc before crashing into the side of the tree. The seat absorbed most of the impact, but his damaged body begged for mercy.

Miller waited for the seat to stop moving, clutched his gear, and unbuckled from the seat. He fell just a few feet, but his legs ached at the effort after being confined in the F/A-18 for six hours.

The roar of jets brought his eyes up to the sky, which had turned purple because of the falling red flakes. He saw two F-16s turning around in a wide arc. He had no doubt they'd do a flyby in search of survivors. But then both planes began flying erratically. A missile cut through the sky and turned one of the planes into a fireball.

Red Horse. The F-22 Raptor gave chase to the second, but was pursued by two more bandits. A missile launched. Small explosions burst behind Red Horse, then the F-22 rose at a sharp angle. The missile exploded well behind the jet, which continued up and over until righting itself behind all three bandits. More missiles fired.

A hand on Miller's shoulder spun him around.

He drew his sound-suppressed Sig Sauer P226 handgun and aimed it at Vesely's head.

Vesely grinned. "Not bad, Survivor. I feared you'd been injured."

Miller lowered the weapon. "Never better."

"White Horse did not make it," Vesely said. "Shrapnel from explosion. Where is Pale Horse?"

Pale Horse cleared his throat, bringing their eyes up. He was stuck in a tree, dangling six feet from the ground, but facedown. If he unbuckled he'd fall hard. Miller and Vesely braced the man. He unbuckled and they slowed his fall, both men grunting as the weight strained three stitched gunshot wounds.

Hidden in a stand of short pines, the three men peeled off their anti-G suits. Each wore black tactical suits with supply belts holding holstered handguns, extra ammo, and small, fifteen-minute pony bottles, just in case. Miller opened a case of disassembled weapons and quickly slapped them together, handing an UMP submachine gun to Vesely and Pale Horse. Each carried silenced handguns with spare ammo for both weapons.

Miller took a deep breath. His chest ached, but he didn't notice. His mind recoiled when the air tasted like blood. *Time to get inside,* he thought.

"Ready?" Miller asked.

Vesely opened a duffel bag Miller hadn't seen him bring. He nearly laughed when he saw the man's cowboy hat and twin .38s emerge. He strapped the weapons to his waist and donned the Stetson.

"Now am ready."

They left the trees behind and walked out onto a large parking lot. A *full* parking lot. But there were no people in sight.

Los Alamos National Laboratory was comprised of more than fifty buildings, but one stood out from the rest. In fact, there was nothing like it for hundreds of miles. The seven-story, 275,000-square-foot National Security Sciences Building (NSSB) towered above everything else in the area. And its design was no less impressive. The building's all-glass front face curved like it had been cut away from a much larger circle. The sides of the building dropped down in a series of one-story steps where it merged with an all-glass square lobby area, a large circular auditorium, and a long stretch of terra-cotta wall that contrasted nicely with the blue-tinted windows covering the rest of the building.

While he and Vesely had never been to the NSSB before, the building had been constructed in 2005, which was when the rumors of the underground rail began to surface from workers who'd been hastily laid off. No one ever investigated their claims. *Until today,* Miller thought.

He started through the parking lot, weaving his way through the endless sea of vehicles. The first cars to arrive had parked in the designated spaces, but as more and more cars and trucks arrived, the vehicles parked in the roads between the rows of early birds. The vehicles slowed their approach, but the organized parking job created long alleys through which to move.

Halfway to the National Security Sciences Building a shrill buzzer sounded and froze the trio in their tracks.

"Sounds like a halftime basketball buzzer," Pale Horse said.

Miller shushed the man and listened. A distinctive whirring sound reached his ears. It approached from the right. Pale Horse was right in a sense, the game *was* changing. Miller was about to order the men to run when the thing shot into the thin, car-lined alley.

"Faster than Antarctic variety," Vesely said as they all stared at the now-motionless robotic weapon. It looked essentially the same as the robo-Bettys they'd encountered before, but instead of a flat disk at the center, it was a semicircle. The thing looked like a bona fide UFO on wheels.

"What's it doing?" Pale Horse asked.

"Nothing good," Miller said. "Time to go."

As Miller turned to run the other direction, a second robot rolled to a stop, thirty feet in front of him. These things were being coordinated. But by whom? Or what? "We're boxed in!"

The two robo-Bettys zipped toward them in unison.

"Over the cars!" Miller shouted. The three men leapt over the nearest vehicles—a new compact car and an old pickup.

The whirring grew closer still. The robo-Bettys could drive beneath the vehicles! Miller jumped from the hood of the compact car onto the back of a big black SUV, and threw himself on top. A moment later, the compact car exploded from beneath. The impact flung him onto the hood of the SUV, knocking the wind out of him.

The pickup truck exploded a moment later. Vesely, who had reached the front of the next car, was spared the majority of the impact. Pale Horse was sent flying and landed in the gap between vehicles.

Miller rolled off the hood and saw Vesely picking Pale Horse up. "Everyone okay?"

"Fine," Pale Horse said.

Vesely gave him a thumbs-up.

"They're not Bouncing Bettys anymore," Miller said.

"Too many hiding places," Vesely said. "Ineffective."

The problem was, the weapons had been adapted so that they could turn the vehicles into giant shrapnel bombs. If any of them had been closer to that car when it exploded, they would have been shredded. A second explosion made them all duck. "Gas tank!" Miller said.

They were surrounded by bombs, just waiting for a fuse. When he stood, Miller saw the pickup truck engulfed in flames. The blaze would soon spread to the surrounding cars, which could also explode.

The sound of several more approaching mobile bombs sent Miller into action. He climbed to the roof of the next car and searched the parking lot. The small things whizzed between and under cars as they converged toward the three men. "Stay on top of the cars, and don't stop moving!"

Miller led the charge. They needed to cover one hundred yards over the roofs of nearly fifty cars. What could have taken fourteen seconds on flat ground would take more than a minute leaping from roof to roof. The bombs closed the distance quickly. The first exploded a little prematurely, four cars behind Vesely, who brought up the rear. The red hatchback flipped into the air. The explosion stumbled Vesely, but didn't knock him over.

Miller glanced back to make sure the man was okay, but when he saw Vesely, the man was stabbing his finger ahead. Miller spun forward and found one of the robotic bombs tearing toward the Cadillac upon which he stood. There was no time to leap away, so he raised his sound-suppressed UMP, took aim, and squeezed off a tight three-round spread. The first two rounds found pavement. The third hit the red light dead on. The small engine fell silent and the vehicle rolled forward. It came to a stop against the wheel of the Caddy, and didn't explode.

A car behind Vesely exploded, and this time the impact sent him sailing. He crashed onto the roof of the next car. Pale Horse jumped back to help him up.

"Aim for the light!" Miller shouted. He wasn't sure what it was, but thought it was some kind of sensor, probably tracking body heat. And now that it was blind, the thing couldn't see him, and thus, didn't detonate when it came within range. It was his best guess, anyway.

As Vesely was pulled into a sitting position, he whipped out his pistol and squeezed off a single round. The bullet streaked past three cars, sailed past the red light sensor on the front, and struck the domed disk in the middle.

The explosion knocked Pale Horse and Vesely down. Though it was farther away, the force of the blast wasn't dulled by a vehicle. Miller ran back and yanked both men up. There were still five of the little bastards on the way.

"I said aim for the sensor," Miller said to Vesely.

Vesely shook his head, clearing it. "Aim can't be perfect every time."

"Thought you were gunslinger?" Miller said.

He took aim in the direction of a distant whir and fired twice. When Miller peeked around the man, he saw two disabled robo-bombs, fifty feet away.

Before Vesely could gloat, several more whirring engines grew louder. The sound came from the direction of the National Security Sciences Building. Miller realized the vehicles were approaching from beneath the cars. They'd only be visible for a fraction of a second as they passed through the open space between cars. "Go back!"

The trio jumped back over the next line of cars. As Miller slid over the hood of a black Corvette, he rolled onto the ground and quickly saw a single red light approaching in the shadow of a car just twenty feet away. He pulled the trigger four times before the red light winked out. It was replaced by two more, coming in fast.

Miller jumped up, scrambled over an old Chevy station wagon. He dove from the back of the wagon, sailing over the cab of a Ford F150. The station wagon exploded a moment later, its front end lifting off the ground. As Miller moved to the back of the F150, the wagon's gas tank exploded. The jolt knocked Miller from the back of the truck. He couldn't see the last of the robo-bombs through the smoke, but he could hear it closing in. He turned left and bolted down the alley between cars.

The robo-bomb entered the alley just seconds later and accelerated. Miller had just seconds before the thing slid up behind him and blew him to pieces. He fired several rounds over his shoulder as he ran, but none found the mark.

"Survivor!" Vesely shouted.

Miller turned forward. Vesely stood over the alley, each foot on a car to either side. He lifted his gun, aiming toward Miller's head.

Miller dove forward, rolling beneath Vesely as he pulled the trigger.

The loud report of the .38 Super drowned out the sound of the robo-bomb's engine, but Miller knew Vesely's aim had been true when the thing rolled to a stop against his leg.

Miller bent down to look at the robot and several things happened at once.

A breeze kicked up just over his head.

The car next to him imploded.

And he heard a very loud, rapid buzz that sounded an awful lot like a minigun.

53.

Contrary to how it sounds, the minigun is anything but small. The heavy machine gun's six rotating barrels can fire up to six thousand high-caliber rounds per minute. And judging by the sound of it, Miller thought that there were actually two miniguns firing in tandem. A glance at the ruined car confirmed it. Twin streaks of destroyed metal ran from back to front. If Miller hadn't ducked to look at the robot, he'd be missing the top half of his body.

"Down!" he shouted as he dove to the pavement and slid beneath a truck. Vesely dove beneath the truck with him. Miller searched the area for any small red lights and found Pale Horse beneath a vehicle two rows over.

A loud pulsating electric hum filled the air. It sounded like the Beehive, but crackled with energy. The hum grew louder, passing above them.

"Is Bell," Vesely whispered, pointing up.

The thing was airborne.

Movement to the side caught Miller's attention. He turned as Pale Horse rolled from one car to the next. The hum grew louder for a moment and then the two miniguns opened up on the pavement where Pale Horse had just been.

"Don't move!" Miller said.

While the little robo-bombs seemed to be attracted to

body heat, zeroing in on the source before exploding, whatever patrolled the air above them responded to motion.

While the thing wouldn't climb under the cars looking for them, they couldn't move.

Unless, Miller thought, *it can't see us.*

The air was already thick with red flakes and smoke from a number of burning vehicles, but the wind was blowing in the wrong direction. What they needed was a fire in the other direction.

Miller shifted back toward the alley.

"Survivor," Vesely whispered loudly. "What are you doing?"

But Miller didn't respond. The hum was off to the side and Miller didn't think the thing would have a good line of sight. At the edge of the vehicle, he peeked out and glanced at the now red sky. Nothing. He rolled out from beneath the truck, grabbed the robo-bomb, and rolled back. The maneuver took just two seconds, but had somehow attracted the sentinel's attention. It hummed loudly as it closed in.

Miller moved back under the truck and slid up next to Vesely. "I'm going to take this a few cars down and—"

"Give to me," Vesely said, reaching for the robot. "I build things. Electronics. Will start motor."

Miller let him take the device. The Cowboy seemed to understand his plan.

Using a knife, Vesely removed four screws from the bottom of the robot. He removed the black cover from the outer ring. The internal design was fairly straightforward, like an oddly shaped remote-control car. "Still functional," Vesely said. "Just lacks input to tell it 'move forward.'"

Vesely found the throttle and pushed it forward. The little wheels spun quickly as the engine whirred. He pushed the throttle all the way forward and pinned it in place using one of the free screws. The two men lay side by side, looking down a line of cars that stretched a hundred feet. Vesely lined the robo-bomb up as straight as possible.

Miller rolled to the back side of the truck. "Go!"

Vesely let the robot go and it zipped away, moving

quickly beneath the line of cars. The hum grew louder as the hovering sentinel tracked the robo-bomb's movement.

Miller rolled out from beneath the truck and got his first look at what was firing the miniguns. The black, vaguely bell-shaped craft hovered thirty feet above the parking lot. A bright light glowed at the bottom, flickering in time with the loud crackles. A minigun had been attached to either side. Miller was happy to see the weapons tracking the robo-bomb as it appeared and disappeared between each car it passed.

The guns opened fire, tearing into the line of cars as it chased the fast-moving robot.

Miller ran the other way.

Behind him, Miller heard what sounded like a war. The guns never stopped firing. Spent shell casings rained down from the craft, rattling against pavement and metal. There was a loud *whuff* as one, or more, of the vehicles ignited. And then, there was an explosion. Miller recognized the sound as the robo-bomb detonating. The sentinel had destroyed one of its own.

Miller stopped, bent down, grabbed what he needed, and sprinted back the way he came. The chaos that greeted him was far better than he'd hoped for. At least four cars were on fire and billowing thick black smoke into the air—smoke that was being pulled in his direction. In fact, his plan had worked so well that he could no longer see the minigun-wielding Bell. But he could hear it, hovering in the smoke, no doubt trying to make sense of its surroundings.

Miller reached the spot where Vesely lay hiding and continued past.

Smoke rolled over him and he held his breath. The hot grime stung his eyes, which began to tear. But he kept searching the haze for his enemy. He found the dull glow moving toward him just a moment later. He stopped, took aim at the light, and waited.

A gust of wind cleared the air around the Bell and Miller tossed his explosive payload like a discus player. The sightless, but still explosive robo-bomb sailed through the air.

Off target.

But Miller didn't need to strike the hovering Bell, he only needed it to see the robot. A moment later it did. As the disk-shaped bomb closed to within ten feet of the Bell, both miniguns opened fire.

Miller dove beneath a car.

The bomb exploded, sending a wave of hot air over Miller.

But there was no secondary explosion. Or the sound of the Bell falling from the sky. Just the hum of the thing. But the hum was different. Instead of pulsating, it was now intermittent. The sound began to fade.

Miller came out from hiding and watched the wounded machine come down at an angle. The bright light at its base flickered. Every time the light went out, the device lost altitude. A loud crash rolled over the parking lot as the Bell slammed into, and through, the front of the NSSB. Glass shattered and exploded inward.

Vesely and Pale Horse ran up to Miller.

"Holy geez," Pale Horse said. "What the hell was that?"

"Is Bell," Vesely said.

"Long story," Miller added, and ran toward the building. He wanted to be inside before any other automated security joined the party. They reached the ruined front end of the building. There was a wide hole where the Bell crashed through. "Open sesame," Miller said, and stepped inside.

The trio entered the large, open lobby one at a time, weapons at the ready. Only Miller had training with breaching and clearing a building, but Vesely and Pale Horse had apparently seen enough movies to be competent. Or they were just following Miller's lead as he swept his weapon back and forth, looking for targets. Convinced they were alone for the moment, Miller said, "Clear," and relaxed his stance.

The place looked like a tornado had moved through. The once chic lobby, decorated with tall, living plants and modern art sculptures, was coated in a layer of human detritus. Food wrappers, empty bottles, strewn papers, lost luggage, even a tipped-over moped. Not to mention a smoldering Bell. Miller steered clear of the Bell and worked his way toward the back of the lobby.

"Now what?" Vesely asked.

"Now," Miller said, pointing to a trail of trash leading down a hallway, "we follow the bread crumbs."

The trail of debris led to a now-abandoned security check point—metal detectors for people and luggage. A second security station held rows of computer monitors connected to what looked like rows of miniature centrifuges. There were several large red trash bins marked with biohazard symbols. Each and every one was overfull with used needles. "What the hell?" Miller whispered.

Vesely pointed to the centrifuges. "DNA testing. For purity."

"Unbelievable," Miller said before moving on.

The floor behind the security checks had been torn up. Shattered wood and ripped-up linoleum tiles sat stacked beyond the hole. Miller slid between the metal detectors in case they were still active, and approached the hole. A staircase shot straight down several stories.

"They've been walking right over it for years," Pale Horse said. "Where does it go?"

Vesely started down the stairs. "Down."

The three men took the stairs as quickly and quietly as they could. Nearing the bottom, they slowed. The stairs ended in what looked like a subway station straight out of Nazi Germany. Red, white, and black propaganda posters lined the walls, proclaiming the superiority of the Aryan race, the rise of the Fourth Reich, and the messianic return of the Führer.

Miller stopped at the bottom of the staircase. He heard voices. He couldn't risk looking without exposing himself, but he could hear two men. He leaned close to Vesely and Pale Horse and whispered, "Take me by the arms, like I'm injured. Drag me out. Lay on some more of that German." He placed his hands behind his back, clutching the silenced handgun.

The two men understood the plan and placed their arms under his, hoisting him up between them. Miller hung his head down and let his feet drag as the two men pulled him out into the secret terminal.

"Who the hell are you?" asked a man's voice.

"Help us," Pale Horse said. "He's been shot."

"Are you here for the last shuttle? It's the last one." This was a woman's voice.

"C'mon now," Pale Horse said. "There are *ten* of you."

Ten of them! Miller thought. *Shit.*

"Why do they have guns?" asked another woman.

"Ich werde verschlingen Ihre Kinder!" Vesely shouted.

"What did you say?" a man asked, but it sounded more like, "Vaht dis you say?" An honest-to-goodness German accent.

Busted.

He heard a weapon slide being racked, drew his silenced sidearm, aimed toward the sound, looked up, and fired twice. *Pft! Pft!*

A man in full World War II German regalia toppled to the floor, two neat finger-sized holes in his head.

Two more men dressed in blue security guard uniforms took aim, but were stumbling back from the action, caught off guard. Vesely and Pale Horse wasted no time drawing their weapons, but in the time it took Pale Horse to aim, Vesely had shot both men in the head with his UMP.

The nearly silent gunfight took three seconds and left seven petrified people in its wake. Judging by the similar facial features and variety of ages, Miller guessed this was a family. Three generations' worth.

A baby cried.

Four generations.

The mother of the baby, a pretty blonde who couldn't have been more than a few days over eighteen, said, "Please don't shoot us!"

The family huddled in a corner. The grandparents stood at the front, ready to take a bullet for their brood.

A part of Miller that sought blood for blood wanted to take the baby, gun the rest down, and be done with it. These people had no problem allowing the rest of the human race to be wiped out.

But he couldn't kill in cold blood. He saw an open door in the terminal's white tile wall. He motioned to the door with his gun. "Get in."

The family filed into the large storage closet.

"Please," said the young mother. "Don't leave us down here. The air—"

"If you don't want to die," Miller said through clenched teeth, "then you better start praying we can stop—"

The second oldest man—the baby's grandfather—spit in Miller's face and wound up to take a swing at him.

Miller punched the man in the gut, doubling him over, and then put him on the floor with a punch to the face. He wiped the spit off his cheek and said, "Lock them in."

Pale Horse held the door shut while Vesely wedged a chair under the handle.

Miller's heart thumped with anger. It took everything he had not to shoot that man. He walked toward the boarding ramp and heard an electric zap to his right. Light emerged from the tunnel first, followed by a sleek red subway car. The car was aerodynamic on both ends and the three sets of double doors were emblazoned with the SecondWorld symbol. It hovered over a pair of strange-looking tracks and was attached to a cable above it, that sparked as it moved. The car came to a stop and the doors opened. Miller saw the engineer glance over, looking for his fare, but instead finding three dead men.

The man's eyes popped open, registered Miller's approach. The doors began to shut, but Miller threw himself onto the car and shot the man twice in the back. Feeling no remorse for killing the man who was about to speed away with their ticket into Dulce, Miller dragged the body out of the train and laid it on the floor.

Miller stood over the four dead men. There was surprisingly little blood from the three shot in the head. The rounds had entered the skull, but not come out. Vesely and Pale Horse joined him.

"What are you doing?" Vesely asked, heading for the train. "We must go."

"Hold on," Miller said. "Let's change our clothes first."

Vesely looked down at the dead and gave a nod.

Five minutes later, they stood on the train. Vesely and Pale Horse were dressed as guards. He had debated with Vesely about him still wearing his cowboy hat and holstered .38s, but the man claimed victory after pointing out that they were in the southwest, where a Stetson combined with his perfected Southern drawl wouldn't stand out. "If anything," he claimed, "they will be admired."

Miller wore the German's uniform, which he realized after counting stars belonged to a general. He hoped the uniform's intimidation factor would keep people from inspecting his face too closely. It wouldn't help to have "the Survivor" recognized.

He sat down behind the controls, which were simple enough. Vesely and Pale Horse stood behind him. Miller looked back and said, "I think this thing has harnesses for a reason."

The two men looked at the side-facing rows of seats. Double-strap harnesses hung from each chair. The two men sat down and quickly buckled themselves.

"How fast can it go?" Pale Horse said, sounding doubtful. "It's a train."

Miller put his hand on the throttle. "We're about to find out."

He shoved the throttle all the way forward.

The train accelerated faster than any of the three thought possible. Faster than the F/A-18 Hornets. And without the anti-G suits keeping the blood in their heads, all three passed out and spent the first ten minutes of the twelve-minute, eighty-mile trip unconscious.

When Miller came to, it was to the sound of an alarm and a flashing display screen that read COLLISION WARNING.

Below that text was a distance counter, ticking down feet quickly. When he first saw it, the number was at five thousand feet—just under a mile. By the time he shook his head clear and looked again, it was down to two thousand feet.

Miller felt a rush of adrenaline surge into his body with the realization that he had only seconds to live.

54.

Miller yanked the throttle all the way back. The car slowed, but continued forward. The distance counter continued to roll.

Seven hundred feet.

Miller looked for the brake, but couldn't find it.

Five hundred feet.

Shit!

Three hundred feet.

The car suddenly dropped, struck the bottom of the magnetic track, and slid with an ear-piercing shriek.

One hundred and fifty feet.

The seat's harness dug into Miller's shoulder. His vision began to fade as the car rapidly slowed.

With a jolt, the pressure on his body eased. His vision returned. They'd stopped. To the right was a subway station nearly identical to the one they'd left—white tile walls and Nazi propaganda posters. If anyone staying here had any doubts upon entering, they'd be brainwashed by the time they left.

Miller unbuckled and turned around. Vesely sat frozen with his eyes wide. His hand was raised and clutching a metal cable. A sign above the cable read EMERGENCY BRAKE.

Vesely had saved their lives.

"What happened?" Pale Horse asked as he freed himself from the harness.

"Is maglev train," Vesely said. "Magnets hold train above track. It hovers. No friction."

Pale Horse rubbed his neck. The rapid acceleration had yanked his head hard to the side. "That's why we were moving like a bat outta Hell?"

Vesely answered with a nod. "Emergency brake cut power to magnets. Train fell. Friction stopped us."

"Did more than that," Miller said, smelling smoke. He walked to the doors and had to force them open with his hands. Two men in red uniforms approached quickly. One held a fire extinguisher. Before they arrived, Miller stepped out of the car and did his best to look pissed. Vesely and Pale Horse followed.

"What happened?" asked one of the men, while the other blasted the smoking base of the subway car with the fire extinguisher.

"This piece of shit malfunctioned," Pale Horse said.

Vesely backed up the claim. "I had to use the emergency brake."

"That's not possible, I—"

Miller drew his sound-supressed sidearm and shot the man in the forehead. The silent cough of the weapon was drowned out by the hiss of the fire extinguisher. The man putting out the fire had no idea his partner had been killed.

Miller quickly scanned the area. A large door that looked like it had been taken from a bank vault was the only exit. It was currently closed. A security panel to the right had a numbered keypad and palm reader.

"How will we get through?" Vesely whispered.

The door opened from the other side. Three more men dressed in red coveralls and carrying an assortment of tool-boxes entered the terminal.

They saw the dead man right away, but before they could retreat, Miller and Vesely shot all three. The door tried to close, but stopped against the body of a man who'd fallen in the doorway. The heavy motorized door persisted, squeezing the man's body. Pale Horse ran for the door, but before he could reach it, the door started moving again, and this time, didn't stop until it was securely closed.

Blood poured from the lower half of the man's severed body, pooling around the door.

"Oh my God, what happened!" shouted the man with the fire extinguisher.

He ran to the severed legs, dropping the extinguisher. "What happened!" he shouted again, and looked to Miller. That's when he saw his dead partner and Miller's gun aimed at his face.

The man's hands shot up, which Miller took as a good sign. He wanted to live.

"What's your name?" Miller asked. He walked toward the man, keeping the gun leveled at his head the whole time.

The man cringed and tilted his head away from Miller. "Ch-Charlie!"

"Charlie," Miller said, his voice calm. "Would you mind opening this door for me?"

"Coming here wasn't my idea," Charlie said. "It's my wife. She was going to take my daughter without me. I had to come. Had to play along."

"*Charlie,*" Miller said, putting a little vitriol in his voice. "If you open the door, I promise I won't shoot you."

"Or k-kill me?"

Charlie was quick.

"Or kill you."

Charlie nodded his head and shuffled his way around the pool of blood, stopping once he reached the security controls.

"What's the number sequence?" Miller asked.

"Three, seven, seven, six, two, zero, pound," Charlie replied, and then punched in the numbers. When he was done, the hand scanner lit up.

"Is that number code just for you?" Miller asked.

"For everyone in maintenance," Charlie said. "The handprint checks against maintenance IDs. We can go anywhere but Security."

"If the handprint isn't in the maintenance database?" Pale Horse asked.

"I—I don't know," Charlie said. "Oh my God, you're not going to cut off my hand, are you?"

The handprint screen turned from blue to green. The door unlocked and swung open.

"No, Charlie," Miller said. "We're not." Then he clubbed the man in the back of the head, knocking him unconscious. He quickly bound the man's hands and feet with plastic zip-tie cuffs and left him on the floor. He wouldn't be sounding any alarms.

Careful not to step in the blood, the three men entered the space beyond. Using the two dead men like logs in a river, they leapt over the vast pool of blood left by the top half of the severed man's body.

The door closed behind them. They were in a small, sealed-off, stark white room. A glass door on the far side was labeled AIR LOCK in reverse. A momentary increase in pressure popped Miller's ears. The glass door slid open.

A stark white hallway led straight ahead, lit from above by rows of bright white LED lights. More framed propaganda lined the walls. Miller could imagine that just a short while ago this hallway was filled with Aryan refuges seeking shelter from the oxygen purge that would bring about their utopian SecondWorld. But the hallway was spotless. No trace of human presence remained. *Somebody runs a tight ship,* he thought.

At the end of the one-hundred-foot-long hallway, it opened into a fifty-foot-wide waiting area. The trio stopped, facing a line of ten elevator doors. Benches and small tables lined the walls. Stacks of pamphlets sat on the tables. The posters on the walls were informational, rather than propaganda, featuring pictures of the facility's insides, which looked more like a five-star hotel than a secret underground Nazi base.

A large brass sign over the elevator doors read ARCHE 001.

"Arche?" Miller said.

"German for 'ark,'" Vesely explained.

"As in Noah's Ark?" Pale Horse asked.

"I think so," Vesely said, then pointed to the right-side wall. "Look."

A wall-sized diagram revealed the facility's basic layout. A spiraling atrium made up the structure's core; thirty stories down, each level tapering down toward the bottom. Doors lined the spiraling ramp, which was labeled "General Population Quarters." A large room at the bottom was vaguely labeled "Security and Control." The message was clear: you don't need to be here.

Pale Horse pointed to a yellow arrow with text inside that read "You Are Here." It showed the long hallway and the railcar terminal behind them. "I think they had a mall designer put this thing together."

Above the terminal were several other large chambers that branched out and away from the central core, but some were colored yellow, some green, and some red. *It's all color-coded,* Miller thought, *like the crews on an aircraft carrier.* Miller found a color guide at the bottom that revealed each section's purpose.

Brown—Military
Green—Garden & Seed
Yellow—Menagerie
Red—Maintenance
Blue—Security
White—General Population

Using the color code as a guide, Miller found two different hangar bays, one near the surface, which looked like it could service planes like the F-16s they encountered. But the other descended straight down into the ground and opened up into a large cylindrical chamber.

Vesely noted Miller's attention on the oddly-shaped hangar. "For foo fighters," he said. "For Bell."

Miller understood. They had flying craft that could take

off vertically without a runway. He shook his head. The sci-fi bullshit was a little too much to swallow sometimes. He didn't doubt its existence anymore. He just wished the UFOs actually belonged to a benevolent alien species.

It was all very interesting, but Miller already knew where they needed to go, Security and Control. If there was some way to stop the ongoing worldwide attack from this location, it would be there. He was about to lay out his simple plan when he heard the clacking of fingers on a computer keyboard.

Vesely stood at one of three keyboards mounted to the wall beneath the large diagram.

"What are you doing?" Miller asked.

"Is like bookstore interface. Type in name. Find room."

Miller looked over his shoulder and saw the name "Elizabeth Adler" typed in. He reached out to stop Vesely, just in case the system was monitored, but the man hit the Enter key too fast.

Nothing happened. And no alarms sounded.

Vesely deleted the name and typed in "Roger Brodeur." Same result.

"What was Brodeur's real name?" Vesely asked.

"Eichmann. Lance Eichmann."

Vesely typed in the name and hit Enter. A door near the bottom of the spiral glowed brown and revealed the text: *Level 4. Room 37.*

Miller wanted nothing more than to swoop in and rescue Adler, but the mission had to come first. "There isn't time," he said.

Vesely looked at him with a single raised eyebrow. "I am not being sentimental, Survivor. She has been here longer. She would have come in through hangar. And as granddaughter of a man and woman without whom none of this would have been possible, it is likely she may have been presented to those who might remember them fondly." He pointed at the brown Security and Control area. "Perhaps Kammler himself."

The idea of not finding Adler never sat well with him so

he quickly agreed with Vesely's assessment and said, "Level four, room thirty-seven it is. If she's not there we'll kick down the Security and Control doors. Sound like a plan?"

"Works for me," Pale Horse said.

"Is good," Vesely added.

Miller pushed the elevator call button. A pair of doors to his right opened immediately. All three jumped back. The elevator was not empty.

A single red eye stared at them, glowing eight inches above the floor. Miller recognized the design as being similar to those in Antarctica—a robo-Betty. The engine whirred as the thing turned toward Vesely. The red light pulsed for a moment and then turned green.

"What's it doing?" Pale Horse asked.

"Can't be facial recognition," Miller said.

It turned toward Pale Horse and began flashing red again.

"Is testing DNA," Vesely said with urgency. "Genetics. For purity!"

The light turned green and the device rotated toward Miller. "You're sure?" he asked.

"U.S. Homeland Security has them," Vesely urged. "Were going to be in airports!"

Miller couldn't risk him being wrong. He didn't know if this thing functioned like the ones outside, but he had to take the risk. He drew his pistol and shot the thing's red eye out. For a moment, nothing happened. But then the disk at the center began to spin. *Ding,* the doors began to close. The disk launched into the air and fired its projectiles, but the three men were unharmed. They heard the spray of metal balls ricocheting off the metal insides of the elevator, but not one made it out.

Miller hit the elevator's call button and the doors opened again. A hundred metal balls the size of small marbles covered the floor. "Okay. They scan DNA *and* don't respond well to being shot. Good to know." He didn't see a second payload and began sweeping the metal balls out of the elevator with his foot.

"I think it *had* scanned you already," Vesely said. "The

delay is probably from analyzing. Homeland units take one hour to analyze."

"How could these be so much faster?" Pale Horse asked, helping Miller with the cleanup.

"Because they're only looking for one thing," Miller said. "Racial purity. Looks like half-Jews don't pass the test."

After cleaning out the metal balls and the remains of the robo-Betty, they entered the elevator. Miller hit the button for level four. The doors closed and the elevator dropped. Thirty seconds and five floors later, the doors opened to another long, white hallway.

Vesely and Pale Horse led the way this time to give the impression that they were escorting Miller. The general's uniform was a good disguise, but if too many people looked at his face, someone was bound to recognize him. He lowered his cap, putting his eyes in shadow, and walked with a rigid step, doing his best to ooze malevolence. If people were afraid to look him in the eyes, this might just work.

When they reached the end of the hallway, Vesely and Pale Horse stopped so fast that Miller bumped into them. All three stumbled out of the hallway. Miller quickly looked for witnesses—he might have to smack the two men around if anyone witnessed their bungling—but saw no one. Then he looked beyond the pair and saw what had stopped them in their tracks. He stepped forward slowly, placed his hands on the railing, and looked up with widening eyes.

55.

No one said a word. They just stood there looking up, gripping the white metal railing that followed the spiraling ramp down three levels and up thirty-one levels. It was the up that held their attention.

The diagram hadn't done the structure justice. It was like standing in the middle of a skyscraper and looking up through its core, all the way to the ceiling. Almost everything was white, like one big sterile laboratory. And the place glowed with radiance—like the noonday sun on newly fallen snow. The light came from what had to be millions of bright, and energy-saving, LED lights.

But it was the ceiling, or rather what hung from it, that held their attention the longest. Two red flags, each five stories tall, hung from the ceiling. Both were crimson with large white circles in the center. One held a black swastika in the center of the circle, the other a large black Second-World symbol.

As Miller's shock wore off, his other senses filtered in. The air felt cool and dry, and smelled of ozone—the atmosphere was being conditioned. No oxygenless air down here. His ears perked up. He heard voices. Hundreds of them. Thousands. He searched the levels above and below level four and saw people everywhere, talking, laughing, swapping stories. Their voices echoed throughout the chamber.

Miller looked down and saw a large open atrium complete with what looked like a marble floor and fountain. People walked and talked, sat by the fountain with snacking kids. But the people weren't alone.

"The place is like a giant fucking fun-town mall," Pale Horse said.

Miller saw several robo-Bettys navigating through the sea of humanity. He couldn't count how many as the throng moved and shifted, but there were a lot. And as the Bettys passed people, their lights flashed between red and green.

"They're constantly scanning the people for racial purity," Miller said, pointing out the Bettys.

"Perhaps increasing standards," Vesely offered. "Or looking for stowaways." He looked at Miller. "Like you."

Miller agreed with a nod. He would have to avoid the DNA-detecting robo-Bettys.

He turned toward a group of laughing people. While this was an underground bunker, it was also luxurious. These people were on vacation while the rest of the world suffered. He gripped the railing hard, fighting to control his rising anger, and then remembered why they were on level four.

Adler.

Room thirty-seven.

"Let's go," he said, and started down the curving ramp. The first door he passed was forty-two. He counted out ahead and figured the door to Brodeur's room was halfway around the circle. Three men, one dressed in blue and two in brown, stood in front of an open door between them and their destination.

As he neared the men, Miller realized he was now in front of Vesely and Pale Horse. His face would be hard to hide. He looked to the right, out over the spiraling core, and ignored the men. They, however, did not ignore him.

"Afternoon, sir," the man in blue said.

Miller ignored him, but glanced at the three men. They weren't looking at his face. They were looking at his weapons—a sound-suppressed Sig Sauer and an UMP submachine gun. Both were modern weapons used by American Special Forces. Miller remembered that all of the

Germans he had fought thus far carried vintage World War II weapons. It must be a source of pride. A badge of honor that set them apart from their modern counterparts. Miller looked at the brownshirts' weapons. Mauser C96s. Old-school German handguns. The man in blue carried a newer Heckler & Koch HK4 pistol.

"You see something purty out there?" the man in the blue shirt said.

When Miller passed the man without acknowledging his existence, he lost his patience. "Hey, I'm talking to you."

"Wer sind Sie?" one of the German brownshirts said, then more angrily, *"Wie ist Ihr Name?"*

Miller spun, drew his silenced handgun, and fired four times, hitting both brownshirts in the chest. Both men spilled back into the room without making a sound. Vesely took out the blueshirt just as quickly, but caught him as he fell forward into the walkway. Vesely quickly pulled the man's body into the room while Miller and Pale Horse moved the brownshirts farther inside.

The room looked like a small studio apartment. The walls were a warm brown, not white like everything else, and were lit by a series of sconces. Framed posters of outdoor scenes hung from the walls. A bed sat in the corner, across from a small kitchenette with an eat-in bar. There was a couch. A wall-mounted flat-screen TV. Even a fish tank.

The only door in the place opened up. A woman dressed in a white silk nightgown stepped out of a small bathroom. "Okay, boys, I—" She looked up and saw them, then fell over dead with a hole in her forehead.

Miller lowered the weapon. "Let's move."

They closed the door behind them, made sure it locked, and continued down the ramp. A man in blue exited from room forty, gave them a nod, and turned to the left, heading in the same direction. As he rounded the bend, a robo-Betty paused as he walked past. The blinking red light turned green. Then it headed for Miller.

Vesely got in front of Miller as they reached room thirty-seven. The robo-Betty approached quickly.

"Keep watch," Miller said.

"Won't that be kind of conspicuous?" Pale Horse said.

Miller motioned to all the people standing around on the ramps, just having conversations. "You're two white men, dressed as guards, having a conversation. No one will notice you. And you've already passed—" He pointed at the Betty, just ten feet away. "—that thing's DNA purity test."

Miller tried the door handle and found it unlocked. He opened the door, slid inside, and closed it behind him just as the Betty arrived and began scanning Vesely. The room was nearly identical to the one now holding four dead bodies, with one exception—a blond woman with a bob haircut, petite body, and curvy hips lay on the bed, facing the far wall. Was she asleep?

Miller approached slowly, weapon at the ready. He rounded the bed, gave the open bathroom a glance to make sure they were alone, and then looked at the woman's face.

Adler! They had dyed her hair blond again.

He lowered the weapon, walked to the side of the bed, and put his hand on her shoulder. He opened his mouth to say her name, but never got the chance.

Her hand reached up, snatched his wrist, and pulled him down. A flash of metal caught Miller's eye as she brought her free hand up and thrust a knife toward his eye.

Miller felt the serrated blade tug at the skin next to his eye and slice through a few layers, but his reflexes saved him as he ducked to the side. The attack didn't stop there, though. Adler spun on her back and kicked him hard in the gut. Miller fell back, the wind knocked out of him, and struggled for air.

"Adler," he said, but his voice was raspy and unrecognizable.

The woman lunged, knife raised.

Miller had no choice but to defend himself. He caught Adler's arm and gave it a twist. She shouted in pain, dropping the knife, but began pummeling at him with her free hand.

He kicked out her legs, sprawling her onto the floor. She fell on top of one of his legs, so he wrapped the other around her, locked them together, and squeezed. While she punched his legs, he managed to push himself up and say, "Can you please stop trying to kill me for a second."

Adler's head whipped toward him, eyes wide with shock.

He let her go and she dove on him again, this time crushing him with a hug. She held on to him for several seconds, squeezing him hard, until he asked, "Have they hurt you?"

She let go of him and sat back. "Aside from plotting genocide, they've been perfect gentlemen." She looked him in the eyes. "I thought you were dead."

He stood, straightened his uniform, and picked up his cap. "Came close."

"Vesely?"

"He's on the other side of the door, keeping watch."

She looked relieved. "How did you get in?"

"Not important right now." He took her by the shoulders. "What is important is that you tell me absolutely everything you know about this facility, its security, how to get into the Security and Control center and shut down the Bells."

"How much longer do we have?" she asked.

She doesn't know, he thought.

She noticed the urgency in his eyes. "What?"

"It's already started."

She sat down on the bed. "Oh my God."

"We have hours," he said. "Maybe less."

She said nothing.

"Elizabeth, I need you to tell me everything you know." He crouched down in front of her. "Right now."

She looked at him, as though dazed, and then snapped out of it. Her eyes widened. "I think I know how to stop it."

"Stop what?"

"Everything," she said. "The attacks. The Bells." She turned toward the end table.

Miller looked and there on the table sat the brown leather journal of the first Elizabeth Adler.

56.

The first thing Miller felt upon seeing the journal was suspicion. He stood up and took a step back, looking at Adler with fresh eyes. She was dressed in white—the color designated for the general population, but instead of the plain coveralls that he'd seen other people wearing, she wore a flowing white skirt with white lace trim at the bottom. Her shirt, which hugged her lithe torso, had long sleeves that ended in flowery lace cuffs that covered her hands. Her skin looked soft and radiant, like she'd been to a spa, and her hair—not only had the black dye been removed, but Adler's crude haircut had been cleaned up. Compared to the other people in the Arche 001, she looked like a princess.

With the sting of Brodeur's betrayal still fresh, Miller gripped his weapon a little tighter and asked, "How did the journal get here?" He couldn't remember the last place he'd actually seen it. New Hampshire? She kept it in her oversized purse, and he certainly hadn't seen that, since when? *Poland. She had it in Poland.*

She noted his rigid body language and the skepticism in his voice. She looked hurt by it, but answered, "I kept it with me. When we flew from the *George Bush* to the *George Washington*. And then to the Antarctic base. Tucked into my waist."

"Why didn't you tell me?" he asked.

"I didn't think it mattered. I didn't keep it because I thought it would help, I kept it because I was hoping to find something in it that would vindicate my family. That my bloodline is responsible for global genocide sickens me."

Miller thought about it. Based on what he knew about Adler, it made sense. But still, he'd been convinced about Brodeur, too. And her clothes . . . the way she'd just been lying in bed while the world outside choked to death. It didn't sit well with him.

Adler noted his attention on her clothing. "He made me dress like this."

"Who?"

"Eichmann—Brodeur. I put up a fight before we left Antarctica. Almost got away." She pulled back the hair behind her ear, revealing a sewed-up gash, still swollen and red. "The clothing is part of his program to 'tame' me. Dressing me like a woman will make me act like one, he said."

The wound on the back of Adler's head erased his doubts. "Sorry," he said. "For doubting you." It was a quick apology, but there was no time for anything more. He motioned toward the journal before she could acknowledge or accept his apology. "What did you find?"

Adler picked up the journal and flipped past the pages of handwritten German. She stopped at the math. "There are several different equations in the journal, each labeled by the theory being tested. Anti-gravity. Magnetic force. Field expansion. Oxidization of iron. Ten in total. And despite my best efforts I've never been able to understand one of them. Just when I think something is going to make sense, the following page turns it all into mathematical gibberish."

She turned to the first page of math, written on a left-side page. "This is the first equation. For anti-gravity."

Miller saw a confusing jumble of numbers and symbols that looked more like an ancient language than math. But on the next page, at the top, he saw a single word.

Energie.

"Energy?" Miller said.

"The second equation," Adler confirmed with a nod.

"But the first is incomplete. It never made sense to me." She flipped through the following pages, revealing two more of the equations, each starting on the left-hand page. "None of them make sense. Unless . . ." She flipped back to the first page of the energy equation and pulled it out. Rather than turning the page, she slid it over so that the two right-side pages sat next to each other.

Miller instantly saw how the pages fit together, some lines and numbers continuing from one to the next. "She hid the equation."

"And mixed them up so they would make no sense," Adler said. "I think it was her way of making sure the equations couldn't be understood by the wrong people."

"How did you figure it out?"

"I was thinking about my grandmother, trying to understand her thought process. I remembered a game she used to play with me—a kind of mathematical hopscotch. The numbers in the answer determined where I had to jump, but the track always ended with two separate paths, left and right. I had to pick one and hop it to the end. Ten squares. I always thought it was a strange way to end the game, but I loved making her happy. The first time we played I chose left, and lost. 'Right,' she said. 'When the path is confusing and the numbers all wrong, follow only the right side.' For the longest time I thought it was a morality lesson, about being on the side of right—the good side. It's part of why I became an agent—liaison. But the game had nothing to do with right and wrong and everything to do with this book."

"She wanted you to figure it out," Miller said.

"I think so."

"And did you?"

"Some of the equations are still beyond me, though I think I could make sense of them if I had the time. But only one of them is important."

"Follow only the right side," Miller said. "Energy."

"Exactly," Adler said. "The equation proves the feasibility of the Bell's power source, a 'zero point energy' device developed for the Reich by Hans Coler. My grandmother refers to it as the Coil in her notes. The equation runs for twenty straight right-side pages and despite its length is fairly straightforward, though I suspect it is a simplified version of the original. At the end of the equation is an addendum. Ten additional pages that I suspect my grandmother never gave the Nazis."

Miller felt like a kid with his first lottery ticket, waiting to see if his numbers would turn up. He cracked his knuckles and licked his lips.

"The Coil generates a never-ending supply of power. Perpetual energy. But it is sensitive to rapid fluctuations. It takes a very specific charge to get the device going, and once it does, the charge must remain within a certain range or it will generate more energy than it needs, or can store in its batteries. It is a very delicate balance. Once it is operating, the Coil supplies its own energy, but produces more than it consumes. The excess energy is contained in batteries, which I'm guessing is what powers the Bell's magnetic force, the energy field, and anti-gravity systems."

"Why run off batteries when there is an energy source that can't be depleted?" Miller asked.

"When too much energy is put into the Coil, it feeds more energy into itself. It begins to generate more energy than it can contain, and feeds even more to itself. The more it generates, the faster it generates. Power feeding power."

"Until it reaches critical mass," Miller guessed.

She confirmed it with a nod.

"And then, ka-boom?"

"Big ka-boom."

"How big?"

Adler shrugged. "That's not in the journal. But if the Bells are in orbit, and the world is doomed anyway, I think it's worth the risk."

She's right, Miller thought. Even if the Bells detonated with the force of nuclear warheads, they couldn't do any damage to the surface while in Earth's orbit. "So what's our plan, kick down the doors to Control and Security, find access to the system controlling the Bells, and give them a little extra juice?"

"That is what I was thinking," Adler said.

Despite the odds being stacked against such a thing succeeding, with the fate of the world in the balance, there was no choice but to try. The thought led to a question. "Were you going to try this on your own?"

"Security is too tight. I was waiting," she said. "For help."

"You thought I was dead," Miller said.

"I just . . ." She sighed. "If I tried on my own, I'd probably be dead already and then no one would ever know how to stop it. I wasn't waiting for *you*. I was waiting for *anyone*."

Miller chastised himself for giving her a hard time. She had clearly been desperate to apply her knowledge, but could do nothing on her own. She was strong, and a good shot, but she'd be on her own against an army. And while four people against an army wasn't much better, Miller had at least been trained to be a one-man army if necessary. "You said security is tight. You've been down there?"

"When we first arrived," she said. "He presented me to Kammler like I was a big fish he'd caught."

"Kammler is *here*?"

"And the missing cryogenic chambers. From what I could see, there are just as many unopened chambers here as there were opened in Antarctica. I think the thawing process isn't quite perfected yet—Kammler had some burn marks on his face I don't remember from the photos I've seen of him. They must be waiting until after SecondWorld arrives to thaw out the rest."

Miller thought about the name he'd read on the computer screen in Antarctica. The thought of that man returning to the world was an injustice he could not ignore. Nor could he deal with it now. "Tell me about the security. What do we have to go through?"

"There are four armed guards. Brownshirt Nazis. The blueshirts—U.S. citizens from a variety of law-enforcement agencies—police the general population. As do the robotic devices. They scan DNA, by the way."

"I know," Miller replied. "Found out the hard way."

"The door to Security and Control has a hand scanner," Adler said. "And a code number and a retinal scanner, and—"

"I get it," Miller said. "We're not getting through."

Two quick knocks came from the door.

Adler tensed.

Miller walked to the door, weapon ready to shoot whoever might be on the other side. He opened it, saw Vesely, Pale Horse, and an unconscious third man dressed in red propped up between them like they were three chums. He opened the door and let them in, closing the door behind them.

"What happened?" Miller asked. "Who is he?"

"Is maintenance staff. Pale Horse broke his neck," Vesely said, pointing to the man's shirt. "I have idea. Well, Charlie's idea."

"Actually," Miller said, "so do I— Wait . . . Charlie's idea?"

57.

After hearing Vesely's plan, which was risky as hell, but perhaps their best chance of success, Miller added his idea to the mix. The combined plan was bold and messy, but if it worked, the enemy wouldn't know what hit them.

Ten minutes later, they were ready. Miller put the general's shirt back on, covering the fresh bandage on his arm. He threw on the coat next and looked at himself in the bathroom mirror. The sight of himself dressed in Nazi regalia was disconcerting, though not nearly as much as the dead maintenance man lying in the tub. The man was just as dead as before, but was now stripped to his underwear, covered in his own blood, and missing a hand.

He left the bathroom and found the others ready to go. Vesely was now dressed in red, and had the maintenance man's satchel over his shoulder. He still wore his two guns and Stetson despite Miller's protest. A cowboy to the end. The satchel, which had been full of tools, now held a severed hand—Charlie's idea.

Vesely shook Miller's hand. "Good luck, Survivor."

"You, too, Cowboy."

After tilting his hat toward the other two, he opened the door, looked both ways, and then slipped out into the hallway, heading up.

Miller wasn't sure he'd see Vesely again. They were

about to embark on suicide missions. That both of them
would survive seemed unlikely. Still, they'd come this far,
so he decided to hold on to the hope that he'd see the quirky
Czech cowboy again.

Miller turned to Adler and Pale Horse. "You two ready?"

Adler held out her hand. She had changed into a brown
uniform that was a few sizes too big. The rolled-up sleeves
and pant legs looked a little off, but she looked far less conspicuous. With her loose-fitting clothes and her hair tucked
up inside a brown cap, she could almost pass for a man—a
very short and pretty man. "Have a gun for me?"

Pale Horse handed her his sound-suppressed Sig Sauer
along with three spare clips. "I seem to be a slow draw with
this," he said, and then patted his UMP submachine gun.
"Besides, I think I'll have more use for this in the next few
minutes."

Miller confirmed the man's thought with a nod and
headed for the door. He looked to Adler. "Ready?"

She stepped around him and opened the door. With seri-
ousness Miller hadn't yet seen, she said, "Let's go," and
stepped into the hallway. Miller and Pale Horse followed.

A quick check revealed no one nearby and no robo-Bettys.
They approached the railing and looked down. The atrium
at the bottom of the complex looked like a galleria at Christ-
mastime. The sea of voices. The bustling bodies. The sound
of the fountain. There was an energy to the place. An excitement. Miller saw coins in the fountain and wondered if he
would find George Washington printed on them, or Adolf
Hitler.

He could see a hallway entrance across the way. Above
the doorway was a sign that read SECURITY AND CONTROL.
According to Adler, the vaultlike door was at the end of that
hallway. With all the security, they would never get the door
open from this end, so Miller came up with a plan that
would get them to open the door from the other side.

Miller reached into his pocket and took out the plastic
Ziploc bag in which he had kept his painkillers. Now it was
full of still-warm liquid—his blood. He poked several holes

in the plastic with his knife, then sliced it down the middle for good measure. "Stand back," he said to Adler and Pale Horse. Better if they didn't get the blood, containing his DNA, on them—like everyone below them was about to.

He gripped the corner of the bag and sent it flying out over the atrium with a flick of his wrist. The bag spun out over the open space like a Frisbee, spraying his blood in every direction.

The first reaction came fast, but was confused. A woman below yelped and said, "What was that?"

A chorus of voices soon joined the woman, none too fearful until one person said, "Is that blood?"

Another replied. "It is!"

And then it happened. An alarm.

Miller peeked over the railing. The crowd below was frozen in place, some looking up, trying to figure out where the blood had come from. He could see specks of it covering their faces. But that's not why they weren't moving.

A single robo-Betty at the center of the group was flashing red. An electronic voice spoke from it, "Anomalous DNA detected. Please remain still until security arrives to assist you."

Miller realized that if he hadn't shot the robo-Betty in the elevator, he might have gotten the same message. But at the same time, it might have alerted security to his presence. This turn of events threw a rather large monkey wrench in his plans.

Another alarm sounded. Then another. Ten more followed. All of the robo-Bettys in the atrium had detected his blood and sounded the alarm. But none of them were activating, and probably wouldn't unless . . . someone disobeyed. That's why the crowd had frozen. If they ran, the Bettys would activate. These people had been trained well. Too well.

A loud pinging noise drew his attention up. High above, where the flags were attached to the ceiling, were sparks. When the first five-story-tall flag fell, Miller knew what had happened. Vesely had seen their predicament and fired on

the flags. The giant flags would send people scattering, or
set off the Bettys themselves upon reaching the floor. The
second flag fell moments later.

"Go!" Miller said, and began running down the spiraling
ramp. No one was paying any attention to them.

As they rounded the second floor, the flags fell past.

"Run!" Miller shouted. "The flags will set them off!"

That's all it took. The people below realized he was right.
And ran.

The Bettys sprang into action, even as more of the killer
devices arrived on the scene, alarms sounding. Screams
rose up from the atrium as a thousand metal balls blasted
through the air, cutting down at least fifty people. Miller felt
a moment of regret for the people. They weren't soldiers.
But they were complicit to genocide, so his regret didn't last
long.

As Miller rounded the ramp to the ground floor, he noticed a robo-Betty up ahead. He slowed and let Pale Horse
and Adler catch up. "Grab that thing," he said to Pale Horse.
"Don't let it see the blood, or me."

Pale Horse ran ahead and picked up the device. It scanned
him as he held it, the light turning green. Then the wheels
just spun as it tried to move on. Pale Horse kept the sensor
turned toward the ceiling as Miller passed and said, "Let's
go."

They rounded the ramp onto the atrium floor and were
greeted by a war zone. At least a hundred people lay dead
and dying, many of them wearing blue and brown. A few
survivors clung to the far walls, afraid to move. A single
robo-Betty sat at the edge of the atrium, flashing its red light
at a corpse and ordering it not to move.

Miller led Pale Horse and Adler across the opposite side
of the atrium and headed for the hallway to Security and
Control. As he approached the hall, he saw that his plan had
succeeded. The four security personnel that had been guarding the large vaultlike door had rushed toward the atrium
when the first alarms had sounded. Three of them lay dead.
A fourth, farther down the sloped hallway, was injured.

Miller took aim and shot the man as he walked past. The man would have died from his injuries, so it was a mercy, but Miller also didn't want the man shooting them in the back when he saw what came next.

Miller stopped his advance next to the security station, which reminded him of a bookstore help desk, thirty feet from the vault door. *C'mon,* he thought, *open.*

And then it did. Security was responding to what they must believe was some kind of malfunction. A terrible accident.

As the door slid silently open, Miller turned to Pale Horse and the robo-Betty. "Point it at me!"

Pale Horse complied without pause. The red light on the front of the machine began to blink as it scanned and analyzed Miller's DNA. Knowing full well what the end result would be, Miller smashed the sensor with the butt of his gun, took the device from Pale Horse, and tossed it toward the opening door. He ducked behind the security station with Adler and Pale Horse.

The robo-Betty stopped in front of the door just as it revealed ten guards—ten very surprised guards.

The Betty bounced into the air and fired its payload. The men, who stood at point-blank range, were cut down before any of them could scream. As metal beads rolled up the ramp, Miller jumped from his hiding spot and sprinted toward the now-closing door.

He reached it with time to spare. He stepped into the dimly lit hallway on the other side of the door. Adler and Pale Horse followed him. The hallway grew darker still as the big door closed over several guards' bodies behind them with a crunchy squish. Miller ignored the sound and motioned the team forward. "Almost there."

58.

The hallway was dimly lit by two rows of LED lights running the length of the hall where the walls met the floor. Miller holstered his handgun and readied his UMP, sliding the rack. "Straight ahead, I assume?"

Adler stepped up next to him, handgun gripped like a pro. "This hallway was bright when Brodeur brought me through. There's a set of double doors at the end. No security. Just doors. They open to a large chamber, like we saw in Antarctica, but there's nothing natural about this. It's a smooth dome. There's a control center in the middle, but it's at least four times the size of the one in Antarctica. Security is based to the right of the control area, past rows of storage arranged like a warehouse."

"A warehouse?" It struck Miller strange that they would keep things stored in the space designated for security and control.

"I think it is older equipment. Relics from the war. Maybe art. Gold. Souvenirs. I am not entirely sure, but it is all crated."

"Like the warehouse in *Indiana Jones*?" Pale Horse said.

"*Ja.* But not as big. Security is past the warehouse area, through a pair of double doors that *are* locked. Cryogenics is to the left via an open tunnel. Same as Antarctica."

Miller slid up to the double doors and peeked through

the windows. The space was just as Adler described it. A large octagonal control center lit in bright white filled the center of the large space. A massive viewscreen hung above it all, displaying a mix of active screen captures from the computers below as well as a mix of video feeds. Miller squinted, trying to make out the images, but distance and glare worked against him. Polished walkways outlined by white lines cut through the place, and reflected the bright lights. The ceiling of smooth concrete arched up over the hanging lights, its peak at the center concealed in darkness high above. A maze of large shipping containers, crates, and oversized canisters blocked his view of Security to the right, but he trusted it was there. He counted twenty soldiers wielding World War II–era weapons, which helped level the playing field a little bit. But there were also at least forty other, nonmilitary people dressed in lab coats or white coveralls. Most of them sat at the computers, no doubt monitoring the purification of the human race.

He pointed to Pale Horse. "We'll go in first. Everyone is a target, but start with the brownshirts. They'll be the ones shooting back." He turned to Adler. "Once things get chaotic, come in and make your way to the computers. We'll give you as long as we can."

"I will get it done."

Miller once again wondered where Adler's confidence came from. He remembered how quickly she'd accessed the computer in Antarctica. With Brodeur's traitorous revelation and Miller's nearly melting, and then freezing, he hadn't given it much thought. She'd said it was a "Linux based system," but who the hell used Linux? Certainly not Interpol. Most people hadn't even heard of the operating system. But the woman was a whiz with a computer, and a gun. *And* she could understand complex math. She'd claimed to not comprehend some of the other equations, but Miller didn't believe that anymore. Once she figured out the page confusion, the rest had fallen into place, and she'd understood the math without tearing out the pages and lining them up as she had done for him.

Focus, Miller, he told himself. *She's on your side. For now. Sort it out later.*

"Ready?" he asked Pale Horse.

"Let's do it."

Miller pushed through the double doors, raising his weapon. He picked out five targets, each a little farther away than the other. By the time the fifth registered what happened to the first, they'd all be dead. Then he'd have fifteen soldiers left to deal with, minus any Pale Horse shot, plus however many were behind the locked double doors to Security. Miller's finger squeezed the trigger.

A gunshot rang out so loud and so close that it threw off Miller's aim and made his ears ring. Miller spun around, searching for a target.

He found it at the center of Brodeur's head.

The man's arm was raised. Smoke drifted from the barrel of a handgun. He turned to Miller and flashed him a smile. "Hello, Survivor."

Miller was about to pull the trigger when he saw Adler struggling and a gun to her head. The face of the man holding her made his hands shake: the executive assistant director of the NCIS, Fred Murdock. His friend. He was dressed in a standard brown uniform, but smiled in the same superior way as Brodeur. Miller glared at the man for a moment, but then saw movement to his right and glanced in that direction. The movement came from a twitching foot.

Pale Horse's twitching foot.

Miller looked at the man. Blood covered his chest, flowing from a wound over his heart. His eyes were already glassy. Pale Horse was dead. Just like that.

The two men shared an exchange in German and then laughed.

Miller backed up, assessing the situation. Adler had a gun to her head. He could hear the footfalls of soldiers approaching him from behind. More soldiers filed in behind Brodeur and Murdock.

"I have to admit, Miller," Murdock said, "I always knew you were good, but making it here. Even I'm impressed. But as much as I'd like to pat you on the back and say good job for old times' sake, I think I'll just put a bullet through that Jew-boy half-breed head of yours."

The two men laughed again.

"He's seeing red," Brodeur said. "Better put the boy down." He turned his weapon from Pale Horse to Miller.

Seeing red.

Red.

Red!

An image of Vesely dressed in red coveralls flashed through his mind.

Miller lowered his UMP and held out an open palm. "You win," he said, placing the weapon on the floor. He slowly drew his pistol and placed it on the floor next to the submachine gun. Miller hated giving up his weapons. It went against all of his training. But he needed time. He raised his hands and stood up.

"Sorry," Brodeur said, "I'm going to kill you and then spend the next year breaking this one's will." He motioned to Adler with his head. "I think she'll come around after our first child." He looked to Adler. "Won't you?"

She struggled, but Murdock held her tight.

Miller could tell he was being goaded into action. They wanted him to lose his cool, to seal his own fate. He wouldn't give them the satisfaction. "If I'm dead, who are you going to torture? Or experiment on? Just admit it, Brodeur. I've seen the way you look at me. You'd miss me."

When Murdock, who was notorious for his gay jokes, burst out laughing, Brodeur's face turned red and angry.

Miller realized he might have gone too far.

Brodeur looked down the sight of his weapon.

The hammer tilted back as Brodeur slowly pulled the trigger.

"Wait," said a voice behind Miller. The man's voice was cold and demanded authority.

Brodeur held his fire, the hammer half cocked.

"He is right," the voice said. "This one has earned a slow death. Make it . . . agonizing."

Miller turned slowly and came face-to-face with Hans Kammler. The man looked just like he did in the few photos there were of him, but the scarring Adler mentioned marred his skin. He wore a tall general's cap featuring an open-winged eagle perched upon a swastika. Aside from the number of pins, his uniform matched Miller's.

"The uniform you wear belonged to General Karl Friedrich, a friend of mine." Kammler circled Miller. "He survived the war. Spent a lifetime frozen in a cryogenic chamber. He rejoined us just ten days ago. Do you know how that makes me feel?"

Miller saw that Kammler was inspecting him from head to toe, the way a slaughterhouse worker might inspect a cow. If Vesely didn't come through, he couldn't imagine the kinds of things this man might do to him before killing him. Hell, they could keep him alive and torture him for years if they wanted to.

Miller decided he couldn't possibly make the situation any worse, and said, "If the rest of your men fight like Friedrich, then I shouldn't have any problem taking care of the rest of you with my bare hands."

Kammler looked him in the eyes. It was like looking into the eyes of a great white shark. But Miller held his gaze and waited for a punch. It never came. Kammler continued to circle him.

"Did you take pleasure in killing those people?" Kammler asked, motioning to the hallway. Miller thought of the people in the atrium. He didn't take pleasure in their deaths. But he didn't feel guilty about it, either.

Kammler took his silence as a yes. "You are more like us than you admit. I doubt you would shed a single tear if every person in this facility were killed."

"That's exactly what's going to happen," Miller said, his temper flaring.

Kammler smiled. "As I thought. There are nearly three thousand adults living here."

Miller shrugged, but then registered the man's words.

Three thousand *adults*. He'd been expertly baited and trapped.

"There are also five hundred children, seventy-five of them under two years of age. Surely, you would spare them?"

Miller gritted his teeth, remembering the girl he'd failed to save all those years ago. He'd nearly given his life to save hers. Children were innocents. They didn't deserve to die. But in war, sometimes the wrong people died, hopefully so more people could live. In this case it was a no-brainer. The children living here had to die so that billions could live. Their parents sealed their fates when they decided to take part in genocide; the burden of the children's deaths belonged to them. But he didn't answer. He wouldn't give Kammler the satisfaction.

"Bring them," Kammler said, walking toward the control center.

Miller was pushed forward at gunpoint. He followed Kammler, who stopped when the full array of viewscreens could be seen.

Kammler opened his arms up to the screens, which showed a variety of live video feeds from around the world. A large, ten-foot screen showed the skyline of London masked by a red haze. The smaller screens to either side of the large screen showed several other cities around the world, all cloaked by red flakes falling from the sky. "Behold the birth of SecondWorld," Kammler said with a grin. "It is beautiful. Purifying blood from the sky."

Miller stayed silent.

"What we are doing is no different than what you would like to do here. You would exterminate every last one of us. Because we are your enemy. But this will not happen, do you know why?"

Silence.

"Because we are stronger. We are smarter." Kammler's strident voice became thoughtful. "We are . . . pure."

Miller stayed silent, but Adler couldn't. "Germany *lost* the Second World War."

Kammler grinned. "Did we?" He let the question hang in the air for a moment. Brodeur and Murdock shared a laugh.

"We discovered the iron cloud that made this possible long before the 'end' of the war. After calculating when the iron cloud would arrive, we began work on several projects that resulted in this." He motioned to the screens. "Germany did not lose the war, we merely pretended to."

Miller's jaw dropped a little. "Millions died."

"A convincing ruse. We fought to the end. The Führer killed himself." Kammler chuckled. "And the United States somehow ended up with thousands of Nazi scientists."

"You sent our people to their deaths," Adler said.

Kammler grinned at Adler. "So much like your grandmother. Surely you must understand the sacrifice now?" Kammler said. "We traded our country for the world." Kammler looked at his watch. "Thirty minutes from now, the air will become poisonous. A few hours later, there will be no oxygen. And in several months, when the oxygen in the lower atmosphere is replenished, the world will be purified and the *Fourth* Reich will rise. We have waited seventy years for this day."

Kammler turned to Miller. "Still nothing to say?"

Miller just stared at the man, willing Vesely to come through soon.

"Where does he live?" Kammler asked.

"Washington," Brodeur replied.

Kammler barked an order toward the group of men seated at the control center. None of the men even glanced up. They were either very disciplined or used to being shouted at. An image of the Washington, D.C., skyline appeared on the large viewscreen. The Capitol building and Washington Monument were all in the shot, but were hard to see through the red haze.

"This is your home," Kammler said, noting Miller's lack of reaction. He shrugged, growing bored of his game.

"Don't forget the girl," Brodeur said. "Pitiful little thing.

She worshiped you. Thought you would save her. Thought you would—"

Miller moved like lightning, striking Brodeur's face with a backhand that sent him sprawling.

Kammler was equally quick. The punch came hard and fast. Miller shouted in pain, dropped down on one knee, and clutched his arm. With a single blow, Kammler had managed to strike both bullet wounds. *How the hell did he know?* Miller realized he must have been holding the arm differently. He'd done well ignoring the pain, but his body still reacted to it.

Murdock was chuckling again. The laugh concealed a second sound that Miller only heard because he'd been listening for it. Been praying for it.

The large vents overhead were no longer blowing air into the chamber.

They were sucking air *out*.

Kammler took hold of Miller's face with one hand and pointed a gun at him with the other. Miller fumed with anger. "There you are," Kammler said. "Defiant. Angry. Amusing. You will be a gift—"

Miller glared at Kammler.

"—for Mein Führer."

Kammler shoved Miller's face away, stepped back, and wiped his hand with a kerchief.

Miller grunted as he got to his feet. He held his arm, which had begun to bleed. The pain nauseated him. Exhaustion consumed him. He drew in a deep breath. Then another. And another. Then he stood tall and said, "I'll be sure to say hello to him for you."

Kammler squinted at Miller, disturbed by his sudden confidence. "And how do you suppose you will do that?"

"Well, for starters, I'm going to kill these two," Miller said, nodding to Murdock and Brodeur, who was back on his feet. "Then I'm going to beat the shit out of you, barehanded, and then I'm going to walk in there—" Miller pointed to the open hallway that led to the cryogenic room.

He could see several of the gleaming metal chambers from where he stood. "—thaw out your goofy-looking boss, rip that mustache off his face, say hello from you, and then shoot him in the forehead."

Miller took several more deep breaths as Kammler walked around him.

Kammler stopped by Brodeur and held out his hand. Brodeur handed him his gun.

"No!" Adler shouted. She realized what was about to happen at the same moment Miller did.

But he didn't shout out.

Didn't beg for mercy.

He looked down the barrel of the gun and took a deep breath.

Kammler fired.

59.

Miller fell on his side, clutching his leg and shouting through gritted teeth. Kammler had shot his left thigh, the bullet coming to a stop halfway through the meat. To make things worse, Miller had fallen on his injured arm, sending a cyclone of pain through his body. The bullet wound wouldn't kill him, but it wasn't meant to. He was a dog and Kammler had just swatted his nose.

As the initial pain subsided, Miller heard the men laughing. He was a Jew surrounded by thirty SS Nazi killers. He had three bullet wounds, blinding pain, and felt a level of exhaustion beyond anything experienced during the SEALs' Hell Week.

But he knew something that Kammler didn't.

Something that, in his weakened state, he found very funny.

When he joined in the laughter, the Nazis fell silent.

They stared at him, no doubt wondering if he had lost his mind.

Miller's lungs began to burn as he laughed.

He looked at the guards surrounding them, their faces etched with confusion, and knew they felt it, too. He laughed harder.

One of the larger men stumbled, holding his head. His muscular body required more oxygen to function and he felt the effects first. The other men watched the big man fall to one knee, and then crumple to the floor, wheezing for air.

The sound of the man's wheezing sparked realization.

Kammler quickly ordered fifteen of the men to follow him. They ran for the doors to Security. Brodeur ordered Murdock to stay, and followed after the others.

Murdock's face slowly turned a deeper shade of red, but his weapon stayed trained on Adler's head and his hate-filled eyes remained on Miller. One of the other four remaining men collapsed. Murdock glanced at him, a momentary fear springing into his eyes.

Miller's chest felt like it would explode, but he held his breath without fear. He'd faced, and beaten, this fate several times already and he'd be damned if it would claim him now, especially when it was Vesely's doing.

"Give the bastards a taste of their own medicine," he'd said. He'd concluded the facility would be airtight, with its own air supply. *The Cowboy did it,* Miller thought. He'd not only found a way to shut the air off, but was quickly siphoning the air from the entire facility. Everyone inside *would* die.

Miller had enjoyed the irony of the plan. Not so much now that he was experiencing it firsthand, but that would change in a moment.

He looked at Adler. She'd known to hold her breath, but even though she looked better off than Murdock, her body would eventually take a breath on reflex and when no oxygen reached her lungs, she would drown in the open air.

Just like the rest of the world if you don't move! Miller's subconscious shouted at him. According to Kammler, he had just twenty-five minutes before the air outside became so thick with iron that the world's population would be poisoned and die gruelingly three days from now when the heavy metal settled deeper into their organs. If that happened, a quick death by suffocation would be a mercy.

Murdock blinked, fighting unconsciousness.

Two more of the soldiers fell. The fourth went to his hands and knees.

Miller mimicked the man's position, but instead of falling down, he was getting up. A jolt of pain ran up the left side of his body, immobilizing him. With his right hand, he reached back to his belt, opened a pocket, and pulled out a small vacuum-sealed pack. He lowered himself down, giving the impression that he was succumbing to the lack of air—which he would soon do if Murdock managed to stay upright and conscious much longer. With one hand he tore open the wrapper, plucked off the small rubber stopper on the end, and stuck himself in the leg.

A wave of morphine warmth spread from his leg up into his torso and out through his limbs, washing the pain away. Even the burning in his lungs faded. He felt weightless. Time slowed. And once again, he laughed.

This time when he looked back up at Murdock, the man looked terrified by Miller's laughter. He looked ready to burst and his weapon was no longer aimed directly at Adler's head.

Miller shifted his gaze to Adler. Her face was bright red. Her eyes wide with fear.

It was time to act.

Miller dove forward, snatched up his silenced Sig Sauer, rolled to his feet, and aimed the weapon at Murdock's head. The man looked stunned. He tried to move his weapon toward Miller, but his hand and arm shook violently. Anger filled his face a moment before Miller's bullet froze the expression.

Adler fell forward, catching herself on her hands. Her chest heaved, as she took in breaths of oxygenless air. Miller knew unconsciousness would claim her soon. He knelt down next to her, removed the small pony bottle from his supply belt, unfolded the collapsible mask, opened the air valve, and placed it over her nose and mouth.

She breathed deep, gasping each breath. Miller felt relieved when he realized she'd make it.

But then a pain gripped him so intensely that he felt it through the morphine. *Air!* The morphine had made him forget he couldn't breathe, either. As blackness crept into the periphery of his vision and little specks of color danced

before him, he lunged to Pale Horse's body, found his pony
bottle, fumbled to open it—and then dropped it.

His chest ached. His hands shook as he searched for the
bottle, his eyes no longer functioning.

As the last bit of consciousness faded, he felt something
press against his face. Adler's voice followed. "Breathe!"

He did.

The first breath felt something like the way he imagined
the experience of childbirth—agony mixed with elation.

Ten breaths later, his senses returned. After another ten,
the morphine began to work again. He stood and pulled the
pony bottle's elastic band over his head, holding it in place.
"We've got about fourteen minutes left in these things, and
just a few minutes more to stop that," he said to Adler, pointing at the video screens. "Let's get this done."

She nodded, still breathing too heavy to reply, and headed
for the large octagonal control center. A sea of white-clad
bodies littered the floor, but Miller hardly noticed them. Instead, he looked up at a huge array of displays the size of a
movie screen. Each one showed a city. He recognized several of the skylines. London. Paris. Moscow. Los Angeles.
New York. Sydney. Washington, D.C. Red flakes fell from the
sky in each image. In some, smoke rose to greet it as a panicked world lashed out. The screen at the bottom right caught
his attention last. Vatican City. But it wasn't the gleaming
domes, now hued pink, that held his attention. It was the
crowd filling St. Peter's Square. Thousands had gathered. On
their hands and knees. Praying.

And whether they knew it or not, they were praying for
his success.

Feeling a sense of purpose bordering on divine calling
that was one part true inspiration and one part morphine,
Miller shoved a lab coat–clad man out of his seat. Adler sat
down at the computer station, which was already up and
running, no password required.

"Can you do it?" Miller asked.

"It is the same system," Adler said. "But I'll need a minute to find my way around."

The monitor next to them exploded in a shower of sparks. Miller glanced over the top of the control center and saw at least twenty rebreather-wearing SS soldiers led by Brodeur filing out of the doors to Security on the other side of the vast warehouse area. Most of the men were armed, as usual, with World War II rifles and machine guns, which Miller's UMP would put to shame in a one-on-one situation, but the SS could send a wall of bullets his way that would be hard to avoid. Even worse, the two men at the front of the pack wore body armor and masks like the guards in Antarctica, but the men looked tougher, bigger, like the armor was mechanized. When the two men each raised very large strange-looking weapons at Miller, he had no doubt.

"Stay out of sight!" Miller said to Adler and then dived to the side. He heard a sound like an acoustic guitar string being snapped against the wooden frame as the weapons fired, but saw no effect. No computers destroyed. No ricochet. Had they misfired?

Miller got to his feet and found that he'd dived right out into the open. The morphine that dulled his pain also made his decision-making abilities questionable. The two mechanized men adjusted their aim. Miller grabbed Murdock's body and picked him up, hoping that whatever kind of rounds the strange guns fired would be stopped.

The weapons twanged again. Miller felt no impact, but Murdock's body seemed to be growing lighter. Miller looked down and saw multicolored goop draining from Murdock's pant legs! He dropped the body and it turned to soup on the floor. Those guns had the same effect on the human body as the Bell!

With no immediate cover, Miller thought, *This one's for you, Pale Horse. Time to spray and pray.*

Miller ran and pulled the UMP's trigger. He drew a quick line across the SS men as they were about to unload on the control center. When the last round left the UMP's muzzle and the magazine ran dry, five of the soldiers lay on the ground, dead and dying. But a body count wasn't Miller's goal. He was hoping for chaos. And he got it.

While some of the SS men unloaded on his position, most ducked for cover, including Brodeur, who had unfortunately survived his initial volley. They hid behind the tall stacks arranged on either side of the large space—walls of wooden crates filled with who knows what. There were plenty of places for the enemy to take cover.

The two big men tracked Miller as he ran toward the warehouse area. He heard two loud twangs as they fired, but his body didn't turn to mush, so he assumed they'd missed.

He dove into an alley lined with crates on either side. The rows of wooden crates stamped with swastikas and Second-World symbols reminded Miller of a surreal Home Depot. But the maze of crates worked to his advantage; he could engage the enemy a few at a time. He laughed as his hastily laid plan came together, and realized the morphine was making him slaphappy. Of course, he could live with slaphappy if it didn't affect his aim, a concern he put to the test by rising from his position and squeezing off two three-round bursts.

Two men dropped. Several more ducked for cover.

The return fire was loud and included two loud twangs. The wood around him shattered, but he wasn't hit.

Aim is still good, he thought, then dashed out from behind the control center and dove behind a very large crate. *This thing is big enough to hold a car,* Miller thought. When Miller saw a red stamp that read simply G4, he knew he was right. Hitler's preferred vehicle had been the six-wheeled 1939 Mercedes-Benz G4. He'd read about the vehicle once when a collector auctioned three, which had belonged to Hitler, for three million dollars each. Only eight had ever been built. *Looks like we know where the other five went,* Miller thought.

Two brave soldiers ran toward the control center. Miller gunned them down before they arrived. He crept around the big crate and slid through a gap, into the next aisle. He peeked down the aisle lined with crates. The left end was clear, but to the right he saw two men crouched, searching for a target. A morphine giggle slipped from his mouth. The two men spun toward him, but he let loose a barrage that cut the men down before a single shot was fired his way. *At least my reflexes haven't slowed,* Miller thought as he slid out of his hiding place and ran toward the next aisle.

He paused at the end, peeking around the corner. All clear. As he moved around the end of the aisle, a shadow— from behind him—shifted on the floor.

He spun and fired.

The bullet had no effect on the heavily armored, mechanized Nazi. Miller could only see the man's eyes, but could see by the squint that he was smiling.

Miller leapt to the side.

Twang!

Rebounding off a crate, Miller opened fire on the man, aiming for his head. The barrage stumbled the man back, but the suit he wore must have had a built-in gyroscope, because he remained upright.

Twang! The man fired blind and missed. But he also swung his big, metal-covered fist out and struck the UMP from Miller's hands.

Miller drew his knife and dove at the man, getting in close where he couldn't be shot. He stabbed the knife into the body armor, but it stopped against solid metal after penetrating an inch of bullet-resistant padding. These suits were definitely an upgrade from the Antarctic variety.

The big metal arm wrapped around Miller and squeezed him tight. Pain flared from the wounds in his arm. He shouted and wriggled. He couldn't break free. But he could still fight, and every suit of armor had a weak spot. He'd been able to strangle the guard in Antarctica. Maybe they hadn't fully armored the neck, which was clearly flexible. Miller withdrew his knife and slammed it into the mech's neck.

The blade slid in.

All the way to the hilt.

He could barely hear the man's gurgle through the suit, but he could see the startled expression in his eyes, which quickly became lifeless. The man's arm fell slack, but the body didn't fall over. It stood still, kept upright by design. Miller glanced at the weapon. It was attached to the suit, but was operated like any other handheld weapon, a finger on a trigger.

Gunfire pinged off the suit. Two brownshirt soldiers ran at him, side by side, firing wildly. If they'd stopped to take aim, they might have struck him, but Miller wasn't about to complain. He yanked up the dead man's arm, aimed the weapon toward the two men, slid his finger over the dead man's, and pulled the trigger.

Twang!

The two men turned to liquid as they ran. By the time their bodies hit the floor they were little more than multicolored puddles. The slop slid across the smooth floor and stopped just a foot from Miller's body. He took a deep breath and was thankful the pony bottle mask kept him from smelling the liquefied men.

The loud clomp of mechanized feet approached from the left. Miller spun toward the sound as the second mech exited the neighboring aisle. Miller ducked and spun around the back side of the dead man's suit. *Twang!* The suit blocked the shot.

The sound of the weapon firing was followed by a high-pitched whine, like a camera flash recharging. *That's why these guys aren't just melting everything in sight,* Miller realized. *They have to recharge after each shot!* Miller grabbed the dead man's arm and shoved it toward the other mech. He found the trigger and pulled it. *Twang!*

Miller watched the other man's eyes widen for a split second and then explode into liquid. Bubbles rose up and the melting man's body slipped lower into the suit.

"Miller!" It was Adler. "It's not working!"

Miller picked up his UMP, but it was ruined, so he left it behind, drew his sidearm, and started back toward Adler and the control center. That's when he heard the crackling hum that sounded an awful lot like the robotic sentinel they'd faced in the parking lot. And it was right behind him.

60.

Miller flung himself to the left, ducking down the last aisle just as twin *twang*s sounded out behind him. Were there two more men in suits? He didn't think so. He couldn't hear any heavy feet behind him, just the crackling hum of some kind of bell device. When the sound grew suddenly louder, he knew that whatever it was had entered the aisle. He looked over his shoulder and nearly tripped.

The thing was huge.

At first, Miller thought he was looking at something organic. It had four metallic limbs—tentacles really—each at least fifteen feet long. They reached out and pulled the thing along, moving quickly. For a moment, he thought the limbs were holding it up, but that couldn't be true, because they never really touched anything. They just wriggled hyperactively, moving only to avoid direct contact with the physical environment. The thing was floating.

The body was shaped like an eagle's head sans the curved beak. The base glowed with flickering energy as some kind of bell device kept it aloft. But it was the two weapons mounted on either side of the thing that held Miller's attention. They were identical to the flesh-melting weapons the two mechanized men had carried. Of course, the two mini-guns mounted to the bottom were pretty intimidating, too, but they weren't firing, or even spinning up. Miller's first impression was that he faced an automated drone like the thing outside the NSSB, but then he saw a pane of red-tinted glass at the core. Through the glass he saw a face. Kammler's. The man looked amused. Miller fired three shots, but the rounds just ricocheted off the thick, curved glass. Kammler laughed, his voice amplified through a speaker.

"What do you think?" Kammler asked. "We have thousands of them ready to search the country for survivors."

Miller knew the man was trying to make him think about talking when he should be running. It was a clue that the man was about to fire. Miller had fifteen feet before he reached the end of the aisle, where who knew how many soldiers waited for him. And he was boxed in on either side. He made the only maneuver he could—spun around and ran straight at Kammler.

Both weapons *twang*ed loudly. But missed.

Miller noticed the miniguns had yet to power up and wondered why Kammler wasn't using them. Were they not loaded? Then he realized the answer. The strange weapons melted flesh, but not other elements. If Kammler's shots struck the relics stored here, they wouldn't do any damage. But the miniguns, those would wreak havoc.

"They don't seem very accurate," Miller taunted, but then had to dive to the side as one of the flailing limbs snapped down toward him. He caught a glimpse of the barbed tip as it took a chunk out of the polished stone floor. It looked like it had been designed to punch through a man, but then not come out, not cleanly anyway.

Kammler's voice echoed in his mind. *We have thousands of them ready to search the country for survivors.* They were designed to quickly pick off or tear to shreds any survivors they came across.

Including *the* Survivor.

Miller ducked to the side as a second arm sprang toward his head. It cut a slice in his cheek, punctured the G4 box behind Miller, and stuck tight. Another arm shot out and missed, striking the box as well.

Kammler let out a frustrated grunt.

He's new to this, Miller thought. *He might know how to use the machine, but he's not very good at it.* Why would he be? Generals never get their hands dirty.

Miller was slammed from behind as Kammler retracted the tentacles and yanked the wooden panel off of the large crate. For a moment, the heavy slab of wood covered his body, and if Kammler had been thinking, he could have easily crushed Miller beneath it. Instead, the weight lifted as Kammler tried to free the limbs. As the wooden panel rose up and away, Miller caught sight of Hitler's big, black, solid metal, six-wheeled Mercedes G4, designed to tour battle zones and protect the Führer. The thing was a tank. Without a gun. But still a tank.

Miller dove across the aisle, yanked open the car's passenger's side door, and jumped in. He slid across the seat to the driver's side and found the key in the ignition. He hoped that the car had only recently been crated, perhaps transported from Antarctica with the rest of this stuff, and turned the key.

The power came on, but the engine just coughed and died. He tried again. Nothing. Then he remembered. No oxygen!

"Like a fox in a hole," Kammler said. "No place to go."

But he didn't strike, either. The car must be important. Miller shoved open the driver's side door. It clunked against the wooden box, but there was just enough room for him to squeeze out. He got down and slid himself beneath the car, quickly finding the large gas tank. He rapped on it with his fist. The tank was full.

"I can wait," Kammler said. "In minutes, the world's fate will be sealed and your failed heroics will entertain the Führer when he returns."

Miller drew his knife and stabbed it into the side of the tank. Twin streams of fuel poured out and flowed slowly toward the open end of the crate. He pushed himself back to the other side of the car and stood. Moving in the tight space was difficult, but Miller made his way around to the back of the car as the smell of gasoline wafted into the air.

Kammler wouldn't smell the fuel, but he would see it

once the puddle emerged from beneath he car, which it would in just a moment.

Standing at the rear of the car, Miller saw the fuel peek out and made his move. He jumped out of the box, hoping that Kammler would have his weapons trained on the car doors. But he didn't wait to see if he was right; he dove forward into a roll, just as the weapons twanged, and missed. Again. Kammler cursed in German, his composure melting away.

Miller knew he had just a few moments before the weapons recharged, and this time, he ran away. Toward the end of the aisle. The crackling hum grew louder as Kammler gave chase, but came to a quick stop as Miller turned around to face him, handgun aimed at the gas.

Kammler laughed again. "Your people never knew when to keep running," the man said.

"And you never know when to shut up and pull the trigger." Miller adjusted his aim down and to the right. He squeezed off three quick rounds. A flare of orange light followed the third shot, and then a massive explosion as the gas tank ignited. The powerful blast knocked Miller off his feet and smashed Kammler's machine into the metal frame of the next warehouse stack.

Miller pushed himself up and took a breath. His chest ached. The pony bottle had been knocked from his face. He found it dangling around his neck and pulled it back on.

There was a loud grinding of metal and a crackling hum as Kammler's machine righted itself and yanked its arms free from the large warehouse shelves. The explosion had been powerful, but not powerful enough, and the flames died immediately for the same reason the car wouldn't start. The twin weapons lowered toward Miller. There would be no banter this time. No delay.

But Kammler never got to pull the trigger. The three-story-tall warehouse shelf above the car buckled and dumped its contents. Miller didn't know what the crates held, but when they landed atop Kammler, they struck like a runaway truck. Kammler, and the robotic suit, slammed to the floor as more heavy crates toppled down. Miller doubted the man was dead, but there wasn't time for that anyway.

Not wanting to expose himself to more gunfire, Miller found a gap in the crates of the shelving unit between him and the control center. He slid through and found Adler waving him over. "I cannot get in! The programs running the satellites are protected. The settings are locked."

She tapped on the keyboard, trying something else. *"Scheiße!"*

Miller entered the control center and ran to her side. On the screen he saw a display that showed the status of several satellites. Bars rose and fell, monitoring various systems, none of which Miller could discern since everything was in German. "What is all this?"

"The system is monitoring the satellites, adjusting power, altitude, everything from here. But it's locked. I can't boost the power." Adler slammed her fist down on the keyboard.

Computers were not Miller's forte, but thinking clearly under pressure was. "What would happen if the satellites were no longer being controlled?"

"In theory, without their energy intake being controlled, they would take in more energy than they could handle. Different method. Same result. They might also just shut down. But I can't do that either," Adler said. "Everything to do with the satellites is locked. I'd need a password."

"But you can access other functions?"

"Yeah, everything else, but—"

"Fork bomb," Miller said.

Adler's eyes went wide. She mouthed the word "fork bomb" and then her fingers became a blur over the keyboard, but the windows he saw on the screen looked nothing like the command prompt he saw in Antarctica.

"What are you doing?" he asked.

"Have something to do first."

"What? There isn't—"

"Done," she said. The command prompt opened and Miller saw the fork bomb code scroll onto the screen.

$:(){ :|:& };:

She hit Enter and then said, "We need to get out of here. Now!"

"We should make sure it works," Miller said. "If they get here, they could—"

"They're never going to get the chance," Adler shouted. "Listen!"

Miller focused on his hearing. There were boots. Voices—muffled behind rebreathers. Weapons being cocked. The occasional gunshot seeking them out. And he heard crates being shoved aside from the aisle where Kammler had been buried. But behind it all, there was something else.

Something persistent.

And rising.

A buzz.

Like a beehive.

61.

Miller's head snapped up. A much more modern-looking Bell hung from the ceiling. It was at least half the size of the one in Antarctica. Adler had managed to activate the fail-safe device—what was no doubt meant to be used if the facility was overrun by a hostile force—using Brodeur's own tactic against him.

"Take off your weapon's sound suppressor," Miller said as he twisted his off. "Let's make as much noise as we can."

Adler removed her silencer. "If we're going to get out of here, we need to leave now."

"We're not leaving," Miller said.

"What!"

He pointed to the set of double doors that led to the vault door. "You better believe that's locked down. There's no way out."

Adler looked at the floor. "Then it ends here."

"Actually," Miller said with a morphine smile, "I was thinking it could end in there." He pointed to the cryogenic chamber. The short hall connecting the two spaces was open. "The cavern in Antarctica was one big open space, so I don't think they had much choice. But this place is man-made. It will be shielded. I'd bet my life on it."

"You are," she said.

Miller gave a laugh, forced away his smile, and said, "Sorry. Morphine. Ready?"

She nodded.

Miller peeked over the partition and saw an army. A hundred men at least.

Bullets zinged over his head as he ducked.

Adler saw his wide eyes. "That bad?"

"Don't look. Just point your gun in back as you run and you're bound to hit someone. Don't stop shooting until you run out of bullets."

Adler braced herself, ready to make a suicidal sprint over two hundred feet of open space.

Miller looked back at Adler and a flicker of light behind her caught his attention. The computer screens—all of them, including the big display—went black. The fork bomb had worked, but would the satellites overload? And would it be soon enough? There was no way to know, unless they lived. "Go!" Miller shouted, breaking out into a limpy sprint with Adler on his heels.

The pair started firing right away, which gave them a few seconds to build speed while the enemy flinched. At his best, Miller could finish a hundred-yard dash in just over twelve seconds, two longer than the world record. Injured and hopped up on morphine, he figured it would take twenty.

Five seconds into his run, Miller ejected his spent clip and slapped in another. The enemy opened fire.

Adler shouted in pain, but stayed on her feet and kept firing.

Miller dove into a roll, allowing Adler to pass him, and came up facing the enemy. The control center in the middle of the room had helped block a lot of the fire, but the SS men were running around it now, shooting wildly as they ran. Miller focused, fired several times, and took out the two lead men. But the rest didn't slow. They had numbers and cultlike conviction on their side.

He caught sight of Brodeur, just three men back, shouting for his men to press forward. He lined up the shot, but never took it. A round struck his side, tearing skin and muscle before ricocheting off a rib, which broke.

Miller fell back with a shout.

Brodeur ordered his men to fire.

Adler appeared by Miller's side, yanking him to his feet.

The SS shooters took aim, tracking their targets more easily while not giving chase.

Miller stumbled, tripping up Adler. They both fell into the hallway joining the control center with the cryogenics chamber.

Bullets flew over their heads, kill shots had they not fallen.

A spike of adrenaline cleared Miller's morphine-dulled mind and while he gained a surge of energy, he also felt his pain more acutely. He roared in pain as he jumped up, took hold of Adler, and dove into the cryogenics chamber. He scrambled to the side as bullets pinged off the floor.

Out of sight for the moment, Miller took two deep breaths. His lungs burned. All of the exertion had drained his pony bottle's air five minutes faster than advertised.

He took it off and tossed it aside.

Adler handed him hers, and he took two deep breaths from it before handing it back. He looked down at the woman. She'd taken two rounds, one on the side of her waist and the other on her left trapezius. Both were close to being kill shots, but they were survivable wounds. If treated.

Running feet followed a war cry from the control center. Miller chanced a look. The SS soldiers ran for the hallway door, charging like men on an ancient battlefield, Brodeur at their lead.

Miller ducked back as bullets began to fly.

They were done.

He dropped his weapon.

Raised his eyes, like he could see the sky through the hundreds of feet of stone, and said a quick prayer for Arwen.

That's when he saw the door.

A large steel blast door hung above the hallway entrance.

Just above Miller's head was a red button labeled NOT-FALL in German. He wasn't sure what it meant, but the button's function was clear. He struggled to reach it as the sound of running boots echoed through the short hallway.

Miller lunged up and slapped the button.

The door descended.

The fastest of the Nazis dove under the falling door.

Adler shot him five times.

The second fastest made it halfway through before the door slammed down, cutting him in half.

The dull thud of human fists followed.

Miller stood and helped Adler up.

The thick blast door had a long, thin window. He walked to it and saw a sea of angry faces. Brodeur stood at the center of them, seething. The man shouted something, but Miller couldn't hear him. He pointed at his ear and mouthed, "I can't hear you."

Brodeur just stared at him with the eyes of a predator; the eyes of a man who knew he would eventually get through this blast door and destroy his enemy.

But Miller knew better.

Though the cryogenics chamber was silent, save for the hum of the life-support systems, he knew the control center would be buzzing with the sound of a thousand bees. He pointed to his ear, and mouthed, "What's that sound?"

Brodeur cocked his head slightly, then started shouting and fired two rounds in the ceiling. The pounding on the door ceased. The men surrounding him stopped moving. With a flash of recognition, the color drained from Brodeur's face. He started to shout an order, but it was already too late.

Brodeur itched at his skin as it suddenly reddened.

The men around him began to flail and fall.

Brodeur took a step back, aimed his weapon at Miller through the window, and pulled the trigger, over and over.

The gunshots sounded like distant fireworks to Miller. The glass was several inches thick. He didn't even flinch.

Brodeur pounded on the window with his fist. The blow

left a white smear behind. Brodeur noticed it and looked at his hand. The skin hung loose over his bones as the liquefied meat inside slid down into his arm and pooled at his elbow. The look of horror on his face became disfigured as his muscles, blood, cartilage, and sinews separated into their elemental parts. His face drooped, and then fell away, leaving a blood-covered skull with eyes and bits of stringy flesh dripping down the sides. The eyes stared back at Miller's, burning with rage. A moment later, the two orbs deflated and fell away. Brodeur's liquid brain slid out of the eye sockets a moment before his body crashed to the floor, forming a large pool of human sludge along with a hundred other soldiers and the fifty white-clothed men who had already asphyxiated.

Miller fell away from the door and sat down.

Adler joined him. "We should move away from the door," she said. "Just in case."

Miller groaned and managed to pull himself away from the growing pool of blood surrounding the one and a half soldiers who made it into the room, but could go no farther. He lay back and closed his eyes. The morphine was wearing off. He was bleeding from, well, everywhere. He had killed his enemy, but it seemed they had done him in, too. It would just take a little longer.

But it was a good death.

Or was it?

"Did you do it?" he asked.

"Do what?"

"Save the world?"

Adler shrugged, leaned on his chest, and closed her eyes as they both slipped into unconsciousness.

62.

Arwen looked out the window. The view was distorted through the translucent oxygen tent, but she could see the red flakes well enough. The first flake had fallen two hours ago, and the man on the news said—between sobs—that soon, the people who were exposed to the air would suffer from iron poisoning. They would feel sick. Then better. And then sick again before dying.

But they wouldn't even last that long. Not this time. The rate of oxidization was much faster than in Miami or Tokyo or Tel Aviv. Within the hour, the air would feel as thin as it was at the top of Mount Everest. An hour after that, only those with air supplies would survive. But with the red storm now projected to last a week—no one knew how long the effects would last beyond that—it was doubtful that many people, if any, would survive.

Arwen knew from experience that she could last days in her oxygen tent, but the idea of being alone that long only to die alone didn't sit well with her.

She lifted up the oxygen tent and slid out of bed. Her wounds hurt a little less now, helped out some by the medication she'd been given. But she hadn't seen a nurse in hours. Not since the first red flake fell. The medication would wear off soon.

She eyed the pony bottle Miller left for her. Part of her

wanted to take it, load up a cart of oxygen tanks, and make for the hills like Miller would. But there was nowhere to hide.

An inch of red covered everything outside the window. She looked at the ground and saw some people standing in it, facing death head on.

When she saw smoke rising in the distance, she realized that not everyone was facing the end of the world so peacefully. Some people would probably die long before the air ran out. Some people were probably already dead.

As she feared Miller to be.

He wouldn't have given up. And if there were red flakes falling from the sky, it meant he was dead.

Tears welled in her eyes, blurring her vision.

So when a distant sparkle of light caught her attention, she couldn't tell what she'd seen.

As the newscaster's voice suddenly grew high-pitched, Arwen wiped her eyes dry and looked in the direction the light had come from.

Up.

Then it repeated. A blue explosion of light pulsed in the sky. It reminded her of a swimming jellyfish, bursting out and then pulling in. But then it was gone again.

A moment later it repeated, but near the horizon.

Then again, above her.

And again, and again.

Soon the sky was filled with soft blue explosions.

It was beautiful.

But not nearly as beautiful as the blue sky that slowly emerged from the purple.

The newscaster was shouting now. Dancing. Hugging and kissing a camera crew.

Arwen placed her hand against the glass as the news cut to people and places all around the world. Singing and dancing filled the streets, including the one below her window.

Arwen looked up and saw a single red flake slip through the sky. It struck her window and stuck for a moment before a gust of wind carried it away.

The last red flake had fallen.

63.

Miller wasn't sure how long he'd been unconscious, but figured it had been several hours judging by how stiff his body felt. The flow of blood from his wounds had slowed, if not stopped. Adler lay next to him in a similar state.

He reached out and grazed her cheek with his hand. The movement caused him excruciating pain, but when her eyes flicked open and looked at him, it was worth it.

"Just to confirm," he said. "We did save the world, right?"

She grinned weakly. "I think so."

"You *think* so?"

"I was trained never to confirm something I haven't seen with my own eyes."

"Hey," Miller said. "I just realized something." He took a deep breath. "I'm breathing."

Adler gave a nod. "I think the air came back on around the same time I activated the Bell. Brodeur wasn't wearing a mask when he . . . melted."

"Neither was I," Miller said. "I guess seeing a man melt distracted me."

"It happens," Adler said with a grin.

"So," Miller said. "Who trained you?"

"What?"

"You said you were *trained* to never confirm something you hadn't seen with your own eyes. Earlier you mistakenly referred to yourself as an agent, rather than a liaison. You shoot as well as I do. So who trained you? And don't feed me any Interpol bullshit. I've earned the truth."

"My name really is Elizabeth Adler," she said. "As is my grandmother's, and that really is her journal. And I had no idea Gerlach was my grandfather. All that was true."

"*But*," Miller urged.

A loud *clunk* from the door made both of them jump. Gears within the wall ground. The door slid up with a groan.

Miller searched for his weapon, but couldn't find it.

Shouted German commands echoed from the hallway.

Adler shouted back.

Ten men dressed in black entered. All white. Speaking German. Armed for war.

With modern weapons.

Miller tensed. He wouldn't go down without a fight.

"Relax," Adler said, placing a hand on his shoulder. "They are with me." She flashed a smile and said, "Elizabeth Adler, Special Agent with GSG-9."

GSG-9! The Grenzschutzgruppe 9 was Germany's elite counterterrorism force.

"I *was* working at Interpol. Undercover. Everything I told you was true."

"You just left out some details."

She looked about to apologize, but Miller held up his hand. "Don't worry about it. I'm not a fan of being lied to, even by omission. But I understand the reason."

One of the men approached Adler, said something to her, and handed her her grandmother's journal.

Miller eyed the book and understood at once. "Seriously?"

Adler reached into the spine and pulled out a long thin tracking device.

"You weren't waiting for me," Miller said. "You were waiting for them."

She confirmed it with a nod and said, "But I was glad it was you."

"Good," he said. "Because they were late." Miller pushed himself onto his elbows. "You guys were late!"

The GSG-9 team ignored him as they set up a pair of stretchers. Then the men parted as Vesely entered the chamber. The Cowboy saw Adler and Miller lying on the floor, but alive, and gave a loud "Yeehaw!"

"Cowboy, you made it," Miller said with a smile.

"I told you. I am gunslinger." Vesely knelt down next to Miller and pointed to a hole in his hat. "They ruined my hat, though."

Miller took Vesely's hand and squeezed it. "We owe you our lives."

"You can thank me later," Vesely said, as a stretcher was slid up next to Miller.

"Vesely," Miller said. "Do you know? Have you—"

"GSG turned computers on in next room. Screens show cities around the world," Vesely said. "Blue sky."

Miller felt a weight lift, both from the fight being over, and because someone was lifting him up.

Vesely turned to the GSG medic. "There is hospital here. Tenth floor."

Miller took Vesely's arm. "Wait."

"What is it, Survivor?"

"There's something I need to do, first."

EPILOGUE

The man burned from head to toe, the pain beyond anything he'd experienced before. Consciousness came and went for several minutes. He could feel his heart beating madly. His muscles, so stiff, cramped violently. But he couldn't scream. Something was in his mouth. Down his throat!

And he was cold.

So cold.

His body shook, convulsing, but bound.

Immobilized.

A loud hiss reached his ears.

The burn increased as warm air coursed over his body.

He felt his skin tensing, and cracking, the way ice cubes do when added to a glass of warm water.

Ice.

Frozen!

He remembered.

Was this part of the thawing process? If it was, Kammler had failed to tell him about it. But he would be forgiven. The process worked! He lived! And if he had been returned to the world, it meant that his SecondWorld plan had been successful.

A sudden pain gripped his chest, followed by a surge of energy.

The tubes were pulled from his throat.

He took his first breath in seventy years. It felt good.

He smiled and felt his lip split.

Tasted his blood.

Felt alive!

He opened his eyes.

To his right stood a woman with deep blue eyes he recognized. What was her name? Adler, he believed. The mathematician. Why was she here?

To the left was a cowboy-hat-wearing man he did not recognize at all. *Where is Kammler?* He asked, *"Wo ist Kammler?"* His voice sounded raspy and wet.

"Kammler says hello," said a man's voice. In English. An American.

He found the man between the other two.

The man was covered in blood and sickly looking, but filled with anger.

Before he had a chance to fully comprehend what he was seeing, the man reeled back and punched him hard in the face.

Warm blood flowed down his cheek.

"He looks confused," the cowboy said.

"Can you translate something for me?" the bloodied man said to Adler. She nodded and he said, "It has been seventy years since the war ended."

"Es hat siebzig Jahre seit dem Ende des Krieges gewesen," Adler repeated.

"You murdered six million Jews."

"Sie ermordeten sechs Millionen Juden."

"My great-grandfather was one of them."

"Mein Urgroßvater war einer von ihnen."

"We sometimes ask each other the hypothetical question, if you could go back in time and kill Hitler, would you?"

"Wir fragen manchmal gegenseitig die hypothetische Frage, wenn Sie wieder Zeit und konnte gehen und töten Hitler, würden Sie?"

"Would you like to know my answer?"

"Möchten Sie meine Antwort wissen?"

Instead of answering, the frozen man shouted a German

curse and attempted to spit on the American, but only managed to push bloody drool out over his chin.

The American said, "My answer has always been, yes."

"*Ja*," Adler said.

"*Ano*," the cowboy said in Czech.

Looking through a swollen eye, he saw the American point a gun at his face and say, "Heil Hitler. Welcome to America."

Hitler felt a mixture of despair, fear, and all-consuming shame over his ultimate failure. But it would be over in just a moment. The American would pull the trigger, and he would escape the torment of living with his disgrace. He closed his eyes and waited for the relief death would bring.

But it never came. Hitler opened his eyes and the American lowered his weapon. The man squinted as he looked over Hitler's face.

He saw, Hitler thought. *He knows!*

"But things are different now," the American said.

Adler hesitated, surprised by the American's change of heart, but then translated. "*Aber die Dinge sind jetzt anders.*"

"The Reich is destroyed. Germany is an ally. Second-World failed."

"*Das Reich ist zerstört. Deutschland ist ein Verbündeter. ZweiteWelt fehlgeschlagen.*"

"You are just a man. Small. Nobody. Powerless."

"*Sie sind nur ein Mann. Klein. Niemand. Machtlos.*"

"And I won't kill you—"

Adler's voice sounded surprised as she translated. "*Und ich werde dich nicht töten.*"

The American leaned closer. " as much as you'd like that. I think lifetime in solitary, forgotten by the world, with nothing but your thoughts to keep you company sounds better, don't you?"

Hitler shook with rage and indignation, but most of all, he wanted to die. As Adler translated the American's final words, he began to weep. "No!" he screamed, and the skin at the sides of his mouth tore, but the physical pain barely registered as he thought about his future. "*Mich töten!* Kill me! *Bitte! Bitte!* No! *No! Mich töten!*"

Ten feet into the jungle, Kam's footprints included deep, round heel marks. This was good news because they would catch up to him more quickly if he was walking, but also added one more layer of confusion to the young intern's disappearance. If he'd entered the jungle in a panicked state, why had he stopped running as soon as he'd no longer been visible? Since then, the footprints revealed a calm, measured gait, which stayed on the muddy path.

This is going to be easy, Hawkins thought. Howie Good-Tracks had taught him to notice the minutest aberrations in the natural world. Every scuff, scratch, indentation, or patch of grass bent in the wrong direction told a story. The depth of a footprint in mud could reveal the target's size, weight, and sex. When tracking people, the gait, or distance between steps, and what part of the foot sank deepest revealed a person's mindset—calmly strolling, running flat-out, or ambling randomly like most lost people do. The angle of a bent branch could even hint at the target's speed, and based on the freshness of the break, when they'd passed through. Skills like these weren't taught in many schools, and certainly not by people like GoodTracks, who didn't just know these things, but lived them. With Kam not hiding his path, most of these skills wouldn't be necessary, but if Kam wandered off the trail, Hawkins would be able to follow him just as easily.

Twenty minutes into their rapid-paced hike, the trail rose up a steep grade. They slowed as they followed the path up, occasionally needing to scale short rock wall. At the top of one such stony rise, Hawkins leaned over the edge and reached his hand down to Joliet.

She took his hand and quickly scaled the eight-foot wall. At the top, she sat with her legs hanging over the edge and caught her breath. Hawkins sat next to her and opened his pack. After taking a swig of water, he offered her the bottle and she helped herself. The air in the jungle felt thick enough to drink, and their bodies were saturated. But they still sweated in the late afternoon heat and needed to drink often.

Hawkins took the bottle from Joliet when she offered it back to him, took one more swig, and capped it. Neither had said a word as they followed the path to this point, but the silence wasn't uncomfortable. They'd often spent quiet days on the deck of the *Magellan*, reading books, writing, or just catching some rays. It was one of the things he liked most about her, but the silence was beginning to feel uncomfortable.

Joliet spoke first. "What are you thinking?"

"You don't want to know," Hawkins answered. And he believed it. During the last twenty minutes, he'd allowed his imagination to run wild, filling in the blanks of Kam's disappearance and working out several different scenarios. Some were farfetched and easily dismissed. Others fit, but seemed unlikely, which was unfortunate because they had happy endings. But there was one scenario that nagged at him. The sequence of events lined up and the evidence seemed to support it. Unfortunately, that scenario wouldn't have a happy ending.

"Can't be as bad as what I'm thinking," she replied.

Hawkins knew she wouldn't give up. Her dogged persistence in all things was one of her attributes that he respected, but with which he often felt annoyed. Still, he'd learned that giving in right away kept things pleasant. "Okay, here's my theory. Kam and Cahill had some kind of falling out. Best guess is that Kam somehow screwed up the computers by accident. When Cahill confronted him, he ran and ended up on deck. When Cahill followed into the storm, he was knocked overboard. Kam made it back inside and hid until the storm ended. Fearing discipline or even legal action because of Cahill's death, Kam fled to the island. He wasn't running from a shark, which is why he ran along the shoreline, rather than straight across it. He ran because he didn't want to be seen. Concealed in the jungle, he slowed to a walk. Kam feels responsible for Cahill's death, and possibly for screwing up the ship. That's my best theory."

Joliet sagged. "I came up with the same thing. Do you really thing Kam would run? If it was an accident—"

"There is the possibility that it wasn't an accident," Hawkins said. "That their confrontation on deck ended in violence."

Joliet's eyes widened. "You think he *murdered* Cahill?"

"Not premeditated. But if they fought, and that's what caused Cahill to fall overboard, it's still manslaughter."

Joliet shook her head. "I just can't picture Kam doing something like that. He's such a sweet kid, not to mention half the size of Cahill."

"People do stupid things," Hawkins replied, thinking of the drunk man who'd been gored by a bison after walking up to the sleeping giant and slapping its snout. "Was Cahill a drinker?" It was an awful thing to hope for, but he wanted Kam to be innocent, too.

"I've never seen him drink," Joliet said. "Not even before we left."

Captain Drake had taken the crew out to a restaurant the night before they left. He tried to remember that night now, but his own drinking fogged the memory. He did remember flirting with Joliet, and being shot down, but had no memory of Cahill imbibing.

"You didn't drink that night, either, did you?" he asked.

"Nope, and I remember every word, story, and grope."

Hawkins froze. He slowly turned to her. "I didn't?"

Joliet's serious expression softened with a smile. "Don't

worry, Ranger. Wasn't you." She stood up, brushed off her shorts, and straightened her tight, blue T-shirt.

As she started up the trail again, he stood and gave chase. "Wait, who was it then? If it was Bray, I'm going to—"

Joliet stopped and raised an open palm in his direction. He fell silent and stood next to her. She pointed up the steep, jungle-covered hillside.

"I don't see anything," he whispered.

"Between the trees near the top," she said. "There's something gray."

It took him a moment, but when he saw it, the flat gray surface stood out. "The hell?"

His hand went to his waist, feeling the handle of his hunting knife. Its presence put him at ease. "Let's check it out."

Following the path, they wound their way up the hillside. As they neared the top, the incline grew steeper and the path became a series of switchbacks. Hawkins didn't like that they had to pass in front of the aberration several times. Something about it made him wary, and every pass left him feeling more exposed. Vulnerable.

But nothing happened. They followed the last path to the top where it wrapped around a stand of trees. Hawkins's hand went to his knife again as they rounded the palms, but when he got his first look at what waited for them, he knew the weapon wasn't needed.

Vines covered much of the gray concrete, but given its location at the top of the hill, Hawkins could see the structure for what it was. "It's a pillbox."

"A what?"

"Pillbox. From World War Two. The Japanese must have occupied this island." Hawkins stepped through the open backside of the concrete octagon. A long, thin opening stretched across the side facing the hill. He looked out and could see patches of the path below. "Anyone advancing up the hillside would have had a hell of a time reaching the top without being cut to pieces by machine-gun fire. They probably had a lot of the brush and trees cleared away back then."

"If this island was occupied during the war," Joliet said, "why isn't it on any maps?"

"If the island was never discovered by the U.S., the Japanese stationed here probably just deserted and went home when the war ended." Hawkins searched the small space for WWII relics, but found nothing. "Looks like they cleaned up shop when they left, too. They didn't leave a thing behind."

"Aside from a giant concrete octagon, you mean?"

"Right." Hawkins turned to a pile of dirt and leaf litter on the side of the room. A splotch of red color next to the debris caught his attention. He knelt down and picked it up. The thick cloth was easily identifiable as a piece of baseball cap. The remnant of a B confirmed Hawkins's suspicion that it was Kam's Red Sox cap. That it was ruined was cause for concern—the kid rarely parted from it—but it being here was also the first real evidence that Kam had made it to the island and not drowned in the storm.

"That's Kam's hat!" Joliet said, taking the fabric from him.

"Yeah, but why is it—"

A loud squeak made him jump back, and Joliet shouted in surprise as a black shape shot across the floor and out the door.

"What . . . was that?" she asked, catching her breath.

"A rat," he said. "I think."

Joliet inched towards the open door, looking for the rodent. "Looks like the Japanese left something else behind, too. Where people go, rats follow."

"Mmm," Hawkins said, but he'd only heard half of what she said. He walked back to the window and looked down the hill, scratching his chin.

"What is it?" Joliet asked.

"The rat," he said.

"You don't like rats?"

"Rat," he said. "Singular. Rats tend to live in colonies. Sometimes several hundred in a single colony. And each female in the colony can have sixty young per year, half of which might be females. Eleven weeks after birth, those females start cranking out young of their own. On an island like this, left to breed for the past seventy years, their population should have expanded until the place was overrun."

"But it's not," Joliet said. "This is the first we've seen."

Hawkins placed his hands on the window sill, watching the jungle floor below for movement. "And there are plenty of food sources out there. Rats aren't picky. It's possible that their population exploded and suffered a massive die-off because of starvation, but that still doesn't explain the lack of a colony. Rats live just two years. For there to be one rat, there need to be others, and we run into the colony explosion scenario again, unless . . ."

"Unless what?"

"Unless something is keeping them in check."

"What do you mean?"

"There's a reason Yellowstone is never overrun with rats. They're there—they're everywhere—but their population is controlled—" He looked her in the eyes. "By predators. Mountain lions, wolves, foxes, lynxes, bobcats, eagles, hawks, owls, and a variety of other predators keep the rodent and rabbit populations in check."

"So, what? The seagulls here have a taste for rat?" Joliet said with a grin.

"No," he said, "to keep a rat population down to where they're not scurrying everywhere requires a healthy population of a number of different predators."

"How do you know there are different predators?"

"If there were only one species of predator, they would face the same overpopulation issue as the rat. They'd be everywhere. Predators are kept in check by competition. Other hunters."

Joliet's smile faded. "How come we're not seeing them then?"

"Because they're predators," Hawkins said, eyes still on the hillside below. "They don't want to be seen."

Hawkins let the moment drag out for a moment and then smiled. "Don't worry, any predators on the island would have come with the Japanese, too. Feral cats. *Maybe* wild dogs. And some bird species, like the seagulls, which seem aggressive enough to handle a rat."

Joliet let out a breath. "Bastard."

Hawkins chuckled, but it was only partly sincere. The combination of a dead woman, a WWII fortification, and the presence of an active ecosystem that included predatory animals had him on edge. The island appeared to be as close as you could get to a tropical paradise, but the history of the place trumped the environment. And he had no doubt the lush jungle hid more secrets.

But he wasn't a historian. Nor was he here to speculate on wildlife. He'd come to the island to find Kam and take him back to the ship. He stepped out of the pillbox and scanned the clearing outside. He'd lost Kam's trail before they'd reached the switchbacks, but he couldn't think of a reason the kid would have gone trailblazing. If anything, Kam had cut straight up the hillside, ignoring the switchbacks altogether. He'd hoped to pick up a trail atop the hill, but saw nothing.

Nothing at all. No rocks. No trees. No overgrowth. The clearing around the pillbox entrance looked almost manicured. Grass covered the ground, but it was neatly trimmed.

Not good, he thought, but didn't voice his fears. Once they had Kam, they could theorize about the island all they wanted. Until then, Hawkins would stay on task.

He spun around, looking at the pillbox again, and noticed that the trees surrounding the building were just barely taller than its domed roof. If he stood atop it, he'd have a good view and might be able to gauge the size of the island.

Joliet stepped outside as he walked to the side of the pillbox and tested the strength of the vines with his hands. They'd make decent handholds, but he wasn't confident they'd hold his weight. "Give me a boost," he said.

Joliet looked at him like he was crazy. "You know I'm half your size, right?"

Hawkins found a thick vine high up on the wall and gave it a tug. It would do the trick. "I need to take a look at the island."

"Why don't you lift me up, then?"

"The operative word is *I*," Hawkins said. "No offense. But I need to see the island for myself."

Joliet strode over to him. She linked her fingers together and bent down to take Hawkins's foot. "You know, Tarzan wouldn't need Jane's help."

Hawkins's placed his foot in her hands, held on tight to the vine, and said, "Jane was a helpless damsel in distress."

Joliet lifted and Hawkins pulled. He rose up the side wall and reached over the top with his free hand. Once he had a grip, he reached his other hand up and pulled. Joliet pushed until his foot rose out of her reach. After swinging a leg up and over the top, Hawkins made short work of the climb. He got to his feet, standing on the flat edge that surrounded the dome. He turned back to Joliet and said, "That was a compliment, you know. The Jane thing."

Joliet smiled up at him. "I know."

She stood there for a moment, staring up at him with a smile and squinted eyes. He was frozen in place. His stomach knotted uncomfortably, but his own smile widened. *Screw Bray and his curvy women*, Hawkins thought, *she's amazing*.

Hawkins thought she must have read his thoughts, or at least seen a glimmer of them in his eyes, because she let out a laugh and asked, "What?"

You know what, he thought, but said, "Nothing."

Hawkins thought he saw her blush, but she turned away and said, "Just take a look, will you? We need to keep moving."

Over the past month, he and Joliet had formed a bond neither of them would admit to, and thus far hadn't included a physical element. But he could sense them growing closer, and the way her sweat soaked T-shirt clung to her body made him hope things moved forward sooner than later. Before Joliet could catch him staring, Hawkins turned towards the domed roof.

The structure looked sound enough. But it had been exposed to the elements for seventy years. He stood slowly and gave the dome a couple of hard kicks. When nothing gave, he leaned forward and put his weight on it. The dome, known to be a naturally strong shape, held his weight. Moving slowly, he crawled to the top on his hands and feet.

Then he stood.

And gasped.

He could see over the tops of the tree and had a view of the jungle below. The mottled sea of green fell away as the hill descended, stopping at the lagoon. He could see the crescent-shaped beach and a small moving figured he assumed was Bray. The *Magellan* lay in the lagoon, silent and motionless. From this point of view, he could see the entrance to the lagoon was actually a curved channel through the cliffs. From the outside, it would be hard to see.

How the hell did the ship get through there without crashing?

Beyond the cliffs, the endless blue Pacific Ocean stretched to the horizon. With his eyes on the outer fringe of the island, he made a slow turn, taking in every detail. His wonderment over the view quickly turned to dread. The island was large. The far end was perhaps three miles away, easy to cover in a day, but he figured there were at least nine square miles of land—nearly six thousand acres—to cover. And that wasn't including the many hills he could see. There was enough land to stay lost in for a long time.

Toward the far end of the island, between a pair of hills, he saw the sparkle of water, behind which lay more land. *A lake*, he thought. People were invariably drawn to fresh water. *If Kam keeps moving until he finds the lake, he might stay there. And if we're stuck here . . .* Hawkins pushed that thought aside. *Focus.* Between the distant hills and the lake sat a lighter patch of green. He couldn't see exactly what it was—there was too little to make out—but it looked like a large clearing.

Maybe an old airfield, he thought. "The island is volcanic," he said, noting the raised perimeter. Like most islands in the Pacific, this one had once been the top of a very large, active volcano.

"You don't see any steam, do you?" Joliet asked as she explored the fringe of the clearing.

"No, it's dormant. Probably been for a long time. There's a couple of tall hills, a lake—probably at the island's lowest point—and a large, flat clearing, but all of it is inside a very large crater."

"Probably multiple craters," Joliet said. "Volcanic cones tend to shift in the ocean."

Hawkins heard the sound of shifting vegetation.

"Hey, I found the path," Joliet said from below.

Hawkins looked down. Joliet stood on the far side of the small clearing, holding a large-leafed plant aside.

"I think I see footprints, too."

Something about the word footprints triggered a new question. "Why is Kam barefoot?"

Joliet just stared up at him.

"Did you ever see him go barefoot on the ship?"

She thought for a moment and then shook her head. "He wore sandals all the time."

"So why is he barefoot now?"

"Maybe they fell off in the water."

That made sense, but still felt wrong. They were missing something. "Maybe."

What the hell aren't we thinking of?

"Hey, look at this," Joliet said. She held the plant up in the air. The large leaves were bound together at the bottom. "The leaves were staked into the ground. He covered the path on purpose. Why would Kam do that?"

The mental floodgates opened.

Kam wouldn't.

"We need to go back to the ship," he said, sliding down the dome to the edge of the pillbox roof.

"Why? It will still be daylight for a few more hours. We can—"

"It's not Kam," he said, lowering himself over the front end of the pillbox. He held on to a vine for support.

Joliet rushed up and put her hands under Hawkins's foot, supporting some of his weight. "What do you mean, it's not Kam?"

"Why would Kam—"

The vine supporting most of Hawkins's weight tore free from the concrete above the pillbox entryway. Taking the vine with him, Hawkins fell. He and Joliet spilled onto the grass in a heap.

Hawkins pulled his legs off of Joliet and got to his feet. He helped her up, and as they both brushed off their damp clothes, he continued, "Why would Kam swim to shore, run straight to a path in the jungle, come all the way up here, and then conceal his tracks?"

She had no answer.

"Exactly," he said. "Kam wouldn't. Someone was already here."

"But Kam is missing," she said.

"He might have been lost in the storm with Cahill."

"Or he was taken," she said.

Hawkins didn't think so. The footprints weren't deep enough to suggest someone was being carried, but he couldn't discount the theory, either. Kam wasn't very big.

"Either way, we need to get back to the ship. The island is too big to search on our own, and the presence of an unknown person . . . or people, changes things. We need help." As Hawkins turned towards the path leading back down to the cover, he glanced at the pillbox and noticed something different. Something was painted above the doorway, where the vine had been.

He brushed away the moss and vine bits still clinging to the wall and looked at the writing.

七百三十一

"Is that Japanese?" Joliet asked.

"That'd be my guess, but I have no idea what it means." He looked at each symbol individually, trying to remember them, but stopped when he heard a faint scratching sound behind him.

"Got it," Joliet said, capping a pen and slipping a small

notebook into her cargo shorts pocket. "Now let's get the hell out of here."

As Joliet started down the switchback path, Hawkins took one last look around the small clearing. When thinking about dogs and cats being left behind on the island, he'd made the logical leap to the idea that they'd be feral after seventy years of breeding, hunting, and surviving on an island. But now he had to consider another possibility.

What would people be like if they'd been left here, cut off from the rest of the world, for seventy years?

Read on for an interview between Jeremy Robinson and Jonathan Maberry, *New York Times* bestselling author of *Rot & Ruin* and *Patient Zero*, followed by a bonus question from a Facebook fan.

JONATHAN MABERRY: Your novels are out on the bleeding edge of science and often there are fantastical elements. How much does the realism or plausibility of your plot devices matter to you?

JEREMY ROBINSON: I go back and forth on the subject of realism. My preference is that my plots, characters, creatures, and technologies stay within the realm of plausibility, even if it's just a thread of science or history connecting what I've come up with to the real world. I admittedly push the limits of plausibility in *SecondWorld*, but even the most outlandish parts of the book, like a cloud of iron particles smashing into the atmosphere, oxidizing and making the air unbreathable, was developed with the help of a group of scientists far smarter than me.

The challenge for me is the way I sometimes come up with a story. I frequently come up with a "wouldn't that be awesome" scenario that I then have to back up with real science, or at least, science theory. Trust me, it's not always easy to make animated stone golems sound like a scientific possibility! Of course, sometimes a guy just needs to let his hair down, which is one of the reasons I came up with *The Antarktos Saga*, a YA fantasy series that lets me create creatures, break the laws of physics, and visit supernatural realms without needing to back it up with science, hard or fringe.

MABERRY: Your novels often draw on ancient or exotic horrors and modernize them into thrillers. Walk us through your process of going from concept to finished novel.

ROBINSON: For me, the concept sometimes starts with the creature and then the story is built around it in a way that makes its existence possible. In my first hardcover novel, *Pulse*, I decided to focus on the mythological Hydra, which has been a favorite of mine since I was a kid. The Hydra has seven heads, one of which is immortal and the rest double and grow back if you cut them off. That description seems to land the Hydra square in the genre of fantasy. But for me, the fun is in finding a way to make such a thing possible.

I did research on regeneration and found that several animals naturally regenerate limbs and tails. Even humans can regenerate fingertips up to a certain age! I dug some more and discovered that genetics companies are researching ways to enable humans to regenerate body parts. And finally, I spoke with a leading researcher in the field who revealed how all of this is possible. Once I applied everything I'd learned to the Hydra, it wasn't nearly as outlandish an idea and deeming it an extinct species actually make a freakish kind of sense. Given the intense interest in human regeneration by modern genetics companies, they became the obvious choice for my antagonist and Manifold Genetics was born. And since the Chess Team had already been developed, I now had my story. Making myths real became the theme for the Chess Team novels and we have since touched on wraiths, golems, Nqui Rung (Vietnam's Sasquatch), dire wolves, and the Norse legend of Fenrir.

MABERRY: Ex–Navy SEAL-turned-NCIS Special Agent Lincoln Miller is tough, resourceful, and a man of honor. Readers unfamiliar with the kinds of men who serve in Special

Operations may think he's a superman. How real is a guy like him?

ROBINSON: I would like to think that there are a LOT of guys like Lincoln Miller. Hell, I would like to think that, in a horrible scenario like the oxygen being removed from the atmosphere, that *I* would be as resourceful as Miller. But I think anyone familiar with the exploits of the U.S. Military's Special Operations would know that we're surrounded by guys willing to sacrifice their bodies, push themselves beyond the limits the rest of us believe are possible, and save lives, sometimes on a grand scale. But I also don't think heroes like Miller are limited to the military. A lot of people—military, emergency services, and civilians—rise to the occasion during tragedies like 9-11, or natural disasters like Hurricane Katrina. People like Lincoln Miller exist. They always have. And hopefully, they always will. *Someone* has to save the world!

MABERRY: Your novels are described variously as action thrillers or science thrillers. How do you categorize your books?

ROBINSON: When people ask me this in person, I usually say something like, "They're run-for-your-life-holy-crap-we're-going-to-die-it's-going-to-eat-me novels." Picking a single genre for my books is probably impossible. Calling them action-thrillers is more for the benefit of bookstores, so they know where to put them. Calling them science thrillers reveals that there is a good amount of science involved. But I think the books also qualify as mysteries, horror, creature features, science fiction, adventure, and occasionally romance. I'm not sure I could rein myself in and stick to the conventions of any single genre. I'm not a fan of limitations. And I would probably get bored, which breaks one of my rules of writing—if I get bored writing, my readers will be bored reading, and that's a no-no because my job is to entertain, which is the opposite of being bored. In a way, that might sum up my books best—they're in the "not boring" genre.

MABERRY: You're famous for prodigious amounts of research for your fiction. How do you get that level of information on science, the military, and politics?

ROBINSON: I usually start with grabbing any books I can find on the broad subjects touched on in my books. Genetics, weaponry, robotics, Nazis, conspiracies, and more. I have a strange nonfiction book collection. After going through the related books with a highlighter, I turn to the Internet, printing out websites, articles, Wikipedia pages, government documents, and the occasional schematic. After putting down some more highlighter ink, I'll fire questions at professionals, most often hoping they'll be able to put what I've already learned into layman's terms. Comprehending science (or telling myself I comprehend it) is one thing; translating it into understandable English is another. Once I have all of the details worked out, and my fringe science is making sense, I start writing. The rest of my research takes place on the fly. If I add a weapon, go to a location I've never been, or throw in a surprise plot element, I'll hit the Internet, learn everything I can, and retain it for the hour or two it takes me to insert it into the book. I'd like to say I retain everything I learn, but if I could do that, I'd have a multibillion-dollar company . . . or at least a TV show.

MABERRY: What was the coolest thing you discovered in researching *SecondWorld*?

ROBINSON: You know, that's a really hard question because I mostly discovered horrible things. Human experimentation. Nazi scientists working for and leading U.S. programs thanks to Project Paperclip. Support for the Nazi party by prominent U.S. citizens. And weapons programs that make me cringe, not just because they're so vile, but because they're probably still being developed today. I think the coolest thing, that isn't quite horrible, is that UFOs might be human in origin, and if they are, there are a lot of amazing technologies in store for the human race, just as soon as the military decides to let the rest of us in on them. Kind of like the Internet. And Velcro.

MABERRY: Your books are both critically acclaimed and popular with readers. Which matters more to you—the regard of your peers or your fans?

ROBINSON: Fans. Without a doubt. Reviews from big publications are nice. I enjoy them. They make me feel good. But without my readers, I'd be homeless and probably institutionalized for my paranoid rambling about neo-Nazis, aliens, and evil corporations. I don't write with the intent of getting high praise, and I'm constantly surprised when I get it. I write to entertain people like me, who crave action-packed, creative, and occasionally outlandishly fun stories. If the critics enjoy outlandish fun too, awesome, but the fans and readers come first.

MABERRY: Your books are entertaining reads, but they're also about the war on terror. Do you use the platform of the novels to weigh in on America's efforts to eradicate terrorism?

ROBINSON: I think the books are more about processing the horror of terrorism and the fear it can create in society. My mad scientists, horrible monsters, doomsday organizations, and robot killers are exaggerations of real-life terrorism, and by defeating them, I'm telling myself, and maybe communicating to the reader, that we can overcome evil, even if it's thirty feet tall, has two rows of shark-like teeth, and can regenerate limbs. That said, this isn't a conscious decision on my part. I'm not saying to myself, "Self, let's help readers process the fears conjured by modern terrorism." It's more likely that I'm doing this for myself and putting it on paper for other people to read . . . which kind of means that my readers are getting their kicks by reading transcripts of my conversations with my inner shrink after they've been embellished by my imagination. Is nothing private anymore!

MABERRY: If you had to choose, would you rather your readers come away from your books wowed by your plots, or in love with your characters?

ROBINSON: Ouch! Another tough question. Can I say, "both"? No? Damn. All right, here's the answer: I am probably better known for my crazy plots. Thrillers, after all, are technically plot-driven novels. And I get a lot of e-mails from fans about my plots, the crazy action, the surprising twists, etc. But I think I take more pleasure in the less frequent e-mails about how a reader particularly loved a certain character. This has happened more with *SecondWorld* than any other book. I've received a lot of e-mails asking for more Miller, and more Cowboy, and those e-mails please me more than the plot e-mails. So, it's a close one, but characters win.

MABERRY: *SecondWorld* is another fast-paced, action-packed thriller. How do you simultaneously show so much action yet reveal character vulnerability?

ROBINSON: It's really all about how that character reacts to things. At the beginning of *SecondWorld*, Miller is faced with an unbreathable atmosphere and a nonstop race to acquire air tanks from a variety of sources—ships, scuba shops, drug stores. It's frantic and horrible and nonstop, except for when Miller comes across a poor soul that was killed in what turns out to be an attack. He doesn't ignore the dead and push on. He mourns them. Wants to avenge them. Even thanks them for the resources he manages to scrounge from them. He views them as people, not just corpses. It's these reactions that make him vulnerable. He's not just a shoot-'em-up hero, responding to bad guys with bullets and one-liners. He's a caring guy capable of deep emotion, sadness, and hurt. Though he also has the ability to channel all of that into the tip of a bullet if need be.

BONUS QUESTION—Jeremy Robinson held a contest on Facebook in which fans could ask him any question. The winner of the contest would have their name, question, and Jeremy's answer printed in this edition of *SecondWorld*. The winning question came from Cherei McCarter. Here it is:

McCARTER: Which character have you written that, deep down, you know is YOU? How many of your other family and friends find their way into your characters?

ROBINSON: The answer to the first part of the question takes little thought. While nearly all of my lead characters have a bit of me in them (habits, likes and dislikes, favorite foods, etc.), there is one character who is based, in part, on me. His name is Solomon Ull Vincent, the main character in the *Antarktos Saga*. He and I share a childhood. He grew up in my home, had the same toys, watched the same cartoons, ate the same breakfast cereals, blew up the same volcano, and even had the same best friend—Justin McCarthy. But I cannot claim Solomon is just me. He shares my past, but his heart and soul—his kindness, gentleness, and forgiving nature—are based on the real Solomon, my son, who is also a spitting image of young fictional Solomon. And that leads us to the second part of Cherei's question.

I use people I know *all the time* in my novels. Well, not really them, but their names. I started the habit in my novel, *Raising the Past*, where I used Mark Vincent (my uncle), Brian Norward (my cousin), Brian Dombroski (a friend), by their full names, and several more friends by their first or last name. Eddy, Eve, Steve, and Paul are all based on people I know. I have since used family members in many of my books. In fact, while I killed Mark Vincent in *Raising the Past*, a different Mark Vincent is Solomon Vincent's father. And his mother, Beth Vincent, is my aunt. In fact, anytime you see the name Vincent in my books, that's probably a family member. The most notable use of a family member is probably *SecondWorld*. Roger Brodeur is my father-in-law. If you have finished the book, you know what happens to him. But I don't just use personal friends. I have named characters after my fellow authors as well, including Scott Sigler, Chris Kuzneski, Lincoln Child (*SecondWorld*), Steven Savile, Kent Holloway, David McAfee, and more. I also occasionally grab names from Facebook, so if you're a friend there, you might find yourself immortalized in one of my books someday.

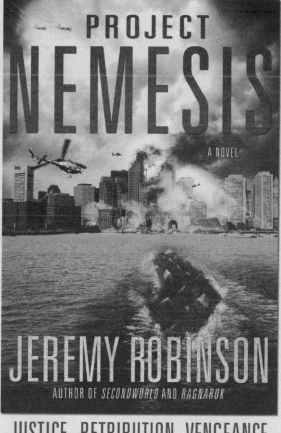